By the same author

NOVELS

The Gilt Cage
Duel in the Dark
The Reluctant Madonna
They That Go Down
When the Wind Blows
Unicorn
The Wise and the Foolish
Virgins
Stallion
Spider
Matador
The Tavern
Return of a Heroine
Who Would Have Daughters
The Lost One
A Candle in the Sun

The Marriage Will Not Take Place
Family Ties
The Sun is My Undoing
Rose Timson
Granada Widow
Twilight on the Floods
Phoenix Rising
Anna Fitzalan
The Bulls of Parral
The Unquiet Spirit
The Little White King
The Swan
The Woman in the Back Seat
The Tower
A Pride of Terrys

SHORT STORIES

A Kind of Insolence

PLAYS

French for Love (with Derek Patmore)

BELLES LETTRES

Hugh Walpole: a Critical and Biographical Study
Reading Aloud: a poetry anthology
The Life of Sir William Nicholson

THE ONE-EYED MOON

by

Marguerite Steen

NICHOLAS VANE
LONDON

First published *1935* (*Victor Gollancz Ltd*)

Reprinted *1949* (*Falcon Press Ltd*)

Reprinted by *NICHOLAS VANE* (*PUBLISHERS*) *LTD*
194–200 Bishopsgate, London, EC2
1964

Printed offset in England by
STRAKER BROTHERS LTD
LONDON

To
my dear friend
LUISA GARCIA ORTEGA

CONTENTS

PART I

PART II

PART I

CHAPTER I

PRELUDE

WHEN THE PRIEST CAME to administer the Last Sacraments to Carmela Moreno, he judged it wise at the same time to baptise the infant so clearly bent on relinquishing its frail hold upon the world to which it was delivered. Freed prematurely from its dark, safe prison, chilled by its separation from the warm, maternal element, it hung, limp and damp, stained with its struggle, in the hands of a stranger. A drowned kitten could have been no weaker, a new-born rat no less handsome. No doctor had eased its passage—for the best of good reasons : it was the last day of the feria in Granada, and Mario Gallego, who combined certain medical offices with those of apothecary, had gone off with a party of friends to see the bullfight.

So when Carmela Moreno, at the end of a long and bitter argument with one of her relations by marriage, suddenly gave a shriek and clapped both hands to her body, a dozen women, understanding what was happening, thrust and bundled her into her unprepared room, while the water-seller's smallest boy was sent tottering for old Juana, the midwife.

Carmela Moreno was at least three weeks before her time : the news ran like wildfire through the alleys and brought half the population out of doors. Not that birth ordinarily created so much excitement among the natives ; but this was the wife of Aurelio López, bearing her first child after seven years of barren marriage, during which,

hating her for her cold, townswoman's ways, they had
never ceased to taunt her with her inability to bear a child
to such a man as Aurelio.

Here, then, was her punishment for her unwifeliness!
The child was being born, three weeks before its time, in
the absence of the father. She had to leave her stall, her
pan of frying-oil, the golden, fatty batter that sizzled over
the charcoal stove, and run indoors to have her baby, just
at the busiest hour of the morning. Had it been anyone
but Carmela Moreno, a dozen volunteers would have
appeared to take charge until she was about again ; but
such was their hatred for her that the stall would have been
left to itself had it not been for the danger of the oil running
over and creating a conflagration among the packed alleys
of the market square. Someone nipped the pan off, someone
trampled out the red embers of the scattered fire, a crowd
of children fought like wolves over the few cakes that had
been made, and over the raw batter. Flour, fat, and saffron
disappeared miraculously among a population that accounted thieving a mark of quick-wittedness, and within
an hour only the little trestle remained, even the pots and
pans having vanished, to enrich some other household.

By the time old Juana had dragged her limbs, crippled
with arthritis, to the house of López, the business was over.
It was as well for the mother that this was so, for the
atrocities committed by Juana's fumbling and all but useless hands could have had but one immediate result.

Carmela lay across the bed, from corner to corner,
unaware of them all, with the naked babe like a drowned
kitten in the hollow of her out-flung arm, in a room full of
charcoal fumes, crowded with Aurelio's wailing relatives
and vociferous neighbours, while someone went hot-foot
for the priest. More and more people, men as well as
women, edged into the room ; flies swam continuously, in

a dense black cloud, overhead, settling on the oiled hair of
the women, on the sweaty foreheads of the men, and
breaking away with loud, evasive protest when slapped at
with hand or apron. A mongrel bitch, which had recently
littered, cocked a leg to scratch, with an air of the most
cynical philosophy.

" And for this to happen when Aurelio is away ! "

" Ay-ay !—and all the years they have been married, and
nothing—and now this ! "

There was as much triumph as pity in the exclamations ;
liking Aurelio, they detested Carmela, and among the hill-
villagers there is little ruth for the misfortunes of an unpopular member of the community.

The crowd was in constant slow, pullulating movement,
first one and then another edging up to the bed, to stare
with detached curiosity at the woman lying there, with a
line of white showing between her eyelids, with the square,
purple line of her lips gummed against her square teeth,
her face olive-green in its pallor, and her hair scattered in
strands like wet serpents across the striped bolster of her
nuptial bed. No one touched her, or the infant ; to do so
was the business of none save old Juana, who mumbled
that it was too late. What remained was business for the
priest ; meanwhile—she lifted a water-jug, allowed its last
drops to spout into the cavern of her mouth, rinsed, and
spat it out upon the floor. She looked slyly at a neighbour,
pointed some maundering jest with a nudge, and settled
down upon the floor, to swell, in a business-like fashion, the
burthen of lamentation. Those who had forborne, in life,
to say a good word of Carmela, were liveliest in raising the
keen for her imminent death.

The priest hurried in, bearing the precious oils ; his
sotana was green with age, and had a cobbled rent in the
back of it ; his breath smelt of aguardiente. He footed the

kneeling peasants out of the way and started his ritual in a hasty undertone. When he had finished, the babel broke out again ; someone remembered the infant and caught it up, thrusting it into his unready hands.

" It can't live, father, it can't live ! Baptise it, for pity's sake, so the poor thing won't get into trouble in purgatory ! "

The priest looked down upon the tiny blackened face, which became convulsed as his awkward clutch tightened on the fragile limbs.

" What's it to be called ? " he asked hurriedly of the nearest person. A barnyard clatter broke out, violent argument interrupted the funerary lamentations ; one said one thing, one another ; someone, it appeared, had heard Carmela say that if it was a boy it should be christened after its father, and someone else shrilly maintained that the godfather should be consulted—the flour-merchant Garcia, who lived across the square. " But Garcia is at the bullfight ! " cried another.

The priest wiped his brow, from which drops were falling upon the infant ; in any case it was not a boy, and if they had no other suggestion——

" Por Dios, here is the father ! Here is Aurelio ! " came a shout from the door. A woman shrieked ; another started to batter her way into the foreground, using her arms as flails ; it was her right, as a member of the family, to break the news to the newcomer ; if any deprived her of her right she was ready to bring her clawed fingers down their faces, to pull out the hair of their heads. The tension of the dark room quickened ; heads dodged one another, each was greedily anxious to observe in its minutest manifesta- tions the effect of the tidings upon the figure that now blocked the blazing square of the doorway with its broad shoulders. A score of voices screamed together ; above them rose the bellow of the priest, with the infant in his arms.

" What name is this child to be given ? "

Aurelio López propped his elbow against the doorpost ; the expression on his face was that of an imbecile or a deaf man. The audience drew in a hissing breath of gratification, feeling in Aurelio's silence a tribute to its own dramatic ability.·

Dust was caked in the deep channels of his face, and lay in a thick white powder upon his shoulders and in the folds of his clothing. The rims of his eyes were reddened, the stare of his eyes was fixed. Presently he put up his right hand and drew it slowly down over the mask of his face. Some kind of returning intelligence trembled in the flesh with an eery effect, as of the dead returning to life. He began to look surprised ; a kind of dull astonishment over-spread his features. Yet it was not the simple, painful astonishment of such a homecoming ; it was, rather, the look of a man who says to himself, " Is it possible that life can hold another, immediate blow, after what I have just been through ? "

The loss of Carmela and her new-born babe seemed to Aurelio, in that moment of elucidation, hardly more than a grain added to the burden which he had carried over the thirty kilometres he had tramped from Granada. He had refused all offers of transport ; people, seeing him, had thought he was very drunk, even for that part of the country ; he had passed a whole night out of doors ; he had no recollection of any landmarks on his way ; nor had he the least idea of what had guided him back to Carmela. He came into his bereaved house as a man who has already experienced to the full the meaning of deprivation. His secret pain lifted him upon its mysterious wings above all these people who were mourning over a simple matter of death—the least of all afflictions. It clothed him in its majesty as he came slowly into the room, staring over the heads of the people at Carmela, stretched upon the bed whereon he had given her this child.

He stood there, unaware of the snuffling and whining noises around him, looking down upon his wife. He had loved her, all through the seven years when she had denied him the fulfilment of his manhood : not with the ardour of the first year of their marriage, but with a matter-of-fact, persevering affection that lent stability to his way of living. Another man would surely have found a mistress, but he had been faithful to Carmela ; his fidelity was part of his dignity.

When they found she was with child, there had been something like a revival of their original passion for one another. Her jealousy and her hard, tart ways had seemed to him again lovable, part of an almost forgotten enchantment she had worked upon him in the beginning. The prospect of fatherhood drew upon the profoundest resources of his nature, and even caused him to glimpse the truth— that life must be something more than a fortunate series of improvisations : that there was a future, for which provision must, as far as possible, be made. He acknowledged that Carmela had, so far, done more than he to secure it. A confused tenderness, which made each of them a little shy, entered into their lusty relationship, and the act of loving her, which had become mechanical, regained something of its original significance for them both. They were still young and healthy, and the belated proof of their power to create life had restored their belief in each other and in themselves.

Had he known, forty-eight hours before, that he was to lose Carmela, rage and resentment, a sense of insupportable loss, would surely have possessed Aurelio ; now, looking down upon her, he felt puzzled to know what there had ever been between them. He *longed* to know ; he felt that in her death Carmela was knowing it, and this seemed unjust and out of place to him. For, during all their years together, he had always been the one to know, she the one to accept his knowledge, often with scorn, often with taunts upon his omniscience, but always, by her actions, accepting it in the end. He had been born knowing things ; that at least, was how he expressed to himself the curious and sometimes uncanny insight he had into the hearts and minds of human beings. His pride lay in it ; and, two nights ago, his pride had failed him. He had met the, to him, unknowable, and he was still suffering from the effects. And now Carmela—even she—mocked him with her silent knowledge of things which, having tried to teach her, he himself had forgotten.

There was flesh he had handled, limbs that had responded forcibly to his passion, hands and feet that had gone about the duties of his household and provided for his personal comfort ; yet none of these objects aroused in him any convincing emotion. It was as if he had been told about, rather than experienced, them ; his mind recorded, but his imagination had no power to animate, their descriptions.

His sister had flung her arms about his neck and was sobbing noisily upon his shoulders ; he felt his hands taken and pressed by people he did not try to identify. In order to show their respect, the company, at his entrance, had beaten up a great wave of emotionalism ; they were frankly, and, in the way of the Latin races, with the greatest enjoyment, drowning in it. Within an hour, almost certainly, they would be singing, jesting, drinking with the same gusto they now brought to their mourning. The priest shook him roughly by the arm.

" Aurelio López ! Do you hear me ? Your child is a girl ; what is she to be called ? "

Aurelio turned his head towards the priest ; his face still

wore its dazed, stupid expression, and his eyes were dull
and dry between their reddened lids. He opened his lips
and moistened them. The priest gave a quick frown of
exasperation.

" Come ; you must be quick, unless it is to die without
baptism."

" Call her——" said Aurelio ; and in the sudden silence
that fell at the sound of his voice the noise of the flies was
like a thin, fierce orchestra above the people's heads ; the
women pulled their aprons hastily down from their faces,
and his sister raised her head from Aurelio's shoulder and
stared into his face—" Call her Maravilla."

A smothered outcry of exclamation was sternly checked
by the priest ; he wanted to get on ; a bowl of coffee was
cooling on the table in his house, and in the painful aftermath of a night's drinking he badly wanted coffee. Glances
sped from under arched eyebrows ; nudges were given and
taken. No such name had ever been heard in the village
before ! Had Aurelio made it up ? The marvellous one !
To think of calling a child that. It was to be hoped some
of the holy saints would not take offence at having their
nomenclature slighted. Just Maravilla—without even a
María to lend it canonical support. Well, well. The priest
was baptising it, and silence was enforced upon the as-
sembly. Aurelio stood with the fingers of his right hand
clasped about the wrist of his left ; a dull purple was
burning up under the weatherbeaten and leathery texture
of his skin. He kept his eyes upon the ground.

" Maravilla."

The mouths of half the women hung open for exclamation ; the men were squinting under their eyelids at Aurelio ;
when there came a groan from the bed.

It was such a groan as appears to be dragged up from
those imponderable depths where the threads of male and

female life are knotted together ; a groan of one tearing
herself loose from the clutches of a dying enemy, who,
under penalty of unendurable pain, drags what remains
out of the talons. It galvanised all who heard it.

" She is living ! "

The old midwife raised her bleared eyes above the level
of the bed, but before she could move she was forestalled
by two of the women. They knew the things to do, as well
as old Juana : had done them for themselves and for each
other, score upon score of times ; it was only the very young
and inexperienced girls, generally the unmarried ones, or
those who had no female relatives, who called upon the
services of the midwife. In a moment it became, not Carmela Moreno, who fought with death under their eyes, but
a woman like themselves, an anonymous woman, who, for
the sake of her sex, must somehow be brought through this
experience which linked her into the sisterhood. As they
fell upon Carmela, Aurelio, with a purely instinctive gesture, snatched up the infant from the place to which the
priest had restored it. Someone gave him a cloth ; he was
holding it, wrapped in a cloth, in his hands. They were
doing fearful things, drastic things, to Carmela—her groans
were coming more frequently, but each was weaker than
the last. . . .

He was holding his own flesh ; this weaker than weak
thing that lay against his breast was himself. He could feel
its feeble movements, like an insect caught in the folds of
the stuff that covered it. Someone—a girl—took it from
him gently, and, baring her breast like a shrivelled gourd,
laid the babe to it ; incredulously he saw it begin to suck.
While it continued to do so he kept his hands upon it ;
people laughed, but he did not hear them. This child, this
flesh of his own creation, this thing which it had been given
to him, Aurelio López, to make—in the condition of his

mind it seemed to him that he was a miracle-worker : that this was the First Child, the mysterious outcome of his own special knowledge ; that God had permitted him to make this child because of all that he *knew*. And then, suddenly, like a shot, came the recollection of that which he had not known.

His hands dropped from the babe ; only his eyes held it with an inexpressible longing. He wanted it, to hold, to lay upon his sore and bleeding heart, to comfort himself by saying, over and over, its mystical name :

" Maravilla, Maravilla, Maravilla . . ."

CHAPTER II

AURELIO'S STORY

Aurelio López did not wish to leave the mountains. Their escarpments of grey and garnet had built themselves about his imagination from infancy; the hard, blue sky, dragged by the savage peaks taut across their summits, could never have that same tented look elsewhere. Nor could he visualise a landscape that did not hold as its focusing-point, the towering pillar known as La Aguja: which sometimes stabbed like a gargantuan finger direct at the staring blue, and at others veiled itself with a virginal modesty in the grace of a trailing cloud. In winter it became a glittering icicle, its sharp and cruel outline softened by the snows.

Nor was it that he loved the mountains; their callous and brutal suggestiveness, which for generations has helped to mould the characters of their inhabitants, meant nothing to Aurelio beyond a sense of security, of the unchangeability of his circumstances; he was aware of them without giving them a conscious thought until this moment, when the prospect of separation from their familiar grandeur presented itself to his slightly dismayed intelligence.

For the twisting alleys of the town, for the white hovels that owed their situations, and, in some instances, their very boundaries, to the rocks themselves, he had a personal and passionate love. The back of his mother's posada was actually hewn out of the mountainside, its façade a mere excrescence, mankind's attempt to improve upon unchanging nature. Many of the homes in Agujasierra were true rock-dwellings, scooped into the mountainside ; during the winter the smoke of their fires poured from a hole cut some little way above the flat cave-entrance that served alike for door and window. Upon a small square of trampled earth, screened by vine or prickly pear, sat, in the summer dusk, the occupants, whispering the town scandal, or silently following the passing of a stranger with their venal and suspicious eyes.

The " modern " houses, with their balconies of verdigris green, their shutters bleached to a frail silver by the sun, their decorative strings of pimientos, and the withered palms of Easter twisted into their rejas, surrounded the irregular space of the market square. This little clutch of architecture was dwarfed to insignificance by the surrounding summits, which had an air of crushing and moulding it between their harsh declivities. Its very existence seemed, in the face of those malignant heights, an act of insane temerity, inviting at any moment its penalty of annihilation.

No sense of impending doom, however, coloured Aurelio's outlook upon his birthplace. The life that went on in the mountain shadow was the most absorbing feature of his existence.

Even as a small boy he had had a deep and insatiable interest in people : in what they did, what they thought, how they looked, and in the correlation of these three different aspects of human personality. He had learnt that only by means of this correlation, which was often difficult and elusive, was it possible to make a correct deduction of character ; and the art of " knowing " people, as he called it, became a game more absorbing than any usually indulged by children of his age. As he grew older, this interest increased until it formed the motive power of his whole life, and, as the curiosity of childhood deepened into something nobler and more thoughtful, it tended to separate him from his companions ; but the separation was rather of a spiritual than of a carnal nature, and neither side was posi-tively aware of it. Aurelio's silences, his slow, quaint pro-nouncements, delighted whatever company he might frequent ; he was applauded, clapped on the back, invited to drink, and regarded as something between a simpleton and a sage. Looking from one to another, his heart would swell, his lips smile, and his eyes grow large and luminous with emotion, as he reflected that there were no townsmen like his people, and no town like his own, in all Spain.

His slow and gentle manner derived rather from the people of the plain than from the mountain dwellers among whom he and his people were born ; the lust and savagery of his townsmen seemed to him to draw too deeply upon the inner well of their life-forces, to be too productive of that which was disagreeable and tumultuary, to evoke a response in his own temperament. He liked to think, and for think-ing one must have peace. The civic and domestic dramas which were enacted about him filled him with as much satisfaction as a dramatic performance, but his natural function was that of audience and not of participant. His pleasure was to comment on them after they had happened ; to draw a naïve philosophy out of them, and to clothe it in words of his own.

He did not in the least wish to go to Granada, because, at that moment, there were things of particular interest to follow in his own town. Mario Gallego had quarrelled with Antonio Haro, and was forming a slow cabala among the members of the casino, whose object was the boycotting of Antonio's stall in the market-place. Without espousing either cause, but with deep sympathy and growing under-standing of the small, complicated motives governing both sides, Aurelio was following each step of the warfare.

And the schoolmaster, Colgas, had his eye upon a plot of land which Pulgar, the cacique, was talking of selling, and had Pulgar in every evening to drink with him. At some point Pulgar would become so drunk he would practically make Colgas a gift of the land, and the latter would quickly produce the document he had in readiness, and get Pulgar to sign it while the loving-kindness of manzanilla was in his heart.

And María Molino had her eye at last upon old Juan Garcia, who was said to have money ; and all his relatives had got wind of it, and were seeping into the town in a fine state of panic—fully determined that the old man, who was more than eighty years of age, should not fall victim, in his infatuation, to María's duplicity.

Old Juan's great-grandson, Inocencio, was beating his donkey in the side-street into which Aurelio turned, lost in his thoughts. The beast was standing tossing up his head, trembling all over, with thin streams of blood running down his flanks : less from Inocencio's beating than from the galled wounds of the panier-straps, which had broken open under the stick. Aurelio leaned dispassionately against the wall until, with another couple of cuts, Inocencio swung round to face him.

" Well, what are you gaping at ? "

Head on one side, smiling candidly, Aurelio answered him.

" I was just thinking . . . whether God meant the sun for the ass as well as for ourselves."

Inocencio guffawed, flung the stick away, and launched a parting kick at the donkey.

" You're a mad one, you are, Aurelio ! Do you always have to be thinking ? You don't catch me thinking—I've got something better to do than think."

" Come now, hasn't it ever struck you that each part of

us is planned out for a special purpose ? " asked Aurelio, his face lightening, as it invariably did at the prospect of argument. " Our hands for work and our feet for travelling, our mouths for food and our minds for thought. That's what Don Pedro says—but he's a Catalan. I told him this is how we'd put it in Andalucía : the hands for music, the feet for dancing, the mouth for wine, and the mind for the copla ! "

Inocencio looked sidelong at Aurelio, as though considering whether or not the latter was a fool. He had forgotten about the donkey.

" They'll be making you alcalde one day if you go on like that," he asserted, with a touch of jealous admiration.

" I dare say they will. My grandfather was alcalde. I'd make a good alcalde if they gave me the chance. The first thing an alcalde wants is to know about human beings ; not to judge by their faces or what they say. A rogue may have a face like Jesus Christ, and an honest man may be vilified in his own flesh."

Impatient of a philosophy he could not follow, Inocencio broke in :

" What's this about you going to Granada ? It's a fine town, fine girls. What makes you go ? "

With a return of melancholy, Aurelio shrugged his shoulders.

" It seems there was no way of stopping my great-grandfather from begetting children," he complained.

" Oh, you ! You always put the cart before the mule. What are you talking about now ? "

" The old sister of my grandmother—it seems she's got a sickness. All her bones are twisting themselves ; if it goes on much longer they'll be able to bowl her down the street like a hoop. I am her godson, so naturally it is to me she turns when she gets into trouble."

" Is she going to leave you her money ? " asked Inocencio greedily.

" Who knows ? Perhaps she hasn't any to leave."

" Huh ! You wouldn't catch me working for any old relative who wasn't going to leave me money. Working for relations is like whistling to a deaf man ; you get no credit for it."

" Who wants money while the sun shines and there's wine in the bottle ? " said Aurelio easily. " When I'm old I shan't get much out of my money, shall I ? But that "—he pointed to the bright patch of sunlight at the edge of the shadow in which they were standing—" goes on for ever. We're all godchildren of the sun, and while it shines we're millionaires."

Inocencio spat into the sunlight in a manner that suggested he did not think much of his heritage.

" Well, what have you got to do ? And is she paying you for it ? "

" I'm to drive the goats and milk them at people's doors. My madrina," said Aurelio grandly, " has many goats— fifty, or may be a hundred, of them. It will be a fine job. Think of the families I shall get to know. It will be better than reading a newspaper every day."

" Get away with you ! Who wants to read newspapers ? " retorted Inocencio, who had never mastered the alphabet, scornfully. " Newspapers are for old men who want to read about the things they can't do any longer. Still," he concluded, unwillingly surrendering himself to envy, " you certainly came into the world with a loaf of bread in both hands. Encarnación Gallego was crying her eyes into puddles this morning because someone told her you were going to Granada."

This news, which should have melted Aurelio with compassion for the young woman in question, merely filled him with intense gratification. It contributed the final, artistic touch to his departure.

For all his twenty-three years among them, Aurelio had never focused his affections upon a single individual, man or woman, to such a degree that his interest in the others was dwarfed. In a desultory fashion, with waxings and wanings of ardour, he had been Encarnación's lover for a year. There had always been girls, whose abandonment to the physical appeal of his manhood he had exploited without a twinge of conscience or responsibility, because one did not necessarily, in Agujasierra, marry the girl one slept with. Marriage had never so far presented itself to him in any overwhelming form of temptation. His two married brothers, who kept stalls in the market, and divided his services between them, envied him openly for having no domestic ties. " Don't you get married, Aurelio," was the sum of their advice to him ; they made him feel there was something fine and enviable about his freedom.

Yet now he caught himself envying his brothers their close, personal ties ; the intimacy between man and wife, between a father and his children, appealed to him, in this mood of sentiment and farewell, as it had never done before. He felt glad of the tears, even of Encarnación Gallego.

The family of López was poor, but, since in Agujasierra poverty was no barrier to distinction, the name was held in respect. The widow of Manuel López, Aurelio's father, kept the posada on the corner of the square ; as many as possible of her children continued to live with her after marriage, bringing their wives and husbands, bearing their children, under the ancestral roof. The women helped in the house, served food to the customers, and reared their young. One of the daughters was a widow, and exacted a special deference on that account. They quarrelled a great deal and made their quarrels up again ; there was always a running undercurrent of intrigue and jealousy that quickened the atmosphere. Nothing Aurelio had seen in his own home disposed him to assume the risks and responsibilities of matrimony.

His spiritual detachment had affected him more intimately in his family relationships than in the contacts which took place outside his own home ; sitting upon his own hearth, he was conscious of being an onlooker, and felt their consciousness of it, and, because he was naturally loving and warm-hearted, this sometimes pained him. It was a thing that could not, in the few hours that remained, be adjusted. Could he now, with conviction, have gone in, involved himself in a violent partisanship with one of the factions under his mother's roof, he could, in a moment, have effected his amalgamation into the family group. He was aware that they looked upon his detachment, his refusal to be drawn into their quarrels, as a little inhuman, not quite to be trusted.

A sudden and burning desire flamed in him to create for himself an environment, a vessel for the fermentation of a love powerful, personal, and composed of every physical and spiritual element, that should convince not only himself but its recipient : a love containing the germs of creation and the mystery of fatherhood. It was characteristic of Aurelio, at this period, that this desire came to him in a guise purely abstract ; that he did not for a moment connect it with any of the girls with whom, hitherto, he had ventured the experiment of love.

Three months later Aurelio drove his goats down a gulley of the Albaicin. The rust-coloured flock stepped slowly, delicately, over the cobbles, with swinging udders and

slender champing jaws ; every now and then a goat paused
to tear at the tufts of weed sprouting at the base of the
walls, or to stare apprehensively, with mad, pale eyes, at the
possessive father of the flock, who stalked among them,
prevented from exercising his natural functions by the
apron slung beneath his shaggy belly. The rank smell of
the herd mingled with, and sometimes overpowered,
the stenches of the alleys ; both were imperceptible to
Aurelio, as they were to the inhabitants of the old Moorish
quarter.

At this early hour of the morning the sun struck a
dazzling whiteness from the walls, and kindled the old,
saffron-coloured roofs to gold. From balconies here and
there dripped the pot-plants, spilling their scarlet and
yellow into the climbing clusters of morning glory. From the
fábricas came a thunder of looms ; long skeins of yarn,
festooning the ancient wooden galleries, stirred faintly in
the breeze which, too soon, would be suffocated in the
blaze of noon. Now and again, through a gap in the leaning
walls, Aurelio caught a silver glimpse of the Sierra Nevada,
but this sight no longer moved him to home-sickness.

The cotton trousers of faded blue material strained across
his buttocks as he crouched to milk a goat, and his bare
heels were pressed downwards in the alpargatas to maintain
his balance. The goat stood still, yielding up its milk with
voluptuous satisfaction to Aurelio's handling ; he had
become an adept at the milking, and would hand the bowl
or jug through the reja with a naïve smile of vanity.
Usually the milking was an honest matter, but there were
days in the late summer when it was almost impossible to
find grazing for the goats, and when use had to be made of a
discreet little bladder of water concealed under one's coat,
and a length of tubing which skilfully conducted down one's
sleeve the modicum of water that helped to eke out one's

litre. Tía Pepa's milk-round was an extensive one, and Aurelio prided himself upon conducting this little ruse, when it was necessary, with a grace and discretion that defied the most suspicious observer. After all, what was the harm in it? A little good Avellano water—it was almost as desirable as milk, if only the customers knew! Tía Pepa had never descended to watering her milk, as less scrupulous persons had been known to do, with the common water of the public well.

The little naked children of the Albaicin, with their skin which looked as though they had been rolled in coffee, and their stupendous bellies, ran out to see Aurelio go by, and, as he laughed and called out to them, a new thought came into his mind. He would nod a connoisseur's appreciation of a glossy, healthy-looking child, and screw up his eyes as though they had dust in them at the sight of the unhappily far too common diseased or crippled little ones. Some day he would have a child : and it would be fine and hard and glossy, and bold and upright, like the children of Pepe Luis, the well-off tavern-keeper.

It was more than milk that Aurelio purveyed round the Albaicin ; for an inconsiderable trifle, or, if his heart were touched, for nothing, he would carry messages ; with an immense gusto for gossip he combined an impeccable discretion, so that the women trusted him with their love-letters, and even asked and obtained his help in writing them. He was known to be kind and generous ; would add a little milk to the just measure for a house in which there was sickness, or bring a few dried figs out of his pocket to coax a peevish child. He revelled in his popularity, in the superiority his gifts brought to him—for example, his power to read and write, his fine manners, the thin, emotional tenor in which he sang flamenco for the patrons of the wine-shops.

It seemed to Aurelio that a world of infinite importance

and interest revolved about his person ; he loved to play with the idea of controlling this world through the power of his own wisdom. Here, as in Agujasierra, he was a looker-on ; but here, instead of distrust, his detachment brought him a certain dignity, the kind of thing which does not often fall to the lot of a milker of goats. He loved it when people flattered and cajoled him for the purpose of getting some favour out of him ; when they asked him for his advice ; when, under the oath of secrecy, they admitted him voluntarily to their confidence ; and when, all involuntarily, they betrayed themselves to him, he suffered an inebriation of power ; he became a hero to himself, and all sorts of splendid possibilities seemed within reach of his outstretched hand.

He had been driving the goats for nearly a year when he saw Carmela Moreno.

It was through an acquaintance he had made apart from his milk-round. The widow Herédia was not a customer of Tía Pepa, but Aurelio had not failed to bid her good day as he drove the goats past her immaculate threshold. She was a woman of severe propriety, rating herself something above her neighbours, and living in a little house of her own—an uncommon thing in that district of crowded dwellings. There were only two rooms, one above the other, to the little house, but the mere fact of having them to herself invested her, in the eyes of her neighbours, with a very dislikable superiority. She was reputed to be very mean, and to have grudged her husband nourishment in his last illness.

She had a thin, bitter, ashen face, scored with many lines, and her plentiful hair was streaked with grey. Her cleanliness, her neatness, and the propriety of her behaviour were offences to a raffish neighbourhood, but Aurelio always glanced with sly eagerness towards her door, hoping to catch a glimpse of the narrow, upright figure to which, for some inexplicable reason, he felt himself drawn.

One day one of the goats dropped a kid—a minute creature, with enormous soft ears and tiny tottering legs too fragile to bear it along with the rest of the herd. Aurelio popped it under his arm and carried it, with a sense of triumph, to the house of the widow Herédia. He shouted in her doorway ; she came angrily from the yard behind the house to scold him for his impudence.

" What do you want ? I don't buy my milk from you." Then her eyes fell on the kid, and, before she could control them, her hands betrayed her with a gesture ; they twitched towards the tiny object with an irresistible although quickly checked movement of compassion. " Why should I take care of the beast for you ? It is like your impudence to suggest such a thing."

" Take it ; in your heart you have always wanted something like this. I have brought you just what you wanted. The more troublesome it is, the more you will like it. That's the way women are with their children," urged Aurelio. " You can't deceive me. All that anger of yours is against life ; it has nothing to do with me, or the kid."

" Indeed ! And how do you make that out ? " snapped the widow, keeping her eyes away from the kid ; for when she looked at it she could feel something coming into them which had no right to be there. She spurted into wilder anger. " The idea of a cualquiera like you coming and saying those things to me ! Be off with you ! I have heard enough about your conceit and the way you tell people their business—as if you were a grandee instead of a common goatherd ! "

Aurelio's eyes sparkled to think that she had heard of him, and he burst out laughing.

" Don't try to deceive me," he repeated. " You are angry

with life because it has cheated you of having children. Well, here's a child for you ! No baby could be more helpless than this kid ; it needs all the things babies need—warmth, and food, and gentle handling. And I will come back and fetch it this evening."

" I wonder you don't suggest I should put it to my breast ! " muttered the widow, in a voice that trembled between rage and tears.

" You should get married again ; perhaps you would have children."

" Who would marry me ? " she stammered, with a sudden lapse into humility, which gave Aurelio the opportunity to thrust the kid into her arms. They closed upon it with a gesture of starvation ; unconsciously her fingers ran possessively over the soft, damp hide. Aurelio stroked the kid's ear.

" Dip your fingers in milk," he muttered, " and let it suck them——"

" Do I need your instructions ? " she snapped. He laughed again, moving a little closer to her. Each was conscious of the other's body—he of the dry, enforced virginity of hers, she of the youthful and lusty masculinity of Aurelio. Her face changed ; she took a step backwards, as though fearing some strange contagion. Their eyes met deeply, with a question in each. She turned with a noise like a sob and ran away from him into the darkness of the house. He called after her :

" I'll come to-night and see how it is getting on ! "

That was the beginning of it : of a friendship often critical and disapproving on the widow's side, complicated on Aurelio's by respect for her age and virtue. She disapproved his light dealings with girls, his interest in his fellow-creatures, which she put down to a low curiosity which had no respect for privacy. She always engineered the conversation away from personal topics, and they talked mainly in abstractions—upon what a revolution might mean to Spain, on the influence of poverty upon a nation, on the growth of civilisations : curious subjects for a woman of her class, and dealt with naïvely by both of them ; but the very fact of her thinking about such matters proved her to be an exception to her kind, and increased the volume of Aurelio's respect for her, while it explained her isolation among her neighbours.

Aurelio himself tired often of these abstract discussions. His intellectual industry was limited to people and places that he knew ; beyond those it flagged ; he would fall silent, drowsily smiling at her, while, stiffly seated in her chair, she would consume in the helpless ardour of a woman lacking normal outlet for her mind's activity.

" I do not know what it is about you," he confessed, one day, when they had been talking for a long time. " It must seem very strange that I come to see you day after day, as though we were novios, yet who would believe we have never exchanged one word of love ? "

" I should hope not ! " cried the widow, but her thin cheeks burned. " The very thought is a scandal—you should be ashamed of yourself for mentioning it."

" Pardon me," said Aurelio, " but the truth is that you excite a part of me which has never been excited before. I cannot put it into words. But inside these four walls—do you not feel it ?—we become something more than ourselves. Such learned and refined conversation ! Do you suppose the Duque has any better at his table ? "

The widow repressed a smile at the naïveté of the suggestion, but retorted sharply :

" If you have so strong a taste for my society, it is an odd thing, the company you keep sometimes."

" It takes all sorts to make a world," answered Aurelio easily. " One does not wear one's Sunday clothes every day ; that way they would very soon get shabby and we should think nothing of them. When I visit you I feel like a bullfighter dressed up to visit his novia ! Can't you see me ? " cried Aurelio, leaping from his chair, hollowing his waist and making gestures. " The Cordobés hat, the elegant trousers——— ? "

" How foolish you are ! " said the widow, letting her fondness steal through her usual severity. " I really believe you think that one must have fine clothes before one can possess a fine mind."

She had given up the kid the day after it was brought to her, but in such a fashion that, had it not been for Tía Pepa, who knew the goat was due to have a kid, Aurelio would have let her keep it. Each day she had asked after it in a dry, ironical voice, and, on the day he told her that it had eaten something poisonous and had died, she railed at him like an Albaicin drab, calling him every name under the sun for his abominable negligence. The day following, she would barely speak to him, and he felt it was a great fuss to make about a kid.

The other women plagued him spitefully about his friendship with the widow.

" Have you got scared of the girls, that you have to take up with an old woman ? "

More malevolent in their comments were the girls from the carpet factory, who accused him of neglecting them for his new friend. They told him to his face he had gone to the widow because he was impotent, and was afraid of the younger women finding it out. Her they accused of hypocrisy, discussing her openly each time they passed her door. He flew into passions ; she took their malice upon a steely sheet of indifference which expressed itself in the bitterness and contempt of her glances at her tormentors. Had they not feared Aurelio's reprisals, they might have gone further ;

as it was, it became by no means an uncommon thing, when she went down to the shops on the Plaza Larga, to hear a stone go clattering past her on the cobbles. She took to walking in the middle of the alleys, to avoid worse outrages from the balconies and upper windows.

There came an evening when she received him coldly and told him that from thenceforth his visits must cease.

" Now, come," said Aurelio. " You are not going to show yourself so weak as to take notice, after all this time, of what people are saying ? What has our acquaintance ever been but pure and noble ? At any moment the priest might have walked in and found us both, as good as angels, sitting at opposite sides of the room, with the table between us, and the doors and windows wide open, so everyone could hear our conversation."

" It has nothing whatever to do with that," said the widow, flushing slightly. " The truth is, my brother's daughter is coming to live with me, to help me in my work and fetch and carry the shirts from the shops for me ; it has become impossible for me to go up and down to the town twice a day, as well as get my sewing done."

" Why could you not have said that before ? " cried Aurelio. " I could surely have arranged something for you."

" Many thanks, but I do not choose to be under an obligation," said the widow drily, but softened the ungraciousness of the words by adding, " that is to say, not more than the obligation you have already laid upon me by benefiting me with your company." He saw the faint colour, like the glimmer of light inside an alabaster globe, that animated the greyness of her cheek, and the evasive look in her eyes which lent her, for a moment, the look of a young girl. He did not believe the tale about the niece ; it was some access of modesty which had come upon her,

some belated recognition of the difference in their sexes—
something that excited and interested him, and reminded
him of a thing he often forget in their intercourse—that
he was male and she female.

" You must have been very beautiful when you were a
young woman, Angustias Herédia," he said, softly. She
shrank back as though he had struck her.

" I forbid you to say these things ! "

" As you like," he answered carelessly ; after all, there
was not much to be gained by insisting upon that aspect of
their relationship. He added formally, " As far as my
visits benefit you—what do you suppose I have gained from
them ? Coming here has been like going to school—no, I
don't say that, because I often ran away from school, or
had to be driven to it like a young bull into a corral ! "

" Nevertheless," said the widow inexorably, " it must
come to an end. When my niece comes to live with me,
everything will be different. I shall not have time to talk
to you, and I shall have my responsibility to her father to
consider."

" I should like to meet your niece," persisted Aurelio.

A look almost of apprehension crossed her face. She
seemed about to give a violent refusal, checked herself, and
then apparently resolved to put her thoughts into words.

" That is exactly what I do not wish you to do, if it can
be avoided," she said frankly. " And I look upon you as
bound by our friendship to respect my wishes."

" Por Dios, I respect them," said Aurelio earnestly. "But
you will at least favour me with an explanation ? Perhaps
you think I shall fall in love with your niece and want to
marry her ? Well, supposing I did ? Would it be so much
of a calamity ? Think what you would gain by it. You
would have the two of us to look after you, and if Tía Pepa
leaves me her money there will be no need for you to go

on sewing. Surely that is an agreeable kind of notion ? "

" It would be every sort of a calamity if you were to fall in love with my niece," cried the widow, crossing herself violently. " For you are not the kind of man she could ever marry."

" What makes you say that ? " demanded Aurelio, offended. The widow looked at him coldly.

" For one thing, my niece, who comes from a refined home, could never settle among your people—which is what would have to happen, for there is no accommodation in her house or in mine for a married couple. And, for another, you have lived a loose life with women, and should think shame of yourself to think of asking a virtuous girl to share her life with you."

" Listen, Doña Angustias," said Aurelio seriously, for the effect of the widow's words was merely to pique his curiosity and imagination. " It is natural one should play with pebbles before one is shown the jewels they represent. One only needs to be shown the gems themselves to fling the pebbles in the gutter, where they belong."

The argument went on for the better part of an hour, but the widow was implacable—all the more so because she realised fully what a deprivation to herself would be the loss of Aurelio's company. It was the first time for many years she had known the pleasure of friendship, and, although the coming of her niece meant she would be no longer solitary, she knew enough of the deep, ineradicable antagonism of sex to be aware that Carmela would not fill Aurelio's place.

She had become aware, moreover, latterly, of a dangerous heightening of her feelings towards him ; had been guilty, on one or two occasions, of looking in the glass, of making some trivial arrangement of her dress, that was planned to attract his attention to her not wholly vanished comeliness.

She despised herself bitterly for these weaknesses, in which she felt not only a lowering of her personal dignity, but betrayal of her husband's memory. For her own sake, his visits must come to an end. Strengthened by her own weakness, she reiterated her determination, until Aurelio rose angrily and slouched towards the door. As he reached it, his broad shoulders and narrow hips outlined in the moonlight which flung a sheet of blue-silver across the opposite façades, there was a hasty shuffle of retreat ; as usual, they had been spied upon, their conversation probably overheard by the ill-natured neighbours who pried upon their meetings. The reminder enflamed the spark of his anger.

" Well, you may forbid me to come into your house," he shouted at her, " but you can't stop me from driving my goats across your threshold twice a day ! "

His words set up a vibration in her ear-drums ; as she lifted her hands towards them a miniature tempest racked her body. The preposterous fact of her love for a man young enough to be her son leapt naked at her from the shadows ; she rose to slam doors and shutters, that none should witness her humiliation. But it was long before she could compose herself sufficiently to get into bed : the bed she was to share with Carmela. A spasm of painful honesty forced her to face the fact that her dismissal of Aurelio was due less to family responsibility than to her dread that he would fall in love with Carmela, and add the pangs of jealousy to those she already suffered.

A day or two later Aurelio saw Carmela. Guessing that the widow would be expecting him on his round, and would take steps to have her niece out of the way, he cunningly altered his route so as to arrive in the street before his usual time. The goats, accustomed to their usual track, took some beating and coaxing into an opposite direction, and when he actually arrived, having surprised most of the customers by his early call, Aurelio was sweaty and breathless, but received, most unworthily, the reward of his guile.

The girl was actually sweeping the doorstep as he came in sight of the house ; she stood aside to allow the goats to pass on their small tottering hoofs. " Bueno' día' ! " called Aurelio as he followed them. She returned his greeting coolly, but, when he actually stood still to smile at her, turned her back upon him and walked into the house. Out of sheer devilment, Aurelio launched a " Guapa ! " at her retreating slimness, and laughed triumphantly as her head went up in scorn.

There was something regal in her carriage ; her back was as straight as an arrow, and the column of her spine supported a head which had less of arrogance in its deportment than of cultivated and conscious self-respect. His first quick view of her had given him the elements of recognition ; he would know her, wherever their next meeting might take place. A pale, oval, serious face, not beautiful according to local standards, for it lacked animation, but correct in every feature—the type of face which acquires a positive beauty only after middle age ; well-shaped eyes, of a deeper brown than his own ; a firm and finely cut mouth. She had firm, full breasts, and, in the action of sweeping, her body revealed a seductive pliancy that was balanced by the modesty of her bearing. Later he was to discover that her ears were small, flushed shells, pressed exquisitely close to the sides of her head ; and that the nape of her neck had a full, rich smoothness like dairy cream. But these beauties were recondite ; he had not done badly for a first observation. Her age he guessed—correctly—to be a little more than his own ; there were, as a matter of fact, four good years between them. Her character resolved itself in her repudiation of his impudent attentions ; she was modest, virtuous, and well trained. It occurred to him that her aunt might have been just such a girl twenty years before. There was something about Carmela that challenged his attention: he was not in love with her yet, but the thought of her clung to his mind like a burr to a woollen garment.

It was not hard to arrange seemingly casual meetings in Granada. Aurelio knew the shop which employed the widow Herédia ; he knew that, to reach it, Carmela would follow always the same route, that led quickly down from the Albaicin heights into the Calle de Elvira ; from which she would go by way of the Zácatin into the narrow churning gulley of Mesónes. What could be simpler than for him to plan his time so as to intercept her evening journey ?

She was never alone, for her own modesty, no less than the vigilance of her aunt, exacted companionship. There were several other girls who went on a similar nightly errand, and she was always accompanied by one or another of these.

At first their encounter was of the briefest ; she gave him no opening for a greeting, as almost any girl of the Albaicin would have done : lowering her eyes, after the first glance, until the lashes rested upon her cheek. He would then follow her at a decorous distance as far as Bibirambla, and, on her return, would be waiting for her at the top of the Zácatin. She was safe to return that way, for what young maiden could resist the lure of the jewellers' shops, the display of fans and mantillas in Granada's most fashionable street ?

In acting thus, Aurelio paid tribute to conventions of which he knew next to nothing ; the girl's demeanour forced them upon him, repudiating the easier manners of Agujasierra, which would have forced an opening long before she granted it.

He had begun almost to despair of making her acquaintance—since it was forbidden him to go to the house of the widow Herédia—when chance played into his hands.

In September the fiesta of San Miguel—that fiesta which starts with the dawn upon the slopes above the Moorish wall—swept all the population of the Albaicin up to the heights. Before daybreak the long procession of ardent holiday-makers who had sacrificed their night's rest to the celebration of San Miguel had started. The dawn came clamorously, to music, to dancing, to the shouts of the stallkeepers, to the rattle of the castanets of the gipsies from the Sacro Monte, whose bright flounces were dim, like the faded petals of flowers, against the blaze of the sky.

Aurelio had followed the widow and her niece unobserved, and managed to keep them in sight even in the turmoil of the fair. His opportunity came when they were torn apart by a group of hooligans who went charging through the mob to separate a couple of dogs which had started a fight under a chestnut-stall.

He could see the ludicrously perturbed expression on the widow's face as she was dragged backwards in the surge of the people from the scene of the combat. Her expression proclaimed that she, at any rate, was not there willingly : that she had yielded, against her better judgment, to Carmela's pleading, and now look what had happened ! He would have laughed had he not at the same time caught sight of Carmela, her too-regular features quickened into living beauty by a flush of excitement. She was a little frightened as well ; hardly less than her aunt she was disliking this thrusting and yelling. With a beating heart he flung himself against the opposing bodies, and by some means reached her side. Their eyes met, with a wild flash of recognition in Carmela's.

That look of hers, the first significant one that she had

given him, took the breath from Aurelio's body. It was exactly as though the girl had reached out with her hand down into some dark, secret depth of his body, and crushed the feeling part of him into the palm of her soft hand.

" I will take care of you ! " he panted, drawing her, as he spoke in the opposite direction from that in which the mob was forcing the widow. In her glance across her shoulder he read Carmela's perfect appreciation of his motive. At best they could have but a few seconds together, for Aurelio must vanish before the widow struggled back to them.

Quick as thought he pulled her round the angle of the church. They were running breathlessly up the steps ; they were in the incense-smelling darkness, in the presence of the plumed San Miguel, listening to each other's hurried breathing, acutely conscious of the lawlessness of their behaviour. At any moment they might be seen, some busy-body would betray them to the widow ; the few devout people still kneeling, after the conclusion of the mass, in the chancel had but to turn their heads to see them as they leaned, trembling, against the leather curtain of the door.

He muttered something ; she said hurriedly, " I will speak to my aunt." She accepted his advances ! In that one sentence, which was tantamount to the removal of the embargo the widow had laid upon him, she confessed herself aware of all his attempts to attract her attention, willing to accept his courtship ! Clutching the curtain, his limbs turning to water, his eyes half closed, he murmured, " I am dying for you."

She flashed him a smile full of heady promise, and was gone ; he stayed for a while, holding the curtain and wiping the sweat from his brow. He knew, with joy and terror in the knowledge, that he had found a thing which was going to alter the current of his whole life, give it a purpose it had formerly lacked, lend shape to his days. He was not sure that he wanted them to be shaped ; he loved the immense fluidity of time, the effortless merging of to-day into to-morrow, the sun on the wall, his own lack of responsibility. Yet here was the woman who, through his desire for her, was to alter all that ; his love for whom cancelled all other loves, upon whom he desired to father his children.

He knew all this, and, when the burning in him had subsided a little, he left the church, and, separating himself from the clamour of the fair, lay down at a distance, behind a prickly pear. The great bowl of the mountains rose, pale amethyst of morning, from the Vega, but the shoulder of the hill upon which he lay hid his own mountains from him. Only the peaks that looked across the valley from the direction of Agujasierra were in sight. He turned towards them. There would they go ; there she would make her home with him, and they would rear their children at the foot of the pillar.

There began their long, difficult wooing : difficult because of the increasing enmity of the widow towards them both. Her will, beaten in its encounter with Carmela's when it came to asking Aurelio to the house, strengthened its malice. Difficult because of the opposition of Carmela's family, who cried out upon her for marrying beneath her station. Difficult because of Carmela's own inviolable determination to yield no jot of her virginity to the demands made upon it by Aurelio's passion until their union had received the blessing of the Church. He had not expected that, and it disconcerted him badly. He had taken it for granted he and Carmela would live together until circum-stances became propitious for their marriage. But she let him know that her people were of the class who could afford, and therefore demanded, marriage for their daughters. She refused flatly to go to bed with him until the priest had given them leave.

Their only supporter was Tía Pepa, who did not like Carmela, but made her free of her dwelling—which scared Carmela by its squalor—because, with the diabolical intuition of old age, she had guessed the widow's secret, and, hating her, took malicious pleasure in thwarting her desires. She was, at the same time, cunningly aware of the advantage to Aurelio of marrying into so respectable a family as the Morenos, and chose, eventually, the most practical way she could have found of helping them out of their difficulty. She died, and her small savings—too insignificant to be called a fortune—together with certain rents on tumbledown property, came to Aurelio, and helped to mitigate the displeasure of the Morenos. On their wedding night they rode under the stars to Agujasierra.

CHAPTER III

CARMELA

THE FATHER of Carmela Moreno was a postman; this meant he could both read and write, and that he cared more about such accomplishments than many in his position. Carmela and her sisters went to a convent school, and remained there until they were each in turn fourteen years of age. Then they came home and helped their mother.

The family of Moreno enjoyed a considerable prosperity, having not only the governmental pay to rely upon, but also the proceeds of the little bakery which the energetic and avaricious Doña Marta had opened soon after their marriage. The door of their house, which stood upon one of the ignoble streets that crowd the lower slopes of the Alhambra hill, had been cut in half, and a ledge fixed upon the lower half, across which the customers were served; Doña Marta was not going to be let in for the expense of a shop window. She did all the baking herself, and, as a little side-line, cigarettes of contraband tobacco were rolled by the youngest girl, who had, in consequence, permanently yellowed fingers, which were regarded with distaste by her fastidious sisters.

In spite of the fact that the house was situated in one of the most squalid parts of the town, among dubious neighbours and the filth to which they were indifferent, which, in the hot days of summer, exuded an unbearable stench of rotting vegetables and sewage, the Morenos preserved an impeccable cleanliness and propriety in their persons, their immediate surroundings, and their lives. To see the Moreno girls going to church on Sundays, with their high combs, their hair burnished beneath the mantillas, their gloved fingers clasping their prayer-books, the neat ankles and smart footwear, discreetly revealed beneath the hems of their skirts, one would have taken them for the daughters at least of well-placed professional men. Doña Marta's vigilance was unceasing, her ideas of propriety derived from circles much higher than her own. This was due to her having been, before her marriage, personal maid to a wealthy lady of the Alhambra, from whom she had eagerly copied all the traits of refinement she now inculcated into her daughters. The names of the Moreno girls were synonymous in Granada with all the ideas of virtue and modesty which other parents, with less success, strove to inculcate into their own offspring.

Carmela was the eldest ; she was nearly twenty-eight when she came to her aunt in the Albaicin. Perhaps, as the years went over her head—and twenty-eight years is a long time to remain a virgin—the aridity of her enforced virtue had begun to suggest itself to her mind.

She was extremely practical, prudent, and conventional, and minded enormously what people thought of her ; but these qualities had not gained her a husband. She was a full-blooded girl, desirous and passionate, but never in her life had she been offered an outlet for her passion. The slightly glacial air of respectability, the too-conscious air of self-respect, had scared off admirers who had been attracted in the first place by her good looks. The general opinion seemed to be that marriage with such a paragon of virtue could only be made worth while by the inclusion of a generous dowry ; and what dowry could a postman with three girls to marry off be expected to provide ?

There were nights when she tossed on her bed, praying to God he would send her a lover who would take from her the secret shame of her burning body. The marriage of her youngest sister five years before (tobacco-stained fingers, it appears, are no detriment when allied to a certain agreeable lightness of manner and a provocative sidelong glance which had many a time drawn upon the lively Dolores the rebukes of her elders) had been a martyrdom to Carmela ; her imagination ran riot upon the experiences which, vouchsafed to Dolores—who, beneath her glitter, was a cold little thing—had been denied to her. In dread of someone's perceiving her state of mind she had become more glacial than ever. It was in some wild hope that, freed from maternal vigilance, she would discover a form of solace at present denied, she had acceded to her aunt's request that she should come and live with her for a while.

Why should she not do it ? She was not needed at home ; her mother was still active, and had her sister to help in the shop. One of her brothers had brought his wife to live with them.

She was in love with Aurelio from her first glance at him. When she was younger her lip would have curled at the suggestion that she should fall in love with a man who drove goats and milked them at people's doors. But these girlish vanities had been swept away from her, as soil is swept from a cliff, by the rising tide of unsatisfied sexual longing, and in that first encounter she saw in Aurelio the one who was planned to save her from the dark abyss towards which she was stumbling.

Not that she would ever have become his mistress. Hard-driven as she was, her innate conventionality prevented her from even considering so simple and practical a solution of her troubles. No ; he must be made to pay tribute to those gods of her idolatry, the social observances of her family, even though the delay destroyed her. It was a curious starchiness of outlook, for a girl of her class, in which the rites of betrothal carry the privileges of marriage. It was part of the affectation of refinement which Doña Marta had brought with her down the Alhambra hill ; and, although she suffered for it, Carmela, like her mother, would rather have died than have sacrificed one tittle of the refinement which, in their own minds, elevated them above their neighbours.

So she pretended to ignore his agonised pleas for a little kindness, though the pulse-beat in her throat almost choked her each time she saw him waiting for her at the top of the Zácatin.

She made her request of her aunt boldly, and was taken aback by its reception.

" What ! " cried the widow Herédia, whitening. " You want to bring across my threshold a ruffian like Aurelio López ! You want to bring the smell of goats into my house ! You must be crazy, girl. Never in my life would I agree to such a thing."

Carmela, who had heard of Aurelio's former visits, became as crimson as her aunt was pallid, but stood her ground ; the same stubbornness and determination to get their own way was planted in them both.

" I did not say anything about his coming into the house ; it is early days to be talking of that. We shall both be satisfied if he comes and talks to me through the reja in the evenings," she said firmly.

" And get the house a bad name, for the scum that hangs about it ! I forbid it," snapped the widow. " Your father would kill us if he heard of such a thing. Aurelio López is not only a common fellow you should think shame of yourself to look at, but he is a bad man. He has been the lover of every puta in the Albaicin, and next thing he will be boasting in the brothels of having conquered your affections ! ''

Such is the contrariness of the feminine mind that, having been reared in a scrupulous regard for chastity, Carmela, although she blanched a little at her aunt's violent words, was attracted rather than repelled by this picture of Aurelio. It surrounded him, for her, with an aura of experience ; and for a moment she, poor girl, was poignantly, humbly aware of her own ignorance. In some ways—in every way save that indicated to her by her own instincts —she was as ignorant as a nun. To be conquered by all that masculine knowledge offered an ecstasy that smote the breath from her body, and her humility was no less than her proud confidence of being able to hold him, once she had got him.

" You may say what you like. I shall find a way of seeing Aurelio if you forbid me the decent protection of your own roof. I am not a girl any longer——''

" That is obvious," said the widow cruelly. " At your age I had been married ten years."

" Well, I mean to lose as little time as possible in following your example," said Carmela boldly.

" What ! You would marry that beggar, that Don Juan Tenorio ! ''

" He is not a beggar, and I have only your word for it he is a Don Juan."

" Go out into the streets, ask the first disreputable woman you meet—ask any woman you like—for her opinion of Aurelio López ! '' cried the widow, flinging out a trembling hand.

" I would as soon trust my own common sense," retorted Carmela. " And, if you forbid us to see each other here, I shall go back home, where at least he can come and buy cigarettes across the counter ! ''

The widow bit her lip. Carmela's threat filled her heart with a bitterness of despair. She saw that there were but two alternatives open to her : either to send Carmela from her house, and suffer all the pangs of imagining their wooing proceeding down in the town, or to bear the equal torment of watching the lovers under her own roof. Appealing to her brother to put a stop to the business might or might not succeed ; she knew her sister-in-law had begun at last to get anxious about the prolonged spinsterhood of her two elder daughters. Who knew whether or not she would take the same view of Aurelio's undesirability ? The widow remembered, with a twinge in her breast, his charm, his gift for ingratiating himself, the disarming candour of his bearing, which had made so fatal an impression upon herself. What if her brother should turn round and say, " This is a very honest young fellow, very respectable—and a woman of Carmela's age cannot afford to be too particular ? " The unaccountability of the masculine mind filled her with apprehension. A year ago Pablo Moreno would have assumed grand and doubtful airs if Carmela had been asked in marriage by a clerk of the Ayuntamiento : would have let her go grudgingly to a well-to-do shop-keeper's son. He might shrug his shoulders now upon this disastrous betrothal, and Marta would, as usual, tune her note to his.

She made some dumb gesture of defeat. The same evening Aurelio was at the reja, whispering his hot words into Carmela's ear. The widow sat above, on her balcony ; she could hear the whispers, although not their gist, and she chewed her lips until they bled. She sat there, drowning in jealousy, while the lovers' conversation went on below.

" Is it true you have made love to a great many women ?"

" But, Carmela mía ! " There was honest bewilderment

in Aurelio's voice. " How is one to help that ? Henceforth I adore you only. I am yours, body and soul."

" That's all very well, but how can I be sure of that ? "

" How can one be sure the moon will rise, the sun will set ? God arranges these things ; he created us separately, and now we join together. It is like a miracle, isn't it ? "

" Miracles are all very well, but one doesn't hear of them nowadays. What made you love the other women ? " persisted the practical Carmela, raising her fan so that all of her face, save her eyes, was hidden.

" Who knows ? When I look back I cannot even remember that I loved any woman but yourself. Only trust me, Carmela mía ! I will make you so happy. Gloria mía, why won't you let me make you happy now ? " he whispered hotly ; his hands, touching her through the bars of the reja, communicated the trembling of his body to her own. She replied insincerely :

" How can I ? There's only one bed here—that I share with my aunt."

" Come to Tía Pepa's ! " he implored her. " She sleeps like the dead. You need not feel shy."

She shook her head positively. Tía Pepa's ! She had been there—once.

" We must just wait," she said, with simulated sadness ; for, of course, nothing would have made her give him that before they were married. " Patience ; there is no other remedy."

She heard him groan, saw him press his brow, which was beaded with little drops, against the cold ironwork. She longed to put her arms about his head, but could not trust herself. When he had recovered something of his self-control :

" We'll go and live in the mountains, and forget in bliss all our suffering," he said. " And we shall teach each other all we know. You will become to me like a beautiful book of a million pages, which I shall read slowly—oh, so slowly ! And as I turn over each page I shall find a new way of making you happy."

" Do you like reading books ? " She asked the question anxiously, with a prickling of vanity. All her family could read and write ; could she bring herself to marry a man who, like most of the peasants, could do neither ? She drew a breath of relief at Aurelio's reply.

" I have read a lot of books," he said carelessly. " But I would rather read people. What does anyone want with books when there are faces and hands and bodies that tell a better story than any of the writers have ever invented ? Oh, Carmela ! I shall read your lips and your eyes and your beautiful breast until I know all of you by heart ! "

She paid for her happiness next morning in the bitter silence of the widow, whose sentences, barbed with acid politeness, fell only at necessary intervals from her frozen lips. An active, almost tangible hatred had sprung up overnight, like a dark plant, within the house ; its clotted tendrils strangled their intercourse. Carmela viciously resented her aunt's attitude, and her responses were barely civil. Had the two women conformed more closely to the class to which they belonged, had their natural instincts not been perverted by civilisation, there would have been open warfare before nightfall, when Aurelio again came to the reja. On this occasion the widow did not go upstairs ; she stood in the doorway, leaning against the wall with her arms folded across her narrow bosom, and her smile, full of malevolence, fixed upon Aurelio.

" Qué tal, señora ? " His impudence maddened her ; she could have struck at him, but she pressed her forearms more tightly against her breast and continued to look and to smile at him. " Come," said Aurelio gently ; he lowered his voice and stepped aside from the reja, so that they stood out of Carmela's hearing. " Do you not see," he said persuasively, " how happy we can be, all three together, if you will be agreeable to me ? There is no reason why we should not all love one another and help each other to be happy."

For reply, she turned on her heel, and, with a gesture of overpowering mockery, invited him to enter her house. Aurelio hesitated, but followed in the end ; Carmela's beautiful, angry eyes met him from her position by the window. They sat down, the widow as well, her hands clenched on her lap, so that the knuckles stared white through the thin flesh. She sat there, looking from the one to the other, with the same diabolical smile, which seemed as though it had been carved into her face. It was impossible to converse—to do anything but sit dumbly beneath such a weight of malevolence. Carmela, crimson, plucked at her gown. Aurelio sat with his hands in his pockets, looking at the toes of his shoes. And the grim woman sat between them, forming, with her soul no less than with her body, an impassable barrier to their intercourse. Aurelio began to sing under his breath.

The widow broke her silence.

" There is a saying that when a Spaniard sings he is either in a fury or penniless ; which is it, Aurelio López ? Which is it ? "

He looked at her with his head on one side, and the uncannily intelligent expression in his eyes which had always baffled her and made her a little afraid of him, although she mocked at his pretensions to wisdom.

" To try to check love is to try to hold back the ocean," he told her quietly.

" You must know a great deal about love, Aurelio López," said the widow, with false sweetness. " It is an interesting subject. Pray, señor, talk to us about love. It is so long since I loved that I have forgotten what it is ; and as for Carmela "—she shot a vicious side-glance at the girl, and moistened her lips before finishing her sentence— " she has never known ! "

For a moment Carmela turned so white it seemed as though she was going to faint. The widow's face, colourless as bone, was carved upon the darkness of the room.

" I will, perhaps, talk about love another day. Allow me, señora," said Aurelio gently, " to wish you good night."

His gentleness slashed at her inflamed heart ; she wanted to cast herself upon his bosom and beg him to take her and to forget all about the girl who had come between them ; and she wanted in the same moment to see him dead at her feet. Sitting in her chair she saw him pass through the door, and heard the rustle of Carmela's gown as she darted to the window to intercept him as he passed by.

" I hate her ! She is a bad shadow upon us both ! I will go home," she panted, with her lips pressed to the bars.

" No, don't go home. It will be so hard for me to see you down there. . . . There's something inside her which is tormenting her," whispered Aurelio hurriedly. " We must try to find out what it is. . . . To-morrow night you had better come to Tía Pepa's."

The following evening, therefore, Carmela climbed the rough track to the whitewashed hutch which had housed Tía Pepa for the greater part of her life. Behind it there was a piece of fenced waste land and some remnants of roofing, where the goats were penned at nightfall ; in the dusk their eyes glimmered at her like pale golden coins among the flat fan-shaped leaves of the prickly pear ; the rasping sound of their hungry dragging upon the bundles of fodder hung above their stalls came to her nervous ears, and their rank odour offended her nostrils, as they were offended by the stenches of her own quarter of the town.

She had been taken aback, on her first visit, by the squalor of Aurelio's lodging : by its lack of privacy (and, consequently, of decency) and its aged smell of uncleanliness. The goats which rambled in and out had left their droppings ; her shocked eyes saw the two beds, with their dubious coverings, in the corners of the single room. The ceiling, arched like a vault, was black with smoke and flies, and the pots and pans of metal, which shone like gold and silver in her own home and that of her aunt, were roughened with collected grime. It shocked her no less to discover that Aurelio was seemingly unaware of these shamefulnesses, in no way embarrassed with them ; surely he could himself have put on a little whitewash, scoured a pot or two !

He led her in by the hand, and pointed with a laugh to the old woman who, bent like a hoop, sat in the hearth, on which were ashes of a whilom fire. They must have been there for hours ; there was no smell or sign of cooking in the place.

" She's fast asleep. Have you ever noticed how old people sleep ? It's as if they are getting ready for death. We can say what we like, she won't wake up until to-morrow morning."

He lit a candle in a lantern ; the shadows swung strangely about the horrible little room. Presently, without speaking, he took her hand again ; his eyes went down deep into hers ; she knew what he was asking her ; she shook her head violently, and dragged her hand from his grasp. That he should expect her to lie with him on that unclean pallet, in this foul room, with that horrible old woman, doubled up like a corpse, by the hearth ! She realised, with a pang of horror, that these surroundings were natural to Aurelio, that he was not disturbed by them, and expected her to be

as indifferent as himself ! While she wondered if it wou.
be possible to go through with it, he took he gently in his
arms, and kissed her with so gentle a sweetness that the
tears gushed to her eyes, while her body went hard lest
her own nature should betray her to him. Stiff, uneasy,
made awkward by her surroundings, filled with a thousand
misgivings that she longed to stifle on his breast, she knew
that she loved him : that, whatever might be his people,
she must marry him.

She could only stay a little while, for convention forbade
him, since they were not yet openly betrothed, to escort her
to her own door, and she was afraid of missing the girl who
had walked up the hill with her. No virtuous woman walked
alone at night, and now, above all things, it seemed to
Carmela vital that she should preserve her character among
these lax and indifferent people.

On Sunday she went to her family as usual, telling
Aurelio he might come down after the evening milk round
and ask for her brothers. Meanwhile she would try to pave
the way for his introduction into the family circle.

That night was a night of the most exquisite torture for
Carmela. Her parents made less fuss than she had expected
about her having acquired a young man ; the widow
Herédia had been right in conjecturing that the relief of
getting their eldest daughter married would overbear any
natural misgiving.

But she had not expected Aurelio to appear at the door
collarless and coatless, with no hat on his springy dark hair.
She saw her brothers, in their smart, ready-made Sunday
suits, looking at one another : felt, rather than saw, the
cruel amusement of her sisters at Aurelio's unsophisticated
appearance, of which, with the good breeding of country
people, he was wholly unconscious.

As modesty dictated, she withdrew into the inner room

ith the women, while the men sat round the open door. She could h☐☐r the rumble of their voices, the pauses in their convers ation ; could imagine the suspicious glances with which ☐ he Moreno men would sum up Aurelio, and t☐eir townsr en's contempt for his simplicity. Her ears burned, her eyes were pricking with tears, the hair on her temples was plastered with sweat. She knew that to them he would appear a fool, a gullible peasant, and her pride sickened. Under her sisters' teasing she was ignobly tempted to repudiate him, to make a joke of the whole affair, to represent it as an act of condescension on her part, and declare there was nothing serious in it at all.

Her sisters, one of her brothers, and Aurelio walked back to the Albaicin with her, and all the way she had to put up with the girls' mockery ; yet, in the midst of her humiliation, the golden ghost of Aurelio seemed to walk beside her, assuring her, in a whisper, of his love for, and power to love, her. They left her at her aunt's door, and she could not even bring herself to say good night to Aurelio, who was the least embarrassed of the party. She had a bad night, during which petty vanity fought with love, and now one conquered and now the other. Her eldest brother called next day to say that the family thought it better she should look for someone else, and, if this was the way she behaved in the Albaicin, she had better come home.

It needed only this to put the final spur to Carmela's stubbornness ; she had wakened refreshed and positive, in the clear light of day, that there was no one she could ever love as she loved Aurelio. She sent her brother about his business, saying she would come down and talk again with her father about it, and she turned an impervious front to the renewed malice of her aunt.

" She is better, is she not ? " queried Aurelio that night.

" Better ? Why do you talk about her ? " cried Carmela

resentfully. " We have not so much time together you need waste it in talking about my aunt."

" But I cannot help being interested in people, and I believe I know what is the matter."

" I forbid you to be interested in anyone but me ! " She added inconsequently : " What is the matter then ? There can be nothing the matter," she answered herself, " but her evil nature, which delights in persecution. You should have heard the things she said to me this morning. I might have been a bad woman from the way she spoke to me."

" There is nothing so evil as unhappiness. The sight of our love pricks her like thorns, for the sap still runs in her, only she is too dry for a man to take notice of her."

" I should think so ! " cried Carmela, with the scorn of the beloved for the loveless.

" There are times," said Aurelio, " when life is very unjust. For a woman with such a power of loving should certainly find a lover."

" What nonsense are you talking ? She can't do anything but hate. There isn't a perilla's worth of love in her whole body ! "

" Human nature is a two-faced coin," responded Aurelio. " One side is love and the other hate ; both images are graven on the same metal. It depends on the spin which side falls uppermost."

" I forbid you to say any more about my aunt," muttered Carmela. " We have only a minute or two, for that is the last candle in the house, and when it goes out you must go away, or the neighbours will begin to say ill-natured things about us."

They fell seriously to their whispered love-making, for all their conversations now took place at the reja, Carmela having now forbidden Aurelio to enter the house. Sometimes, as she pressed her bosom against the bars, she could feel the widow's presence behind her—a hissing breath, the quick rustle of a garment, would betray that unhappy curiosity which made it impossible for Doña Angustias to keep away from the sight of that which was most painful to her.

The better part of a year had passed before Carmela succeeded in talking her family into acceptance of her betrothal. The decisive feature was, of course, the death of Tía Pepa, and Aurelio's inheritance of her infinitesimal fortune. Without that handful of pesetas her cause would have been lost, she would have been dragged home, to pine away, or go crazy for want of the thing her healthy body craved.

She suffered badly at the wedding, when a party of Aurelio's friends and relations came into the town—wild-looking men in corduroy or cotton suits and broad-brimmed hats of white or pale grey, the leather bands brass-studded, and great leather belts that carried a pistol on either side ; the women in shawls and print dresses, hardly better than gipsies, at which her sisters giggled, while her brothers nudged one another and pulled faces of covert mockery. Yet Carmela, with a flash of rare insight, had an idea that, if it came to a show-down, these savages from beyond the mountains might prove themselves better men than her elegant, slightly languid brothers, whose manly exploits, she shrewdly suspected, were confined to boasting in the cafés.

The outlanders showed no friendliness ; their fine manners were worn, like cloth of gold over rags, to conceal a cold, impersonal curiosity towards herself ; they had come down to the wedding because there would be plenty of wine and food.

She was chalk-white, and could eat and drink nothing. There was little mingling between the families : the women shunned each other, forming two separate and slightly antagonistic groups ; the men achieved an indifferent amalgamation under the influence of wine. Doña Marta was terrified of the firearms, and, at her husband's request, these were flung on a table, where they stood, to Carmela, for symbols of her future.

A constant stream of friends and visitors poured through the patio ; Carmela, holding back tears behind staringly bright eyes, knew that curiosity, rather than goodwill, accounted for their presence ; that the neighbourhood as a whole disapproved of the marriage, and was inclined to jeer at it.

As the feast went on the Agujasierrans became very drunk ; the men sprawled senseless on Doña Marta's spotless floors, which they had already sufficiently defiled with their expectorations and by the refuse from their plates, and their women laughed at them, taking it for granted. The women friends of the Morenos, nervous and disgusted, went upstairs. Carmela could feel their enmity, their resentment against her for " letting them down." Her mother's expression was inscrutable, her sisters sneered openly at her.

Strange to say, the only person who supported her through her ordeal was the widow Herédia. A day or two before the wedding took place, a miraculous change came over the widow. Her bitterness passed from her, she became mild, sweet, and a gentle melancholy took the place of her former acridity. She waited upon Carmela with humility, as though begging her pardon for her former unkindness. " Let me do that. You must take care of your hands for the wedding. Let me put on your shoes for you ; it is right and fitting I should perform these menial duties for one who is to become a bride." Her attentions embarrassed Carmela more than her unkindliness ; she would flush and stammer, protest, and end by giving in to the importunacy which was more overwhelming than her aunt's former spite. To Aurelio the widow was even more obsequious, addressing him as " Usted " as though he were her superior, shy and assiduous as a girl in her attentions to his needs. It was she who made him a fine linen shirt for the wedding, paying for the material herself in spite of his protests, and sitting up until the dawn to finish the embroidery of a monogram on the breast. And all the services she performed for them both were veiled with a quiet melancholy, with an air of resignation and farewell which filled Aurelio with sadness and Carmela with puzzled irritation.

" It makes me shiver. She now lays a table for a meal as though she were laying out a corpse."

" Perhaps she is."

" Ave María Purísima ! What things you say ! "

Aurelio was right ; this was exactly what the widow Herédia was doing : she was laying out the corpse of her dead hopes. She had realised at last that this thing was to be, that one could not struggle against it, and suddenly, without any preparation, she resigned herself as, when the time came, she would resign herself to the grave. All unconsciously this resignation had been brought about by Aurelio's attitude to her ; by the gentle and filial front he had presented to her cruelties. Like many others, the widow Herédia was not proof against a continued gentleness.

Her one dread was, now, that the married couple should part from her without regret, and not come back to visit her after they were gone. Her love for Aurelio had become like a withered bunch of rosemary, which smells sweetest in dying. She felt very old.

" Only promise me one thing : that you will call your first child after me," she implored Carmela, on the eve of the wedding.

" How if it is a boy ? " muttered Carmela, with characteristic caution. She did not wish to part from her aunt on
bad terms, for the widow had certainly a little money of
her own, which might come in very useful later on.

" There's nothing to prevent your joining my name on to
his father's, is there ? " snapped the widow, with a return
of her former asperity ; but she softened again, turning to
Aurelio, who, in his proud character of prospective bride-
groom, was having his shoes cleaned at the door. " When
your first child is born, you must bring it here to me ; you
must give me my share of it—just as you gave me the
kid," she added, with a tremulous smile.

At the wedding she hovered continuously at Carmela's
side, touching her, encouraging her with quick smiles,
putting food that she could not eat and wine that she could
not drink into her hand, and coaxing her, as though she
were a small child, to take a single mouthful, a gulp from
the cup ; protecting her as far as possible from the curious
or contemptuous glances of the others.

Excited by the presence of his own people, Aurelio
unwittingly neglected her, but of this she was thankful ; she
could not have endured it if he had indulged in any of the
coarse, premature familiarities she had noticed at other
weddings. To her own dismay her physical desire for him
seemed to be totally extinguished now that the time had
come for her to indulge it ; this terrified her even more
than the prospect of going out to the mountains with
Aurelio at sunset.

Half sick and stunned, with throbbing head and burning
eyes, she thought, looking at him across the room, that she
had made a mistake ; that she did not love him after all.
She saw him, for once, with a terrifying impartiality, as an
ill-dressed, ordinary-looking young man, who, in the
matter of sophistication, compared unfavourably with her

brothers. The thought of suicide flashed through her mind, to be quickly dismissed, for, after all, she was not a child. She had simply sold herself as household drudge to a mountain peasant ; how right they all were to despise her ! Their scorn for her folly was no greater than her own.

When the time came, it was discovered that one of the guests who had come in on horseback was too drunk to return the same way. There was the second part of the feast to be gone through—the celebrations at Aurelio's home, where his mother, who had long been crippled, and could not make the journey to Granada, waited for her share of the festivities. The suggestion was made that Aurelio should mount the horse and take Carmela behind him, their original intention having been to take the diligence as far as the Last Inn, where a conveyance would meet them and take them the rest of their journey.

Carmela had never been on a horse ; she would be terribly conspicuous on her ride through Granada, but she was too miserable to care. " As well contribute the last touch of ridicule to this antic marriage," was her bitter thought as she suffered herself to be pushed up on to the back of the saddle-cloth. She wished now that she had taken more wine, that she was so drunk as not to care what she looked like. Her mother's face was dark with humiliation, her last embrace perfunctory ; Doña Marta was anxious to get back into her house, to verify her secret impression that the strangers were capable of helping themselves to any such small movable articles as happened to take their fancy.

Some of the others were trailing on foot (these would not reach Agujasierra before the following day), a few were on horseback, and a number piled into a cart drawn by mules ; it was like a circus procession, headed by the two figures so unconsciously romantic, the young, ardent husband on his handsome horse, the bride, sullen, reluctant and beautiful, ducking her head to conceal her blushes. The dark rose her aunt had thrust into her hair hung loosely from the blue-black coils, she dragged her best shawl of magenta silk closely across her bosom. In her misery and alarm she pressed close to Aurelio, and gradually the contact of their bodies, the warm, strong feeling of his torso, comforted her as the horse trotted equably along the deep-cut road between the red plateaux planted with olive-trees, and the rustling acres of sugar-cane on their right.

But the sight of the mountains towards which they were travelling—their fearful evening purple, the seeming menace of their ravines, the whole wildness and dissimilarity of the life towards which she was travelling from her former urban existence—revived her terror, and she could not bear it when Aurelio, caught up in the rapture of homecoming, burst into song :

> " Casita que está en la monte
> Y no la ponen puntales,
> Es fácil que venga a bajo
> Por los malos temporales ! "

Carmela struck at his shoulder with her clenched fist.
" Don't sing ! Don't sing ! "
He turned, saw her white, scared face and starting eyes close to his shoulder, and, swinging in his saddle, flung his arm about her, and, heedless of their companions, crushed his mouth to hers. Slowly the upwelling of her passion drove out all save the thought that they were together for ever, and that she loved him.

Agujasierra accorded from the first a dubious welcome to the foreigner whom Aurelio had chosen to foist upon it.

He was the first of his family to look outside the town for a partner, and, indeed, the girl was to be pitied for her intrusion upon a community close-welded, not only by matrimonial bonds, but by family associations that stretched back for as many generations as could be counted upon the fingers of both hands. The bewildering crowd of relations-in-law included an old, senile grandmother, a mother, uncles and aunts, brothers, sisters, and cousins, all stamped with the wild impress of the place itself : primitive in manners and in morals—even to the younger generation to which Aurelio himself belonged, which had received some smattering of the so-called benefits of education.

From the moment of her introduction into this community Carmela felt the impact of their malice and distrust. A weaker or more sensitive girl would have been crushed by it ; Carmela's stubborn nature, her passionate and possessive love for Aurelio, flung back their ill will from the impenetrable surface of her own resistance. At first she was amazed to see the way in which Aurelio took for granted things which offended her morally and physically, and, in spite of her foretaste gained in the house of Tía Pepa, it was a never-ending source of painful astonishment to her that Aurelio, with his mild, genial ways, should have come from such savage stock. She was very miserable, very thankful her own people were not at hand to witness her misery.

She was quick to realise, however, that the name of López carried its own distinction in Agujasierra, and that Aurelio's people were, if not the most important family in the town, at least among the ruling set. She clung to the hope that one day they would make Aurelio alcalde, as his grandfather had been before him ; that, at least, would be something to slap in the face of her own family.

Since their return Aurelio had become a man of leisure ; there had been some talk of his continuing to help his brothers at their market-stalls, but Carmela's small-town pride had set her against that. Stall-keeping was a thing that could well be left to women. Did he suppose she was going to stay in the house all day, exposed to the enmity of her mother- and sisters-in-law, to wait upon peasants and clean the dishes from which they had eaten ? With her mother's instinct for making money she had decided to run a little stall herself—of fried cakes, such as were sold in the square of Bibirambla ; she produced, to Aurelio's surprise and gratification, sufficient capital to establish her equipment of charcoal stove, cooking utensils, and ingredients. She needed no one to help her in this venture, and Aurelio might as well take his time to look about him for other employment, so that they could enjoy a double income and make provision for the future. In the vocabulary of both Aurelio and Carmela " the future " stood for children—who were slow in coming. Each month they hoped, and each month were disappointed. Carmela turned to her cooking-stove as a solace for her bitter ignominy.

She never used rancid fat ; her cakes were very good, very golden ; the little venture prospered. Aurelio was proud of his efficient wife, and, with masculine prudence, closed his eyes and ears upon other expressions of opinion.

She still rated respectability above all the virtues, and the conventions in which she had been reared above any law of Church or State. In the early days of their marriage she tried to impress her ideas upon Aurelio, who listened fondly and tolerantly, but preferred making love to being lectured upon his manners. To Carmela, the education which Aurelio had received—which did not amount to much, but was not so far inferior to her own—was a poor thing, since it had not taught him to wear a collar, to handle a knife and fork, or, on formal occasions, to dismiss the thick Andaluz dialect from his speech.

CM

Yet, imperceptibly, her sensitiveness to these shortcomings became blunted by custom, and the continual excitement of their mutual love reconciled her somewhat to circumstances which, without it, would have been intolerable. Carmela was a wonderful lover ; he had never had the slightest inclination to look at any other woman since he married her. But she minded intensely about numbers of trivial, external matters ; she had none of the penetrative and contemplative qualities that enriched his own character, and no appreciation of them ; yet, in some way, this very *stupidity* of Carmela's deepened his love for her. Or it might be truer to say that it did nothing to interfere with it ; it presented no challenge to that masculine superiority which, in Aurelio, was more conscious, because he was more intelligent, than in the majority of men.

With the passing of time, things became a little easier for her. The first fortunate occurrence, from her point of view, was the death of Aurelio's mother ; followed, shortly after, by a summons from a relative who had actually, at some adventurous moment of his career, migrated as far afield as Atarfe, and who wrote to Aurelio's eldest brother that he was now old and sick, incapable of looking after his business, and plainly stating his intention of leaving the property to Enrique López if the latter would come and manage his affairs for him. This meant the removal, not only of Enrique and his wife and of their tribe of children, but of several other members of the household, who, after the Spanish fashion, could not break away from the herd, and possibly glimpsed the advantages of accompanying their leader to his new home.

Then the grandmother died ; the widowed sister actually found a new husband, and went to live with his family at Málaga. And so the house gradually emptied itself, save for two unkempt girls, daughters of the widow by her first marriage, who were supposed to do the work of servants but devoted most of their energies to baiting Carmela, who was too proud to complain of them to Aurelio. Also, she loved him too dearly ; she understood the responsibilities that relationship fastened upon him, and her love freshened under circumstances that set her free of so much of the strain she had suffered since her marriage. Now, with her heart at rest, she might easily conceive a child.

The one chink in the armour of her pride had been her childlessness. The town said, openly, that she was barren, but in her soul Carmela knew this was not the case. Without any kind of biological knowledge, she linked up her inability to bear a child with the continual strain of her existence, and, with a touch of superstition, to the enmity with which she was surrounded. Privately, she thought it possible they had put the evil eye on her—especially the old grandmother, who had been her most implacable enemy.

She had been seven years married before she knew she was with child. Out of sheer devilment she kept the discovery to herself until it was no longer possible to conceal it, and her lip curled with a bitter triumph when once her secret was out.

Her pride and her jealousy were the strongest emotions Carmela had ever experienced. There were days when Aurelio's manliness, his unconscious grace, were a positive torment to her, and she could hardly bear to let him out of her sight ; for it did not seem possible that some other woman would not tempt him to betray her, especially during the months when she had to watch the waning of her own attractions.

He had been, to the best of her knowledge, faithful to her for seven years, although, as was natural, the keen edge of his passion had worn a little dull with the passage of time. Carmela attributed this, justly, to her failure to give him

a child. Man's instinct is to fulfil himself by the perpetua-
tion of the name, and the woman who does not help him
to his fulfilment risks more than the mere waning of his
passion. She had grown a little haggard, her tongue had
acquired a tang in those anxious years : always conscious of
the fact that she was older than Aurelio, she was terrified
of old age creeping visibly upon her before she had accomplished her female destiny. For the first months of her
pregnancy the removal of this terror made her positively
beautiful, and, like a princess, proudly aware of her own
beauty, that drew other eyes than Aurelio's to her when she
walked abroad.

But as the beauty of pregnancy passed into its repulsive-
ness, as the lines of her face and her body blurred and
thickened, her jealousy took possession of her, driving her
nearly crazy. In common with the majority of jealous wives,
Carmela held the belief that her husband was irresistible
to other women, and, during the onslaughts of her suspicions, she grew to hate the very qualities which, originally,
contributed to her love for him.

Intuitively Aurelio was aware of these mental disorders
of Carmela's. They made him tender towards her, but most
of all tender to the child she carried in her womb. It seemed
a pity, to him, that the babe should be nurtured in such a
bitter vessel. He thought much of the child, with a loving
emotion of paternity and pride : sometimes planning its
life, and his own share in it—rehearsing, as it were, the
incidents of his fatherhood. Its sex troubled him little : boy
or girl would be equally welcome, as vindication of his
procreative power. For the first time in his life he lost that
sense of being an onlooker : fate at last had provided him
with an intimate part in the drama of his own family.

He was very happy, although Carmela now made ceaseless, and often unreasonable, demands upon him, and, if

he seemed slow in response, accused him of secret meetings with other women. He tried to tell her that the dim rival whose presence she sensed was the child itself : but she would have none of the explanation. He would have liked to tell her of the dreams he had about the child : of the hold it was establishing on his imagination, so that everything he did and thought seemed in some way connected with the child and for the child.

But of latter years he had grown a little silent ; he no longer talked of the things he thought about—he turned them over lovingly in his own mind, smiling over them, but keeping them to himself, because Carmela's practical nature made her impatient of the discussion of abstract subjects, and gradually he had given up the attempt to interest her in them. There were days when he remembered the conversations with the widow Herédia, and felt that had she been at hand he would have sought her sympathy ; but ever since their marriage Carmela had refused to go near her aunt, although, with the idea of keeping prudently in her good graces, she wrote to her at long intervals : proud letters, a little boastful, and not strictly adherent to facts—for what facts were there about her life at Agujasierra which were not shameful ?

Without knowing it, Aurelio was a little blighted in his expectations of marriage. He had said he would read Carmela like a book of a million pages ; it had not taken him long to discover that the book was meagrely printed—that many pages were blank. For all her sophistication there was not nearly so much subtlety in her as in his own people. She was not exactly shallow, but her mental processes were all given over to material and external things, and her perceptions, save when sharpened by her love for him and her apprehension of losing him, were non-existent. He knew her, and she did not know him—that was the trouble. It was a trouble he could easily forget when they were clasped in their intimate embrace ; but in the separation of their flesh he thought sometimes how like to her aunt Carmela was growing, and thus the fatal element of pity encroached upon his love for her.

Yet he was faithful to her, and only left her for the companionship of his friends in the casino, where he would drink, and sometimes be delivered of one of his old philosophical sayings that drew their laughter and applause upon him. He still disassociated himself from individual quarrels, still shrugged his shoulders upon the mistakes and misjudgments of other people, which brought about their sufferings ; his pity and his impersonal love and interest were still at their disposal. But, like Carmela, Aurelio was ageing ; like her, he felt a little apprehensive of the frosts.

CHAPTER IV

THE OTHER MARAVILLA

THE GIRL CALLED MARAVILLA picked up the cracked mirror from the bench at which she was sitting and, lifting a candle in her right hand, closely scrutinised her own face. The candle she was holding was old and dusty, silted into its tin socket with the accumulation of drippings, and streaked down its sides with beadings of black : for it was the candle in which she melted, on the prongs of a hairpin, the cosmetic she used to stiffen and colour her eyelashes.

The face anxiously peering at its original from the mirror seemed to her to be losing some quality which it ought to possess, which it had formerly possessed. Deprived of its professional animation, it hardened into a sculptural pretti-ness that suggested less youth than agelessness ; it might pass, with equal success, for the face of a girl of sixteen or a woman of forty-six. Actually, her age lay half way between the two, and she usually deducted six or seven years when obliged to reveal it. Latterly she had begun to wonder if her deception was successful : whether people really believed she was in the early twenties when she told them so.

The light fell full on the quivering spread of her nostrils and the translucent circles of her eyes, in which the pupils were shrunk to pin-points. The frail texture of the skin, which she scrutinised with such anxiety at the angles of chin and jaw, was covered by a thin shining film of grease, whose faintly unpleasant odour had become so familiar to her that it no longer offended her senses. For more than twenty years she had been greasing her skin at this hour of the night ; wiping the grease away with a stained towel, veiling her eyelids with a mauve shadow, and blackening her lashes. She knew exactly the angle at which to hold the worn-down stick of vermilion, to produce the fine, sweeping line about her mouth. She sometimes performed the whole make-up with her back to the glass, talking with the other girls, and scarcely troubling to verify its success before holding out her arms for the bodice, with its faint clamminess and prickle under the arms of sweat-stained material, into which the dresser put her for her appearance on the stage. Sometimes it hurt her to lift her arms, because the stage-clothes were almost always damp ; rain got into the baskets, or the walls of the dressing-rooms sweated. She no longer paid attention to such things ; they were the natural incidents of her profession.

But to-night she lingered, gazing into the mirror, until her companion of the dressing-room, the older actress, Emilia Mera, said to her :

" The call will come in a minute or two ; remember you were in trouble last week for being late for your entrance."

" You are kind," replied the girl quickly, putting down her candle. " Any of the others would have let me be late, to see how angry Echaurri would be with me."

Emilia Mera, who was fully dressed, sat resting her whitened hands upon a towel, waiting for them to dry ; she was the only member of the company who paid attention to such details, but she had played in first-class companies, and took a melancholy pride in preserving the traditions of her better days. The broken lines of her face held the traces of a delicate and almost refined beauty, which was enhanced by the grey wig she wore for the part she was playing.

" You said that as if you were sad," she observed. The other hunched her shoulders, rummaged among the litter on her dressing-table for the sausage she had been eating, and filled her mouth before replying.

" On the contrary. For the first time in my life I was thinking that if they offered me a comedy part I should accept it."

" You are very wise, very artistic," said the elder woman. " One must have experience of life—one must have suffered —before one can be a successful comedienne. For a *farceuse*, on the other hand, nothing is necessary but a sense of the ridiculous."

" There is more money nowadays in comedy than in heavy drama," resumed the girl. " Get me some water, Lola, to wash my hands—and for God's sake try to let it be warm this time. Money, money, money ! If anyone offered me enough money, Emilia, I would leave the stage to-morrow. I suppose that to you, with your lofty ideals, that sounds blasphemous."

" To speak of ideals in connection with my career sounds like mockery," said Emilia Mera sadly. " You see what they have brought me to ! There is nothing idealistic in mouthing puerilities in a play of this kind, with a producer like Echaurri, whose one idea is to make us deliver every line as though it were a pistol shot. No subtlety, no atmosphere, so long as the leading actors get plenty of opportunity for their ranting."

Maravilla laid her hand for a moment over her companion's.

" I am sorry for what I said, Emilia ; it must be torture for you."

" You will be a success," said the Mera, brushing aside with a gentle dignity her companion's sympathy, " because you have accepted the things I refused to accept—until it was too late. You are sensible for doing so ; I applaud you. Has Echaurri asked you again to go out with him ? "

" What is the use ? He knows I know about his wife and the four children, to whom he sends his salary every week."

" Be careful ; he can be very unpleasant when he is offended. One day you may find yourself in the street. But I forget ! Of course it will not be that way with you, because he knows how valuable you are to the company."

" Why do you flatter me ? " said Maravilla, almost wistfully. " I am a mere barnstormer to the people with whom you have been used to acting." It was rarely she made so complete an act of humility, and it surprised her to find herself completely sincere.

" No. You are undisciplined, of course, and your style is coarse, because you have not had the opportunity of playing with finished actors : but there is something about you which is very fine, very distinguished ; even in moments of extravagance you convince your audiences—I mean not only the facile, easily emotionated people who come as a matter of course to see our kind of show, but the rarer ones, who come in to fill an hour between engagements, or to laugh at our clumsiness. They do not laugh at you. When you get to Madrid——"

" Oh, when I get to Madrid ! That is the way I used to talk fifteen years ago. Dear Emilia, we are good enough friends to dispense with compliments. Shall I tell you something ? If I could find a rich and not too unattractive lover —someone who is not an actor, or anything to do with the theatre—I would burn my baskets and tear up my contracts to-morrow ! "

" Does acting mean nothing to you, then—for itself ? "

" I will tell you what acting means to me," said Maravilla, as the dresser returned with a tin bowl of lukewarm water, into which, with an exclamation of dissatisfaction, she plunged her hands. " It means a traffic in bodies, a system of bargaining, a rivalry in deception, an exploitation of ignorance by cunning, an unprincipled opportunism ! That is what acting means to me."

" But when you are actually on the stage ? " persisted Emilia Mera. " When you are given fine lines to speak, do not the sentiments, does not the rhythm of noble words, give you some kind of emotion—carry you beyond the baser aspects of the profession ? "

" When I am on the stage I think of one thing only," said Maravilla. " When I cross the stage, when I lower my eyelids, when I pick up a book, I am thinking whether there is someone in the audience who will send me a present, or wait for me outside the theatre. I bend my body, I lift my chest, I display as if by accident the length of my leg, so as to excite that unknown individual, to make him anxious to possess me. I am on sale—to the highest bidder. It was not always like that, Emilia. I can remember the time when I thought of nothing but my rôle, when the idea of betraying the intention of the dramatist made me tremble with anxiety. But now—can you blame me ? In what other way am I to make palatable the squalor of our existence ? How am I to buy the small luxuries, the refinements, which are necessary to people like ourselves, because, acting the fine lady night after night, portraying women of quality and wealth, our imaginations are continually inflamed with desire for that which we have not ? "

" Take care," counselled the Mera, with a sadness of experience in her voice. " Because by the blunting of your sensibilities you imperil your art. I have known many actresses, who held the same opinions as yourself, to lose their hold upon the very quality which recommended them to their public. Their acting became mechanical, lost its fluidity——"

" To the devil with my art ! You are one of the chosen, Emilia ; your work is vocational, whereas mine is a business, exactly as my employers have intended it to be. You set out to make something of the theatre ; I have allowed the theatre to make me—just what I am. Does it ever occur to you that, although you are so much older than I, I have been on the stage more years than you ? They christened me La Maravilla when I was a child of six or seven, running on the stage from my mother's dressing-room to present my song and dance to an audience which, I was perfectly persuaded, adored me ! In those days I had plenty of ideals. I was going to become the greatest actress in Spain ; I was going to act in all the European capitals ; all the famous playwrights were going to offer me their plays before they were seen by the managers ! I was not sure whether I would take a king or a matador for my lover ! And now. Do you remember in Zaragoza, where the rain came through the roof of the theatre, and our costumes were soaked when we put them on ? I remember you complaining there were bugs in your lodgings, and in mine the sheets had been used before they were spread on my bed. I gave myself to a middle-aged wine-merchant for the night, so as to enjoy a little comfort, a little cleanliness, for a few hours."

" Hurry up, ladies, the curtain will be going up in a few minutes," said the call-boy, opening the door without knocking and staring hopefully round, on the chance of finding one of the women in undress.

" Look at this rag ; you would have thought the management would have found something better, knowing we had this date for the feria," protested Maravilla, standing up while the dresser hooked her into her dilapidated draperies of chiffon, which stood, on the playwright's direction, for " an elegant tea-gown."

" Take a little of my perfume," said Emilia Mera, also rising to her feet. " It will perhaps inspire you to play your love scene with more abandon to-night ! "

" It is more likely to inspire Baenza to take liberties with me," muttered Maravilla. " Many thanks, Emilia. I had no idea you had an admirer—although it does not surprise me in the least," she ended politely.

Emilia Mera gave her beautiful, melancholy smile.

" You would have every right to be surprised ; wrinkles do not attract admirers. I saved up a little of my salary and bought a small bottle, because, you see, I also have your craving for luxury at times."

" Emilia, you are an angel ! " cried Maravilla, flinging her arms about Emilia's neck. " Next week I will get myself some, and you shall fill your bottle from mine. How beautiful you are ; how elegant. You are the only one among us who ever looks an aristocrat ; the rest of us are just mongrel dogs, aping the tricks of the thoroughbreds. What fools men are ! "

" I must go down now ; the boy will not think it worth his while to come up again for so insignificant a member of the company as myself," she said—without bitterness, but with an acceptance of her humble lot that fired Maravilla with passionate resentment against all those people and circumstances which had contributed to Emilia's failure in the theatre.

" No, wait for me, darling ; I will not be more than a few seconds. I wonder what sort of an audience there is in front to-night."

" Granada is a rich town," said Emilia Mera, raising her shoulders. " I have played here many times. But the people with money are too mean to spend it on the theatre, and the poorer classes are too indifferent to leave their favourite tables at the cafés. It may be a little better as it is the feria."

" What a prospect ! " laughed Maravilla, as she dragged
on the high-heeled shoes in which she had to walk carefully, for the heels were so worn down she was liable to
turn her ankles. She kept these shoes for this scene, in which
she wore a long gown that concealed her feet, but she never
put them on in Emilia's presence without a slight feeling of
shame. Emilia would have gone without a meal, she knew,
to have had those heels repaired : it was part of her religion
of the theatre to appear on the stage as immaculately at-
tired, with regard to the unseen details that most of the
other women neglected, as she was in private life.

They went arm in arm down the stone staircase, which
was fouled by the spittle of the stage hands ; on either side
the wall was marked by a greasy band of dirt from human
hands or clothing ; the smell from the open door of a urinal
overpowered the theatre smells of grease-paint and size. It
did not occur to the management that the players' comfort,
even their efficiency, could be affected by these sordid conditions. Maravilla was so used to them that she took them
for granted. Emilia's lips were moving, and Maravilla preserved a considerate silence, for she knew Emilia never
went upon the stage without a Hail, Mary, and that
she travelled in her clothes-basket a small and battered holy
picture which, whatever dressing-room she occupied, was
hung above her bench, with its tiny oil lamp beneath it.

Echaurri came towards the two women as they stepped
into the darkness of the wings. His eyes ignored Emilia
Mera and took possession of Maravilla. She knew he was
wondering whether he would succeed in persuading her to
sleep with him ; she wondered whether, in spite of Emilia's
discouragement, the evening would bring forth an admirer
whose offer would make it worth her while to continue in
her resistance of Echaurri's desire. She had given herself
to many men, usually from a pecuniary motive, and had

once or twice been in love ; but latterly she had become uneasily aware of the ephemeral nature of these adventures, of the fleeting nature of the benefits to be derived from them, and on that particular night she would have sold her soul to the devil to have had her future assured.

She was thinking, as she waited for her cue, of an admirer she had in Cádiz : a dotard whom she had permitted to fondle her because he showed himself more ready than the majority to pay in hard cash for any favours she accorded him. This man of good family was, she knew, infatuated with her. He had offered her an apartment, attendants, anything she liked to ask for, if she would become his mistress. Something—some unaccountable relic of a nicety she had not believed to have survived from her girlhood— had made her refuse. The man was over seventy, was senile, was impotent, depended upon stimulants to produce a parody of love, and tried her endurance to breaking-point with his degenerate and perverted endearments. His family, she knew, was terrified of his contracting another marriage, for his sons and daughters waited impatiently to realise their expectations from his will, and, although the law prevented his cutting them out of it, there were ways and means by which an infatuated old man might be persuaded, during lifetime, to part with possessions his children already looked upon as their own.

And her refusal had been half-hearted ; in saying " No " she had visualised with a painful clearness the luxuries which she was foregoing, the ease with which she might influence him to provide handsomely for her future. So deep was his infatuation, so feeble his mind, she might even trick him into a secret marriage ! And what would be the price of a few months of discomfort beside the years of plenty that would succeed them if she brought off her scheme ? He had never properly accepted her rejection of his offer ; he let her see he was hankering after her still, by gifts which he sent her at towns where he knew the company was appearing.

And as the draught struck between her shoulders from the scene-dock, whose doors had not been properly closed, as a drunken stage hand jostled her and the irascible hiss of the prompter warned her not to forget her words that night—as every possible combination of circumstance revealed to her that she was the slave of a system she had grown to detest, Maravilla made up her mind.

In the front of the house, in the highest and cheapest gallery, sat Aurelio López, with his friends. It was a great event, for him, to come to the theatre ; he had only twice before been there in his life, but at feria time one made all kinds of exceptions to one's usual rule, and spent money with a foolish lavishness one sometimes regretted in the lean days that followed. So Aurelio sat in the gallery, eating almonds and cracking jokes with his companions, while they waited for the curtain to rise.

Carmela had given sour acquiescence to his declared intention of going to the feria as usual. What else could she do ? Everyone who could afford it was going to Granada, and, whether she agreed or not, Aurelio would certainly go his own way. That is how things are when one has been seven years married.

Every year save this one she had accompanied him, and they had slept at her mother's. Carmela had been anxious that he should do the same this year, when her heaviness disposed her against the trailing round and late hours of the feria week. She was disappointed, and peevish in her disappointment ; resented his going without her, and tried to drive him to the promise he would at least get a bed

under her mother's roof. That way she could at least be
sure of Aurelio's nights.

But Aurelio, anticipating the pleasures of three days of
bachelorhood, and honest in his desire to spend his time
with his men friends, had refused to give her the promise.
What did he want with a bed during the feria ? They would
be carousing all night ; they would fall asleep with their
heads on a café table at daybreak, and a few hours later
would refresh themselves with cognac and coffee. No one
wanted to waste time in bed during the feria, when the
town was full of gaieties, when the matadors' cuadrillas
were to be seen and talked to outside their favourite cafés,
and the streets were alive with amusements not to be found
at any other season of the year.

Foiled of her security, Carmela next tried to find out
with whom he was going ; and this also he good-temperedly
refused to tell her. He was used to Carmela's jealousy,
which amused and touched rather than annoyed him ; it
was as much part of a woman's make-up as her physical
functions, and it was, of course, exaggerated by her condition. Nevertheless, he saw no reason for pandering to it.
In return for his long fidelity she owed him her trust ;
besides, she could find out what she wanted to know merely
by questioning one of the other women : no one has secrets
in Agujasierra.

He made his escape in the twilight of early morning,
while she was still heavily sleeping. It struck him as an
excellent joke as he climbed into the diligence, which he
and his friends had arranged to catch as it passed the foot
of the mountain. He had kissed her sleeping face, damp with
night-sweat, thinking how much he loved her, how wrong
she was not to trust in him. More than once, as they
followed the dusty ribbon of the road, he flung back his
head and laughed aloud, to think of her rage when she

discovered he had gone without waking her. Poor Carmela ! Why could she not love him simply and trustfully, without making a pain of it, as he loved her ? After the child came —in a month's time or so—he would try to make things different for them.

The night before his departure, she sat up in bed after he was asleep to light a candle-end and gloat upon the face she loved and hated. She did not understand what constituted the beauty of that face : the fine, thin bone-structure that underlay the tough brown flesh that had coarsened from its youthful fineness, and which, when Aurelio was awake, fell into one or two deep lines, miraculously smoothed away in sleep. His hair was tossed upon the bolster ; his forearm rested upon it. He was sleeping naked, because of the heat ; all the exposed design of bone and muscle that made up his masculine body filled her with an obscure rage of possession. Rather than allow any other woman to enjoy that body she would destroy it with her own hands !

Her fingers trembled, shielding the candle-flame, as her eyes travelled down the long, straight line of his limbs under the cotton counterpane. Cautiously she edged it down, inch by inch, so that she might possess with her eyes the whole of that fine body, and comfort herself, after he had gone, by remembering the privilege which was hers— and only hers ! A grimness of concentration spread from her to her hobgoblin shadow on the whitewashed wall— the unwanted third that intruded upon their privacy of man and wife ! Becoming aware of it, seeing in it the symbol of all she feared, she struck at it with the flat of her hand. The sound disturbed Aurelio.

" Jesú ! What's the matter with you ? "

" A mosquito," she muttered, drawing up the counterpane with quick dexterity. She blew out the light and lay
down close to his side, possessing him with her thoughts
as she had just been doing with her eyes.

Something leapt across the line of footlights, travelled
through space, and struck Aurelio in the breast—something
that made a demand upon him such as he had never before
experienced. The roof of the theatre opened to the heavens,
and there were the angels, all chanting together, row upon
row, their wings like pale flames among the stars. His
breast was torn ; his heart became like the bleeding heart
of Jesus ; his limbs burned with an angelic heroism, like
San Miguel's ; solemn and tragic words were sounding in
his ears, words spoken in the voice of the soul, calling upon
his chivalry.

Some chance gesture of the actress altered the atmosphere ; he became burningly aware of her person, of that
very quality which Carmela was always preaching to him,
which seemed on her lips a kind of flimsy joke : of the refinement of all her movements—more convincing, because
more practised, than Carmela's—of her speech ; of the
inconceivable delicacy of her apparel, that tempted one
with its glimmer of the half seen.

He strained his eyes towards the yellow glare of the lights
across which she sent her words, her gestures, like arrows of
destruction. He had no means of judging of the quality
of her performance, or that of the company in which she
appeared. She stretched out her arms in a gesture of tragical
appeal, and his soul leapt into them ; she lifted her head,
and in spirit he sank at her feet. *I know thee not. Thou art
miraculous. I submit. I believe.*

From the distance at which he sat he accepted the mauve

shadows about her eyes, the carnation of her lips, for an authentic beauty which had a heavenly, rather than a mortal, origin. The falling of the curtain at the end of the piece came upon him like the stroke of the guillotine that severs spirit from flesh. He felt, as his friends, laughing and joking, propelled him into the café after the performance, like a dead man ; he was dimly aware of his own corpse, which was outraged by their liberties. Presently the life came trembling back into him, while he sat with his elbows on the table, his shoulders pushed up to his ears. He took no part in the conversation, cared nothing for the winks and smiles the others bestowed upon his condition. It seemed to him that he had just witnessed a spectacle of great privacy and spiritual significance which had been intended for him only, which the others had not perceived.

As the room began to swim back into his consciousness, the woman of whom he was thinking walked into the café with a female companion.

They behaved in the usual circumspect manner of women in public places : sitting at a table apart from those occupied by the usual crowd of men, ordering coffee, neither giving nor inviting greetings. But their presence in the café at that hour marked their inclusion in a society more emancipated than that of the town. Their calmness and repudiation of the stares of recognition with which they were favoured proclaimed the fact that they were accustomed to such attentions, and not to be discomposed by them. They talked in low voices, looking at no one save each other.

Their clothes were neat, but shabby ; the elder woman was in black ; the younger, from whom Aurelio, trembling in every limb, never took his regard, wore a light checked coat of brown and white material, and a hat with a bird's wing that stood up above the crown. This, in itself, marked her as an unusual personage, for only foreign women, and a few very advanced young women coming from the capital, wore hats.

Beneath its shadow she looked jaded, even melancholy ; the aftermath of a vicarious tragedy lent pallor to her face, upon which the scarlet, the mauve eye-shadows, still remained to emphasise its significance. Her demureness was more conscious than that of her companion ; it robbed her expression of what might have been its nobility. In the flutter of her eyelids lurked an immense awareness of the eyes that tried to force hers to return their scrutiny. Presently she raised her head, and directed her gaze, with a deliberate blankness, across the café. Whispers of " Guapa ! Guapisima ! " went rustling among the tables, as by a prearranged signal ; she ignored them with an assurance that revealed her sophistication.

Following the direction of her gaze, Aurelio's eyes met hers in an opposite mirror. His whole being trembled, and it was through a sudden mist that he saw the momentary parting of her lips. Her eyes held his steadily for a moment, as though by this means they could photograph his image on her mind ; he could feel an ache, a straining of all his being towards her, in his own. Then she turned again calmly to her companion ; he was too far away to hear what they said to each other.

" I would not have come if Gálvez had not said he would be here," Emilia Mera was saying.

" Surely you did not expect Gálvez to keep his word ? So far as I am concerned, I am used enough to going into the cafés without an escort. It rather amuses me to see everyone staring, wondering what sort of a person I am ! How behind the times we are in Spain ! I am sure it is the only country in the world where a virtuous woman is not supposed to order herself a cup of coffee in public unless her husband is there to pay for it."

" If you can attract the waiter's attention, let us pay our bill ; I am terribly sleepy," said the other.

A moment or two later the pair of them left the café, without a glance at any of the tables.

When Aurelio went out into the darkness, they were slowly crossing the square. They appeared to be talking together ; their arms were linked and their heels made a faint, brittle click upon the pavement. He felt himself drawn after them, knowing he dared not accost them, but was bound to follow wherever they might go.

One of the innumerable churches of Granada sent two strokes of its bell quivering among the stars ; a lull followed the hectic gaiety of the feria night ; the façades of the houses were green with moonlight, and that mysterious purification which falls upon cities when their streets are empty lay upon the town, as it lay on the invisible mountains.

Up the narrow streets towards which they mounted were pits of shadow, that swallowed their figures from time to time. In many places the pavement was broken away, or twisted so abruptly that, for a moment, he believed, with an unbearable sense of deprivation, he had lost them. No one else seemed to be abroad in those silent and furtive byways of the town.

The girl must have said something to her companion, for Aurelio, fearing to gain too closely upon them, and lingering in a doorway, saw, with a thrill of emotion, the elder woman leave her and walk briskly ahead, while the girl's step became more slow and deliberate than before. The conviction came to him that she was aware of his pursuit and meant him to overtake her. By a carefully calculated regulation of pace he caught up with her in a patch of darkness. Both stopped. In the silence each could hear the other's breathing, and to Aurelio's nostrils came the perfume of her hair, or her body, or the cosmetics she was wearing. A romantic ecstasy so exquisite as to exclude, for the time, all baser physical craving, prevented him from speaking.

" You aren't very bold, are you ? " she was whispering ; her voice had a rustle like leaves in a wind. " A nice thing —I have to get rid of my companion before you will come up and speak to me ! "

" I didn't want to speak to her," he stammered. He could feel that she was laughing in the darkness, and the knowledge stabbed his pride.

" Who would suppose you did ? You would have had a very cold reception if you had tried that game on Emilia Mera ! "

" What is your name ? " he questioned boldly.

" Caramba, didn't you buy a programme ? " she countered. " It is too bad of the patrons not to buy programmes. How else are the artistes to advertise themselves ? I hope you are not mean. I can't bear mean men."

" I lost it," he lied, unashamedly.

" What a pity ! You would have learned from it that they call me Maravilla. It is not the name by which I was christened, but I was given it when I was a little girl, because I danced and sang—well, divinely ! Maravilla del Monte."

Maravilla ! The name itself seemed like the lovely fulfilment of a dream. The Wonderful One. It was a dream ; to-morrow he would wake, and all would be as it was before. But for the moment he stood within the blue confines of a dream, and spoke to the girl who called herself Maravilla.

" And what do you mean by making love to me with your eyes in the café ? " she continued, on her note of raillery. " It was enough to cause a scandal. In the theatre it is different ; people have paid for their privilege of staring, and it is their business and ours to see they get their money's worth. Haven't you got a sweetheart you can look at, the way you were looking at me ? "

" Don't mock me," he muttered. " The way I look at you is the way I feel about you ; I have never felt that way for any other woman."

" But why ? " she persisted, with feminine insistence upon a direct avowal.

" Your sorrows—all you are suffering——" he managed to say.

She started ; then, with a strange softening of the heart, she understood that, in his naïveté, he was confusing her theatrical character with her private one. The solecism was not uncommon among the simpler members of her audiences ; it had not ceased to touch, while it amused, her. For all the mercenariness of her nature, she felt a curious attraction towards this countryman, who looked at her with eyes of such a lost and despairing adoration across the café. He was something more than the average, she decided ; neither clod nor animal ; something misplaced in its present situation. It was in her nature to get fanciful about such encounters, because, although pecuniary need almost always drove her into love-affairs with men whose physical attraction—if it had ever existed—was a thing of the past, her own taste was healthy enough to predispose her in favour of youth and virility, when she had the chance of it. Alas, how seldom it went, in her experience, with a well-filled purse !

" All women suffer," she murmured, playing to his idea of her. Was it not true ? Was she not suffering now at the prospect of delivering herself up to her aged admirer at Cádiz ? Already her flesh cringed in anticipation of that to which she was committed.

" If you would let me comfort you a little——" he stammered.

" How ? "

He made a wordless movement which she avoided.

" Come into the light, where I can see you," she suddenly commanded. He put up his hand to hide his collarless state as she dragged him out of the shadow ; without a word, this girl had accomplished that with which Carmela had struggled in vain : Aurelio was, for the first time, conscious of his slovenly attire. In that moment he paid the penalty of his neglect of all Carmela's admonitions, for it appeared to him an act of unpardonable disrespect to approach this refined, mysterious woman save in seemly and proper clothing. His face burned ; he struggled with his shame as she lifted her face to his, feeling unable to meet her eyes : certain that she would reject him when she saw what a ruffian he appeared.

But for the moment she chose only to see that which had attracted her to begin with : his hard-bitten, countryman's face, with the lean cheeks cut into leathery folds by the deep lines that ran from the nostrils to the corners of his lips, whose fine modelling appealed to the artist in her ; she had seen such lips in sculpture, in the towns to which her profession had taken her, and they belonged, invariably, to people whose names inflamed her imagination, and to the history of whose exploits she thrilled. His age she assumed, correctly, to be near her own ; they had each reached a period of life when the current of the blood runs at its swiftest, with a deeper reverberance in its human channels than in the bubbling, chattering days of youth. To love, at their ages, was something serious ; if they chose to will it so, it could leave its impression on their lives for ever.

But in her own case Maravilla knew that this thing, this impression of soul on soul, must not be permitted to take place. She had that very night come to an important decision that would direct the whole of her future course. She was not a girl, to jettison security, in however distasteful a form it might present itself, for the sake of immediate gratification.

But something—whether it was the part that she had been playing, more romantic than those which commonly fell to her share, or whether it was the hour, and that strange purification of people and places that went with it—drove her, it might be for the last time, towards an unmercenary love. For the last time, before delivering herself to her wealthy lover, she would follow her own inclinations, without regard for the material value they represented. It was not often that opportunity came to her in so wholesome a guise. The suddenness of it appealed to her dramatic sense, and offered immediate relief from the tedious routine of her theatre life, with its constant manœuvring of expediency and diplomacy, its petty rivalries and betrayals, and troublesome change of scene, which afforded so little opportunity for making permanent contacts. In the present instance it was well that it should be so ; after to-night they would part, and in time would cease to think of each other. She had an idea Emilia Mera would approve of such an affair as this—of its freedom from the corruptive influence of pecuniary gain, of its directness and purity of motive.

Inevitably, when the outlines of the furniture began to resolve themselves from the anonymity of darkness, Aurelio, the more prostrate of the two, the more deeply affected, began to stammer phrases whose import she was, at first, slow to understand. She lay high on the pillows, her arms flung outwards, her eyelids half closed, her lips slightly open ; upon her lifted breasts showed dark circles, like bruises upon the *grisaille* of the pale flesh. She was at peace, whereas dawn-horror, that bane of lovers, had laid its chilly finger on him, quickening as the light quickened into a thin film like water upon polished wood and marble. Her insensibility sent a shudder through him ; it was as though she had retreated from him into a region whither he could not follow her ; he had the same dread of touching her flesh that he would have had of touching a corpse. And the enemy light slid naked into the room, to destroy him with its white sword.

At some moment during the night the separation between her and her theatrical self had defined itself to his senses, and he had seemed, for a moment, to be lying with two women : with the victim of the evening's tragedy, the mystical *inspiratrice* of a heroic passion, and with a girl like other girls, save for her superiority over every woman he had ever known. And after that, through all the hours of darkness, the two individuals seemed to dissolve into one another, to draw apart and define themselves, again to merge and again to part, so that he became maddened with his inability to seize upon the one and wholly to dismiss the other. His passion leapt towards the one, only to receive a rebuff as he found it was the other he held in his arms. Fear ran like a thread of scarlet through the ecstasy of his loving. She exalted him, she reduced him ; all that he knew was lost to him in his perception of her superior knowledge. And, when dawn came, it brought him the exhaustion of one who has dreamed of love and spent upon a phantom all the resources of passion.

At last she became sensible to her companion's mutterings, and her eyes flew open. He could see her sitting up in the bed, with the beautiful crescents of her ribs lifted like so many delicate arches, as, with a single movement of decision, she swept her hair into a knot at the back of her head.

" What is it you are saying ? Now I will tell you what we can do. Quickly ; because I must let you out of the house before they wake up. Yes, indeed ! There are proprieties. . . . I am not a *cocotte* ! It would be a little awkward if Emilia Mera were to come in, as she does sometimes, and find you still with me. Of course she knows ; but there is a difference between knowing and seeing ! "

Her words were mysterious and hurtful to him ; they seemed to belong to another person, an intruder upon his obscure pain, that quickened into fear as she pointed to the foot of the bed, across which his clothing was lying.

" Did you hear ? Quickly."

" But—you want me to go away ? "

" Madre mía ! " she whispered, exasperated by his stupidity, yet conquered by the lost and mystified expression of his face, which she caressed lightly. " You must not be foolish. You are still asleep. Come, rouse yourself. Listen ; I have somebody . . . Well ? What did you expect ? Why do you grow pale ? Have you not got somebody as well, up in the mountains ? "

It seemed to him that he had at some time heard of a woman called Carmela ; but that name belonged to a period of his life ended, irrevocably, between candlelight and dawn. He clung to her, pressing his hands hard down on her thighs, so that she could feel the marks of his fingers forming in bruises on her flesh. For the second time slipped away for her also ; she had a flash of quick, professional anxiety— would the marks show when she went before her public ? Then she remembered how long it was since the type of work she did compelled her to expose her limbs in that fashion, and she thrust against the masterful clutch.

" Do not let us separate like this. At the thought of parting from you I feel death in my body ! "

" Is it not enough—what we have had ? Do you expect pleasure to go on for ever ? Come, do not make me angry with you," she added more tenderly, but it annoyed her he was making so bad an end of it.

" I am destroyed ; you have destroyed me," he muttered, as though he had not heard what she said ; his hands were clasped to his forehead. " You have taken from me that without which a man cannot live. Like air, like water, like bread—that is a man's love to him. You have taken my love from me, and you have given me nothing in return. You are very fine, very noble, very good, but you are also very bad. Yes, I say it, you are very bad. You do not understand that to take everything from a man and to leave him nothing is to destroy him."

" How can you say such a thing ? " she said, now seriously vexed with him. " It has been the same—for both of us," she ended—for her, clumsily.

" That is not true. It has not been for you what it has been for me, or you would not be sending me away now."

" Love is an illusion," she answered sadly, swept from anger into the profound melancholy of Aurelio's mood. Her fellow-actors said it was one of her great qualities that she could catch an atmosphere unfalteringly, and render it back to its creator enhanced by the mysterious emanations of her own spirit ; they called it " never spoiling a scene." Now her actress's instinct would not permit her to spoil Aurelio's scene. " Love is an illusion." The phrase pleased her. "All the beauty that is in the world is illusion, a thing that does not exist save in the minds of those who are very happy. We have been very happy." She suddenly dragged him to her, pressing his face between her breasts as she told him quickly about her old admirer, about her plans for the future. She could feel the long, powerful tremor which shook him from time to time, but she continued inexorably with her narrative, the more inexorably because she herself, for some reason, now felt a little shame.

" We need not entirely lose one another," she pleaded, with a woman's folly : for was not this exactly the argument which she had used with herself when she had made her decision with regard to Aurelio—that when it was over they would pass completely out of each other's lives, and, in time, forget ? " I will tell you what we can do. You must not try to get in touch with me in any way ; that would be dangerous. All men are jealous, but his jealousy will be worse than the ordinary, because he is so much older than I ; he will always be watching to see if I get a young lover ; he will pay people to spy upon me. Oh, I know ! I have known women who have done what I am doing ; it was not easy, but it came right in the end. . . . But I will find out a way to get a letter to you once a year. I shall send it to the post office, and you can ask for it at the restante. Is not that a very good plan ? "

He reflected that a year ago, when his father-in-law was still at the post office, it would have been impossible ; but Pablo Moreno had succumbed to the germs of tuberculosis which were in his family, and had been forced into retirement twelve months ago. It seemed like a true instance of divine intervention on behalf of the lovers.

" I shall grow fat," she was babbling. " Madre mía, how fat I shall grow, with nothing to do save drink chocolate and order my servants about, and buy all the clothes and furniture I have ever wanted in my life." She saw his face, with all the lines dragging downwards, like the face of the Crucified, and the slackness and abandon of his body that drooped on the edge of her bed, as though bone and muscle had lost their power to co-ordinate. " If you like, I will promise you something more : you shall be my last lover. After you—nobody. There ; does that comfort you ? Do you now believe I have loved you ? "

" As the scrapings of vegetables comfort a beggar ; as I believe figs grow upon thistles," he answered her bitterly.

" How ungrateful you are ! You are so lost in your own feelings you do not stop to consider what it means to me ! "

He lacked the power to retort ; his strength was gone from him with the tears that slowly poured down his face, for he had never before known what it was to shed tears for a woman. He felt himself like a devastated area, upon whose accursed soil no plant could ever again take root, incapable of fertilisation or of being fertilised. His flesh, his bone, crumbled ; the remainder of his youth died upon him suddenly, like flowers scorched by the sun. Her words made a noise inside his head like insects that run about inside a skull.

Presently, seeing it was useless to talk to him, she began to force him into his clothes. It piqued her that he suffered her to do this as though he were a child or an imbecile, staring with vacuous non-comprehension at the garments as she put them upon him. She had never dressed a man before ; the unfamiliar act filled her with a contemptuous compassion, and at the same time she was angry that he was not capable, like herself, of making the renunciation firmly and lightly, with thanksgiving for the past rather than chagrin for the future. Tears were trembling in her own eyes, but she flung back her head and they were gone ; she had to bite her lips to steady them, knowing his grief blinded him to hers. Nor, had he perceived it, need it have comforted him, for she wept, not for him, but for the sacrifice of her own freedom to the need of the future.

Finally, with a gesture of surely ill-timed friendliness— she whose timing, whose sense of the appropriate, upon the stage was so impeccable ; indeed he had swept her from her moorings !—she gave him her hand, saying seriously :

" And now, if there is ever anything I can do for you in the future, you have only to let me know of it, and I shall find a way. Money is a necessity, as some day you may find out. Remember, you must never send a letter directly to me ; but I will discover some trustworthy person, and let you know how to get in touch with her."

The whole town was pink with the dawn when she let him out into the street.

" Go with God ! "

When he had gone, she stood a moment clutching her wrapper across her bosom, looking about her at the shabby walls, the dust and refuse swept into a corner of the patio by a careless servant, at the tattered posters of theatrical performances and bullfights that no one troubled to destroy, at the framed photographs of the patron saint of Granada, Nuestra Señora de las Angustias, which is in every house. The image of the Miraculous Virgin was dust-covered and fly-spotted, like everything else in the house. What else could one expect in a five-peseta fonda ? At least she and Emilia had not, so far, found bugs in their rooms.

" Emilia ! I am sorry to disturb you, but have you a little water ? My mouth is as dry as though I had been eating sand."

" I have no water, but over there are some sweets I bought yesterday ; there may be one or two left."

Maravilla thirstily popped a caramel into her mouth ; the sugary flavour nauseated her and increased her thirst, but she masticated as though she were ravenous. Emilia, with her elbow propped on the bolster, watched her.

" What beautiful hair you have. What do you put on it ? "

" I shall do a great deal of good when I am rich, Emilia."

Ignoring the question, Maravilla spoke suddenly. " I shall feed beggars and give money to all who ask for it. All my friends shall benefit by my good fortune. You will see ; I am not one to forget my promises. I shall become quite famous for my generosity."

" You have decided, then ? " said Emilia sadly.

" How can you ask, when you look at a pigsty like this one ? " was the passionate reply. " I am not a slut, but, living in such surroundings, I should sooner or later become one."

" I have not become one," said Emilia Mera diffidently.

" You, as I have often told you, are an angel. You see your vision, your ideal of the theatre ; half of what actually goes on never even crosses the line of your sight. If I were like you I should go on, working nobly, giving always of my best, disdaining compromise—rewarded only by my own integrity. But I find already that the few things I had which were good are gone. I find I have lost the power even to love—except in a certain way . . . I found that out last night."

" You should go back to bed," prompted Emilia. " Do not forget there is a rehearsal to-day."

" For which play ? " asked Maravilla carelessly. " I have a good mind not to go down to the theatre at all until to-night. I am tired of rehearsing, and I know all my parts."

" In a decent company," said Emilia, with one of her rare flashes of resentment, which were always for others, never for herself, " your understudy would spare you the annoyance. But the play is *The Lawyer from Andorra*, and the rehearsal is called for the new young man who has joined us to play Silvestro's parts."

" Well, I have only one scene. I suppose, for the sake of ' the new young man,' I shall be there," yawned Maravilla.

DM

" Unless I desert the company ! I should do that if it were not for leaving the rest of you in the lurch."

" What ? Before you have got your fare to Cádiz ? " inquired Emilia, with a twinkle of humour.

" What a pity I have not the courage to finish it !" said Maravilla quietly. Emilia got out of bed and came to her side, putting her arms about the younger woman, and pressing her head against her shoulder.

" Do not say such things, my little one. Fortune will change for you, and when you have done with the theatre it will seem no more than a bad dream."

" But for last night I should do it. If I live, it is because of that. Oh, Emilia, I ought to have let everything go, and done as he wished me. After all, what I want is to get away from this ; what would it matter, when I took off the paint for the last time, where I went, or whose wife I became ? I am sure I could be as happy in a peasant's hut——"

" You are overwrought," said Emilia calmly. " You know that that would not suit you any better than the theatre. You are a creature of luxury, and, remember, it is coming to you. God bless you ; go to your sleep, hija. You have only a little longer to wait. . . ."

CHAPTER V

AURELIO AND CARMELA

No one cared to tell Carmela about the fate of her market-stall ; no one, in fact, admitted to knowing anything about it. The stall, the stove, the pots and pans, and the cooking materials might have been swept away by the devil on a high wind. Aurelio was many times pressed to drink in the casino, and his opinion was flatteringly consulted by many people who, as they held his sleeve and poured their troubles, real or invented, into his ear, tried to find out with their eyes whether, on his wife's behalf, he was bent on reprisals. Murder had been done for less ; but the López family, as a whole, did not run to murder ; they had the infinitely more inconvenient and troublesome habit of haling their complaints before the alcalde.

There was a lot of wife-beating in Agujasierra on the night the men came back from the feria. Ordinarily, in their domestic relations, the Agujasierrans were peaceful enough ; only when in drink, or under provocation of secret masculine troubles, were their hands laid upon the women who shared their beds. But on this night yells and thuds echoed in the alleys ; in the morning the women exhibited their bruises to each other with furtive pride. To have a husband who could beat one up to that tune was something ! The men had heard all about it in the casino, from the nondescripts and dotards who, from one reason or another, had been prevented from going to Granada. One inferred that the destruction of Carmela's stall had offered them very agreeable compensation for what they had missed; the affair was discussed more than the form shown in the Plaza de Toros. Then the men went home—to ask no questions, but to beat up their wives, the innocent equally with the guilty : not because Carmela was any more popular with them than with the women, but because it was well to put oneself on the same side with the López. Several made a point of referring, casually, in Aurelio's presence, to the wife-beating, but none was sure that he listened. As the days went on, a faint contempt took the place of their apprehension, for Aurelio continued to ignore the occurrence in a manner that was an offence to every local tradition.

"Give me a little water for my face. Hand me a cloth to wipe the child." These were the requests which Carmela, as her strength returned to her, made of Aurelio. "Do not permit those sluts to cross my threshold !" was another of her commands, spoken in regard to the nieces, who carried on the housework, after a fashion, while she was laid in bed.

And if he was a little slow in interpreting her commands —for he moved always like a man in a dream, and his face was the colour of ashes ; and, besides, is it a man's business to wait on a woman in sickness ?—"The least you can do now is to wait on me, after leaving me alone for this to happen to me !"

If left by herself, she sulked ; if he remained with her, she ignored him for the child she held against her bosom. One day, looking down upon the small, palpitating head, which looked as though it had been rubbed in coal-dust, she began to talk in a crooning voice, as though her words were spoken to the child, when really they were intended for Aurelio.

"Before you came, I hoped you'd be a son. How am I

to raise a daughter among all these brutes and beasts ? Now you've turned out to be a girl, and you must take your chances with the rest. Dio' mío, what is to come of you ?— And you ! " She turned furiously upon Aurelio. " What gratitude have you shown for all I have suffered for you ?— for all I have given up ; for the sacrifice of all my personal feelings and comforts ? How many women do you suppose would have been as brave as I, accompanying a man into a den of wild beasts ? Ay, the good home I left, to follow you into your mountains ! I suppose you think I have been quite happy, with your relations all biting at me and making up lies about me ? "

These words of Carmela's, which would formerly have saddened him, were to Aurelio no more than the sound of rain on the roof. He sat speechlessly against the wall, resting his chin upon his clenched right hand ; he did not even turn his head to look at her. Absorbed in her self-commiseration, as she had been ever since the birth of the child, she paid no attention to his abstraction, continuing her mournful, egotistical speech, which she punctuated by kissing the infant.

" Ay, to think you have it all to go through, because it was God's will to make a girl of you ! At least you shall have your mother's spirit to help you make the best of it ; she will teach you all her own tricks of self-defence, when the time comes. Pobretica mía ! That you should have to learn such lessons. And now, I suppose, no one has thought to send word to my people that the baby is born ? " she flung at Aurelio.

He lifted his head ; truly, at that moment, he could not remember whether or not a message had been sent to the widow Herédia, or to the child's maternal grandparents. Carmela flew into a passion.

" And my aunt expecting to be the godmother ! Probably

you have even forgotten the money she is going to leave us when she dies ? Mother of God, what a world it would be if there were nothing but men in it ! "

" You are right," said Aurelio humbly ; he roused himself with an effort. " I will go to the house of Colgas and borrow some paper and ink to write to her."

For the first time, looking at him sharply, she seemed to realise the change that had taken place in him ; her lips loosened their bitter line, and, shifting the child a little into the angle of her arm, she spread out the other with a gesture that invited him to her bosom. Her querulousness was the direct result of the nervous and physical strain through which she had passed ; like many of her kind, when she suffered she had only bitter words in which to express her suffering, she was not really motivated by any desire to pass it on to Aurelio, whom she truly loved. Seeing now, for the first time, his aged and stricken look, his mouth that did not smile, his eyes that looked dully at her from half-closed lids, a feeling of tenderness completely routed her baser feelings ; for it seemed to her that he, in some strange fashion, had been taking part in her agony, and, like every woman, she knew that men have neither the physical nor the moral fortitude of women.

Even to her limited powers of perception, it was plain that, while she was ill, Aurelio had been through some painful experience which had impressed itself upon him physically : for that mild and easy bearing, that air of acquaintance only with things which were pleasant and agreeable, which differentiated him from the rest of his family, had vanished, and to Carmela's infinite disquiet the lean, wolfish, and furtive look of the typical Agujasierran, the relic of their former brigandage, had taken its place. She felt as though a stranger stood there ; so keen was this feeling that, with an access of modesty, she hastily covered her breast, and, lying against her bolster, she was unable to take her eyes from his face.

For all her former jealousies, curiously enough, it did not once occur to Carmela to connect this sinister change with a woman. She would not, in fact, have believed any woman could so affect Aurelio. She racked her brains for a possible solution of the mystery, and her essential ignorance of this man who had given her her child defeated her. It was as impossible for her to say to him, quite simply, " What is the matter with you ? " as it would have been to coax a confession of infidelity out of him, had she suspected it.

In a silence that shocked them both, they stared at one another, and, while the air trembled with their unspoken thoughts, the door was pushed open, and the priest entered, without knocking. He was wiping his mouth on the back of his hand, for he had been drinking with the nieces in the room which, in the days of Aurelio's parents, had been the tavern.

" Well, Carmela Moreno, are you getting better ? It is high time you were on your feet again, you know, in the —on your feet," he concluded hurriedly, for he had been about to say, " in the market." He knew he was in part to blame for what had occurred, for he had heard the noise they made over breaking up Carmela's stall quite clearly from the casino ; he had even peeped through a window and seen them at it, and had not interfered because his stomach was more precious to him than the well-being of his flock, and the wife of the man who kept the casino had just dished up for him a fine paella, which he wanted to carry through to the presbytery next door. He had bribed the old woman not to say anything about his being there, but his conscience made him uneasy in the presence of Carmela, to whose wits he paid reluctant tribute, and whom, for that reason, he had not visited since the day he had baptised the infant.

Carmela's face took on its habitual expression of contempt and dislike, for she despised the priest, his unseemly familiarity with the people, and his greasy fumblings with the town girls, who made a joke of them, and went to confession prepared, they said, for anything. Carmela herself had been aware of the lascivious eye which took stock of her charms while she knelt in the confessional, but he had not ventured to try any tricks with the wife of a López.

" No doubt God will decide when I am fit to be about again," she answered drily. The priest shot at her the look of malice which a base nature directs towards a nobler one.

" Come, I can't have you blaspheming, Carmela Moreno," he said sharply. " The truth, if you want to know it, is that you women of the towns have not the stamina we look for up here. Why, the day after La Pelluda had her twins she was helping her husband to kill pigs."

These graceless words filled Carmela with astonishment ; they could only mean one of two things—either the priest was very drunk, more drunk than ordinarily, or else, for some reason, he had lost his respect for, and fear of, her husband. She looked quickly at Aurelio, to see what kind of retort he was preparing, and, to her complete bewilderment, saw Aurelio staring vacantly, as though he had not heard, or the purport of the words had not penetrated his understanding. Taking advantage of the silence, the priest came unsteadily towards the bed—to look, ostensibly, at the infant.

" And the little one ? It is to be hoped the little Maravilla inherits her father's constitution, rather than her mother's."

Carmela snatched the infant closer to her bosom, pulling the cloth over it so as to conceal it. She was not appeased by what she took for the compliment to her baby ; all children were marvels, and, in any case, he was too drunk to know what he was saying.

" My Angustias will not be living the life of a little animal like the rest of the children here," she muttered.

The priest's eye lit up with a glint of intelligent malice. Ah, that was it ! That was just what he had suspected, the thing which had brought him here. His awkwardness at encountering Carmela was not proof against his over-mastering curiosity—fomented by certain gossip which was abroad in the town—about the name which had been given to the infant.

" Not so fast ! Not so impudent ! " But his voice was soft and cajoling, rather than severe. " If you speak so dis-respectfully, I shall have to give you a penance. But you are quite right not to approve of so outlandish a name as Maravilla ! The child might as well be a heretic as grow up with a name like that. It is an insult to the holy and blessed saints—to ignore their protection——"

Carmela could feel a whiteness and tightening in the flesh of her cheeks ; her fingers dug themselves into the bed covering.

" What are you saying ? My child is called after her great-aunt, Angustias Moreno, the widow of Herédia ; we promised it before we were married."

" Caramba," said the priest, thoroughly enjoying him-self. " Aurelio, surely you have not been deceiving your wife ? This is a great deal more serious than I had im-agined."

" Aurelio ! " cried Carmela. " What does it mean ? What has happened ? Why are you tormenting me ? " Unable to say more, she pressed her trembling mouth to the dusky head of the babe, but her eyes fixed themselves upon Aurelio's with the expression of a dying animal's.

" Now, now, Carmela Moreno, you must not distress

yourself. How sorry I am for you. No doubt Aurelio has behaved very badly," said the priest unctuously, " but you are not the first woman to be deceived by your husband. Nothing can be done about it, so you must resign yourself."

" Por Dios ! " she gasped, crossing herself, almost swooning.

" I baptised the child myself, acting on Aurelio's instructions," said the priest, mouthing each word with deliberation. " The name it was given was Maravilla."

Carmela gave a great shriek, which brought the two nieces running to the door. She pointed with a trembling hand at their inquisitive, scared faces.

" Get rid of everyone ! Empty this room ! " she cried. Though the priest made a jest of it, made as though to sit down, and shouted to Carmela to calm herself, it became apparent that unless her wishes were regarded she would scream herself into some kind of a fit. He took his chagrined departure, and, weak as she was, Carmela flung herself out of bed, to drive the wooden pin through its socket behind the door. At the unglazed window, whose shutters were flung back to admit what little air there was at the dusk of the June day, appeared the gaping faces of neighbours. Aurelio stood as though turned to stone, looking at the wall, with his hands hanging at his sides.

" You worm ! You deceitful hypocrite ! You have allowed me all this time to speak of the child as Angustias ! You must have bribed those sluts of women to help you to deceive me ! What did you bribe them with, you false traitor ? Which of them have you got for your mistress ? Tío ! Granuja ! Oh, if I had a knife and the strength to use it, I should carve you in pieces for what you have done to me—as you have carved me in pieces for your own brutal satisfaction ! "

In her rage, which made the whole of her face tremble, so

that the vibration of flesh and muscle was like the shudder-ing in the wings of a stationary moth, she looked capable of carrying out her threat. Her body hooked itself over the babe that clung to her breast like a little monkey, her upturned face and the blackness of her eye-sockets were those of a woman of sixty.

Again she voiced her accusation against him in connec-tion with the nieces, and at last, as the meaning of her words reached him through the wall of separation which had reared between them, he answered her.

" You need not say any of these things. They are not true ; I have not laid a finger on either of them."

" Then after whom have you called my child ? " In the transport of her rage she held the wailing infant in both hands above her head, as though she would dash it on the tiled floor. A sympathetic hiss of emotion went through the audience. " She's out of her mind ! He'll have to take her to the madhouse ! "

At last she had hold of the right thread. But Aurelio's face hardened like lava ; he refused to speak another word. With all her raving she could not make him open his lips ; he stood there defeating her with his silence, whatever angle she might choose for her attack. He might have been blind and deaf, as well as dumb. At last he went towards her, took her by the shoulder, and, without either roughness or tenderness, put her aside, as though she had been a piece of furniture, unbarred the door, and went out of the house.

The immediate result of this terrible scene was that Carmela became unable to suckle her child. Fortunately it was not difficult to procure a wet-nurse ; the girls of Agujasierra are famous for their milk, and for this reason in great demand among neighbouring well-to-do families, and in Granada. Carmela relinquished her infant to the wet-nurse without a sign of regret.

She was up and about a week later, but, to the surprise and disconcertion of all, she gave no signs of resuming her place in the market. Neither then, nor ever afterwards, did she make any reference to the destruction of her stall ; it was a thing that might never have been. Carmela knew, or, rather, could guess well enough, what had happened ; but her pride, and her abhorrence of these people, triumphed even over her avarice and her distress at the loss of her stock-in-trade. But they had now done her a factual injury, and it was stored in her mind, to be repaid, with interest, at a convenient moment. She would not give them the satisfaction of seeing her anger or her mortification ; she would wait, and one day her revenge would descend upon them out of a cloud—cold as snow, and sharp as steel. That she promised herself ; and they, taking her inaction, like Aurelio's, for pusillanimity, began again their verbal persecutions, with more freedom than formerly, because among the Agujasierrans the act of turning the other cheek is plain declaration of cowardice. The name of López had lost its dignity, and, among the rawer members of the community, was even synonymous with weakness—incapacity to take care of oneself.

" He acts like a López " ; " If you do that you're no better than a López "—these were phrases that crept into the local vocabulary. Carmela knew of them, and the knowledge drew a new line of bitterness at the corner of her thin lips. Aurelio neither knew, nor, in his present state of mind, would he have cared.

Moreover, it became gradually apparent to Carmela, whose perceptions had become evilly alert, that the townsfolk knew the thing that was withheld from her. The secret had leaked out, first among the men ; then one of the wives got hold of it and scurried with half a tale to some of her friends ; the women, agog, had not rested until they had the whole history out of their husbands. The alleys screamed with scandal : Aurelio López had been with a woman in Granada. If that did not serve his stuck-up wife as she deserved !

She could have had the whole tale in a minute ; it bubbled on the lips of women who passed her, their eyes flashed knowledge into hers a dozen times a day. And how polite, how gracefully courteous they were with her ! But once someone spat furtively on her gown as she went by. They were like mischievous children who band together to torment a playmate by letting her know they have a secret and refusing to share it.

They despised her, as well, because she was not suckling her child.

In those hours of torment her brain evolved a plan which finally, in curt sentences, she communicated to Aurelio. She had the Moreno greed for money, and had been casting about her for means to support them both ever since she lost her means of livelihood in the market-place. She was determined to show them they could not defeat her, and at last she found the way.

She announced that she intended to reopen the tavern. She coldly reminded Aurelio that Enrique López, when he migrated to Atarfe, had borrowed a sum of money which should have come to Aurelio at the death of his mother, and suggested that Aurelio should write, or go, to Atarfe, to claim the return of this sum, which she needed to restock the tavern with wine and eatables. He shrugged his shoulders in token of submission to her wishes, but he could not understand why Carmela, or anyone, should have this pre-occupation with money, or what money could do to restore the thing that lay broken between them.

The only thing for which he cared, in those stupefied days, was the child : over which he brooded tenderly, rarely venturing to touch it, yet clinging to it with his soul as though it were a frail angel that alone could save him from the abyss towards which he was sinking.

Its tiny face, the colour of old ivory, its eyes of milky brown, that completely filled the space between the lids, its little sucking mouth, that seemed perpetually to be seeking the breast, could not bring him joy : but they stood to him for something stable—something sane in the confusion of all his ideas. Often he would have picked it out of its cradle to nurse it, but some silent opposition on the part of Carmela prevented him from exercising his fatherly instinct.

He and Carmela were now living, under intimate conditions, lives of the utmost separation. Realisation of this sent a trail of sadness floating occasionally, like a thin cloud, across the surface of his deeper sorrow. Night by night their bodies lay together, one or the other sleeping, the wakeful one listening to the other's heavy, regular breathing. Once or twice he had had a crazy impulse to wake her, to tell her all, to share with her the burden of his suffering.

All of this pain, it seemed to him, arose from his lack of knowledge of Maravilla : of her life, so exotic by comparison with his own ; of her thoughts, concerned with so many things of which he had never heard ; of her actions, so problematical, so incomprehensible, so coloured with her existence in the theatre, that in her company he had had the dizzying sense of being forced into some drama whose rules were unknown to him. The only live part of him seemed now to be his thought of her. His mind ran back and back, like a squirrel on a wheel, over every moment from his first sight of her to their farewell : remembering, analysing every action, every spiritual and sensual experience, beglamoured, dazed, and possessed by this woman to

whom he had been no more than a night's adventure ;
trying in vain to fit his knowledge of human beings, on
which he had so prided himself, to this inhabitant of another
sphere.

The way she had looked upon the stage of the theatre—so
mysterious, so possessed by the tragic part she was creating,
the very emdodiment of a suffering and outraged virtue
that seemed to him positively saintly, and yet, with her
tragic beauty, invoking thoughts that set his soul and body
on fire.

The way she looked in the café, when, it seemed to his
imagination, she had divested herself of the supernatural
elements so profoundly unnerving and so repudiative of
human contacts, and chose to reveal herself simply as a
tired woman, exhausted in both a physical and a spiritual
sense with the part she had assumed, still sodden with it,
seeking an antidote for its subtle poison, seeing in him this
possible antidote.

Her light, almost trivial, reception of his advances, and
the skilled manner in which she handled them—exhibiting
herself as a woman of the world beyond the limits of his
experience.

And, finally, her surrender to him in the sophisticated
setting of her bedroom, whose every small detail was fixed
upon his memory before the extinction of the light. Her
watch, which she hung on a nail close to the head of the
bed ; the perfumed handkerchief she thrust under the pillow ; the delicacy and cleanliness of the garments she took
off ; the inexplicable equipment of her toilet-chest—all
these things were present to his memory with a torturing
fidelity ; instead of helping to recreate her image, he found
them obscuring it. It was as though her soul coquetted with
him behind the multiplicity of detail that surrounded her ;
and every now and then, in the midst of whatever he was

doing, he became quite still, fighting back some scrap of matter that interposed itself between her image and himself; or he would be so overwhelmed by a momentary recrudescence of the physical emotion she had inspired in him that the blood, charging to his brain, destroyed his balance, and he caught at the nearest object to prevent himself from falling. Nothing he had previously known corresponded with any of his experiences during that strange night; stripped of his knowledge he suffered the shame and humiliation of nakedness, and his manhood seemed to shrivel away.

Very slowly his mind returned to the normal. He became aware of what was going on about him—rather as a man coming home after a long absence uncertainly picks up the abandoned threads of his former existence. The year was growing old, and he saw that alterations had taken place.

The most intimate of the alterations was in his own home. He found it in possession of a middle-aged woman, whom he knew to be Carmela : an acid, active creature, who conducted with cunning ability the business of the house. She had the peaked face of a virago ; she rang every coin before putting it in her pocket, and at the end of the day, without reference to him, counted her takings and entered them in a little paper-backed book which she produced from the top of her corsets. She put her money in a canvas bag, which, when they went to bed, she thrust under the mattress ; where she kept it during the day he had not the least idea. She seemed neither to expect nor desire him to help her by taking any part in the work of the tavern ; she treated him as though he were a customer or a stranger, eyeing him with the same suspicious look, refusing, in the same way, to talk with him. She was as thin as a rail, and the last traces of her comeliness had vanished ; after the birth of the baby she had suddenly lost two upper teeth, and their loss drew her mouth into a wrinkled shrewishness. She now looked remarkably like her aunt, the widow Herédia, and there were moments when Aurelio found it hard to remember she was his wife.

Had it not been for the child, there would have been nothing whatever to draw him to his home during the daylight hours. But the baby was enchanting ! It was a miracle. And the first grimaces a worshipping mother might have interpreted as smiles were reserved for Aurelio. Kneeling beside the cradle, he first, with a delicious temerity, ventured to touch with one finger the blind, waving hand ; then, growing bolder, reminding himself the child was his as well as Carmela's, he lifted it up, at first overwhelmed, awestricken by the imperceptible weight of the thing, then cradling it triumphantly, asserting his fatherhood by crooning to it beneath his breath.

It was some little time before he noticed that Carmela took no part in the ritual of love which surrounded the baby. At first this puzzled and repelled him ; he was to come but slowly to realisation of the obsession which had taken possession of Carmela's mind—an obsession connected with the fatal name which, to her perverted way of thinking, did her out of her share in the babe ; an obsession which was to strengthen with the years, until, by the time Maravilla was in her teens, her mother had ceased to regard her as the fruit of her own womb, but looked on her as a changeling which Aurelio's infidelity had foisted upon her in the place of her own child.

Even now, thought Aurelio, the child might not have been hers. She kept it clean, rated the wet-nurse if she was unpunctual in her hours of attendance, and ignored Maravilla for the rest of the day. If the baby howled, she peremptorily hushed it with a foot on the rocker, or a slap, not hard or cruel, but strong enough for the infant to be aware of an authority which forbade such assertions. If it had pains she shrugged her shoulders : all infants had pains. It was warm ; it was well fed—it did not reject the nourishment it drew from the rich breast of its nurse. It cannot have had many pains, for it throve. In spite of its thriving, the tale went round that Carmela Moreno ill-treated her baby. Mothers of scabby, half-starved children terrified their offspring by dragging them to their bosoms and calling on the Virgin to witness to their own maternal virtues. Spotty, half-blind infants, suffering from the prevalent disease of pink-eye, were plucked from withering breasts, smacked, and told how fortunate they were not to have Carmela Moreno for their mother.

The little Maravilla never had sore places, was never scabby ; her eyes grew wider every day, and more clear ; it must have been accident that it was so, for there were enough microbes in the dust of Agujasierra to have provided for a massacre of the innocents, and Carmela, although cleanly, had no ideas on hygiene. It did not occur to her to cover the cradle to keep the flies off the baby's face ; these same flies gorged themselves on the street offal, descended on the putrescent meat on the stalls, entered the house, and found their way, sooner or later, to the cradle. The baby screamed, beat with its hands, while the creatures punctured its brow, its cheeks, raising lumps that quickly inflamed the delicate skin. But eventually some kind of inoculation must have taken place. The lumps came, but they were not so angry ; she seemed hardly aware of them ; within an hour or two they vanished. What would have killed a northern child was accepted by the child of the south as a necessary evil of existence.

The cradle stood on a broad sill, caused by cutting

window-space into a wall as thick as that of a fortress ; clouds of dust poured in through the reja, the horns of steers scraped the iron bars as cattle were driven along the narrow gully ; the sill was just above the drain that carried the sewage from the house into the common gutter. The only advantage of the situation was that it protected the baby from the inquisitive noses of the mongrel dogs that sneaked, scavenging, into the tavern, and evaded capture with reptilian cunning.

There was a little medal of the Blessed Virgin fastened to the wooden hood of the cradle ; Carmela did not know who had put it there, but she did not remove it.

CHAPTER VI

WINTER

THE SHORT, SAVAGE WINTER of the lower mountain-slopes was upon them. For many days both men and women had been cutting firewood, dragging or carrying home the bundles of faggots, filling their rooms with them, so that it was almost impossible to get in for piled brushwood. Few could afford to buy charcoal, none coal; the schoolmaster had made a great storage place under his class-room, which was on the first floor of the town hall, and, under threats and penalties, had compelled the elder scholars to contribute to the wood store. Part of it was for the warming of his own dwelling (the school-room itself had a grant of charcoal from the alcalde), and part was to be " given " to those who were too old or feeble to do their own wood-gathering. From these it was his intention to levy pay in kind, since the majority were too poor for the question of money even to be mooted. Colgas knew all about an old painted platter which he had long coveted from the widow of Amalio Ortega ; Cecilio Pérez had a skinny fowl or two that might be palatable in the cazuela. He reflected, with satisfaction, that he was not likely to be out of pocket on the transaction.

In the same way the priest was securing his own comfort through the arduous efforts of his flock. The presbytery must be stocked before individual households were considered. Nothing could be more offensive to God and to the Blessed Virgin than the neglect of their chosen ministers. Wrapped in his cloak, with his florid face blackened by the wind, he intercepted the homecoming wood-carriers, confiscating a portion of each load to his own use, and driving the un-willing victim before him—if necessary with blows of his stick. Warm with wine, the discomforts of those whose half-starved bodies had been exposed for hours to the mountain wind did not trouble him. Men˙dropped in dead stupor on the floor of Carmela Moreno's tavern, overcome with the mere wine-fumes before a drop had passed their lips ; the fortunate few who had not found it necessary to go out tucked the table-cloth more snugly round their knees, and toasted their lower parts in the glow of the brasero, while aguardiente kept their blood in circulation. There were one or two tales of deaths among the mountain shepherds ; the stall-keepers neglected their trade to cower over their stoves, and peered like tortoises out of their hastily contrived wrappings.

Each morning looks of anxiety were directed towards the peaks whose dark *chevaux de frise* stood like black iron across the steely arch of the sky. Snow was expected ; it lay already upon the upper pinnacles ; La Aguja bore its frozen coronet, and each day the snowline crept lower on the slopes.

There was no need for Aurelio to trouble himself about wood-cutting, for Carmela had the house amply pro-visioned with fuel. Theirs was one of the few houses in the village that had ample storage room, and, in her usual thrifty fashion, Carmela had started at the beginning of the autumn to store charcoal, kindling, and logs, so that winter should not find them unprepared. She had it all soundly under lock and key, so there was no danger, either, of her thrift being wasted by pilfering.

The first flakes of snow were falling when, returning from a walk up the mountain with his gun under his arm, Aurelio came face to face with Colgas the schoolmaster, who looked very self-satisfied, with a large earthenware platter, painted with a blue and yellow design, in his hand. Aurelio owed his permission to shoot over the jealously preserved estates of the Duque de Alora to the family's historic friendship with the cacique ; it was, in fact, the cacique's father who had presented his grandfather with the ancient fowling-piece which Aurelio had learned, not very skilfully, to use. He did not like killing things, but there was no denying that a rabbit or a pheasant made a very agreeable variation in the daily diet.

Colgas made a point of not quarrelling, openly, with any of his neighbours, so he greeted Aurelio with great civility, at the same time giving him a sharp, inquiring look out of his little, inquisitive eyes.

" Good afternoon, Aurelio López. So we are to have snow at last ! I hope you are well provisioned for the cold weather. But, with a wife like Doña Carmela, I hardly need to ask ! Whatever people may say about her, I am sure there is no better housewife in Agujasierra."

" Many thanks for the compliment, Colgas," replied Aurelio, and was about to pass on when the schoolmaster detained him.

" That is a fine fat bird you are carrying. Dear me, what a thing it is to be able to handle a gun ! I heard this morning that you had gone shooting ; a more agreeable occupation—ha-ha !—than cutting down trees." With which fatuous observation Colgas claimed the right of familiarity to pat Aurelio on the shoulder. The friendly gesture immediately aroused the latter's suspicion. He knew the town held little friendliness towards him and Carmela, and the knowledge, which would once have wounded him, left him indifferent. He cared for none of them, and for nothing in the world, save his little daughter. Their contempt or their enmity were nothing to him so long as he had his little daughter. The stars twinkled and the almond-trees broke into flower for him at Maravilla's crowing laughter.

" Excuse me, Aurelio López," Colgas was saying. " But I cannot help thinking, from your manner, that you have not heard of a little trouble at your house, since you went away this morning ? "

Aurelio stared, with eyes red-rimmed with the cold. The one fear that was always present to his mind leapt to his lips in his reply.

" Is the baby ill ? "

" What an idea ! " laughed Colgas, chuckling and grimacing as if this were an excellent joke. " If all the children in Agujasierra were as healthy as yours, our friend Gallego would do well to close his shop. Oh, no ; put that out of your mind at once. If you have really not heard, and would like to step into my house for a moment ? There is no need for us to take all the neighbours into our confidence."

Aurelio followed, scowling ; this was just Colgas's way— to pretend friendliness and sympathy, when really all he wanted was the personal gratification of enjoying the dis- comfiture of his victim when he got him to himself. He always made a point, under pretext of soothing, of keeping people on the rack as long as possible. This was his method with his pupils, as well as with older people, and Aurelio remembered, with uncertain relief, that the more trivial the matter, the longer, as a rule, was Colgas's preamble.

" Now do sit down. Pray take this chair—it is more com- fortable than the other. Put your legs under the table—let me stir up the brasero ! A person needs to be as comfortable as possible when he has anything unpleasant to listen to. I am sorry to start in such a manner, but it struck me that it would be much better for you to hear the details from a person like myself—a man of the world and a personal friend—than go into the middle of the business unprepared."

"He can hardly contain himself for pleasure in the torture he fancies he is putting me to," thought Aurelio, becoming, on the contrary, more and more reassured by the schoolmaster's manner. What an advantage it was to know people and their ways. In order to throw cold water on Colgas's ardour, he first smiled sceptically, and then made a totally irrelevant remark.

"That is a very handsome plate you are carrying, Colgas."

"This? Oh," said the schoolmaster, feigning surprise. "I had forgotten about it. It is touching how grateful people are, in this weather, for a handful of sticks or a lump or two of charcoal." He put the plate carefully down on the table, and, clasping his two hands together beneath his chin, looked across them at Aurelio. "So you have not heard what has happened to your niece Conchita?"

The elder of the two girls Carmela so detested had got herself with child by one of the men of the town ; Aurelio knew about that, but did not consider it a matter to make a song about, and wondered how it concerned him. He shrugged his shoulders.

"She is not a great favourite with Doña Carmela, I take it," said Colgas slyly.

"They are both as lazy as snakes in the sun," agreed Aurelio, and, getting no immediate reply, wandered off on one of his characteristic soliloquies. "Yet nothing is more certain than that God created sloth as well as industry ; and why did he make the sun, unless he intended us to sit in it?"

"A little family ill-feeling hardly justifies the act of turning a woman—in her condition as well !—out of doors

in weather like this. That, at least, is how the town looks
at it."

The snow was now whirling against the rejas ; Aurelio
frowned. The necessity seemed to be upon him to do
something, and, to one so long accustomed to playing the
watcher's rôle, to adopt suddenly an active one, in what
was evidently a public drama, was distasteful. He lifted
his shoulders.

" One does not interfere in women's quarrels. Unless one
is a priest."

" Now, come," said Colgas, in a propitiatory voice. " You
know I cherish feelings of warm affection towards you. You
were one of my best pupils, and your family has always
commanded great respect in this town. You are not, I
hope, above taking a little advice from an older person who
wishes you nothing but the best."

" What do you want to tell me ? " frowned Aurelio.

" Now do not misunderstand me," said Colgas fussily.
" In a population like ours a man like yourself is always a
little out of order. I understand very well what you are—
how you live all the time over people's heads, and pay no
attention to what they think or say."

" What a fool you are, Colgas," Aurelio was thinking.
" All my life I have known these people's hearts as I have
known my own. I could tell you more in ten minutes
about them than you have learnt in all the twenty-five or
thirty years you have lived among them." But since the
days of his naïve simplicity were past, and also, perhaps,
because the time when he had come to the limits of his
knowledge was fresh in his memory, he bent his head in
apparent acceptance of Colgas's words.

" You do not understand, for instance, that you have
allowed yourself to become very unpopular. Of course not
with me, my dear : as I have said, you were always my

favourite pupil. But with people who do not understand your character. Who find it difficult to understand, for instance, why you allow your wife to govern you. That is very unlike a López, you know ! It is always a little suspicious when a man does not rule his own household, and people are apt to think that therefore he is not capable of looking after himself outside the casa."

The idea that he was governed by Carmela had never before occurred to Aurelio, and the more he thought about it the less true it appeared to him. All the same, his pride was touched by this revelation of his neighbours' opinions, and he began to pay attention to what Colgas had to say.

" It's not as if she had you pinned down by her money, as is the case of Pepe Luis and his wife. Everyone is sorry for Pepe Luis, because it must be formidable to have married a woman with all that fortune behind her ! But so far as that goes you are entirely a free agent. Now all this trouble under your roof," continued Colgas. " It is just a commonplace when it happens in other families. A little gossip, perhaps, among the women, but no serious person takes note of it. But in the house of the López ! Then, let me tell you, it becomes quite a different matter."

Aurelio began to wonder what Colgas, in his circumlocutory fashion, was driving at. He was naturally aware of the constant quarrels between Carmela and the two daughters of his sister who had married again and gone to live in Málaga ; but all his life he had been accustomed to female bickering, and had cultivated the art of closing his ears upon it, unless it was more than usually interesting. The two girls were lazy, and he had gathered that Carmela considered them dirty and immoral in their habits. Immorality was a subject whose heights and depths Aurelio had never fully explored. It was to him a matter of philosophies, of points of view, of subtle, circumstantial

modifications. Sexual immorality was what it is to any
Spaniard—a thing which takes place outside the casa and
in no way affects family relationships.

" It seems your wife has been beating both the girls,"
went on Colgas. " Now, it is very well to give a person a
good beating—there are very few women who are not the
better for it. But the elder one has been with Paco Ledesma ;
it seems she is in the family way, and if her novio's people
get wind of it there will certainly be a very inconvenient
scandal."

" I will go and see what is going on," said Aurelio,
getting up. Even now it did not seem to him a serious
matter. Carmela had given one of the girls a drubbing, and
she had run out and shrieked about it in the market-square.
All the natives would take her side, because they were at
odds with Carmela. The more he thought of it, the more
trivial it appeared to Aurelio, as he approached his own
house. To his surprise the door of the tavern was closed, and,
when he tried it, bolted. When he hammered, Carmela
herself jerked back the shutter of the small grill in the
upper part of the door. Without a word she flung it open
and let him in.

She had evidently been scrubbing out the wine-shop ;
there were no customers ; the lamps were lighted, for by
now it was completely dark indoors, and darkness was
rushing upon the town—a darkness made tremulous by the
whirling dance of the snow, which Aurelio shook off his
hat-brim as he stepped into the house. The quietness told
him that no one save Carmela, and the presumably sleeping
child, was indoors ; ordinarily there would have been the
parrot-shrieks and clatter of the girls, the rumble of men's
voices.

" What has happened ? " he asked shortly.

She faced him with her hands on her lips.

" You are a nice lot—you López ! " The violence and directness of her attack took him by surprise ; almost it gave him a feeling of relief, for, the frost-bound politeness of her speech removed, she was the old Carmela—a withered and battered version, but familiar and reassuring in her anger. Without saying another word she went into the room where they slept and brought him a canvas bag, which he recognised as the one in which she kept her savings. At the end of every month she took it to the alcalde, who, in her presence, locked it into a leather wallet, and, in due time, took it into Granada and banked it for her. It was a favour he undertook for several of the more well-to-do tradespeople. It was now the end of the month, and the previous night, when Carmela had added the day's takings to the contents of the bag, he had noticed that it was fat and heavy. Now she handed him a limp fold of canvas, and he knew the money was gone.

" That's what I found this morning—after that slut of an Asunción had got leave from me to go to the Fonda Fidel, to ask if those cases of Valdepeñas had been left there by mistake, instead of being delivered at our place. Ay-ay ! I gave her two hours, because the way back is all uphill . . ." Carmela stopped ; she caught the corner of her lip in her teeth, and all her face quivered. Aurelio, understanding her as he had not been able to understand her for months, felt pity gush up in him. Why should she take the loss so hard ? There must be plenty in the bank by now. They would soon save some more. But something warned him not to speak these thoughts aloud ; he stood, holding the bag, and shaking his head.

" There was I," she resumed presently. " When the time to eat came, instead of one or two, there were seven wanting food, as well as something to drink. That Concha—she could do nothing but be sick ; you'd think no one had ever had a child before ! " she threw in viciously. " I had to get Zoraïda Zubia to help me—and that meant the baby was not fed at its proper time, and it got wind on the stomach and screeched without stopping, till I could have smothered it ! "

The baby ! Aurelio's eyes strayed towards the inner room, and his hand towards the pocket where he had a root he had picked up on the mountain ; with a little trimming it would make a doll—a delicious hard thing for the relief of little aching gums. Carmela saw the look ; it drew from her a fresh shrill outcry.

" Of course you think of nothing but the baby ! I could be dead before you would think of me ! "

" Go on, Carmela, tell me the rest," he said gently. He had not used her name for so long that it felt odd and unexpectedly sweet upon his lips.

" When they were all gone, and that slut had not come back, I began to wonder. And then—something whispered in my ear ! May the devil destroy them both—scheming bitches that they are ! One of them must have spied on me —I wouldn't put it past her to have hidden under the bed, or in that old cupboard that holds your grandmother's clothes—oh, if I had only caught her at it ! I'd have bolted her in till she was black in the face—suffocation isn't bad enough for such a one——"

" Come," stammered Aurelio, taken aback by her violence. " Do not be too hard—curiosity is a woman's failing."

" I suppose you will next say thieving is a woman's failing ! " screamed Carmela, by now beside herself. " And when I went to find the other slut, to question her about it, believe me or not, she denied knowing anything about it. That's likely, isn't it ?—with them always in each other's pockets, sniggering over their secrets, calling me names——"

" And has Asunción not come back ? "

" What do you suppose ? By now she's twenty miles away, with my money in her pocket. And good riddance to her ! At any rate I've sent her fine sister to look for her."

" What do you mean ? " said Aurelio, catching her by the arm. She looked up at him with eyes that held a red glitter.

" I'll tell you what I did to her ! I thrashed her till she screeched for mercy. I terrified her out of her life. I soon let her see there was no room in my house for thieves. I beat her until she ran out at that door, bellowing—of course she did it on purpose, so as to let the neighbours know what was happening to her. Her eyes stuck out of her head——"

" Where did she go ? "

" How do I know ? " said Carmela, suddenly calm. She made a grand gesture of washing her hands of the whole affair. " I have cleaned my house of filth."

" You had no right ! The house is mine. She is of my family."

" A fine family ! "

" Do you know it is snowing ? "

" I did not cause the snow to fall. Now stand out of my way : I have my floor to clean." She took a lamp from the wall and stood it upon the stone flags. Aurelio looked down—at first incredulously. There were dark spots on the floor ; at first he took them for wine-stains, then he realised they were too dark. He remembered, as he came in the dusk from Colgas's house, seeing other stains, similar, on the ground. He had recognised these as blood, but that was nothing out of the ordinary ; there might have been an argument, or someone might have been beating a donkey, or dogs might have been fighting. Carmela flung him a defiant glance as she went down on her knees ; in that glance he perceived suddenly the contempt of the Aguja-sierrans for a man who could not govern his household. He said quietly, " When I come back, I will beat *you*," and opened the door.

A blackness of mountain night met him ; a few orange squares showed round the market-place, but most people had their shutters, as well as their doors, closed. The old oil-lamps clamped to the sides of the buildings shed a sickly light. The snow was now coming down in heavy, relentless flakes, large as goose-feathers ; already the whole surface of the square was white.

He did not, for a moment, know what to do. Where was he to search for the girl whom Carmela had driven away from his door ? The fact that there were no people about— none of the usual knots of commentators in the doorways— made it appear to him for a moment as though it must be Carmela's imagination ; as though Concha must have crept back into the house to hide. Or she had taken refuge with one of the neighbours. Someone must have seen her if she had gone out of the village. Yet he remembered, with an uneasy sureness, the spots of blood he had seen on the ground, along the alley which led past the house of Colgas. Colgas could tell him more. He stumbled over the ruts and hammered on Colgas's door.

The room, when he entered it, was full of men, and it was instantly obvious to his perception that they were talking about the matter which had brought him there. Their faces turned towards him in the thick cloud of tobacco smoke, and they became silent. There was not one man present, save, probably, Colgas, who had more than a rudimentary sense of morality. Pity was an emotion as unknown to them as it is to a cannibal ; they lived, meta-phorically speaking, by cutting one another's throats, under cover of that exquisite politeness which is the Andalucían's cover for all his peccadilloes. They did it languidly, elegantly, with a word rather than with a knife. Too indolent, in the main, for revenge, they had their own way of getting even with the person who annoyed them. They feared no man, save the alcalde, an official whom they themselves had helped to elect ; the majority took pains, from motives of superstition, to keep on the right side of the priest. As is often the case in rural populations, the men were, taking them on the whole, gentler, more civilised, than the women, but the male populace of Agujasierra still carried cutlery and firearms, which inevitably appeared when arguments sprang up.

The look they turned upon Aurelio was mainly one of curiosity, to see how he was taking the upset in his household, but the curiosity was blended with contempt for a member of the community who could not force his women to keep their squabbles within doors, or at least within the bounds of what constituted feminine convention. It was agreed that, on this occasion, Carmela Moreno had gone too far. Their own method was to beat up their women periodically—without malice, but merely with the motive of reminding them who was master of the household. It was known that Aurelio had never so much as laid a finger in wrath upon Carmela. Well, he was a López, and the López had always managed to get on without wife-beating.

Aurelio had a sense of acute isolation ; his resentment leapt to meet it. In an instant he knew that these people knew what had happened, had probably been summoned by Colgas, the moment his back was turned, to talk it over. Talk was the staple means of entertainment in Agujasierra. The roar of voices had reached him through the door, before Colgas had opened it, and he could guess what they were saying. What was Ledesma, the maltreated girl's lover, going to do in the matter ? The Ledesma had gipsy blood in them ; they did not take their troubles to the alcalde, they settled them after their own fashion, and prudently vanished until the hue and cry had blown over.

" My dear Aurelio López ! " Colgas was crying. " This is a most unfortunate matter ! " His eyes were sparkling with excitement ; it was plain he had other information, which, in his usual fashion, he meant to reveal at his own leisure. " One of the López women ! What a very unfortunate thing ! "

" Which of you has seen her ? " said Aurelio, ignoring Colgas, and addressing the ring of men, among whom he now saw one who was, at least traditionally, pledged to friendliness with the López family. It was towards this man, Pulgar, the cacique, that heads were turned or jerked. Pulgar pulled down his lip, lifted one shoulder, and gave every possible sign that he disclaimed all responsibility.

It turned out that Pulgar had been riding up the steep hill that led from the valley a little before dusk. Above him looped the main road, spanned at intervals by bridges across the narrow gorges that cleft the mountain-side to a depth of hundreds of feet, and fed the river in the valley-bottom with its scores of small, savage streams. Such a bridge hung, spanning air, at the very point where the main road, mounting upwards, merged itself into the principal street of the town. The rise of the ground was so rapid that, although on a much lower level, one could see, from certain points of the valley, right up this street—or, more correctly, track—as far as its first bend, at which was the house of Colgas the schoolmaster.

Allowing his horse a breathing space, Pulgar had been sitting in the saddle, looking upwards, when down the track came a woman—running as though devils were after her. Pulgar swore she was screaming, although he was

E𝗠

unlikely, from that distance, to have heard the sound, which would surely have brought the neighbours out of doors. She was running at an uncontrollable speed, which ended by dashing her against the low stonework of the bridge. Whether she actually threw herself over, or whether she was carried over by the impetus of her mad rush, Pulgar was not prepared to say. The parapet was very low ; it had a rounded top. A child had been killed there a few years before. It was a place of terror for the mothers of children, and therefore it had become incumbent upon the honour of every small daredevil of the town to walk barefooted across the sickening chasm at least once in his career.

Pulgar saw the body toppling over and over in air before it vanished in the gorge below. It was growing darker every minute ; it would have been unwise, even had there been any point in doing so, to attempt the clamber down into the gorge, whose sides became perpendicular before they touched the rocky bed of the stream. Aurelio realised that it could have happened only a few moments before he himself crossed the bridge, on his way home. Had it not turned so suddenly cold, driving everyone indoors, there must have been a dozen witnesses of the tragedy. Pulgar had stopped at the house of Colgas on his way into the town ; as yet the news was not known. Pulgar himself had not known, until then, that the victim could be no other than Conchita López.

Every eye was fixed eagerly, greedily, upon Aurelio while this tale was told. The blood was singing in his ears, the thudding of his heart almost choked him. Although he had taken small notice of the girls, had accepted them as an unwelcome but unavoidable legacy when the rest of the family migrated to Atarfe, the blood relationship which forms so intrinsic an element of Spanish character called upon his deepest resources of horror and pitiful emotion. He felt, for a moment, almost a terror—it went deeper than loathing—of Carmela, who was no doubt responsible for this fearful happening. It appalled him that this woman should be in charge of his child. Surely the baby was in the hands of a madwoman and a murderess !

These initial thoughts, which came from the profoundest depth of Aurelio's nature, and were deeply individual, and which, a few months ago, would have wholly and solely conditioned his actions—he had a fleeting thought, so fleeting his imagination had barely seized upon it before it was gone, of taking the babe at once to Granada, and putting it in the charge of the widow Herédia—passed in the succession of others more in accordance with the alteration of his character since Maravilla's birth. Suddenly he was a López : a member of a family whose standing no Agujasierran had ever challenged. The curiosity, the eagerness to see what he would do, goaded him, stimulated him into a supreme assertion of himself in front of these scornful, incredulous neighbours. They said he could not govern his household ! He would show them !

" I am going home ! " he shouted at the top of his voice. ' I am going home to beat my wife ! "

The atmosphere suddenly altered. There was a burst of shouting, of laughter. This was just the thing that appealed to the Agujasierrans. A good wife-beating, when it took place in public, was the next best thing to a bull-fight. Aurelio repeated his words again and again, while the company thumped him on the back, congratulated him, laughed with and not at him, forgot entirely the grim business which had brought them there, and cried aloud for wine to celebrate the occasion. Colgas, too mean to provide wine for so many, wrung his hands and protested that he had finished the last bottle for his midday meal, and would have bought another but that the López affair put it out of his mind.

So they all stumbled out into the street, now velvety with snow which thickened every moment ; and Aurelio, still shouting, as though he had gone crazy, that he was going to beat Carmela, was dragged into the casino, where half a dozen more were sitting, who were instantly given the news, and responded to it after like manner. The death of Conchita López was unanimously considered to be a matter of less importance than the beating up of Carmela. Red wine made its appearance ; Aurelio was given glass after glass, until he became wilder than he had ever been in his life. A few slipped home to tell their wives ; the women would not want to be out of this—their resentment, if they were not informed in time, might have trying consequences for their husbands. The old woman who served in the casino deserted the customers for a moment to pass the news on to a few of her cronies. The noise presently drew the priest from the presbytery ; he poked his nose inside the door, got wind of what it was all about, and hastily withdrew. He cuddled himself with delight, only regretting that his office prevented him from being a spectator. No one in the town hated Carmela Moreno more bitterly than he.

When the company passed from red wine to aguardiente, someone cried, " Hold ! " At this rate Aurelio, who was already uncertain on his feet, would be incapable of wife-beating. Thrusting him ahead of them, they poured out into the square. A few, overcome by revelry, tumbled in the snow, and were trampled by their companions. Women swarmed out of the houses, children joined the crowd and swelled its insane excitement. The alcalde, whose house stood at some distance from the square, and who was in the habit of falling into a heavy sleep after his meals, was roused by his household but appeared rather late upon the scene. He laid about him with lusty blows in the darkness, but was unable to penetrate further than the fringe of the riot. In his sleepy haste he had forgotten his revolver and had no weapons but his hands. He could not distinguish friend from foe in the mob that poured towards the López posada. In a few minutes they were like snow men, or a company of ghosts. At any moment the alcalde expected the place to go up in flames ; he could not get any succinct idea of what it was about from the inebriated gaiety of the crowd that thrust with limbs and bodies as it thrust at the entrance to the bull-ring.

Someone—accidentally—let off a gun ; the report echoed from the peaks, invisible in darkness ; there were female cries, but it was impossible to tell if anyone was wounded. The only buildings round the square which did not now show lights were the town hall and the López posada : for even the few steadier and more serious people, who had forborne to join the riot, could not resist throwing open their shutters to see as much as possible of what was going on.

The shutters of the López house were closed ; suddenly there was a rattle of stones—flung by the women, no doubt, against the rejas.

Aurelio had been pushed to the front, right against his own doorway. His head felt as though it contained bright burning things that split into fragments. He was not now certain of what it was all about, although he continued to shout, as he had been doing for the last hour, " I am going to beat my wife ! " The curious uncertainty of the drunkard's mind now turned suddenly against the mob itself, with whom, a few minutes before, he had been on terms of passionate affection. What did they mean by it ? Why were they thrusting and jostling a López ? He unexpectedly kicked out against the nearest man, and there was a yelp and a groan, drowned in the unsympathetic laughter of the others near enough, if not to witness the accident, to surmise its cause. A woman thrust her face close up to Aurelio's and screamed, " Fetch her out here ! Beat her out here, where we can see."

It was at this point that a number of the older men detached themselves from the company. In their estimation the joke had gone far enough ; to carry it farther would be to lose one's dignity. They gave their hats a tap, eyed one another solemnly, and walked virtuously back to their houses with their hands behind their backs. Aurelio was left with the rabble—the rapscallions, the nondescripts, who had no dignity to lose.

He stood with his back to the door, and his gun, which he had forgotten, in his hands. He shouted :

" Friends of Agujasierra ! I am going to beat my wife ! I am going now, into this house, which is mine, to beat my wife ! " There were ironical cheers, cries of " Vivan los López ! " Aurelio's fuddled mind caught at the last words. " Friends of Agujasierra ! I am a López ! The wives of the López are as the López ! I am going into my own house to beat my wife ! "

Here a light shone out suddenly on a level with his cheek ; Carmela, wondering what it was all about, half scared and half excited, had opened the shutter in time to hear Aurelio's last words. With the light glaring upon his face he yelled above the outcry caused by Carmela's appearance, " I am going into my house to beat my wife ! And the first man who crosses my threshold I shall shoot dead. The López say a thing, and it is done. The López do not beat their wives in public, like the Ribas, the Carbonnels, the Inclάns——" He reeled off the names of a dozen families in Agujasierra, which brought a doubtful growl from the crowd : was Aurelio now insulting them ? " Stay where you are, and you will hear enough ! " He swung unsteadily round, and Carmela found herself staring down the muzzle of the gun. " Open this door, Carmela Moreno ! Open this door for your husband, who is going to beat you ! "

She could not slam the shutter, for the barrel of the gun was through the grill ; trembling in every limb, convinced that Aurelio was out of his mind, she drove back the bolt ; he turned and pointed the gun again towards the crowd, which threatened to thrust in with him as he forced his way backwards through the open door. With one hand he slammed the shutter, with the other he shot the bolts.

Carmela faced him, panting ; his eyes, rolling round the room, saw that the cradle was not there. Suddenly, without warning, he launched a blow, that would have felled an ox, at the wooden counter across which the drinks were served. Carmela shrieked. Aurelio, by now appearing completely mad, lifted a chair above his head, and brought it down splintering upon the stone floor. She shrieked again. He lurched further along the counter, and sent a pile of empty bottles crashing to the ground. This time she did not shriek, but a deep, satisfied, admiring roar came from the mob outside. There was no doubt Aurelio López was beating his wife up in fine style.

Aurelio had lost all sight of his objective. He was now drunk purely on sound : on the crash of things—on ring, jingle, and thud. Never, in all his mild, inoperative life, had he known himself author of so rich an uproar. He punctuated it with an occasional short, grunting shout. Picking up a bottle, he hurled it deliberately at the wall, from which a splinter of glass, ricocheting, caught Carmela just across the eyebrow and temple.

With the blood running down into her eye, she began again to scream : short, high shrieks, thin, and spaced as regularly as notes upon a stave, issued from the tightened circle of her lips, while her face, white as paper, became as the fact of an idiot.

Catching her wrist in his hand, Aurelio said to her, in a quiet, even reasonable, tone :

" That is right, Carmela ; that is right. You are right to scream. Go on screaming. That is what you should do——" And, raising his other hand, he brought it down, the fingers clubbed into a fist, heavily on her shoulders, so that she staggered, and, but for his hold on her, would have fallen.

Perhaps it was the strange, dull sound of beaten flesh that checked the progress of his violence. If Carmela's body had given forth a crash, or a ring, or a crackle of destruction, Aurelio, lost in his madness, would have struck again and again. But there was only that dull, heavy sound, that fell upon his mind like a cloak of darkness over crimson, and through which he heard another scream—the convulsive shrieks of his daughter Maravilla.

While Aurelio rushed into the inner room to see after the child, Carmela stood stock still in the middle of the floor, clutching her shoulder, leaning a little forward, in a stupid attitude which allowed the blood of her wounded temple to drip upon the floor. Through her mystification was breaking something new, something purely primitive that owed its inception to the incredible violence of Aurelio, his unexplained wrath, and fearful, unprecedented expression of it. She felt awe—the awe of the traditional and religious subservience of the female to the male. Something that, so far, she had only experienced in its physical manifestation now took possession of her soul. All the invisible as well as the visible part of her was now for the first time delivered to Aurelio, and the love and passion which they had enjoyed together in the early days of their marriage seemed almost meaningless beside the dark core of utter oneness which Carmela now felt with her husband.

The noise out of doors had died to a few mutterings and chucklings ; evidently most of the audience had had enough of the entertainment, and had dispersed to talk it over in the casino, or in their homes. But through the lesser noises now came a rapid, imperative hammering on the shutter of the grill. " Carmela Moreno ! Carmela Moreno ! Open ! "

For some reason she obeyed ; opened the shutter, and the dark, blubbered face of Zoraïda Zubia, quick with curiosity, impatience, and excitement, appeared panting between the iron bars. Her bulging cheeks were crimson, and the whites of her eyes showed.

" Por Dios, Carmela Moreno ! When is your baby to be fed ? It is long past the hour ! "

As Carmela silently opened the door, all the triumph and bitter laughter of her enemies seemed to sweep in with Zoraïda Zubia. This latter, gasping out invocations of the saints, clutching her great breasts like melons in her hands, allowed her eyes to gulp the details of the wreckage that lay about her feet. A ludicrous terror, mingled with importance, shook her pulpy body. Soft, timorous and sensual, she had had to be thrust and patted and urged towards the door, her foolish eyes overflowing with tears as her breasts with the milk which told her the baby's feeding-time was long past. " Oh—oh ! Supposing he was to turn on me ! " " Go on ; go in, and come back and tell us everything ! " " Blessed saints, what has he done to you ? Holy Virgin, there's a devil in the house ! Protect us, blessed Mother of God ! "

Carmela vouchsafed no word. Aurelio came, having by some means reduced the infant's shrieks to a drooling whimper ; the softness of its nurse's breast concluded the pacification. Crouched on a stool, Zoraïda Zubia's eyes continued to take possession of the scene : of Carmela as she leaned over a bowl of water, phlegmatically staunching the flow of blood from her brow ; of Aurelio, standing very still and calm, as though he had no association with the scene, his feet a little apart, his hands turned with the palms outwards, and his eyes fixed upon some point higher than themselves. His attitude was reminiscent of sculptured figures of the martyrs with which Zoraïda Zubia was familiar ; she trembled as the milk ran out of her between the baby's sucking lips, and, when at last the milk ceased to flow, she dragged her shawl over her head and ran out of the house without a word to either of her employers.

Most of Agujasierra put on its funeral black and arrived with the utmost decorum to pay its pésames to Aurelio López for the death of his niece, María Concha. It was disappointing to find the tavern, although a little empty, perfectly neat and tidy, and its dueña pale but composed, although the cunning eyes of the women noticed that her hair was pushed a little more forward than usual, on the right side. It rather discounted Zoraïda Zubia's story that Aurelio had smashed up his house and cut his wife's head open.

CHAPTER VII

SPRING

AURELIO became conscious of two things; of the new, dark, desperate attachment of Carmela to himself, and of her deepening enmity towards their child. From both he recoiled; he became a creature in flight from elements which disturbed his inward peace.

His first hope had been, in the renewed intimacy between himself and Carmela, to quicken her love for the baby, whose every look and movement was to him an enchantment. At first he would pick the little thing out of her cradle and carry her to her mother.

" Look, Carmela ! The way she points her little toes—already. She is going to be a dancer ! "

Carmela's face would stiffen, and she would turn her head away, but later, when Aurelio had put the child back in its cradle, she would come to him and rub her cheek against his shoulder. It was as though she said : " I am here ; what more do you want ? You must not pay attention to anything but me." And he would caress her, but a little sadly, because the happiness he had hoped for was not to be had in this way.

He was too much of an Agujasierran to feel, even for a moment, ashamed of having struck Carmela. The matter, which had made so deep an impression upon her, dropped easily from his mind the day after it happened. He would never have believed that Carmela herself would take seriously that which was a commonplace in the lives of other women, any more than he could have imagined himself, sober, indulging in wife-beating as a habitual pastime. Everything that militated against peace and order was naturally abhorrent to Aurelio, and became more so as the years went by.

He loved Carmela, but he desired that love to be calm, quiet, and peaceful as grass. He did not wish to be reminded of it, to be made conscious of it, or to submit to claims on account of it. It was a thing to be taken for granted, the more so now the pair of them were no longer young. All of romance that remained to him in loving he now prepared to transfer to his little daughter, and it seemed to him unnatural that Carmela should resent this transfer.

Yet he could feel her, beneath that harsh, almost stony exterior, forcing upon him something feverish, insatiate, and all-possessive, that sought to drive itself into him, to subjugate him, to render him blind, deaf and insentient to all save itself. He could feel himself perpetually on guard against this thing, in constant dread of surrendering to something that would destroy his most inner self. It was as though Carmela had assumed a male initiative, that threatened with rape some virgin element in himself of which, up to the present, he had been unconscious ; which, now he had discovered it, he desired most jealously to preserve.

Yet how difficult it was to fight against the invisible enemy. For outwardly she was the soul of submission. No complaint now ever crossed her lips regarding the hardship of her lot. She waited on him hand and foot, cooked for him at all hours, kept his clothes in order and his house clean, and ran the tavern with very little help from himself. Upon his making some effort to occupy himself actively with a business which did not in the least interest him, she had said, quite sharply, that she could manage better by herself, with the assistance of the hired boy who came in now to wash the glasses and serve the clients who came to sit in the patio. Through her efforts a modest prosperity was coming to them, and, unknown to Aurelio, ambition had taken root in her soul.

He never glimpsed that ambition until the time came for Spring to cast her emerald-spattered trellis across the hills ; when the thin, fierce, starved carnations broke into reluctant cressets along the balconies, and their stalks were snapped and thrust between the teeth of maidens in whose veins pulsed the irresistible sap of Spring. Then the alcalde died.

There were, inevitably, rumours about the manner of his dying. The blame was fixed in a score of directions ; but his death, as it happened, was a perfectly natural affair. He was a man of plethoric habit ; he had over-eaten ; he had had a kind of fit, and rendered up his soul to God. The thing was so simple most people could not believe it. He had not been a popular alcalde.

The funeral was peaceful and an impressive affair ; more than a hundred candles were carried by the friends of the dead man ; the great blond wood coffin, brought specially from Granada, had been much admired, as were the wreaths of black and purple feather flowers for which the better-off townsfolk had subscribed ; and the town band excelled itself, until the musicians became too drunk to handle their instruments.

That night Aurelio was more than ever aware of Carmela's dark possessiveness. There was flight in her movements ; a shimmer across her face, when she looked at him, like the shimmer of lightning across water. Once she seized his hand and pressed her lips to it furtively, then, as though ashamed, rushed from the room. He felt his resistance to her stiffening him physically ; his body gathered

itself into a hard knot, as well as his mind, to hold her off.
She was like a pan of liquid that bubbles over a stove ;
every now and then the liquid rises hissing to the edge of
the pan, which is snatched aside to prevent its boiling over.
Sooner or later, he knew, Carmela would boil over.

To make a diversion, he turned aside, with his plate half-
emptied, and held out his arms to the baby, who was
rolling on the floor.

Maravilla had just arrived at the incomparable accom-
plishment of standing up without assistance. For some time,
clutching her father's finger, she had been toddling, but
the triumph of raising her own little body from its animal
to its human position had only just been revealed to her,
and all of her baby will was now bent to the avoidance of
adult interference in the important act.

At her father's word, at his loving invitation, she first
sat very still, then smiled warningly. Her smile said :
" Very well—I am coming ; but don't you dare to touch me
until I give you leave ! " Then she solemnly rolled over, so
that her little haunches were exposed to her father's enchanted gaze, while, using hands and knees, gaining slow
purchase first with one foot, then with the other, with many
a miscalculation, overbalance, and topple, the grave state
of equilibrium was at last attained, and Maravilla stood
upright, very serious and uncertain, swaying a little, making
up her mind.

With a shout of delight Aurelio leapt from his chair, to
catch her before the beloved flesh should make unkind
acquaintance with the stones ; she gurgled as he held her
to his breast, ruffling the silken flakes of hair with his
kisses.

" Who made thee so beautiful ? " he murmured in
ecstasy. " Say ' Papá.' " Her great eyes blinked at him.

" Pa-pa-pa ! " bubbled Maravilla, poking lovingly at

Aurelio's eyes, while her toes drummed enthusiastically on his stomach.

" Now—say ' Guapo ' ! " prompted Aurelio. Maravilla drew the immense sigh of the surfeited coquette, and delivered herself.

" 'Uapa-pa-pa-pa ! " she improved upon the original.

Carmela, coming in from the wine-shop with a bottle in her hand, stood still in the doorway.

" So you do not like the cazuela I have prepared for you," she said quietly.

" But of course. It is good ; very good," said Aurelio absently ; he was riding Maravilla upon his knee. Carmela made no reply ; she calmly picked up the plate, with half its contents untouched, and shot them into the rubbish bowl.

" But Carmela—— ! " He stopped petting the child ; he was genuinely shocked—not at the waste of the food, but that Carmela should be capable of wasting it—she who found a use for every crust, every fragment left over from their meals.

" It will do for the hens. There is no need for me to cook if you are not hungry," she replied, in the same flat voice. " And it is time the child went to bed."

" I will see to it," said Aurelio eagerly.

" That is as you please," she rejoined, with an exaggeratedly submissive gesture of the hand.

She occupied herself in washing the pots, in putting them away, in raking out the stove, while from the inner room came the ridiculous shouts, the laughter, and disjointed babble of endearments which were Aurelio putting Maravilla into the cradle which was now almost too small for her elastic little limbs. Had it been left to Aurelio, she would have stayed up half the night, sagging and nodding on her parents' arms, wrinkling her little nose in the smoke and wine fumes of the tavern, waking now and again to cry or demand her nurse's breast. That is how it would have been had Carmela loved her child ; not loving it, she did, without intention, the very best for it : justifying her actions to Aurelio by asserting it was the way in which she and her sisters had been brought up—Doña Marta having learnt Alhambra ways from her mistress up the hill. It was Carmela's unspoken compulsion that laid Maravilla in her cradle each night after the evening meal, from which, since the milk of Zoraïda Zubia had ceased to flow, she was not roused till cockcrow of the following day.

When Aurelio had finished playing with his daughter he passed through the back door of the tavern into the little patio, full as a tank with blue darkness, and silent save for the trickle of the water spout which fed the trough where Carmela washed her clothes. One wall of the patio was the rock itself, a star-crowned precipice ; the other three were the whitewashed walls of the posada, blank as featureless faces. Hesitating on the threshold, Aurelio had that unmistakable sense of a presence to which eyesight contributes nothing.

Close to him, within touch of his hand, facing the mountain-side, sat Carmela, in idleness so unwonted as to drive a shaft of uneasiness into Aurelio's heart. They were both deathly still, feeling one another without physical contact ; in silence his hostility to her renewed itself.

Maravilla's yells of resentment at being deserted by her father rang lustily through the silence. He made as though to return to her. Carmela's words checked him as though she had laid her hands upon him.

" They are going to make you alcalde," she said swiftly.

Aurelio thought at first he had not heard her rightly.

" What is it you say ? " he said, after a moment of doubt.

" You are to be the new alcalde. They are coming to see

you about it in the morning." There was a breathlessness of youth in her voice.

" Who are coming ? " He sounded stupid, incredulous.

" Colgas," answered Carmela, " and Pulgar, and others. They wanted to see you after the funeral, but you were nowhere to be found. Where have you been ? Why do you go away and hide yourself, so that no one knows where to look for you ? "

Aurelio's eyes travelled up the mountain-side without re-plying ; up there he had been—somewhere up there, where of late he had formed a habit of going. He filled his lungs with a sigh ; her hand sought his in the darkness, and her strength dragged him down on the bench beside her.

" They will make you alcalde," she whispered intently, pressing his hand as though to force him to give her his whole attention. " Do you hear what I am telling you ? Answer me."

" With what can I answer you ? " he said wearily. " Who thought of this ? "

She gave a cry, and flung his hand away from her.

" After all I have done—the way I have talked about you : reminding them about your grandfather, and saying how wise you were, and educated—and the presents I have made to that skinflint of a Pulgar, and making friends with their women, and all ! You would not notice—oh, dear, no ; it is beneath you !—how many bottles of wine I have given away, and how often I have refused, when it was an important person, to take money for the drinks ! Oh, no ! I might beggar myself for you—you'd never notice it, so long as there was money in your pocket and a shirt on your back. I suppose you will find plenty to say when they come and fetch you your badge of office, but not a word of thanks to your wife ! "

Aurelio was completely taken aback by this revelation of

Carmela's activity on his behalf. He was horrified to think that such things could go on unknown to him, and alarmed by the unknown obligations to which he was committed. On her part, she had conquered her anger, and her hand was again seeking his.

" Come, tell me what you will say to them. You will have to make a fine speech, full of grand language, to show them how right I was about your learning ! How will it begin ? "

" It will be over," he said, " in the falling of a leaf."

" What do you mean ? " Her voice trembled with nervousness.

" I will not allow them to make me alcalde."

She flung up her hands.

" For all you care I might be dead at your feet ! " Before he could answer her wild accusation, the words started to pour from her lips. He had been right ; the pan was now boiling over.

" After all I have borne for you in all these years ! After the way I have slaved for you ! What have you ever done but treat me like a beast of burden from the day we were married ? And the scorn I had from my own relations for marrying you ! Ay-ay, what would my mother say if she knew all I have suffered ? What would my aunt think, after her warnings ? Hasn't it been like vinegar for me, when my brothers came from their fine houses and found me in this hovel ? And now, when I might have my little reward, you snatch it from me ! "

" But, Carmela," said Aurelio, with petrifying mildness. " Why do you want me to be alcalde ? How should we be better off if they made me head of the town ? "

" You do well to ask me that ! After letting me be reviled by every slut in the market, abused by your relations, insulted by a priest on my sick-bed——"

" But all that is over now," said Aurelio, with the same deathly self-control.

" Yes, it is over," she answered, in an exhausted voice, as though, suddenly, the last of her strength had gushed from her. They sat, she sobbing quietly, and he pitying her, in the dark.

" I will not be alcalde," he said presently. " When I was young—yes, in those days I used to say to myself, ' Some day I will be alcalde.' I had not then learnt the difference between the little and the great. I had not learned to know myself."

" What folly you talk," she said with weary fretfulness.

" Folly is the beginning of wisdom. Before a man can be wise he must first be a fool. And a fool is not fit to be alcalde of Agujasierra."

" Now you are stupidly belittling yourself," she retorted in vexation. " Who is there knows the town and the people as you do ? You are a López ; it is right you should be their leader. Why, even Colgas—even he—now says there is no man more fitted to govern the town than you. He was not at all in favour of it to begin with, and there were plenty of others of his opinion ! You are too quiet ; you do not assert yourself enough. But I talked and I talked, and I went on making presents. Now I believe they are all, under Pulgar's orders, ready to accept you. They will obey you because you are a López, and because your ancestors governed them before you were born."

" I have not time to govern Agujasierra," said Aurelio.

" Madre mía ! " she cried. " What have you to do, I ask you ? Do I not look after all that goes on here ? Aurelio, my dear, my adored one ! " She had not used such words to him since their marriage. His soul took fright, darted into its farthest stronghold against her irresistible, her impious, advances. She was pressing her body against him, her arms were wound about his neck ; she became a pythoness, strangling him with her love. "My beloved one ! Remember all I have done for thee ! Do this now for thy Carmela, who worships thee as she worships no other thing in this world or the next ! "

From his fastness he answered her.

" You do not know about these things. For some people it is right and proper to be active—to perform deeds of their own, and to direct the lives of others. But they are not always the wise ones. For the rest, it is better to watch, to listen, and to be silent. To do nothing. By doing nothing one is sure of making no mistakes."

" Oh, you idle good-for-nothing ! " she cried, starting away from him in a fresh access of rage.

" It is your doing that I am idle," he answered her swiftly.

" Oh, it satisfied you very well that way," she retorted, with unwonted astuteness where he was concerned. " Ay ! " she cried, lifting her clasped hands and bringing them down heavily on her knees. " I do not know what I am to do with you ! "

" You do not know. There are many things you do not know," he repeated coldly. " Perhaps if you learned to be a little idle these things would come to you."

" Like yourself, I suppose ! Oh, to think I have a husband who is all laziness and conceit ! "

" Why do you abuse me ? " he asked mildly. " You only hurt yourself by it ; for you love me so much that your abuse twists itself round and strikes into your own heart. Could you not manage to love me a little less, Carmela ? Then we could be happy together, and not want things we cannot give each other."

" You say things it is impossible for me to understand," she answered, weeping. " You loved me—once——"

" Por Dios, I love you now," he replied, but something inside him was aching, and he found it as difficult as she to put his thoughts into words. " But you are asking for more than love, and what I give you does not satisfy you."

" I want you to be alcalde," she whimpered foolishly. Her very soul longed for it ; it was for this she had toiled and endured during their married years. The hope of it had been the lamp on her way of darkness. Latterly she had striven towards it consciously, striving to ingratiate herself with all the influential people of the town, particularly with Pulgar, the Duque's representative, who would have the principal say in the matter : labouring to efface the unfortunate impressions of eight years—no easy thing for a woman of her proud disposition to accomplish, even though the tide had turned and was running in her direction. She had been quick to perceive the alteration in the demeanour of their neighbours after Aurelio had, supposedly, beaten her—as though, in some way, his act had appeased their resentment against her. She had the cunning to make the most of their tentative offers of friendliness, while in her heart abating no whit of her scorn and hatred of them.

Never for a moment had she imagined Aurelio refusing the honour she had so assiduously sought for him ; it was the first thing she had thought of when the more important families of the place—the Pulgars, the Gallegos, the Ribas —had begun to take notice of her existence. They had not been among her tormentors ; but they had held themselves aloof from the unpopular wife of Aurelio López. She saw at once the possible advantage to be gained by taking advantage of the acquaintanceships now, if tardily, held out to her. To be wife of an alcalde, even of an obscure hill town, would give her a position not to be sneered at even by her own relations ; and, deep hidden beneath her

fleers at his impracticality, was an unshakable belief in
the wisdom and knowledge of Aurelio. Now, when she had
succeeded in impressing her belief on those others—oh,
surely he must see he owed her something for her pains !
Her disappointment gushed from her in sudden, dangerous
phrases.

"You care nothing for me. You care for nothing but
that——" She flung her hand backwards, towards the house,
whence came the now hushed whimperings of the child.
Maravilla was falling asleep ; he thought of the small
flushed face pressed into the pillow, of the dark crescents
of her lashes that lay upon her little cheek. The slow,
deep spring of pity welled in his heart for this woman who
wanted more than he was able to give her. He took her
hand ; it burned and vibrated, her anger, the jealousy
which was devouring her, stung him through the work-
roughened finger-tips.

"You are wrong. Just now I care for no one but myself."

"Oh, you are a monster ! A horror !" she breathed.

"You do not understand. It is only by knowing and
loving myself that I can be anything at all. I have a
plan——" He stopped short. How could he tell Carmela of
his plan, woven as it was about the tiny personality at whose
very mention she froze into stone ? Of how the serious
pre-occupation of his life was fatherhood—the preparation
of his heart and mind to give the child, so strangely motherless, the dual parentage that is the right of every child ?
"Carmela," he said, from some far-away green pasture of
the soul into which he had forgotten she could not follow
him. "Have you ever seen a blade of grass ?"

He felt her start from him, caught her outraged exclamation. "Yes ; you think I am crazy. But try to have a little
patience with me. The other day I saw a blade of grass for
the first time. How beautiful it was ! So straight, so strong,

so upward-leaping, with all of its life-force gathered in that little rib that stiffens it from end to end. Man's life and the life of grass are the same thing, part of the same great mystery which men have been seeking down all the ages. How old is grass, how young are we ; and how little we know of the life that is within us ! Once I thought I knew everything ; now I know that I have not even the wisdom of grass, that roots itself in all kinds of unlikely places and is not destroyed, because it bows to the storm. I have lived like a blind man, and now my eyes are beginning to be opened. I must not let myself be blinded again——"

" Oh, you and your fine speeches ! Why don't you save them up until the child is old enough to listen to them ? Every time you come into the house, your first look, your first word, is for her. Even your food is neglected : when I have spent half the day getting it ready for you. There is nothing else for me to do, I suppose, but wait on you, while you take your time, like a sultan, to amuse yourself ! Oh, yes, I am your slave ; you will teach her to tread on me as you have trodden upon me——" Her words flowed on wildly, for she could not bear him to talk, as she considered, insanely ; it frightened her, set her outside his interests. " Go your way," she continued. " It does not matter now. You shall see, the pair of you, how humble, how obedient I will be ; I shall be the dust for you to trample. It is a fine thing that you are a father !—to have all the pride and the pleasure and the easy way of things from the moment you take the woman to possess her. How fine to sit in the sun with your child on your knee, boasting that you have made her, and taking credit for every good thing she does and is ! It's a pity you can't see what an advantage it would be to her if you were the alcalde. That would give her something to hold her head up about among the other children. As it is, poor little thing, she will have to put up with their pointing their fingers at her and asking what her father does to earn his living. But you don't think about that. All you think about is idling on the mountain while others labour for you."

A great heaviness lay on his soul. He wanted to tell her about those long hours of idleness when his spirit took its excursions into the invisible world ; when the creative miracles of nature, which he had never before seen, revealed themselves to his senses with such overpowering distinctness that his brain reeled with them. He had got into the habit of slipping away and climbing the hill-side, to lie in the sun. Several times, risking Carmela's displeasure, he had taken the child with him, to savour to its full in solitude the exquisite sensation of paternity that such a responsibility brought him.

In some grassy saucer of a rock ledge he had taken the swathed garments off the babe, and left it to kick and curl, like a bit of growing nature, in the sun. In those days, before Maravilla could speak, she was to him more like a lovely little plant than a child ; a thing purely and wholly natural, like blossom. He liked to fancy her absorbing the sun and the air into her tiny body, which, to his loving eye, held promise of its future grace.

He would often forget her, so complete she lay, in her goodness and content, her little toothless mouth curled into a smile of utter no-knowledge, her fingers and toes enclosing air like the tendrils of a plant. And his mind would slip back to his own youth, to that restless proud curiosity which he had taken for wisdom, whose emptiness he was now beginning to understand.

He wondered, sometimes, whether, if he had never met the elder Maravilla, he would have gone on being content with the lesser wisdom ; whether it had truly been that coming face to face with the limitations of his experience which had shattered his self-content and made him dissatisfied with that which had previously been sufficient for him. And the conviction grew in him that in very truth he owed it to her—to that strange duality in her which had terrified, attracted, and repelled him during the brief night of their love.

What was she doing now? Had she yet married? No letter had reached him, although he had been down once or twice to inquire. Nor did he yet regret it, for the past had come to him as a dream that might be shattered by the intrusion of a material reminder of itself. Instinctively he knew that Maravilla would not write a good letter, and he shrank from anything that might tarnish his memory of her.

Now, when he was alone, it seemed to him that he became two men—himself and his soul. And that in this strange companionship of himself with himself lay the mystery of a great reinforcement of strength and peace.

One day there came to him—as he lay alone upon a ledge so narrow he seemed to be cradled in space above the infinitely tiny town, whose clustered roofs resembled a faint patch of saffron in the valley below—a singular revelation.

For the first time in his life he *saw* that which lay about him; saw it entire, in crystalline detail, as though a telescope had drawn heaven and earth close to the seat of his consciousness. A terrible and clamorous rhythm went ringing about him; the scoriac rage which expressed itself in ridge beyond ridge of escarpment communicated itself to some secret part of his being, so that each razor-edge bit at his consciousness and seemed to inflict upon it an individual pain. He saw the jawbones of leviathans, and pieces of ravine that looked as though the steel-clawed limb of a monster had torn a wound in the earth's side.

And he saw all that sonorous accumulation of colour that builds itself in chords upon the mountain-sides resolved in the one pure note of the turquoise sky, so that he became stupefied by the nerves of sight, and cowered upon his ledge, dizzy and overcome. A single word shaped itself in his mind : God.

Then, into his stupor, stole a cool, unearthly clarity of moving air ; he could feel it upon his flesh. He opened his eyes to look at the spread palms of his hands, upon which, involuntarily, he expected to see traces of the miracle. But they bore no mystic stigmata. Slowly he realised that this was the wind.

Aurelio sat very still ; his hands, pressed upon the grass, made contact with tradition ; through the earth, through the grass, through the palms of his hands, into his innermost being flowed a wordless, mindless message, whose echoes started in the world's primeval shaping. A marvellous security, for himself and for the child, filled him with peace.

If he could but have communicated this to Carmela ! But no such hope crossed his mind. The message the earth gave him was a message of solitude ; he resolved to learn this message, so that in time he could pass it on to little Maravilla. All manner of things now appeared to him in a new light of significance—a rock, with its surfaces of grit and smoothness, with its colouring ; to the uninitiated eye so drearily uniform, but gradually revealing all the subtleties of a pigeon's breast beneath the shadowing grey ; with its multitudinous carvings and unreadable hieroglyphics graven by the centuries—until, as a result of these observations, a sensation of indescribable awareness stole upon him, and from every direction would flash upon his sight flakes of living gold, soft shades and darknesses, inviting his spirit to awareness of his unity with them through the creative spirit which was author of them all.

How, indeed, could one talk to Carmela of such things as these ? She, with her close, tight crowd-life ; her pre-occupation with matter that drained away her perceptiveness for all save material things ; her ordinary human tendency to take for granted all that the eye could see, the ear hear, and the flesh make contact with, without pausing to reflect upon any of these—how could she enter into this curious phase of life through which he was passing ? For her, physical indolence was a sin ; her active, busy mind could see no virtue in the stillness of contemplation.

And how could he assure for the little Maravilla the happiness which was beginning to be his ?

He was coming to a belief which is common to all sages and philosophers of all the ages : that in order to live at peace among men the mind must be trained to disassociate itself from all teasing and uncomfortable thoughts. That which cannot be remedied must be ignored ; a blind existence is the only true form of bliss. To be like a stone, a cloud, or a blade of grass—not to have in one even the quickness of a stream—this condition of mind and body comes so naturally to the country-bred Andalucían that Aurelio's whole being drifted towards it like a filament of steel towards a magnet. There was nothing to prevent it, save Carmela, with her dangerous, dark demands.

From her advances he saw himself sinking deeper and deeper within himself, like a shell-creature, pressing further and further into the utmost dark and delicate convolution of its brittle dwelling while some invader threatens the threshold. He would relinquish nothing. Like a mild, warm sap running through him, he could feel the beginnings of wisdom beyond all that his mind had ever conceived. He must be supine before it ; he must deliver himself to it, for it was the vehicle of a power that he could use for the blessing and good of his little daughter.

And of this she wanted to cheat him ; she wanted to deliver him bound to the small material world which was the whole of life to her.

He could hear her weeping in the dark ; her tears afflicted him, yet he knew that with a single effort of will he could rid himself of the affliction, and, knowing this, he allowed himself to suffer them a little longer. It was like sitting near a door in a stifling room ; one had only to make a single movement to escape into the cool air. He enjoyed the knowledge, and postponed his deliverance.

Customers were now crowding into the tavern, voices shouted both their names. Carmela rose sharply, putting, as always, business before sentiment. With her going, peace fell upon Aurelio. He could almost feel it caressing his face with its thin, sweet fingers. A guitar twanged. How they clustered together ; how they relied on each other's company ; and all that mattered was silence, solitude—a man and himself together in the perfect communion of the soul.

They would be seeking him presently ; he sighed. Who would they make alcalde in his place ? And what did it matter ? What had he ever been, to think it mattered ? A thread of moon showed like a glittering scratch upon the dark blue slip of sky. Someone came to the door and called to him.

" Olá, Aurelio." It was one of the older Gallegos, Mario's second cousin : a thin, unrespectable scarecrow who clung on the fringes of society by virtue of his patronymic alone. He had come in search of Aurelio because Carmela would not serve him with drink unless he paid for it. A peseta or a drink—either might be coaxed from Aurelio. He sat down on a bench, and laid his arm familiarly across the latter's shoulder ; he leaned forward and spat between his knees. He had a disease of some sort that kept his body a-twitch, and the dried skin and bone rustled like parts of a skeleton.

" Qué tal, Esteban ? "

" So they've planted Pedro," began Esteban, in his oblique fashion. " I was in Granada, and missed the fun."

" It was a good funeral," conceded Aurelio, wondering how Esteban, who never had a centimo of his own, had got to Granada.

" Naturally. He's been alcalde for nine years." Now, thought Aurelio, he will begin to talk about me ; but there was a silence that lasted several minutes. " There's plenty going on down in Grana'a."

" How so ? " yawned Aurelio.

" There is a lot of fuss about the elections. Alfonso can't be finding his bed very cosy these days. They say the monarchy is to be overthrown."

" They have been saying that as long as I can remember," said Aurelio, with the limitless indifference of the peasant. " King or President, what difference will it make ? There will still be as many empty bellies in Spain."

The melancholy of the idea drew a heartfelt grunt from Esteban.

" I saw Vargas. He gave me a message for you. I thought I'd better give it when Doña Carmela was not there."

" What's Vargas doing these days ? "

" He's working in the post office. He told me to tell you a letter is waiting for you ; I offered to bring it along with me, but he would not let me—you know what a fuss these public officials make of their bit of authority ! "

" . . . I must get it one day," said Aurelio. They went into the tavern, where Esteban, grinning expectant, received payment in aguardiente for the message he had carried. The shop was crowded from counter to walls ; a little apart stood a serious group—the priest, Colgas the schoolmaster, Mario Gallego the apothecary, and Pulgar, to-night the most important person in the town, for he represented the political and personal authority of the local landowner. They were politely avoided by the rest, whose eyes and ears, however, were cocked for developments.

" Come, my dear fellow, my dear boy ! " Colgas was saying, smiling, and stroking Aurelio's sleeve. " Where have you hidden yourself all day ? Such modesty—not appearing at the funeral either ! You should really be more careful—such delicacy is not always appreciated, or inter-preted in the way it is intended."

The priest smiled and bowed, his fat face creasing itself into greasy folds ; for the Church found it expedient to stand well in with the civic authorities. There were certain transactions at which the late alcalde had winked ; it was as well to make sure, from the start, that one's relationship with the new alcalde would be as conveniently agreeable.

" There is too much of a crowd here," began Pulgar, in his autocratic voice, thrusting his lean elbows right and left and his face close to Aurelio's. " Come ; you know what we want to talk about. Let us go to Colgas's and get it all fixed up, so that the election can take place to-morrow."

" Why not now ? " Mario Gallego, who was very tipsy, clapped Aurelio on the back, raising his glass to Carmela, who was watching them, and whom he rather admired. " Come, let us fill our glasses to the health of the new alcalde ! There are no secrets among friends." He beamed on the eagerly attentive company. " It is good to think of a López being our alcalde again."

Aurelio had dismissed them all in his mind. He was thinking of the letter which was waiting for him in Granada. Not with impatience, for the letter would wait as long as he did. But with a quiet wonder that she had kept her promise and written to him. He knew he had not expected her to do it.

The urgent faces of the men recalled him to the present, and brought a crease between his brows. He wanted to escape from them and their badgering ; he wanted to go and look at his sleeping daughter, and assure himself that all was well with her. Slowly he shook his head.

" You must find someone else. I will not be the alcalde," he told them.

The outcry was enormous, but in the midst of it all, jostled and shaken and attacked by those who wished to force the undesired honour upon him, Aurelio had a sense of escape that lifted his soul on wings above their turmoil.

CHAPTER VIII

LITTLE MARAVILLA

To FEW MEN is given the inspiration of an immaculate love : a love so fierce, so strong, and yet so stainless that it lifts the whole of a man's life on to a higher plane. There were days when Aurelio moved like a man in a dream : conscious always of his love, moving delicately as though to protect it, seeking tentatively for that which should reinforce, strengthen, and render it richer and more productive. For, like most people who have in their possession a new treasure, he was apprehensive, lest by some careless or ignorant touch he should impair its perfection. It was as though he could not at first trust himself with this angelic love : could not believe in the strength of a thing that was stronger than himself—because the vessel which contained it was so fragile that with a single movement he could have destroyed it.

All of his seriousness and responsibility as a husband, all the wild and upward-reaching passion he had known as a lover, became fused and sublimated in his adoration for his little daughter ; the baser elements of each vanished, their beauty and purity remained to do her service.

In essence a poet, Aurelio saw this love of his in many forms ; sometimes he laid it in the little cupped hands of Maravilla like a captured pigeon, and, when her baby fingers caressed it, the sensation penetrated to his own soul, so that bliss took on a new meaning for him. And sometimes he built it about her like a palace of mother o' pearl, so that she sat, smiling and crooning, in the heart of a rainbow.

For many years, depending on him, watching him, identifying herself with him in every possible way, all the experiences of Maravilla's life came to her filtered, as it were, through the personality of her father. Almost she was cold because he was cold, hot because he was hot. Certainly, if Aurelio was tired, Maravilla drooped, and his moments of elation acted upon her in a way that never failed to draw upon her the disapproval of Carmela. " Look at her ! She is like a mad thing. Come and sit down by me, I tell you, or people will say you have taken leave of your senses." And Maravilla, who knew no fear, because she had never seen her father fearful, would break into peal after peal of laughter, and please herself about obeying her mother or darting away up the mountain-side.

" That Maravilla López—she is more like a boy than a girl," was the neighbours' not too flattering comment. She had the freedom of a boy, a boy's lively assurance. For many years she had none of those wriggling, simpering mock-demurenesses that drew upon her schoolfellows their parents' sentimental admiration.

Maravilla had become accustomed to her mother's chill ways; besides, she knew she had only to turn to her father for warmth. He was like the sun, and Carmela was like the moon, which Maravilla did not much care for, because it turned everything to black and white, and the shadows cast by moonlight were altogether different from those cast by the sun. With the latter one could play—particularly with one's own shadow : making flowers and odd creatures with one's arms and hands, inventing grotesque shapes that crawled and pounced along the wall. But with the shadows of the moon one did not play. They stalked beside one like strange, hooded Good Friday figures, checking one's natural effervescence—just as it was checked in church.

FM

This fancy of shadows was almost the only one which Maravilla entertained. She was her mother's child in that she was almost without imagination, although she chuckled with delight when Aurelio made up foolish tales for her diversion, or adapted historical or literary legends for her childish ear. " Tell me about the eggs of Colón, papá " ; or, " Tell me about the silly gentleman who thought windmills were giants." There was quite a spice of cruelty in the merry laughter with which she greeted Aurelio's description of the pains and agonies suffered by the sorry knight. Already she was a true child of her country, in that she was quicker to see the ridiculous than the pitiful ; in mind and in body she turned towards the sun. But that her tender sympathies could also be aroused on occasion she revealed to Aurelio on a morning when she had returned with Carmela from church.

" Poor Blessed Virgin Mary ! " she confided, with her elbows on Aurelio's knee and her face upturned with that confidence in his unchanging sympathy which never failed to thrill him.

" What is it, my little pigeon ? "

" Always in there "—she pointed a disparaging finger at the church. " Always in the dark and cold." She wagged her head reproachfully, as though Aurelio were responsible for the discomforts of the Virgin. " Why don't they take her out in the sun sometimes ? " she accused him. Aurelio shook his own head ; this was too difficult for him ; perhaps Don Baldomero, the new priest, who was good with the little children, would know.

" She can do miracles, can't she, the Blessed Virgin Mary, papá ? " persisted Maravilla. Aurelio agreed.

" Then why doesn't she walk out all by herself on the mountain, instead of spending all her time in that old church ? I should think she would like to walk up the mountain. Wouldn't it be nice, papá, if one day, when we were coming home, we met the Blessed Virgin Mary, in her blue dress, climbing up by the berry-bushes ? "

" Ojalá ! What would you do, queen ? "

" I'd pick her some lavender to make a nice smell in her clothes," responded Maravilla promptly. " Oh, I do wish she would—one day——" She pounded urgently on Aurelio's knee. " How can I *make* her, papá ? "

" You would have to say a lot of Hail, Marys," he told her seriously.

" How many ? "

" A hundred," answered Aurelio, at random.

" But I can't count a hundred ! "

" When you can count a hundred——"

Maravilla nodded, a little quenched. When would that be ? She hated lessons. With a flounce of light-heartedness she postponed miracle-working to the indefinite future. Dark or light, the Blessed Virgin Mary heard one's prayers, so she had been told, and rewarded one when one had been a good girl, and was grieved or angry whèn one had been bad. She was fairly often bad—according to her mother. With a cunning glance at Aurelio, she thought his rewards were always better, because more immediate, than those of the Virgin Mary, and that he was never, never angry, whatever one did.

From the top of her head to the soles of her small feet, Maravilla was a child of the sun ; the sun had gilded her body wherever Carmela's sense of decorum permitted it to be uncovered—and in other places as well. Aurelio and Maravilla never betrayed the secret of those days in the mountains when—in memory, perhaps, of her babyhood— he would encourage her to take off all her little garments, and to prance like a small, wild mountain spirit, with her feet in the wiry grass. And always, afterwards, they would find a spring or a stream, and Aurelio would lave the grimy little feet, so that nothing should remain to arouse Carmela's suspicions. The joy Maravilla took in her nakedness was no less than Aurelio's ; he gave thanks for the new power of observation, which seemed to give him possession of every fraction of the precious body. They would merely twinkle at each other when Carmela, undressing Maravilla, would remark, in her cold tones of detachment, " The child is a gipsy ! She's black all over ! " But she was proud of the child's lithe sturdiness ; proud to the extent of announcing abruptly one day that she should be called by another name. " It is not right she should be called as though she were a heathen. Let them learn to call her María, then she will at least have a saint's day ! "

Aurelio made no objection, and Maravilla, taking her cue from her father, made no ado either when she was informed of the change. María was shorter ; therefore it would be easier to write. María López Moreno. She went capering among her playmates, informing them she was now called María, and Carmela set her lips and prepared for another bout of gossip. But there was little ; the old animosity had died down, and the child was a López, whatever her parents chose to call her.

By the time María was twelve she had almost forgotten she had ever been called Maravilla, and Aurelio was aware that the change of name had in some way mysteriously affected the attitude of Carmela to her daughter. She now spoke freely to and of the child ; if not affectionate, she was complacent, though her complacency was always liable to be replaced by sombre and vindictive moods which reflected, not only upon the child, but upon Aurelio. They affected him wretchedly, but he did all in his power to keep his feelings from the sharp eyes of María. While she was little, Carmela's moods seemed to roll off her like water off a duck's back, and Aurelio was determined this should continue for as long as possible. But she had that awareness of him which many children have of those whom they love : could tell that he was coming, and almost what he would say, long before he came in sight ; and he feared it would not be long before this instinct deepened into a profounder knowledge, an exact estimate of his thoughts and feelings, in which, because of their love for one another, she was bound to share.

For this reason, when Carmela was under her evil shadow he would absent himself from the house. He had not done this without considering whether it was fair to leave the child alone to bear the brunt of her mother's morosity. But his one-time fear that Carmela would, under its influence, do harm to María had proved to be without foundation. She would sulk ; she would rave ; she would be silent ; but she would not lay a finger on the child ; and the resilience of María's spirit was too great to be affected by these manifestations. She would run out and play with the other children ; would fret a little for his absence ; but such fretting would harm her less than the discovery of Aurelio's distress. Fortunately, such moods were not of long duration ; experience led Aurelio to connect them with Carmela's change of life.

One day, when he and María were up on the mountain, and she started to undress, Aurelio stopped her.

" No, my little love ; no, my pigeon. The time for that is over."

" But why ? " questioned María, looking up at her father with an angelic pout. " Why must I wear clothes, when it is so much nicer without them ? "

But Aurelio, who had recently, with an almost unbearable quickening of the heart, observed certain signs, took the small cajoling hands in his own and squatted on his

heels to bring his face on a level with María's. She crooned
with pleasure, and laid her cheek against his unshaven
one as though the bristles were velvet, rubbing it up and
down with little sensual noises of delight, like a cat.

That day they had climbed very high ; they were almost
at the edge of that strange region where the lavender merges
into the purple-flowered gentian, and where little frosty
plants spread out their stars close against the earth. The
snows looked very near, spread out upon the hollowed
slopes like drying linen. " Giants' bedclothes," Maravilla
called them. A flock of sheep poured over a distant ridge
and an unearthly tinkle of bells floated to them across the
valley.

" Listen, little pigeon ; tell me this. If Pepe, and Blas
and Baldo "—he named her playmates—" were here
would you take off your clothes ? "

" Pues—no, I don't think I should," replied María
after a long pause. She had never thought of this before.
She became, for the first time in her life, shy with her
father, and pretended to look for snakes among the thinning
grasses.

" And why ? " pursued Aurelio, capturing her hand. She
twisted her shoulders.

" Pues—because I am a little girl and they are little
boys."

" Claro. And thy father was once a little boy, and in
not so very long Pepe and Blas will be men, like thy
father. And you, little fish, will be a señorita."

" But I am not a señorita yet," protested María, perfectly understanding the line of reasoning.

" Very shortly you will be," answered Aurelio. She
looked at him wide-eyed, as though he had promised her
crown of gold.

" How do you know ? "

" Only see how tall you are growing ! " he said fondly. And how the sex was beginning to articulate itself, he thought ; love and awe had swept him the last time he had seen her dance naked before him, and a sweet sort of melancholy that all that budding beauty was consecrated to another hand. The days of María's childhood, now numbered, seemed to Aurelio to have passed like the little flowers of the plain, whose loveliness comes upon them, and passes, in a day. With a pang, he accused himself of having treated them too lightly : like the beads of a rosary that slip through drowsy fingers. Those exquisite, flashing moments, like flung spray from a fountain ! Had he but foreseen, he must have counted them drop by drop. What strange power had beauty and content, that it made a man forgetful even of its very self ?

In how short a time would those clear eyes be shadowed with the secrets of maidenhood, and that angelic shamelessness become a conscious demureness ? And how would such changes affect his love for her ? Aurelio knew he could but love her more, but that between his love and hers would stand thenceforth the shadow of the cursed tree at whose roots perished the innocence of mankind. The future gripped his heart as he thought of seeing in María's eyes the image of her first lover.

María went to school, but she did not like it, for the old schoolmaster, Colgas, dribbled and mumbled, so that the scholars paid little attention, save on the days when Don Baldomero swept in, his sotana flapping, his eyes bright and compulsive so that even the idlest (among whom, let it be confessed, was María López Moreno) sat up and pretended to be on the alert.

On one side sat the boys, on the other the girls ; Don Baldomero was continually trying to get a separate instruction for the girls, but there was apparently no money for

the foundation of a convent school in Agujasierra. Because
the disparity in ages was very great, there were always some
who wiled away the time with unhallowed devices.

It bored María to hold a pencil in a sticky hand, or make
marks on a slate. She did not see why anyone should trouble
to read or write, since Colgas could do it for one. He still
wrote letters—on matters of business or love—for the illit-
erate, and his phrases were no less resounding than of old.

She liked arriving at school in a clean frock, with other
little giggling girls not nearly so neat or clean as herself,
and seeing the boys stare as she sat down, flouncing her
petticoats. She liked to play a game of smiling one day at a
boy, and the next day pretending not to see him and
smiling at another. This meant sometimes that the first
boy, furious, would lean over and pinch the second, or hit
him on the back of the neck. Then there would be trouble,
and Maravilla, leaning low over her desk to conceal her
smiles, would express by the mere angle of a side-tilted
head her demure disapproval of it all.

She liked to make fun of Colgas with the other girls, and
to scandalise about the senile passion he had developed for
one of the town girls, which was well known to all his
pupils. Like little devils, they would chant this girl's name
in whispers all round the room, until Colgas's ears were
burning, and he would descend upon the boys with his
stick and scare the more timid girls—among whom was
not María—with his shouting.

But, although she would not work in school, she did so
for Aurelio. With many sighs, smiles, sidelong looks of
appeal and open cajoleries, she mastered her alphabet, and
came at last to read from the little five-centimo books
Aurelio bought her from the market-stalls—nursery tales
of an incredible naïveté over which she yawned, because
they were much less diverting than the ones her father told

her, and which one did not have to pick out painfully, syllable by syllable, from the printed page. She learnt to add, doubtfully, on her fingers, and she managed, by the time she was eight or nine, to write the word " Maravilla " in a clumsy hand, although, for her own taste, she preferred its shortened form, María, which was so much less troublesome.

Carmela said she must learn to use a needle, and to this she took as a duck to water : especially when she was given her own garments to sew. She even went the length of stuffing bits of material in her pocket when she went up the mountains, and instead of skipping about, or sitting attentive while her father showed her the veins running through a leaf or the strange markings of a stone, would sit placidly stitching, with no eyes for the miracles which her father longed to share with her. To see her thus occupied, when all his desire was to bend that tender mind towards the things which were absorbing him ever more deeply—the mysterious changes of earth and air, the shapes of clouds and the small, secret life that went on in the roots of grass—saddened Aurelio a little ; it made her less his own. Yet he was glad Carmela should claim her share in the child. He had noticed, or fancied he had noticed, of late, a kind of guarded friendliness between them, on which he was too wise to comment.

One day, when she was just nearing her thirteenth birthday, María felt very ill ; all her limbs seemed heavy, and there was a dull, dragging ache below the waist of her gown. Her body hurt her ; for some days it had been tender to the touch ; and her sleep at night was disturbed and full of dreams, so that she awoke unrefreshed, with black circles under her eyes.

She might have told her mother had not her sickness coincided with one of Carmela's black moods. Aurelio, as

usual, had absented himself from the sight and sound of
Carmela's venom, and, for the first time, María resented her
father's absence, and felt he had deserted her.

She crawled away up the mountain—not very far, but it
seemed a great distance to María—and found a little hollow
where she allowed her body to drop, with a groan. The
ground ran precipitously downwards ; nothing but a
gnarled olive-tree prevented her own descent into the valley
below. She wedged herself behind it and closed her eyes.
A heavy weight seemed to press upon her head, and her
eyeballs burned ; the glitter of the sun turned her giddy,
and she felt inclined to vomit. She was hot and uncomfortable ; her hands burned dry as ashes, but her frock was
soaked under the armpits.

She knew what was happening to her. She had known it
happen to older girls than herself, and that it lent them a
proud importance which she herself had envied. But she
had not expected it to come to her so soon, or in this form
that gave her a loathing of her own body.

An appalling loneliness came at her from the mountains,
as though no one but herself had ever known this pain, this
humiliating sense of uncleanliness, for which she had not
known how to prepare. The tears began to course down her
face ; her lonely wail went out into silence, so that an
eagle checked its swinging circuit of the valley, to hang
motionless against the background of adamantine blue,
with predatory eye upon the hollow wherein María
crouched. She would have to sit there until it was over,
until she had finished seeping away into the grass ; while the
sun went down, and the stars came, and dawn and moon
and dusk—for how many days ?—passed over her head
hungry, frightened, alone. She howled with self-pity and
terror.

Aurelio found her. A glance told him ; his heart strained

towards her, sitting in the grass, with her face streaked with tears and her eyes which, starting towards him, accused him, her father, of all she was suffering. Her lips were pale, her face shiny with sweat, her eye-sockets blackened. He had known this was coming ; he should have been on the watch ; he should have warned Carmela—if, indeed, a mother needed warning of so momentous an event in her child's career.

He dropped on his knees, tore up handfuls of the wild lavender and thyme that grew about them—sweet and cleansing herbs. He crushed them between his hard palms so that the leaves gave out their aromatic essences, and thrust them under her nose.

" Smell that, my little one ! How good, how beautiful. The little children of the soil—God gives them a sweet perfume to comfort them for their humble little flowers. Look, how gracious is the thyme, that suffers itself to be trodden underfoot and only betrays itself by its incense to the traveller ! " Her eyes closed ; he wondered if she were about to faint. " Come home, my treasure."

" I can't ; I can't move ; I'm ill."

He unknotted quickly the white, folded kerchief from his neck, dropped it on her knee, and left her to do what she could with it. When he returned, instead of telling her to get up, he sat down beside her and gave her a peach out of his pocket. Her teeth sank through the hard, downy skin into the golden flesh ; presently she lay against his arm.

" There is nothing in the world so strange and mysterious as growth," he began slowly. " Nothing stands still. As the olive ripens, and the grape, so we ripen : child into youth and youth into man ; child into maid and maid into woman. This is a holy day for both of us, because my little marvel has become a maid ; she has become a princess ; one day she will have a queen's crown."

María turned, flung her arms round her father's neck, and began to cry heartily ; but her tears were no longer of fear and anguish, but of love and relief. They stopped as suddenly as they had begun, and she smiled at Aurelio, through eyelashes still glittering with their moisture. " I am now a señorita," she announced shyly.

A thin sacramental veil had fallen upon her, to her father's eyes ; a delicate foreshadowing of her destiny as a woman. With yearning, he saw the chubbiness of childhood fining into something that roused more complicated emotions than those of simple love for her gaiety and lightness of heart. She chose this moment to announce, with portentous gravity :

" Blas Mejías is my novio."

" What grandeur ! Really, I had no idea of it."

" We are going to be married, and have a little house of our own in the mountains, and Blas is going to look after sheep, and I am going to have babies. But you must come and live with us, papá mío ; it would not be at all nice if you didn't."

" And your mother ? " he could not forbear adding.

María's fine brows gathered themselves together.

" She will be too busy with the tavern," she said, with conviction.

" And I, am I not busy as well ? "

" Are you ? " The idea seemed to intrigue María. " Tell me how you are busy, papá mío." Then she yawned. Already, thought Aurelio, she had developed that woman's trick of speaking to the man she loved humouringly, as though he were a child ! If there was anyone in the world she was in love with at the present, he thought, with a swelling of the heart, it was himself ! Blessed Virgin, let him gather the rosebuds, even if the full-blown flower was reserved for another hand !

"I am very busy indeed," he told her gravely. "It takes a great deal of a man's time, I can tell you, to sit up here, and count the birds as they fly across the valley, and see which way the clouds are rolling, and whether the wind blows east or west——"

"But you don't get paid for that, papá," she startled him by replying. She gave him a look that was almost all Carmela. He was so taken aback that for a moment he had no answer. Feeling she had hurt him, she instantly flung her arm round his neck again. "Never mind ; perhaps one day we'll win the big prize in the lottery. And perhaps I won't marry Blas," she added, as a crowning consolation. "Perhaps we'll go and live in a little house by ourselves, just we two ; that will be best, papá mío ; yes, I think that will be best."

He wondered, as they walked down the mountain track hand in hand, how far her words, her reiterated suggestion of a house apart from Carmela, expressed her realisation of her mother's attitude to her.

With the duplicity of childhood, Maravilla had known, and kept to herself, more than either Aurelio or Carmela would have ever believed. Her eyes and ears wide open, she perfectly realised the difficult situation that revolved about her own small person, although it was a little less than a year since she had, by a rather ignoble piece of eavesdropping, discovered what it was all about.

In the spring of the previous year a letter had come from the widow Herédia. She was now a very old woman, and her arthritis had made it impossible for her to continue living alone in her house in the Albaicin. So she had moved to a house in the lower part of the town, and she wrote to tell Carmela of the change and to remind her of a long overdue visit Carmela had promised to pay her when the winter was over.

" And when am I again to see the little one ? This is a nice way to treat me, I who should have been her god-mother ! Soon it will be the feast of the Santa Cruz ; that will make a good excuse for you to come and spend a day or two in the town. Remember how dearly I love you both, and do not treat me so badly, for I have not deserved it of either of you.''

" That is quite true," said Aurelio, as Carmela read aloud this part of the letter. " We could easily spend a night with your mother. How often she has written that she would be pleased to have us, now your father is dead."

" And who is to look after things here ? " she retorted, as she folded the letter and thrust it into her bosom.

" We can lock the house up for a day or two," answered Aurelio easily. Maravilla, standing behind her father, jerked Aurelio's coat-tails. A visit to Granada ! She had only been two or three times since she was old enough to remember it, but she loved her grandmother's house—the hot, sweet scent of the bakery, the tiny little shop, with—always—a basket of kittens under its counter, which at night so mysteriously closed up and made the door ; and she adored her aunt Dolores with a slightly romantic adoration that took the form of praying very earnestly that when she grew up she might be exactly like her—a prayer which seemed likely to be fulfilled. She had the same tiny features, the same lovely little Moorish nose, slightly flat-tened, the same small, round head. She also liked, but a little feared, her mother's aunt, the strange, thin woman whose face and hands looked as though they were made out of dim glass ; whose eyes had a queer, penetrative quality, that made them seem as though they could look right down into a little girl's soul. And María was not sure whether she always wanted her soul to be looked at.

" And throw away good money, while we idle about in Granada ? " Carmela was saying, with asperity, above her head.

María gave a gasp of disappointment ; she knew, when her mother spoke like that, her mind was made up. Why couldn't they go alone, she and her father ? But she was too wise to suggest such a thing. She was sorry for her father. She was sure Aurelio wanted, just as much as she, to go to the feria ; to see the fireworks, and the holy crosses in the patios—which she had heard her mother say were so much finer than those they had in a few houses in Agujasierra. " You should see the cross we had in our house the year before I was married ! " Carmela had said. " It was all of crimson carnations and as tall as—*that* tall ! And my mother's brother was a torero, and we had his two fighting-cloaks spread out on the wall, with such an elegant arrangement of fans—very artistic. Hundreds of people came in to see it, and we got the first prize—a hundred pesetas. We girls had new dresses out of it ! "

The days passed by. One evening, when Aurelio came in, about sunset, and she and María were polishing glasses that the boy who helped in the tavern had washed, Carmela said :

" To-morrow is Santa Cruz."

María was so startled that she dropped a glass. Could it be that her mother had reconsidered her decision ; that they were to go after all ? She picked up the pieces, wholly oblivious of Carmela's scolding.

" You " said the latter, to Aurelio, " can sleep at my mother's."

" But you ? Are you not coming ? " He also was dumb-founded. They had never, since the night before María's birth, spent a night apart ; even had he desired it, he would not have suggested it, fearing that she might misinterpret his suggestion.

" How do you expect me to come ? Is there not the tavern to look after ? "

" Surely Rodrigo——"

" That imbecile ! That drunkard ! " The glasses rang on the tray as she pushed them together. María, breathlessly watching, came to one of those quick decisions of which children are sometimes capable. Her mother did not wish her father to go ! Then why had she suggested it ? She was terrified for fear he would say " Yes," yet she herself had put it into his head !

" I could spend the day there, and come back at night," said Aurelio doubtfully.

" No, no ! What is the good of that ? Waste of the journey-money. You know that nothing happens until after dark—there is music and dancing in the streets. You will find plenty of girls to dance with you at the Santa Cruz ! "

María scowled and bit her lip ; for some reason, this picture of her father dancing with other girls did not please her. She knew it did not please her mother ; for once she was completely in accord with Carmela.

" And María ? " he asked slowly ; and she clenched her hands under the little apron that covered the front of her dress.

" What of her ? "

" They will want to see her ; your mother, and Doña Angustias."

" Then let them want," said Carmela crisply. " There is plenty of time, when she is older, for María to go to the Santa Cruz."

At this (to her) unjust decision, María's face grew crimson, and her eyes filled with angry tears. She threw an agonised look at her father.

" . . . I will think about it," said Aurelio, and left them.

To María's surprise, and annoyed discomfort, Carmela sat down and covered her face with her hands. She did not weep, but, like many people who are not used to abstract thinking, she needed to shut out everything that was not connected with her thought.

Aurelio had not accepted ; but he had not refused. With the pitiful contrariety of her sex, she now desired to force, at whatever personal cost, his acceptance. She had made an offer of great—for her, of unprecedented—generosity, only in order to hear him refuse it. He had failed her.

María was wholly puzzled ; her bewilderment almost for the time conquered her rage at being deprived of the treat. More than ever, she was sure her mother did not want her father to go to Granada ; what did she mean ? Giving up the problem, she crumpled up her face, began to cry, and ran out of the room to escape her mother's scolding.

It was after midnight when Aurelio returned. In their bedroom he found Carmela stitching, by the light of a candle. She was sitting up in bed, darkly companioned by her own shadow, that kept up its rhythmical accompaniment to her movements on the white wall.

He looked at her, yawned, and stretched himself. His eyes went to María's bed in the corner of the room. María was pretending to be asleep ; her face was crimson still and her eyelids fluttering, for she was fearfully excited. Had it not been for the long discipline they had imposed on themselves, she would have leapt out of bed and thrown herself into her father's arms. Aurelio, believing her to be asleep, felt the angel of his love for her take shape and pass out of his bosom to enfold with its wings of divine protection the body of his beloved child. Another year, when they could go together ; there was plenty of time.

Carmela's needle went clicking in and out. Aurelio started to pull off his clothes ; he thought, with a gentle

glance at her, she would be pleased to hear he had given
up the idea of going.

" It's late," he said, as he got in beside her ; he put his
hand over hers to take the needlework from her, but she
jerked it away.

" Go to sleep ; I have this to finish."

" What is it ? " he asked her curiously, fingering the
stuff, which pleased him with its smooth, green, leaf-like
surface.

" I suppose you thought," she retorted, " I should let
the child go to Granada in her everyday rags ? " She wil-
fully traduced her own care of María, for no child in the
town was dressed more neatly, with such care and cleanliness. But Aurelio gave no thought to the self-depreciation ;
for the second time that day she had stunned him with the
unexpected. He heard María's bed rustle ; knew that she
was awake.

" Do you mean we are both to go—together ? "

" They will begin to think things if they never see her,"
she defended herself. " Besides, it's what you wanted—
both of you ! " she flung at him.

" What a good mother you are ! " he said warmly. He
stroked the crude green silk which, an hour ago, Carmela
had rushed out and bought from a market-stall. " Carmela
mía, won't you change your mind and come with us ? "
He did not want it ; passionately he did not want it ! But
the words came to his lips unbidden, and were out before
he could check them. In María's corner there was dead
silence.

" No. I will do as I have always done ; I will see after the
house," she answered, but without bitterness. He took heart
of it to kiss her, and a tremor of response shook her body,
although she said sharply, " Lie down and go to sleep ;
how else are you to waken in time to catch the diligence ?

I have put out your best suit and mended the pocket ; you had better wear the shirt my aunt made you ; she will take it as a compliment I take such care of your clothes they do not wear out."

" You are like a deep well," he told her. " Your surface waters are bitter, but in your depths lies a sweet and wholesome draught." The prospect of being together, wholly together, for a couple of days, with María ; of being wholly responsible for this dearest part of himself ; of being free to indulge, without the modifications imposed by the cold presence of Carmela, the exuberance of his love, almost suffocated him with bliss.

The candle had long been out. There was an uncertain light in the room, or, rather, a pale darkness ; it might have been moonlight, or it might equally have been dawn. It crept through the cracks of the closed shutters. It was restful to aching eyes.

Aurelio was long in getting to sleep. Presently she felt him get up. He was long in coming back—so long that she turned from the wall, to call out to know if anything was amiss. The words were arrested on her lips, for Aurelio was there, kneeling by the child's bed ; they were locked in each other's arms.

Had he but known, when he got back to bed, he was lying with a woman of stone.

María never forgot that visit to Granada ; not for the feria, for the gaiety, the celebration, the spoiling she received from her grandmother and her aunts, the sweets they bought her from the stalls, the little pink comb and the cluster of carnations her aunt Dolores fixed in her hair, the laughter, music, and dancing of holiday-making Granada, the fireworks she watched from the balcony of her aunt's lodging-house down near the Puerta Real—but for a conversation she most abominably overheard between her father and the widow Herédia.

She always a little dreaded those visits to the one little room which her mother's aunt had taken in the lower part of the town. There was something so fine as to be almost repressive in the old, crippled woman to whom, since her father did so, María felt it her duty to pay her tribute of affection. When she pressed her kiss upon Doña Angustias's cheek her lips felt chill ; it gave her a feeling not entirely agreeable to see her father kissing her as well, as though she were his mother.

" How evil you have been to me ! " she began, pretending to chide him. "All these years, and how few times you have been to see me ! Of Carmela I expected it, but hardly of you."

" And you—when have you been to see us ? " he rallied her. " Not once since we were married. We do not live quite at the world's end, you know."

" I know, I know ! But I do not come where I am not invited," she answered with dignity. " Carmela did not give me an invitation."

" As though you need to wait for that ! " But he knew that Carmela's curious shame of her circumstances had prevented her asking her aunt to visit her in the days before the widow's travelling was curtailed by her disability. Had she been in a position to show off a fine house, a grand hospitality—oh, he knew his Carmela ! Not her friends only, but her enemies, would have been bidden, to envy.

" And how is the little one who should have been my godchild ? " María blushed, hung her head sideways, and wriggled a little in her chair. This oblique accusation was levelled at her every time they visited the widow Herédia ;

she was made to feel it was, in some way, her fault that Doña Angustias was not her godmother. She herself had begun to feel curious about it. Why was she not Doña Angustias's godchild, if it had been promised for her? " This is a very little, humble room," went on the widow. " There is not very much room for a little girl to move about, and little girls like moving. Look here, my child " —and she produced from under a napkin a plate loaded with bread fried with spice and sugar, a sweetmeat dear to María's soul. " In the room across the landing there is another little girl, who is alone all day, because her mother goes out to work. Take these sweets and share them with her—you have only to open the door and go in."

Now, although María adored spiced bread, she was not at all anxious to share it with a strange little girl whom she had never met before ; neither did she care for being sent out of the room while her father and the widow talked about things she very much wished to hear. So, although she took the plate in her hand, thanked the donor politely, and stepped out on the landing, drawing the door behind her, but not quite closing it, she then did the most wicked thing she had ever done in her life—although it did not strike her in that light. Instead of going through the opposite door, where the poor little girl whose mother went out to work would no doubt have welcomed her, she sat down on the top step of the stairs and began to eat the crisps by herself, masticating carefully so as not to drown the sound of the voices which came clearly to her through the half-open door.

There were many things which María did not understand in the conversation which her ears took in as greedily as her lips received the sweet spiced crumbs ; long adult phrases that conveyed little to her eleven-year-old mind, but of which she would not willingly have missed a syllable.

" Tell me—tell me everything," the widow was saying. There was the scraping sound of a chair drawn across the tiled floor, and María knew jealously that the pair of them were sitting close together. She felt deeply her own exclusion, for she was not used to being dismissed when grown-up people talked together. She resented her father's having permitted her great-aunt to send her away. In revenge she prepared to listen all she could. " How changed you are ! How much finer ! Why, I believe you are all I wanted you to be as a young man ! Come, do you realise this is the first time we have been alone together since the old days ? Tell me what has happened. What has altered you, and given you this fineness ? "

" I do not know exactly what you mean," María heard her father reply. " A man grows older ; he is bound to learn more as the years pass over him."

" All in you that I regretted, all that angered me about you, has gone. Your conceit, your shallowness, your parade of your little empirical knowledge—you have lost your cleverness and have found wisdom. Yes, you need not contradict me ; it is in your eyes. What has Carmela to say to that ? "

" At any rate she has got over her anger with me for not letting them elect me alcalde."

" You did rightly not to allow yourself to be sacrificed to her ambition. I too, once, had ambition of a kind. It poisoned my youth for me. Ambition is an evil thing ; it steals the peace from the heart's core. How few people know what a valuable thing is peace ! It is the most blessed of all the virtues. There are things in the world more important than governing a town. And I daresay you now find people respect you quite as much as if you had let them make you alcalde ? "

" That is certainly true," said Aurelio.

" What do I tell you ? In fact, they will respect you more, because, although it is a fine thing to be offered a crown, it is an even finer one to refuse it. But why do you let me tell you these things which you know already ? "

" Because I have the habit of listening to you. And besides, I have not gone so much beyond knowing what I do not know, as yet. But I have found a leaf, a stone, a puff of wind. I do not know if these are important things. It only seems to me that they are more important than anything I have ever found in my life, up to the present. I think that if I could understand them I should be a wise man, and wisdom has come to mean more to me than it ever did before. But it is a new kind of wisdom I am now seeking ; one that will benefit other people rather than myself. Sometimes, in the mountains, I have a great desire to lose myself ; not my limbs, my body, only, but to lose all that part of myself of which I have become tired, which is of no use to anybody. To find a new self ! That must indeed be the one desire of the human being as it becomes conscious of its failures and its sins."

" You have not reached these conclusions without suffering," said the widow shrewdly. " And are you and Carmela happy together ? " In the long silence that followed, María pricked up her ears. " Do you still love one another ? "

" Love," said Aurelio, " is an illusion. . . . It has no existence save in the minds of those who are very happy."

" Where did you hear that ? " cried the widow sharply.

" I will tell you," answered Aurelio.

María forgot her sweet bread, forgot the new frock which she had carefully lifted so as to avoid contact with the dusty stairs, forgot almost to breathe, as she listened to a story as strange and unreal as any she had ever listened to : stranger, because her father was the principal actor in it, and because her own name, Maravilla, was mysteriously woven into it. She thought at first that it was of herself her father was speaking, but she presently realised that it belonged to a beautiful lady—or were there two ladies ?— one of whom her father had seen at the theatre, and the other with whom he had gone home for a night. It was an entrancing story ; the only thing which spoilt it for María was that she could not run in and, resting her elbows on his knees, look up in Aurelio's face while he told it ; he had so many faces—angry and laughing, sinister and gay—when he told a story, when he became each of the characters in turn. But something warned her that it was better, on this occasion, not to claim her privilege as chief and cherished audience of Aurelio's tales ; for the first time in her life she was conscious of hearing something that she was not meant to hear, and this added to the thrill of listening.

" Why have you stopped ? "

" I was waiting for you to rebuke me, as you used to do."

" How foolish you are ! So that was why the baby was not called Angustias ! I knew there was something behind Carmela's letter, in which she made out it was to avoid family jealousy ! Such an excuse might do for my sister-in-law, but it did not take me in. So that is the meaning of the name Maravilla. Well, that was a long time ago ; has she now forgiven you ? Are you as fond of one another as you used to be ? "

" You know, Doña Angustias, love is like a flower ; either the bud is opening, or the petals are trembling towards their fall. Nothing remains the same."

" But there is always the heart of the rose ; that which contains the precious seed—the germ of re-birth."

" But if there is a canker within ? "

" Is that the way it is with you and Carmela ? "

" When we are alone together, she is just as she was when

I fell in love with her. And that—digo ! It was an enchantment. But at other times she goes out of her way to show
me that the past is not forgotten ; she does all in her power
to destroy and deny my love. She will not speak, withdraws
herself in every way from me, and acts as if it were I and
not she who is to blame for it."

" All the Moreno women are stupid," pronounced the
widow, " and obstinate as mules. And there is something
else. Carmela has always been a strange girl. Her nature is
a very jealous one ; she likes always to appear better than
her companions. Now, as she cannot fail to know in her
heart that she is much less clever, much more ignorant,
than you, she fears to betray her ignorance when other
people are there. Do I not know her ! She is exactly like
my sister-in-law, who is very clever in business, but apart
from it is so stupid it is a penance to be with her. Do you
know they asked me to live with them ? Very kind and considerate ; but I should have gone out of my mind, listening
to the girls' gossip and Marta's heavy breathing as she adds
up her money ! And, you see, Carmela started with the idea
she was so much better than you in every way, it has perhaps come as a little shock to her to find out what you are
really like. She is not one to take kindly to a second place."

As Aurelio made no immediate reply, she continued :

" Probably you try to talk to her in your own way ? About
ideas and feelings, instead of things and people ? She will
certainly resent that very much ; for she only knows about
the price of hens and rabbits, and about keeping the house
clean, and mending your clothes. It is not kind to expect
more than that of her."

" You are wise and you are right," said Aurelio wearily.
" But the root of our trouble goes deeper than that. She is
jealous ; but not on that account. She is jealous of María ;
the child is like a drop of acid in her cup. Not always ; but

there are days when she hates her, and me because of her."

" Ave María Purísima ! How unnatural a thing ! For a mother not to care for her own flesh and blood ! But of course she is a little mad ! She married late, and it was late in life for her to have a child. And besides, all her mother's family do odd things when they get to a certain age. There was María Luisa—she forgot everything, and had to be looked after as though she were a little child. And there was Doña Clara, who became so crazy she took her own father for her son, and used to pat and fondle and scold him and tell him he would be late for school ! What is to be done ? There is no remedy but to have patience."

" For myself it is easy to have patience ; but, when things get worse every year, what is to become of the child ? "

" She does not ill-treat her ? She is not inhuman with her ? " said the widow quickly.

" Por Dios, no ! There is no better cared-for child in the town, nor any bolder. You should see how she climbs among the boulders, like a little goat ! But those things are coming to an end—and what is to take the place of them ? Whatever I do to show and assure Carmela that my love for her is no less real than my love for the child, she will not be convinced by it. I know that every time I caress María I am driving a nail into her mother's breast. She has made her own cross, but it is I who crucify her upon it ! But what can one do ? I can no more withhold from María what is hers than I can deprive Carmela of her own dues. She believes the child has stolen my love from her : whereas since the little one was born I have learnt ways and means of loving I never knew existed before ! I am a thousand times more capable of loving Carmela than I was before, if she would but believe it of me ! "

" Yes, indeed," said the widow gravely, " you did well

not to let them make you alcalde. Your life is already
dedicated. If things are that way with Carmela, you must
give up everything for the little one. You will need all your
wisdom," she said, with a woman's loving doubt, " and
more, if you are to be father and mother both to Maravilla.
But there is always myself ! Once you brought me a little
kid, and I hated you for it, thinking you were mocking me.
But now you can bring me a little girl, and you will find
my arms no less ready to receive her than if my own womb
had given her birth. Only it will have to be soon. I can feel
the life is beginning to run out of me. My poor Aurelio !
Life is very hard. Very difficult. There are some of us who
seem to be born under a one-eyed moon. God grant the
little one is not one of these ! "

For some reason, these strange words afflicted María
with a spasm of positive terror. She had always disliked, and
a little feared, the moonlight, and she knew that it was very
bad luck to meet a one-eyed man in the street. There was
a boy in her village whom they called Paco Tuerto, and
she and her companions always ran down side-streets when
they saw him coming, to avoid the dim glance of his one
eye. The combination of the moon and a one-eyed man was
so terrifying to her that she, who was as bold as a lion
with all normal and daylight fears, began quietly to
whimper. Coming on top of the revelation of the mysterious
import of her own name, and the half-understood explanation of her mother's dislike for her, of which, for a long time,
she had been childishly aware, but which had not distressed her, because her mother was of so much less importance in her life than her father, the mention of the one-
eyed moon made it impossible for her to stay alone any
longer on the darkling stairs.

But it must not appear as though she had been eavesdropping. Some deep-rooted, childish cunning warned her

to check her tears ; the pieces of spiced bread which she had not eaten she hastily shot through the opposite doorway, where, no doubt, the other little girl would receive them with gratitude, and María walked boldly, plate in hand, into her great-aunt's room.

But not even the gift that the widow produced—of a little old shawl of celestial, faded blue, with pink and yellow roses on it ; not even the rapture of walking with her father in the streets where the lamps were already lighted ; not all the delights of the feria, could eradicate from María's mind the guilty secret which she carried, which from that day influenced her attitude towards both her parents.

Into her love for Aurelio had entered a deep curiosity, held at bay by a totally new awe that held some blurred, childish conception of her father's masculinity, a thing of which she had never before been aware, save in its general sense ; and a new caution, a new mistrust, no longer sub-consciously copied from Aurelio, but springing authenti-cally from her own soul, coloured her relationship with her mother. She did not hate Carmela ; she merely felt for her a cold dislike, which prudence warned her must be kept in check, since they had, unhappily, to live together.

PART II

CHAPTER I

ANDRÉS

A PHLEGMATIC GROUP of loungers round and about the Café de la Alameda watched the erection, on that piece of waste ground that faces upon the square, of a dingy-looking tent. It was a sluggish time in Granada—the month of August, when all who can afford it go down to the coast, and the café tables, even at night, are all but deserted. The tent itself spoke of a forlorn hope on the part of some itinerant entertainers, who had chosen to bridge a geographical gap between a couple of ferias by a night in Granada.

A suffocating heat lay upon the town, and a corresponding lethargy upon the spirits of its occupants. The majority were too languid to stretch out their hands in acceptance of the thin green leaflets offered to them by a narrow-shouldered boy on the edge of the pavement. Not that he brought to his task any effort of interest or compulsion. Unsmiling, he merely stretched out a thin brown hand, and seemingly made nothing of the complaisance or otherwise of those whom, with his mute gesture, he indifferently accosted. It was a mechanical movement, bereft of hope or despair ; a certain drawn look about the curiously well-cut mouth suggested that, when one was as hungry as all that, it really did not matter what happened.

Very few of the drifting couples troubled to observe the boy, who was a stranger, and who, from his clothes, might have been a beggar. A pitiful suit of cotton hung loosely

on his narrow frame, and his feet were thrust into alpar
gatas. The few who accepted his leaflet glanced at it
grinned, and crumpled it in their hands before allowing
it to drop into the dust. He saw the action and gave n
sign ; there were yet a handful of bills to be distributed—
no matter to him what people did with them so long as h
disposed of them.

A few habitués settled at the tables of the café ; th
waiters moved indifferently about their duties, and two o
three shoeblacks rose from the fountain steps and began t
solicit custom. The members of the orchestra drifted lan
guidly on to their wooden platform, and seemed to agre
among themselves that the custom was worth a tune. Afte
uncovering their instruments, they began, with an almos
insolent carelessness, to play a paso doble. The air wen
blue ; the bats swooped down from the chestnut-tree
overhead.

With the first bars of the music a singular change too
place in the manner of the boy who offered bills on th
pavement. The deathly languor which had informed hi
body and deadened his actions vanished. His thin shoulder
went back, his carriage became something like that of
bullfighter entering the ring. Instead of shoving his bills a
people, he now handed them with a flourish that drew
attention to himself and made one or two of the passers-by
laugh at him ; a grand air of the theatre imposed itsel
upon his actions ; instead of being one of the negligible
whose very bones seem to be made of Granada dust, s
dusty of body and soul are they, he began, in some odd way
to dominate his surroundings : so that the patrons of th
café looked at him with curiosity, and a couple of girl
stood still to gape at him with the naïveté of their class. H
magnificently ignored their attention.

It was only to men he offered his bills—for the best o

reasons. In doubtful type, and with still more doubtful spelling, they advertised an entertainment " for gentlemen only " : they described with luscious adjectival profusion the pulchritudinous delights of the performance to be given that night in the marquee across the street. As he disposed of the last of them, he was saying to himself, " And now I can look for some place to sleep." A café, he meant, or some low-class tavern where he could lay his head down on his arms and become unconscious until his duties called him at ten o'clock. The performance ran until midnight, or after ; when it was over, he had to take his share in the shifting of the tent and the disposal of the properties in their insecure baskets. How he cursed those baskets—which, being long past the use to which they were destined, were continually getting him into trouble by shedding their contents. Still, life might be worse. Life had *been* worse.

Just as he swung on his heel, with a whistle of relief at having completed his tedious task, one of his companions of the show lounged up to him and caught him by the shoulder.

" Well, here's a nice bit of news for you."

" What's happened ? "

" They're saying Juanón's thinking of clearing out after the show : leaving us stiff ! There's no money in this hole —and look what we did at Loja. If I don't turn up to-night, you needn't say anything about it. I know a woman who keeps a house in the Albaicin ; I'm going up there now, to see if there's any work to be had."

" Thanks for telling me," returned the boy slowly. His eyes were narrowed, his face sharpened into immobility. The other looked at him, not unkindly.

" Mala suerte, niño. You haven't struck much luck since you joined on with us, have you ? "

The boy lifted his shoulders. " Why talk of luck ? " he

seemed to say. " What is luck ?—and who are the fools who expect it ? "

" Now you think you were better off where you were before," jibed the other. He shook his head.

" No, I don't. I wouldn't have run away if I'd been better off."

" Vaya ! You didn't know what you were coming to ! "

" It was all right," he replied laconically. The other pulled a face.

" I know which I'd choose if I had the luck ! I'd put up with a lot of running round after the customers for the sake of a good meal in my belly to-night."

" If you think they gave us good meals at the Casa de Apolonio——! I ran away from being a waiter because I'd had enough of it. I knew what I was doing. I always know what I'm doing," he boasted. " I know what I'm going to do next."

" That's all right for you ; hasta luego," mocked his companion.

It was a lie, of course. He had not the slightest idea of what to do. What does one do when one's occupation has been to sing dirty ballads in the intervals between the naked posturings of the girls ? What a place—Granada— in which to be stranded, in which to look for the only kind of work one wanted to do. Horrible as his job had been, Andrés felt a cold chill at the thought of its deserting him. The blaring of the band, the artificial lights, the atmos- phere of entertainment—these had been near enough his ideal of the theatre to satisfy, for the present, his cravings.

His eyes filled with tears as he thought of those few moments he had each night between two of the numbers, when the ignoble nature of his performance never so much as crossed his mind, so filled it was with the joy and excite- ment of being alone on the little square platform, called by courtesy the stage : of feeling the attention of the audience focused upon himself, of doing lawfully, and even for an infinitesimal pay, the thing for which, as a small boy at the orphanage where he had been reared, he had so often been punished (he had had, even as an infant, a diabolical gift of caricature ; his dramatic gift had not been applauded by the fathers—truth to tell, because it was too often employed in the exploitation of their foibles).

To relinquish already the opportunity he had at such expenditure of cunning and boldness secured for himself seemed to Andrés the bitterest experience of his life.

It had been by the merest accident he had taken this step towards the achievement of his, up to then, unconsidered goal. The miserable little vulgar show had come to Loja ; he and another boy who had also been at the orphanage, and was now, with Andrés, a camarero in the greasy café that called itself La Casa de Apolonio, had contrived to slip for a few minutes into the tent. Andrés ran away that night, and joined the show on its way to Archidona. If they had asked him his reason, he could not have given one ; the lure of the music, the lights, and the figures that moved upon the little stage was too subtle for Andrés to summarise it ; they called to some depth in him which so far had been unstirred.

It was another accident which, in the first place, had given him his position on the programme. One of the girls was taken suddenly sick, and he, up to then a mere hanger-on, a baggage-boy, a nonesuch of the show, had, at a moment's notice, taken her place. He had sung a couple of lewd little verses he had learned from the other camareros, and something about his young, fresh impudence had so tickled the fancy of the patrons—coming between the jaded posturings of the beauties—that he was allowed to keep his place as part of the entertainment. And now it was over—if Pedro spoke the truth—like the fading of a dream.

That night he performed, for the last time, with a kind of desperation. The tent was not more than a quarter full ; the audience apathetic to the point of insolence. " Las niñas " launched in vain the faded battery of their charms, the innuendoes of their accustomed bodies. Half the audience conversed among themselves, paying small attention to what passed on the stage. As Andrés stepped on the rickety boards a wave of antagonism hit him in the tenderest spot of the artiste : in his *amour-propre* as a performer. His whole nature rose to the challenge.

He had changed his clothes ; the suit he wore, although not made for him, fitted passably well, with only a little superfluous breadth in the shoulder seams to betray its present ownership. His linen appeared to be clean—at least from the front of the house. He had a frail, slightly dissipated type of good looks ; it was an effect of the lighting that plunged his eyes into shadow and imparted an overripe bloom to his lips. His thick and over-long hair shone from an application of stolen brilliantine. And he threw his farrago of innuendo at them as though he had a quarter of a century's experience of the theatre. Many a worse performance was to be seen in the music-halls of Madrid.

He stood with his heart thudding as they shouted corroborative obscenities and clapped at the end of his song. His eyes took painful note of the many empty seats ; there was not money enough in the house to pay for the lighting. No question of salaries this week ; half the girls had been crying ; and Juanón himself, since the rise of the curtain, had been invisible. Pedro (who had not made his appearance) had told the truth.

A stout person with a toothpick sat immediately below

the steps he had to descend when his all-too-short turn was over. As he came down them, it seemed to him that all the lights went out. He was moving blindly towards the ragged curtain that cut off the artistes' quarters from the audience, when a shout checked him : " Oiga, niño ! "

The stout man with the toothpick was beckoning him with that curious downward sweep of the hand that has more the air of dismissal. And ten minutes later Andrés found himself engaged to sing nightly in a cabaret which, its proprietor informed him, was due to open in a few weeks' time. It was not easy to believe. He gave a vague, superstitious thought to his patron saint.

It was that look of dissipation, coupled with Andrés's youthful good looks, that had given the dueño of Las Estrellas his idea. He had been in Barcelona, and he had seen things that he thought he might at least try out in his own cabaret. He had one or two elderly clients . . . and he had a hard, commercial mind, which felt that Granada was behind the times. The experiment, at all events, was worth trying.

Meanwhile, thought Andrés, how was the time to be filled in, while he was waiting for the cabaret to open ?

The fonda known as the Casa Fermín did not offer very distinguished amenities to the travellers who, attracted by its cheapness, elected to stay there. It was, in the main, a commercial house, with a regular clientele who patronised it when business brought them to Granada.

The somewhat unsatisfactory husband of Dolores Moreno had inherited the proprietorship of the fonda, which lived rather on its past reputation than upon its present attractions. There were half a dozen dingy little bedrooms, a dark dining-room in charge of a thieving waiter, and the patio was free to visitors as well as to the family, when they had not the inclination to entertain themselves elsewhere.

When she left her mother's house, Dolores Moreno prepared to make changes ; she worked hard, with all the Moreno passion for cleanliness and propriety, until the little strength which remained to her from six successive pregnancies gave out. Four of her children had been still-born ; of the surviving two, a fever epidemic had deprived her before she came to the Casa Fermín, and the year after her removal a major operation had made it impossible for her to conceive again, and had reduced her to a state of semi-invalidism very trying to her husband, Don Luis. When able she looked after the fonda ; but, during the longer periods when her ailments would hardly permit her to drag herself from one room to another, the fonda looked after itself. Her mother and sister were too busy to come to her assistance, and Don Luis had certain important and private negotiations of his own which kept him out of the house most of the day and a good part of the night.

The joy of Dolores's days was when her niece María came to pay a visit to Granada. On these occasions, the most perfunctory hours of her stay were passed with her grandmother. Invariably she schemed to spend the greater part of her time with her aunt Dolores—a state of affairs not wholly approved by the family, who did not wholly trust Dolores's chaperonage. How, indeed, could she, sick as she was half the time, look properly after a young and devastatingly beautiful niece ?

For María was, by the standards of her country, devasta-tingly beautiful. Her prayer that she should grow up like her aunt Dolores had not quite been answered, for she had not Dolores's beautiful square mouth, with its still match-less teeth. María's mouth was small and scarlet—too small in the opinion of foreigners, but conforming perfectly to

Spanish ideals. The local saying that she was " worthy to
be a Sevillana and an Andalucían " was frequently applied
to her, for there was a suavity in her beauty which suggested
rather the Sevillan type than a girl reared roughly in the
mountains ; and she had the confidence which only the
consciousness of beauty bestows upon its fortunate posses-
sors. Her strict rearing at the hands of Carmela had at the
same time given her a modesty of demeanour by no means
common in the present day, although general enough in
Carmela's girlhood, and this veil of modesty was shot
through with the golden threads of laughter and gaiety
which, at little more than the same age, had found Dolores
Moreno her husband.

" How I wish they would let me come and help you to
look after the fonda ! " breathed María, when the two
women, having concluded their embraces, sat down in the
patio.

" Ojalá ! " returned Dolores, with the smile that played
like lightning across her little ruined face. " One does not
wish for the moon ! "

" But why not ? It's not as though I were allowed to do
anything at home," pouted María. " Do you know, they
never even allow me to go into the tavern when there are
customers. I don't know what you think, but it seems to
me a very old-fashioned upbringing. I see plenty of girls
here doing things I'd never be allowed to do in the village :
going about in twos, for instance. Mamá never lets me off
the doorstep unless Carlota Ŕiba and her sister Paca come
for me."

" She knows two girls together can easily come to an
agreement," said Dolores, twinkling. " It's not so easy to
dispose of the third one ! That's the way we were brought
up ourselves. Ay-y ! If we so much as blinked an eyelash
in the wrong direction—— ! Have patience, niña ; when

you've got a novio he'll make things more agreeable for you."

"Well, there is Carlos Gallego," admitted María. "I think she would be very pleased if I were to marry him ; but mi papá knows I am not at all in love with Carlos. It's very difficult, all the same ; because I'm not allowed to talk to anyone but Carlos, and sometimes I really don't know what to say to him ! I don't mean to marry him, anyhow."

"Marriage for love is a very good thing," sighed Dolores, "but sometimes there are other things to be considered. It is really time you had a novio."

"I know ; but what is one to do ? And, besides, I don't really want to leave mi papá. Sometimes he looks so old——"

"And the tavern ? Is business good ? "

"I suppose so," said María indifferently. "Oh, yes, it must be good, because we've got a new counter, of marble, instead of the old wooden one; and we've got little tables and potted bamboos in the patio, and lots of foreigners come when they drive out to look at the church. I see them from the hen-loft."

"But you haven't fallen in love with any of them ? " said Dolores sharply. María shrugged her shoulders.

"What would be the good ? I'm never allowed near enough to talk to them. Ay, it's a dull life. I'd like to come down here for a while——"

"There's not much in Granada since the Republic," said Dolores, sighing. "Nobody seems to have any money— at least, the rich people won't spend it, and the others haven't got it to spend. Come in ; come in," she cried suddenly, to someone who stood, invisible to María, at the door. "What is it, niño ? Come and sit down. What were you wanting ? "

To the lively interest of María, a youth near her own age

came shyly into the patio, carrying under his arm a bundle,
of which, on seeing the two women, he seemed to become
painfully conscious. His bow to them both flung a lock of
hair across his brow—loose hair, with an unusual amount
of colour in it for boys of his nationality. A glint of chestnut
broke out of the darkness here and there, and the same red
gleam was in his eyes, which he modestly lowered to his
own shabbily shod feet. He had reached the half-way house
of adolescence, and the dignity of manhood was enhanced,
in his case, by an air of rather weary experience that contrasted with his apparent shyness. He stood upright and
faced them dumbly, not immediately availing himself of
the reiterated invitation of Dolores to take a chair.

" Is this the Casa Fermín ? " he asked. His tone sharpened Dolores's professional instinct, and she replied,
rather shortly :

" Sí, señor. Were you looking for a room ? " Her sharp
glance, travelling over him, decided that he could not even
afford to pay the modest terms of the Casa Fermín.

" No, señora." He bit his lip, looked sideways at María,
and continued : " I heard you were looking for a waiter.
I came to offer myself."

" Well," said Dolores, now settled into her role as dueña,
which hardened her little face and brought out its fleeting
likeness to her mother's. " That is quite right ; I am looking
for a waiter. But you seem to be very young. It is not an
easy place ; the hours are very long, and there is a good
deal of responsibility. What experience have you had ? "

" I have had a great deal of experience, señora," he
hastened to inform her. " I was at the Casa de Apolonio, in
Loja, for four years. They have a great deal of company
there. And the hours were long."

" Four years ! But you must have been a child when you
went there ! "

" I am now seventeen years of age, señora," he replied, with a great assumption of dignity. María's eyes sparkled ; just a year—or perhaps only a few months—younger than herself ! She had never come so closely into contact with an unknown youth, and she had already decided that he was very handsome, and that she hoped her aunt would engage him. A strong current of sympathy of youth for youth established itself between them as their eyes met. A searching catechism from Dolores kept Andrés fully occupied, in replying, in vaunting his own capacities, and, when necessary, in lying : for he did not wish to betray the fact that he had arrived in the town with the scrofulous little show, which he was sharp enough to realise would surely prejudice his future employer in his disfavour ; or to tell her that in a week or two he would be leaving her to take up his cabaret work. He was, as a matter of fact, very nearly down and out ; for a week he had been sleeping in alleys, begging crusts at restaurants, and keeping his aching stomach drugged by smoking the tobacco he had collected from derelict cigarette-ends, and rolled in scraps of news-paper. He could, very likely, have earned a peseta or two by entertaining the patrons of the taverns by a display of his art ; but he had a nervous horror of being recognised later, when he made his appearance at Las Estrellas—his pride jibbed at it. He was grateful for the chair Dolores had offered him, for he was very weak with lack of food, and he sat upright, striving to take in the lengthy description of his duties she poured upon him. Without the hardness or the acrimony of her mother or of Carmela, Dolores had a sound business sense, and, even to María, it became apparent she was driving a hard bargain. Andrés accepted it.

María was left alone, while her aunt took the new waiter into the dining-room and instructed him as to his duties, which began at once. "Wash all these tables and sweep the floor ; be sure the water is fresh in the bottles ; count the cutlery.—I'm a fool to take him," she announced, returning to María. "How do I know it's not all a parcel of lies—his having been at the Casa de Apolonio ? He isn't much like a waiter, is he ?—Niño ! " she cried, having felt in her pocket for money. "Go to the Casa Morales—do you know where it is ?—and buy yourself a white coat, to wait on the patrons. Tell them it is for Doña Dolores, and bring me back the bill.—And now, very likely," she said, as Andrés vanished, " we've seen the last of him ! Don't you dare to tell Carmela what a fool I am ! "

" I am quite certain he isn't dishonest ! " said María indignantly. "What good manners he has !—and what a nice voice ! He doesn't speak like the people here ; he shapes his words more carefully—like a gentleman ! "

" What do you know about gentlemen ? " teased Dolores. " And a nice voice and good manners won't pay for the plates he breaks ! He was just the age my Antonio would have been," she added, and put her hand to her head. " I don't know what it is—there is somebody he reminds me of——"

" How strange that you should see it ! " cried María. " I noticed it myself. Is it the way he walks ? " she added doubtfully. Her eye, trained by Aurelio in observation, had noticed a certain springing lightness in Andrés's step.

Dolores stared at her.

" It might be that. He certainly doesn't walk like a waiter. But—no ; it isn't his walk. It's something—something——" She made a gesture of brushing away a trouble-some thought. " I can't get hold of it. Wait here a little, hija ; I'm going to make some coffee. And I suppose there's no reason why I should not give the boy a bowl—if he comes back ! He looks to me as though he could do with it."

" There ! " said María, caressing her. " I always said you were as soft as a ripe fig ! " She felt she should offer to make the coffee instead of her aunt, but for some reason felt she could not forgo the possibility of seeing the youth again, on his return from the shop. She picked up the cat, and began to fondle it ; the clean little patio, with its ring of pot-plants round the little central fountain, had suddenly become a place of exciting possibility. María ran and turned the tap of the fountain, which suddenly spurted its thin silver jet a couple of metres into the air ; the gold-fish in the tiled basin stirred sluggishly.

It was thus that Andrés saw her when he returned : a girl and a fountain, two slender spires of grace—frail, evanescent, and sparkling. The tortoise-shell cat was outspread on the bosom of her black gown—both the women were in black for the death of the widow Herédia, which had taken place in early spring of the same year.

The two pairs of eyes met with a mutual recognition of loveliness. Each drew, visibly, a long breath ; each smiled. " Señorita——" began Andrés.

" I'm María López Moreno," she said quickly. " Doña Dolores is my aunt."

" Do you live here ? " he asked her, with an equal hastiness. Each was anxious, subconsciously, to get as much said as possible before the return of Dolores.

" Oh, no ! " she answered him. " I'm only in Granada for the day. I live in the mountains—in a village called Agujasierra ; have you heard of it ? "

" No ; nor of the lilies that blossom in the mountains," he came back at her, with true Andalucían grace. " One day, when I have a holiday, I must go into the mountains. I should like to see—Agujasierra ; with your permission, señorita ? "

María coloured and buried her face in the cat's fur ; but

her eyes gave the desired reply. It would not be easy,
though—if Carmela got to know ; if she heard María's
visitor was a camarero at her sister's lodging-house there
would certainly be a great deal of trouble ! As if it mattered—as if it meant anything. Hundreds of strangers came
to the López tavern ; it had even become, thanks to
Carmela's good management, quite a little Mecca for
tourists—for evening parties of the gay young Granada
bloods, who drove out there, with their novios and their
guitarristas, for an evening's merrymaking. " We keep a
tavern," she informed him hurriedly. " Everyone knows it
—on the corner of the market-square. Buenas tardes, señor,"
she added, as her aunt rejoined them, and Andrés hastily
turned to give Dolores the change and the bill.

" Yes, now you look more like a waiter," said the latter
briskly. " Go along and do your work—and you will find a
bowl of coffee and some bread waiting for you. And remember it is your duty to wait upon me as well as the
lodgers."

" Sí, señora," replied Andrés respectfully, making a little
bow. He had put on the white linen coat, and suddenly he
hated it. What bad luck he had—to appear before María
López for the first time in such menial attire ! The first
money he earned he would order a suit from one of those
tailors who let one buy by instalments—there were many
such in Granada.

" And when are you coming to see me again ? " Dolores
was asking over her coffee. María did not know, but it
would be as soon as possible. " You had better make it next
month, because it is the October feria, and you know
Nuestra Señora de las Angustias is being taken through the
streets ; it is the first time since the Republic was declared,
and a great many people think it is very dangerous and
should not be allowed. But who would touch the Blessed

Virgin ? It would bring ruin upon all Granada. Ask your
mother to let you come then, if not before, and we shall see
the procession together from one of the balconies."

On her way back with her father, by the new tramway
route which had replaced the old diligence to the Last Inn,
María shuddered and thrilled alternately over the prospect
of being visited by Andrés in her home. She could not
imagine what Carmela would say. She would certainly
want to know where María had made his acquaintance, and
would make unpleasantness for Dolores, if María told the
truth. Better to pretend she had never seen him before.
But why make a worry of it ? " When he had a holiday,"
he had said ; and, of course, waiters never had holidays.
She was quite safe—too safe, she acknowledged ruefully, as
she tucked her hand under Aurelio's arm.

" Is my little one tired ? " he inquired tenderly.

" When are we coming to Granada again, papá ? " she
asked instead of answering him.

" Now, let me see. Escribano, whom your mother wanted
me to see about that last order of La Riba wine, was not in
his house, so I shall almost certainly have to come again in
a few days—in a week or so," answered Aurelio. " How will
that suit you, my señorita ? "

María's cheeks flamed, and she squeezed her father's arm.

" And you'll make her let me come with you ? "

" What ? You like the streets and the tramlines and the
shop-windows better than the mountain paths ? " he teased
fondly.

" So long as I am with you, papá, it does not matter
where I am," she answered, with an equal fondness—quite
unaware of her own insincerity. The pleasure they took in
each other's company seemed to have grown deeper for the
restrictions now placed upon it. It was no longer possible
for María to accompany her father in all his travellings, but

this lent a precious excitement to the times they were together : to the rare occasions when, for instance, the Gallego
family planned an excursion to one of the mountain inns,
and invited Aurelio and his daughter to accompany them.
Such moments of delight were only spoilt, for María, by
the presence of Carlos Gallego, who utilised them to impress
his passion upon her with songs and sidelong glances—all
highly approved by his family, which was as anxious as
Carmela herself that Carlos and María should make a
match of it. But, because there were always plenty of
Gallego women on these outings, María usually found herself able to avoid any more pressing declarations of Carlos's
inconvenient love. She liked better to listen to her father's
explanations of the scenery than to Carlos's singing ; she
always contrived to sit next to Aurelio at the table where
they ate.

The chief part of the pleasure of coming to Granada,
apart from seeing her aunt Dolores, was the time she and
Aurelio spent alone together upon the journey ; but now,
for the first time in her life, she had a reason for wishing to
go in which her father had no part ; which, for this reason,
she could not share with him. She had always known it
would be a great blow to Aurelio when she found a novio.

But the depth of María's distress must be imagined rather
than gauged when, being brought again by Aurelio to her
aunt's house—which they usually visited on the way up to
Doña Marta's, to inquire at what hour Dolores could most
conveniently entertain her niece—their entrance was
barred by a stranger—by one of those elderly, sinister-look-
ing waiters one saw at the cafés—a personage whose soiled
white coat and baggy trousers exuded a kind of hopelessness
only too readily reflected in María's poor heart. He took a
cigarette out of his mouth to inform them that Doña
Dolores was sick in bed.

Hastily bidding farewell to her father, María ran down the passage to her aunt's room. As soon as decency allowed it, she said in a trembling voice :

" You've got another—he's *gone* ! " She concluded in tones of despair. Dolores, whose thick black-and-silver hair was scattered across the frilled pillow-case, who, in spite of it, looked more like a sixteen-year-old virgin than a woman shattered by her marital experience, made a gesture of inevitability.

" What did I tell you ? Your ' gentleman,' with the good manners and nice voice ! A great deal of consideration he showed me when the time came for him to look after his own affairs ! "

" Why ? What is it ? What happened ? " implored María. Her aunt looked at her wisely.

" Well, now—— ! So that's the way of things, is it ? And I suppose I'm expected to take part in it ? To act as the go-between and all that ? Get away with you ! I may not be as strict as Carmela, but I know what's right. Just listen to me. Your ' gentleman ' is simply a nobody. He doesn't even know who his parents are. He was brought up in a foundling hospital—not that one thinks less of him for that. We are what we make ourselves, and to be sure he is to be congratulated for his cleverness and the way he manages to earn his living. At least he isn't one of those idle good-for-nothings who live on honest, hard-working people."

" I beg you—tell me about it," implored poor María, certain now, as she had not been before, that she was in love.

" What an egoist you are—worrying me with your affairs when I'm helpless in my bed ! " grumbled Dolores, in pretended annoyance. María cast herself upon her aunt, stroking and murmuring and caressing until the elder woman was placated. " Where is he ? " she whispered, when Dolores's head lay in the angle of her shoulder, and her small, work-roughened hand was prisoned in María's own. Even in that attitude Dolores managed to achieve a shrug.

" If you ask me, he's fast asleep at the top of the house," was her astonishing answer. " You see—I'm always the fool ! Taking people in for charity—well, that's what it amounts to, the money he pays me. Only, of course, that little room was hardly ever let ; people do not care to climb so many stairs," she added, anxious to convince herself, as well as María, of her fundamental prudence. " One doesn't know what a boy of his age gets up to, if he hasn't a respectable bed to come to. And working at a place like that—— ! I was in two minds whether to have him when I knew about it. One can't keep an eye on all that goes on—this house has always been decent—God knows what mother would say—— ! " She ended incoherently.

" He's living here ! " María drew a deep breath of relief.

" And working at Las Estrellas—the new cabaret that has opened in opposition to La Montillana. I don't know what he does—it isn't a place where respectable women go," said Dolores virtuously. " I've told him if he wants to bring any of those girls home he must look for other lodgings. If one keeps a house of this kind one expects all sorts to go on, of course, and one knows when to shut one's eyes ; but I should certainly lose some good custom if the lodgers found that class of girl about the place."

" But what does he do ? Does he help with the music ? Is he a waiter ? " pressed María breathlessly.

" No, por Dios ! He tells me he sings songs—he sung one of them one night for us, and it was very amusing. Quite like being at the theatre ! Pobrecito ! It is a bad thing for a young man to have no mother. He is so clever, too ! What a pity he could not have had an education. Plenty of boys with only half his accomplishments are being trained for lawyers and schoolmasters. But he—all he wants is to be an actor, if you please ! To hear him recite poetry, and pieces from the plays, is to bring tears to the eyes."

A slow happiness was taking possession of María's heart. She had only the dimmest possible conception of social distinctions ; the classes in her own village were so faintly differentiated, and according to such subtle standards, which had nothing to do with money or possessions, that she was often puzzled when Carmela spoke of herself and her family as being infinitely their superior. She realised the difference in the degree of refinement between her grandmother's house and that of the Gallegos, but she knew that in Agujasierra the Gallegos were looked upon as one of the most important families. She felt, however, that, from Carmela's point of view, there would be a distinct difference between a waiter and an actor, and thought it might be possible, with tact and patience, to introduce a rival to Carlos Gallego.

While she was in her aunt's room, Andrés, who, as Dolores said, had been sleeping—small blame to a person who sleeps until noon, when he has finished his work only a little before dawn starts to whiten the roofs—was wakened by the waiter who brought up his coffee. This luxury, to which he was not entitled, he owed to Dolores, whose thwarted motherhood reached out to the motherless youth, and treated him in most respects as the rest of her lodgers were treated, although the sum he paid her was less than half of theirs. The room he occupied was very empty, very squalid, but to Andrés it represented luxury. He had not known a room of his own in all his life ; nor, since leaving the orphanage that educated him, had he slept in a bed. The only thing of beauty that the room contained was, strangely enough, a possession of Andrés's which, through all the rough and tumble of his career, he had managed to preserve fairly intact. It had often been a nuisance to him. He had several times been tempted to leave it behind in his wanderings ; but some motive of sentiment or superstition had always ended in his tucking it under his arm, rolled in the bundle of his garments, and now, for the first time, he had a place in which to put it.

He had been told, at the orphanage, that his mother had left it with him ; that it was found with him in the revolving cradle in the wall of the foundling hospital where mothers deposited their unwanted children : the old painting on glass of La Divina Pastora, the Virgin of the Fields. Only a miracle could have preserved it during Andrés's travels ; a crack ran across it from corner to corner, but the deliciously absurd drawing of the Mother and Child, in beflowered hats—with lambs, that, poised in air against a background of magenta, nibbled at flowers the size of cabbages—remained complete. Its bright colouring met Andrés's eyes when he awoke ; he was not sentimental about the mother he had never known, but he gained a certain optimism from seeing it there.

The gossip of the waiter accounted for Andrés's hurried rising, and for the fact that, when María crossed the patio from her aunt's room, to carry some message to the servants, he was waiting there. She hardly recognised him, at first sight, in his new suit of striped grey, his smart shoes, his butterfly tie, and the wave he had put in his hair for his work at the cabaret. A young man of elegance and sophistication, such as she had never seen the like, bade her a shy though confident good morning with all the aplomb of previous acquaintanceship.

" Oh—it is you ! " gasped María, when she had recovered from her shock. He smiled more broadly, and advanced towards her.

" Yes, you are quite right ; this is really *I*," he told her. " The other wasn't ; the other was just—a joke." It was as though a prince doffed his disguise before her startled gaze. " I have been wondering when you would come again."

" Well, you haven't been to Agujasierra," pouted María, regaining her own aplomb.

" No ; but I am coming—very soon. I and some friends are arranging to come out one morning and eat at your house," he told her boldly.

" Oh—be careful ! " she gasped, taken aback by the definiteness of the suggestion.

" What of ? Have you a dog ? Is it savage ? " he taunted her. " Surely that is very bad for the business of a tavern ? "

" No ; but I am not allowed—my mother does not allow me—to talk to the people who come into the tavern," she stammered.

" We must think of something to please her. If I bring her a present—a pot of flowers ? "

" She would wonder what you meant. Please do not do anything—strange," gasped María. He drew closer to her, drawn by her beauty and her distress.

" I would not for the world do anything you did not like. I want—always—only to do the things that please you. You are quite right. What does your mother want with a pot of flowers when she has you ? Tell me, have you a novio ? "

" What do you think ? " replied María, instantly the coquette. His face became so white that she relented. " There is a boy in our village—my mother is very anxious——"

" Do you love him ? " His fingers pressed her like steel.

" Why do you want to know ? "

" Because ever since seeing you I have never thought about anyone else. Listen. The other night I made this up for you :

" ' Yo cubriría su cama de un lecho de pétalos de rosas, en el cual su cuerpo desnudo daría envidia á las flores por su pureza y elegancía. Cuerpo el suyo digno de ser modelado á besos por los propios ángeles. Quien fuera angel ! ' "

Her head swam ; she felt the hot words, muttered with youthful emotion, pouring over her like the petals of the roses invoked by Andrés. Her heart passed from her keeping.

CHAPTER II

WAR BETWEEN WOMEN

Was it true, then, that Carmela was out of her mind? He had thrust back the thought whenever her fits of passion and senseless backbiting forced it upon him. For in between these fits she was capable of such exaggerations of tenderness, such acts of reparation, that she shamed his anger and his infrequent reprimands of her injustice to himself and María. The painful oscillation of her nature between its two extremes sickened him, called upon his deepest pity, and awakened in him a sense of heavy responsibility towards her ; for he regarded it as a sickness, as symptomatic of the changes which he knew must be taking place in her body.

It seemed outrageous that no doctor could prescribe for such a state of affairs, and that Carmela must, for an unspecified number of years, suffer this penalty of her sex, aggravated by the idiosyncrasies of her own nature. And, try as he might to shut his eyes to it, it had become impossible any longer to ignore the fact that the condition of Carmela's mind was affected by the presence of María in a way that spelt ruin to all their lives. A single incident opened Aurelio's eyes to the fact that he had eventually to make his choice between an absent daughter and an insane wife.

She and her mother had passed a peaceable enough morning on the day the thing—the dreadful, definite thing that forced Aurelio's hand—took place. They had these moments of approach, largely owing to María's cool,

healthy-minded acceptance of a situation which was not
to be avoided. María's childish dislike of her mother had
passed into a calm indifference ; secretly, she had come to
the conclusion, years ago, that Carmela was quite mad.
So long as she could keep her outbursts of insanity focused
upon herself she was satisfied ; when they were extended
to include Aurelio they became unendurable to her, and
she ran away to indulge her angry tears, the pain she
shared with her father. She had the wit to realise that her
presence only acted as fuel to her mother's rage while it
continued, and that she could do nothing to palliate it.
Time had taught her a great cunning in dealing with
Carmela ; a high-spirited girl, gay, self-assertive, and
candid in her expressions of feeling and opinion, she knew
exactly what would give rise to an outbreak of Carmela's
evil demon, and developed a form of duplicity that often
saved an awkward situation. She was housewifely, and
conventionally religious ; these two things gave her
grounds on which to meet her mother in a fashion which
would at least have convinced the casual observer.

On the day it happened, María had helped her mother
to count the household articles which the laundress collected and bore in a head-bundle down to the stream. She
and Carmela together had washed their body-linen, and
laid it to dry on the flat stones of the patio, which had
been scoured by one of the servants Carmela now kept to
relieve her of the heavier part of the housework.

Carmela had then proceeded, in the old-fashioned way,
to oil her daughter's hair, pressing and kneading the
golden bubbles of oil into the roots of the long, virile
tresses that sprang in an arch above María's broad, low
brow. " That's the way to prevent the hair from going
white when one gets older," she said grimly. " Look at
Dolores ! She was always too lazy, as a girl, to have her hair

oiled, and look at it now ! And here am I, years older, without a grey hair in my head." María thought, but was too wise to remark, that she admired her aunt's hair, with the two wide bands of white that ran parallel across the crown of her lovely little head. She herself had had ideas of cutting her hair, in accordance with the fashions of Granada, but Carmela had slapped her for suggesting it. " None of that nonsense under my roof ! " María wondered what she would have said if she had taken it into her head to peroxide her hair, as a great many young Granadinas were doing ! That, indeed, was an ugly fashion ; the yellow hair did not go with the deep, olive skins and colourless complexions of the majority of the girls. And how ugly when the black showed through the yellow, which it did very soon ! No, María did not wish to be a rubia ; she was very well, in her own as well as other people's estimations, as she was.

The two women then took it in turns to stir the stew, which they sat down together to eat when Aurelio came in at noon. It was a good stew, having as its foundation all the odds and ends of ham Carmela saved from the sides she served to her customers, with little bits of sausage to add further flavour : thickened with beans, with macaroni, and with bread ; there were cockles in it, pimientos, and the indispensable onion. Into each individual platter Carmela broke the yolk of an egg, and, while María was beating up the white, she poured the soup upon the yolks, stirring quickly, to prevent their setting. A squeeze of lemon, a glass of wine in each plate, and the whipped white folded into the whole—a dish for a king ! It was to be followed by little cold birds, which had been stewing for days in wine. Acting on her mother's tradition, Carmela kept a much better table, now she could afford it, than any of her neighbours.

For she was, by now, as local standards had it, a rich

person. The fall of the monarchy had not affected, had
even improved, her business. People seemed to be drinking
more, to forget their troubles, their confiscated lands, the
steadily rising tide of taxation that threatened to swamp
their remaining means. During the summer she had done
excellent business—when the town taverns languished, and
the gay young sparks of Granada compounded with their
friends the chauffeurs to drive them and their girl friends
out to the country for the night. Carmela had begun by
wondering what she should do about these ambiguous
parties. She was no fool ; the epithets for the hard-faced
women who were brought out by these foolish young men
came readily to her tongue. But she also knew that parties
of this kind meant lavish spending ; that the desire to cut
a dash in front of the town girls and of each other was the
finest inducement to spending that could be offered to the
young bloods of Granada. She had heard of tavern-keepers
who entered into contract with the girls themselves : she
would not do that. There was María to think of—María
who, with nightfall, was forbidden the threshold of the
tavern—and at least half of her clients were respectable.
It did not do to mix respectability with the other thing ;
but there was no reason why one should not profit, as far
as was compatible with the dignity of the house, from the
easier morals of some of one's customers.

She had made many improvements in the property ; the
new counter, with its top of brown and white marble, had
replaced the old wooden bench on which, on one memor-
able occasion, Aurelio had wreaked his rage with her. The
glasses, instead of being piled in the sink, were now ranged
in glittering rows on shelves of plate glass—a great extravagance, for which she had trembled ; but she had seen
such an arrangement in a tavern in Granada and could not
forbear emulating it. She had given *carte blanche* to a local

painter to decorate the walls with horrible little friezes and medallions that seemed to her the apex of refinement, and framed pictures cut from the catalogues of wine-merchants had replaced the old, dirty bull-fight posters—which she had sold to an American aficionado at a price satisfactory to both parties. Now and again she brought out from the fábrica in Granada a few plates, which were sold to tourists at a profit for Carmela ; she also undertook to dispose of shawls for one or two of the dealers, and succeeded in making enough on them to repay her for her efforts. No means of gaining money was too insignificant to attract her ; she played her game of finance with the skill and absorption of a chess-player ; her thoughts, waking and sleeping, were of the steadily mounting balance in the Banco de Crédito. It was known she had all kinds of negocios " on the side " ; that she was always the person to approach for advice in matters of business ; that the cacique himself did not think it beneath him to go to Carmela Moreno for information ; that no one ever got the better of her in a bargain ; that she knew when to give a present and exactly what to expect in return for it. Neither was she backward in extending inexpensive charity to the poor ; there were always people who tried to get employment at the Casa López, although Carmela was known to be a hard taskmistress.

She had grown to be, in short, a leading figure in Aguja-sierra, that town of mañana, of *laissez-faire*. The rumours of her evil tempers only lent force to her character, in whose shadow moved that gentle, grey figure of her husband, the rich and bounteous one of her daughter María.

It so happened, upon this day, that when Carmela offered him bread, Aurelio, with his mind on other matters, refused. María had gone to fetch the pot of olives, and, on her return, seeing that her father had no bread beside his platter, she broke off and offered him, in all innocence, a twist of the loaf. Equally innocently, Aurelio accepted it, bit into it, and smiled lovingly at María as he chewed his mouthful.

Neither was prepared for Carmela's action, although, as she sprang to her feet, they turned quickly towards her, remindful, as always in her presence, of their guarded love. But their mild embarrassment quickened into horror as they saw that Carmela had snatched up a knife, and was making hideous movements with it towards her own person. Her eyes rolled up until there was little visible of them save the whites, and froth appeared between the clenched teeth bared by her empurpled lips. With a smothered shout, Aurelio leapt from his chair and seized her wrist. She struggled, and began screaming like a madwoman :

" So you will eat from her hand, will you ? And not from mine ? Holy Mother of God, see how I am scorned at my own table ! " As María, horrified, came to her father's assistance, and caught one of her mother's arms in her young, strong clasp, she added : " Take your hands off me— interloper ! Keep your hands for the one who gave you birth ! I have nothing to do with you ! "

After a short, ugly struggle Aurelio mastered her ; María, with a pale look, had fled to the loft. The food grew cold on the table, while Aurelio held Carmela down on their bed and sought for words to penetrate the barrier of her obsession. They came suddenly—out of space. Afterwards he wondered what devil prompted him to speak them—the vile words that betrayed his beloved : " Be calm ; María shall go away for a little while."

He must have been mad—madder than Carmela. He felt her relax under his hands ; the softening of her tense muscles almost into seductiveness. The contortion of her face smoothed itself away, so that he was no longer holding a devil or a virago, but a pliant woman, who looked up at him with eyes full of voluptuous submission, and who murmured, " You hurt me, Aurelio mío, the way you are holding me."

He loosed her in bewilderment, and her hand immediately caught his. Her eyes closed, as though, on the heels of her frenzy, sleep overcame her. But he knew this trick of Carmela's of taking refuge behind closed lids to work out some dark scheme of her own. If I had first cut out my tongue ! She would now leave him no peace until he had ratified his words. Yet, as though that same devil now assumed complete control of his organs of speech, he found himself reiterating the fatal syllables : " Yes—yes, she shall go away." The best—the safest for them all : but more particularly for her, the innocent cause of the trouble. He heard Carmela murmuring that María must stay at home and find herself a husband. Behind that deceitful murmur he could hear the voice of her thoughts : " Yes, yes, send her away ! Get rid of her ! Let the two of us be together in peace, for Christ's sake. That is what you owe to me, your wife." And weakly he felt himself submitting to this silent, fierce demand of Carmela's, felt the slow strangulation of his will by hers, which had fought so long for ascendancy over him.

" But where should she go, Aurelio mío ? " Carmela was now saying, in the soft voice of appeased passion. Her voice sounded exactly as it had sounded sometimes after he had been loving her ; he realised with a thrill of horror that she had actually extracted some morbid kind of sensual satisfaction out of the scene that was past. For a moment he hated her completely. It was because she knew she had gained her victory that she could now speak of María as though she had not a thought of the girl that was not dictated by maternity. She knew—none better—that, with his mind once made up, Aurelio would carry out at all costs the promise he had given. With a soft, diabolical duplicity she now began to insist upon the impossibility of María's leaving home. She pretended to oppose the idea, so that, through his insistence, her triumph might be the greater ; so that all the responsibility should rest upon him. For the first time in his life, sober, Aurelio knew the desire to strike, to batter—even, for an instant, to murder her. His mind recoiled, and a groan broke from his lips. The harshness of his words, far from wounding her, sent a thrill of satisfaction through her body. " It is done, woman. The thing is done."

But it was not done. For many torturous weeks he puzzled and agonised over the problem of putting his words into effect. And throughout his life Aurelio was never to forget or forgive the way in which, when all was settled, when the victim of their plotting had been informed of her fate, Carmela came to him, weeping bitterly, imploring him, with a sincerity beyond question, to let the matter drop. In her contrition she even knelt to him, to find him, for the second time in their married life, implacable.

In the meantime he had talked with María.

" You could not, my treasure, marry Carlos Gallego ? " He spoke tentatively, and for the first time openly, on the subject which, for many months, had been stirring Aguja-sierra as a wood is stirred by a breeze ; everyone knew Carlos Gallego was after María López.

She raised to his eyes sullenly beautiful, as though she accused him of siding against her ; she knew she could never love anyone but Andrés, but so twisted into the fibres of her being was her love for her father, so conquered was she by his broken look of an old man, that she flung her arms about him.

" It is for you to say, papá mío," she whispered, making a supreme act of daughterly duty. At that moment María, who was a very ordinary and, in a few ways, selfish young woman, felt herself capable of any sacrifice, if it would bring back a little happiness to her father's face.

" Calla ! " he said, stroking her head with a hand that trembled. " What does thy father want save thy happiness ? You and Carlos are not in love ? "

" *He !* " She shrugged her shoulders upon the emotions of the unhappy Carlos. " For me, I'd as soon marry Paco Tuerto."

" Now, now ! Carlos is buena persona, and his people are the best in the town," said Aurelio wistfully.

" Como tu quieres." She shrugged again. " So I must marry myself ? That is *her* idea ? " They were, for once, alone ; Carmela had gone marketing. Seizing him by the arms, María cried passionately : " What is it, papá mío ? Tell me—for the love of God don't tell me a lie about it : am I her daughter and yours, or am I not ? "

" Por Dios ! What is this ? What lies have you heard ? Let me meet the author of them, and I will strangle him with these very hands ! " cried Aurelio.

" You heard it, papá—*she* said it. ' Interloper—keep your hands for the one who gave you birth.' It wouldn't go out of my head."

" Why did you not ask me before ? "

" Why should she say it if it is not true ? " countered María, with something of Carmela's own steely obstinacy.

" She did not know what she was saying. One cannot tell the reason of a woman's ramblings when she is sick, like your mother. You must forget it, my precious, my darling."

For all her common sense, however, and her usual philosophical acceptance of her mother's ravings, María's nerves had been so shocked by the scene with the knife that she was unable to dismiss the subject from her mind.

" What have I done," she cried, " to make her always like this with me ? Of course, I know, it is natural women should be jealous of one another. But a mother of her daughter ? That's a bad thing, an unnatural thing. Why don't you speak to me, papá mío ? Speak to me as though I were thyself—as you used to do when I was little. She is jealous of me ; well, what are we going to do about it ? Things can't go on in this way. I might just as reasonably be jealous of her, because you are always so gentle and so good to her ; but I am not. If God had given me brothers and sisters, I think I might have been jealous of them—if you had seemed to love them the way you love me."

" Foolish one. If you had had a dozen brothers and sisters, I should not have cared for the whole lot of them together as I care for the tip of your little finger. One day," said Aurelio heavily, " I shall pray you to forgive me. . . ."

Their eyes met : and in hers he saw a look dawn that he had never seen there before : a look of ignorant and naked fear. He saw her moisten her lips ; her eyelids flickered, and the look was gone ; she could not be afraid of him, her father, in whom all her trust and confidence were rooted. She caught at his hand.

" Never mind, papá mío ! We are always so happy together ; we have always got each other, and, for me, that is enough. So long as I need not marry Carlos Gallego. Certainly I don't want that, though, if you told me to, I'd marry him. After all, it would hardly be like going away ; we could see just as much of one another as ever——"

The sore temptation came to Aurelio to take her at her word : to command her to marry Carlos Gallego and have done with it. But, as a man and as an Agujasierran, he

knew what he knew. Carlos Gallego might belong to the
only family that the López acknowledged to be their equals
in the town, but they were a sickly lot ; they had " the
cough " ; generation after generation succumbed to it.
And as for Carlos, neither his family nor occasional bouts
of sickness prevented him having much more to do with
the girls of the town than was good for him. How could
he offer up his María to such a marriage ?

" But you cannot continue to stay with me all your life,
hija mía," he said, with his loving hand upon her head.
" A time will come—a bad time for us both, but worse
for your father—when nature will have its way. What
then ? " Still his courage failed at the prospect of telling
her that he had already betrayed her. María gave a little
laugh.

" That is mañana," she replied, using the word which
may mean to-morrow or the indefinite future. And she
also thought of the way in which she had betrayed her
father's love, and a little shadow fell between them. They
were conscious, for the first time, of being *two*, instead of
the indivisible one which all their lives together had helped
to consolidate. Aurelio began to speak clumsily, with his
head turned away.

" It is not good for my little girl to spend all her life
up here in the mountains ; she must go among other
people, learn other ways."

" Why, papá ! I thought you had always said there was
nothing in the world like the mountains ! That the most
important thing was to be up there, alone—with God ! "
cried María, startled.

" That is for when one grows old, when one has learnt
the little value of earthly things," replied Aurelio. He
caught her arm almost roughly. " Thou hast always obeyed
thy papá, isn't that so, little one ? "

" Are you sending me away ? " she whispered, her lips blanching.

" Listen, hija. For many years—for all the years of your life, which is sacred to me—I have put your good before my own and hers ; I have done things which to you have seemed strange, but behind them all was the guiding hand of your father's love. Now you are a woman ; you no longer need my hand to help you to walk. And there are things you do not know about as yet, that lie in silence between people who are married : things that sooner or later rise up and make their claim, whether one wills it that way or no. For a while my duty is to her, towards your mother : and you must have patience."

" Madre mía ! " wailed María. " What is to become of me ? "

" Come now, can you not trust your father ? " said Aurelio reproachfully. " If you were not at home, where would you most like to be ? " he asked her, with a dreary attempt to lighten the heaviness of the atmosphere. María checked her tears to consider.

" With my aunt Dolores," she answered eventually ; but her head went down, to hide a burning blush. Even in this most simple and truthful answer she was deceiving him.

" And did you think your father did not know the answer to his question before it was given ? We shall see what can be arranged."

Overcome by her feelings, María leapt at him and began kissing him. Taken aback by her enthusiasm, Aurelio caught and held her away from him, to look into her sparkling eyes.

" So it's that way ! Doña Dolores has stolen away my girl's love from her father ! Who would ever have suspected such treachery ! "

" No—no ! " gasped María ; she stammered, flung back

her head, and made up her mind. " No, papá mío. Please
don't be angry with thy María—I will tell thee all !
Andrés—next Sunday——"

Her confession flowed from her on a flood of incoherence.
Aurelio sat as though turned to stone. So it had come at
last ! She had gone from him. He found himself thinking
of her as though she were dead, and of this unknown youth
who had stolen her heart from him as though he were her
murderer.

But when, later on, Carmela knelt to him, he told her
certain things in a cold voice of resolution.

" It is arranged. There is no more to be said."

" Por Dios, what is arranged ? " cried Carmela, with
tears of mortification streaking down her face. She dried
them with her skirt, still on her knees, but her spirit had
sprung upright, was again in opposition to him. " What
can be arranged in such a manner ? No good comes of
things that are done in a hurry. Don't forget there is her
grandmother to be consulted ! I don't want trouble made
with my side of the family—they can be very useful if they
are not offended." She scrambled to her feet and stood
facing him with an ugly expression of enmity. " Do you
want to make a scandal ? If you persist in this notion that
María needs a change—heaven knows what put it into
your head—there is no reason why she should not go down
to Granada for a week or two. My mother will be glad
of the extra help, because María Pepa is expecting another
baby——"

Aurelio smote the table with the flat of his open hand.

" Our daughter is our daughter. No grandmother in the
world has anything to do with the affairs of my house.
Cease to molest me, woman, with your changes of time
and tune. I know the words, the steps I must take. Santa
Madre de Dios ! Have I not given in to you ? Have I not

deprived myself of my very flesh and blood for your sake, and have you the insolence to demand more sacrifice ? Am I to give this flesh of my flesh, this blood of my blood, to your mother, so that it is no longer in the least sense my own ? "

She was silenced by his outburst. She stood there, twisting her apron, while his head sank on his arm ; presently she said, in her mildest, most falsely submissive tone :

" What is it, then, you have thought of doing ? "

He answered :

" She is going, for the present, to your sister Dolores."

" Jesú María Santísima ! " breathed Carmela slowly. She stooped to peer into Aurelio's face, as though unable to credit her own hearing. " Is it that something has sent you out of your mind ? Are you drunk ? Or dreaming ? Do I understand you to say that María is going to live among strangers ? After the way she has been brought up, never allowed out of our sight for a minute, never sleeping a night out of her own home ? You'll send her to live in a common lodging-house, among men—and my brother-in-law Luis no better than he should be where women are concerned ? "

He looked at her with a deadly expression, and remained for a few moments silent. Then :

" Woman," he said, " there are times when the remembrance of my duty to you is like the pricking of a goad. Take care of the ass's heels when the point sticks in too far."

" Ay-ay ! " cried Carmela, too excited to heed the warning. The old, smouldering resentment against her sister Dolores, she who had been the first to get married, who had aggravated her sisters with her (relatively) flighty ways as a girl, and who still annoyed Carmela at their every meeting by some indefinable levity that should, heaven

HM

knew, have been knocked out of her by her experiences, burst into flame. " That Dolores ! It is not for one to speak ill of one's own sister, but how is she fit to take charge of a girl of María's age ? Running that fonda—that houseful of men—with heaven knows who running in and out all night long ! A place very little better than a brothel ! Oh, I don't blame Dolores for it ! When she is sick in bed, who is to know what goes on ? And how is she to keep an eye on a girl like María, up to all sorts of pranks and ready to give herself away to the first rapscallion who makes eyes at her ? She thinks herself too good for Carlos Gallego, but I know the young lady ! No ; for once I assert myself ; I am not to be ordered by you in a matter that concerns my own family ! If the girl goes anywhere, she goes to her grandmother, where she will be looked after strictly, as we were when we were girls, and where she has a chance of meeting the proper sort of young men——"

" It is arranged ; she goes to Dolores."

" What ? You have been plotting with my sister behind my own back ? I will have justice for this ! I will go to Granada myself ! María shall stay here. What would the neighbours say ? What would everybody think, if she went to the Casa Fermín, after the way I've kept her out of the tavern ? She might as well go to a house of ill-fame and have done with it——"

" Quiéta ! " roared Aurelio. " The neighbours can be told the truth—the whole truth."

" And who is going to believe the truth ? Isn't the truth the last thing anyone pays attention to ? "

" Think of it any way you will," said Aurelio, recovering his self-possession. " The thing is done ; nothing will alter it. For the sake of the peace of this house, María goes to Granada. Listen, Carmela. Twenty-five years ago we were two, you and I. God joined us, and we became one. That is to say, there is but one body, one soul, between us. Whether or not we desire it, that is the way of things. That which the one suffers the two must suffer. To live with suffering is to live in a diseased air ; is the disease to be passed on to one innocent ? You cry to me. You tell me you are suffering. There is no need for you to do that, because I know it. How can I fail to know it, when I am joined to you in the mystical body and flesh of our coming together ? I, because I am the stronger, can pull the roots of suffering out of your body ; but just as a tooth, after it is pulled out, leaves pain behind, so I shall suffer, and so must you suffer, because I am part of you. Only our suffering will not be shared by another. It is not seemly that youth should learn the meaning of suffering, because suffering is evil, and acts like a canker which twists the young bough. *She goes*."

The storm, once spent, was succeeded by one of Carmela's phases of mildness and placability towards both Aurelio and María. Although she continued to shake her head over María's going to the Casa Fermín, and actually sat down and filled several pages with a long letter to Dolores, up-braiding her for having conspired with Aurelio behind her back, and adding as many instructions about María as though the latter had been a babe in arms, incapable of looking after herself, she wasted no further moments in reproaching either of them. All those impure depths of her being that held the secret desire to get the girl out of the house seethed with a dark triumph, but she kept it under control.

As for María, she alternated between wild fits of high spirits at the incredible thought of being under the same roof with Andrés, and fits of weeping at her approaching parting from Aurelio. She was like an April day, veering between sunshine and storm ; yet she succeeded in concealing both of these moods from Carmela, to whom she presented a dutifully cool exterior, agreeing ironically with Carmela when the latter said to her, " See what a fortunate girl you are ! What some of your friends would give for your opportunities "—which was perfectly true. The Riba girls, and the younger sisters of Carlos, were openly envious. That María López ! She had all the luck. Ay, what they would give to be going to live in Granada ! " For how long ? " " Vaya, tonta ! Until she has found a novio, of course. Pobrecito Carlos ! It is to be hoped he will console himself." " That you may be sure he will," retorted one of Carlos's sisters, tossing her head. " There are plenty of girls waiting with their mouths wide open for Carlos to drop into them ! " So the conversations ran under the clump of olive-trees a little way up the hill-side, where, in the evening, the younger girls were wont to collect and giggle and gossip : while María's cheeks flamed. She had not confided in any of them, partly for fear the news would reach her mother, but she longed to tell them about the wonderful young man she had found, beside whom Carlos Gallego seemed even more stupid and unattractive than she had always considered him.

When, on the following Sunday, a party of young men arrived just before noon, with such excellent and formal manners that even Carmela was impressed, María, scared out of her life, fled to the little bedroom which, since she grew up, she had occupied. It opened out of her parents', and had no means of egress save through theirs. Although it had no window or other means of ventilation save its doorway, across which a curtain was drawn, María did not seem to suffer from her nocturnal incarceration.

The party, which consisted, of course, of Andrés and his

friends, ordered chicken and wine : an order which kept
Carmela busy, for she always saw to the cooking herself.
Knowing her mother was in the kitchen, María rushed
across her parents' bedroom, one window of which, through
a miniature reja, looked into the tavern, beyond which was
the patio. She had to clap her hands over her mouth to
keep from laughing at the sight she saw there : of the four
youths, sitting primly at a table among the potted bamboos,
so stiff, so self-conscious, and, she knew, so taken aback to
find her presence totally denied them ! Andrés had his back
to her ; her heart leapt at the sight of the smoothly cropped
back of his head, the soft bit of neck that appeared above
his immaculate collar.

There were several people in the tavern, and they kept
interrupting her view ; also she was afraid that she would
be seen spying between the bars. She bit the tips of her
fingers, wondering what she could do. Aurelio was in the
tavern, talking with Pulgar and the other men. She hissed
sharply through the reja, and dodged out of sight before
the heads were turned. Aurelio came to the little window ;
her little face glowed like a rose through the iron frame.

" Papá ! He is there ! In the patio ! " She bit her lip
with excitement. " The one in the striped suit of clothes—
with his back to us. Oh, papá, couldn't I—couldn't I —— ? "
Couldn't she—what ? She herself did not know. So strongly
was she imbued with Carmela's scale of proprieties it would
have covered her with shame to have walked, unsupported
by another woman, into that stronghold of masculine pre-
rogative, the tavern, when there were strangers present.

She saw Aurelio look sharply across his shoulder ; saw
him dismiss her with a movement of the hand ; and shrank
back, panting, against the wall. Her father would do something—something !

When she next stole a glance, Aurelio was standing by

the table of young men. She saw that Andrés had risen to speak to him—significant gesture of respect from a young man to the father of his prospective novia ! They were talking ; presently the pair of them strolled together into the tavern. Aurelio was inviting Andrés to take a glass of wine ; Andrés was making the usual polite refusal, preliminary to acceptance. They were both standing by the counter, Aurelio with his back to the little reja, Andrés facing it. It was her opportunity !

Andrés, making agreeable conversation with the man who was his mistress's father, saw, incredulously, a white hand slip through the reja : the glass, raised to drink, remained motionless in his hand ; his sentence broke in half ; he was unheedful of the close, sad scrutiny of his companion as he looked towards the little window, where, for a moment, fleeting as a dream, María smiled at him—and then slipped away.

It was his only glimpse of her. Some might have thought it was a long journey to have made for so little reward ; Andrés burned, but he was content.

" I suppose you know," said Carmela to Aurelio sharply, when they were in bed, speaking in a whisper so as not to be overheard by María, " that that young man is a lodger of Dolores ? You see what kind of thing we may expect when María goes down to Granada." As Aurelio did not reply, she pushed him with her elbow. " Well, what did you think of him ? I saw you walking up the hill-side, after the meal, together. You had plenty of opportunity of talk."

" After a meal a man wants to sleep rather than to talk," he answered evasively.

" At that age ! " Her retort was scornful. He grunted and turned over. He did not wish to talk, himself. That boy. Buena persona. And serious. But there was something . . . something . . .

CHAPTER III

YOUNG LOVE

THE LIFE OF ANDRÉS swung upon a thin thread, attached somewhere in illimitable space, between the civilisations and formalities of the Casa Fermín (not that these amounted to much) and the haphazard existence of the cabaret. He now had clothes—respectable ones—and a bed, his professional vanity, and his love for María López. Otherwise he was one of the drifting thousands of young Spaniards who deceive the eye with their smart appearance and their excellent manners, worn with careless aplomb over under-nourished bodies. In the well-cut pockets are rarely more than a few centimos : just enough for a cup of coffee and a shoe-shine. Their friends the waiters are as courteous to them as to other customers ; threepence is enough to assure them of an hour, or two or three, at the tables in the shade ; a cigarette gracefully extracted from the full packet of a wealthier friend lasts a surprisingly long time, smoked with elegance and art, as the Spaniard smokes it.

The only way in which Andrés differed from the majority was in his desire and resolution to get on in life ; it was not sufficient for him to indulge in golden dreams, to pin his faith to the lottery ; he was willing to put both physical and mental effort into the act of advancement—but, like all whose ambition takes the form his did, he found it bitterly difficult to know where or how to direct his energies. Granada was certainly not the town to provide him with opportunities, and it was not easy, on his pittance from the cabaret, to save money for the railway fare to Madrid. Las Estrellas was not proving the success its dueño had hoped ; its rival, the older established La Montillana, continued to draw upon the relatively small section of Granada society that had the money or taste for that kind of thing ; every night there were more empty than occupied tables, the girls were melancholic, the atmosphere half-hearted. It took Andrés all his will-power to put his stuff across in such unpromising surroundings.

What hope was there, either, of his ever gaining the consent of María's parents to their marriage ? And it was clear enough they would not accept the easier relationship. Marriage was not a thing that had ever entered into his calculations so far, but he had, through his contacts with the López, had a baffling glimpse of standards other than his own, the standards of people who complicated their lives by all kinds of rules and regulations of which Andrés could not perceive the reason, but which he tried to understand because they governed his María's life. He realised, already, that he could not ask her bluntly to come away with him, or treat her easily, as he had treated other girls. Their relationship was " una cosa seria," difficult to amalgamate in the rest of his life, and infinitely difficult to live up to. It would have surprised María had she known how difficult Andrés found it. There were moments when it was almost a relief to relax in the company of the cabaret girls —to indulge the loose habits of speech and epithet which María did not understand, to be permitted familiarities he knew he must never attempt with María. But he was crazily in love with her, and driven to distraction by the obstacles raised by Dolores Moreno between him and his love.

The family had their own private sitting-room, and here, in a darkness of plush-seated furniture, old enlarged photographs of Don Luis's parents, a forest of artificial flowers, some under glass sheaths, others dustily exposed, María was obliged to pass most of her time. She had only the radio for amusement, since she could not play the old piano whose top was crowded with ornate little vases and photographs of Dolores's family at various stages of their careers. Her own photograph was there, very shiny and glassy-eyed, the face seemingly swollen with the effort to keep utterly still during the operation. Andrés was never allowed there.

Her bedroom, also on the ground floor, was next door to her aunt's, and, every night when María had gone to bed, Dolores locked the door and took the key away with her. In one way or another, María did not find her life in Granada so vast an improvement upon her life at home, save that, when she went out, there was more to amuse her. She had made delirious acquaintance of the kinema, seated, always, strictly at the end of a row, with her uncle's and aunt's bodies interposed between her and any adventurous neighbour ; she loved strolling, as her mother had done, up and down the Zácatin ; she found it exciting to drink coffee out of doors, listening to a band ; and she enjoyed walking in the gardens of the Generalife on Sundays. But there were long hours indoors, which hung very heavy on María, since she had almost nothing to do with herself, had not the habit of reading, and was not allowed to help very much in the house. These she filled with letters to her father, writing almost every day, although Aurelio came down to see her faithfully each week. She and Dolores had talked themselves out on the subject of the state of affairs at her home, and had both agreed that no good end was to be served by telling the grandmother about it. Doña Marta had come down in a fine state of excitement on the day she learned that María was living with Dolores.

" Now what is all this about ? Who is responsible for making all these arrangements without telling me about them ? " she wheezed, her fan beating the black shelf of her bosom with irritation.

" Well, now, mamá, you know how hard I have found it to get on by myself," said Dolores placatingly. " It is very nice for me to have María to help for a little while."

" Indeed ! And what does a girl of that sort do to help ? " snorted Doña Marta. " It's a nice thing if a granddaughter of mine is to wait on male lodgers. She had better come straight home with me."

" María does not go into the public rooms at all ; but there is plenty of sewing that I can't attend to without help. You know how my back aches when I use a needle," returned Dolores. It was fortunate that María was occupied, at that very moment, in hemming some bed-linen ; she looked up, with virtuous reproach, at her irate grandparent.

She was living, in fact, almost entirely upon the excitement of her few encounters with Andrés, on the conversation which took place at the reja of her bedroom window at night, when Andrés was just going off to his work. Poor food for lovers !—and galling to María, who had noticed the easier encounters of other Granadina maidens. The old order was changing ; the reja no longer played its supreme part in the courtship comedy. She said as much to Dolores, who shook her lovely little head. " Perhaps you are right, but it is a pity. It made the girls more valuable when their lovers saw them only like pretty birds behind the bars of their cages." Dolores knew of the conversations with Andrés, but decided to close her eyes to them. It was not reasonable the girl should have no young man to talk to her. The house was in a small side street ; it was unlikely that anyone but their immediate neighbours would notice, or the Morenos, her mother and sisters, hear of it. It was good for the boy to have a respectable girl to talk to. She had taken a childless woman's affection for Andrés :

petted and spoiled him as far as decency allowed it, and secretly sympathised with his hopeless passion for her niece. She was even guilty of having encouraged him—on an occasion when he had sobbed out the despair of his heart regarding María.

" Hombre ! Don't take it so badly. Think of the time when you will be rich and famous, and you can take your pick of all the pretty girls in the big towns you go to. By that time you will have forgotten all about María ! "

" Never," he replied, with the desperate earnestness of youth. " Not when I am lying in my grave will I forget her. If I am ever rich, I will come back and take her away with me. But, madre mía," he cried, beating his brow, " she may be married by then. Well, I shall get her somehow. We are meant to belong to each other—I can feel it here. Already I can feel a kind of belonging—I do not know how it is—as though we were already close to one another."

" Do you know nothing of your mother ? " Dolores asked him quietly, smoothing back the disordered hair which hung over his brow.

" Nothing of either of my parents. Well, what does it matter ? " he said defiantly. " There are plenty like me. She couldn't have been worth much, my mother, or she wouldn't have left me in the basket. I sometimes wonder about my father ; it's a pity I can't find him. Perhaps he was an actor. One doesn't have instincts like mine for nothing. Always, since I was a baby, I've been acting, without knowing what I was doing. It was only when I left the orphanage that I began to think there might be money in it—because people used to give me coppers for imitating them. . . . "

He came one night to the reja, wildly excited.

" What do you think ? " he stammered, when their usual greeting was over. " I may be going to have a chance !

Nothing is certain yet—you know how a thousand things happen—but the manager of the theatre may be going to arrange a vaudeville show later on. You know the kind of thing," he babbled, forgetting that to María the subject was as Greek. " There will be one big star, and they will be engaging smaller people to support her. It may be La Estreso—I don't know ; she's a great favourite in Granada. But he—the manager—was at our place to-night, and he saw me ; he has promised to engage me, if the rest of the thing is arranged ! " It was not absolutely the truth. Gómez, the manager, had seen Andrés do his crude little act, had grunted, thought he had found a cheap fill-up if he needed one, and exchanged a few completely non-committal words with Andrés, into which the question of engagement never so much as entered. It was one of the girls who had afterwards beckoned Andrés to her, and had said, " You were lucky to catch Gómez's eye. Sometimes he does a variety show at the theatre, as a change from the cine, and he nearly always goes to the cabarets for some of his performers." The wish being father to the thought, Andrés's imagination had instantly supplied the rest of the tale with such a wealth of detail that he himself was immediately convinced. It was, obviously, not hard to convince María. She clasped her hands in rapture, without fully understanding what it was about, and flamed with enthusiasm.

" How wonderful you are ! How clever ! Then we shall be able to come and see you perform. Dio' mío, what a proud moment for me ! "

" Of course. You must have one of the palcos right over the stage," he said triumphantly. " Don Luis must pay for it. It is good for one of the artistes if the management know he has rich friends in front who can afford to pay for their seats. And perhaps your father will come as well, if you ask him. I want everyone to see me ; I want them to know that

I am worth something, that you will not be marrying a nobody if you marry me ! " His face was very flushed, his hair tumbled ; he was exquisitely drunk, and he had not a penny in his pocket, because he had spent all his money in inviting his friends to drink to his future success, at his expense. They had all taken his word that it was assured ; for the first time in his life Andrés had felt that he was surrounded by good friends, that he was not a mere crawling nobody, dependent upon luck or charity.

It was three in the morning, he had wakened María by tapping softly on her shutters, which she had flung open, revealing herself to his beglamoured eyes in her white nightgown—most chaste of garments. Carmela had seen to that.

" Will all the people clap for you ? How important I shall feel ! You must be sure to look at me."

" At whom else should I look ? And after that I shall soon be earning a lot of money. Enough for us to get married and set up house together. María mía, you will come away with me then ? " he pleaded hotly.

" Oh, yes." What objection could there be, if he were able to support her ? And, naturally, the practical María knew that she herself would be by no means a beggarmaid. As Carmela's only daughter she was bound to get the tavern and all the money in the bank. She was, however, Carmela's daughter in not mentioning this to Andrés.

" Your father is bound to give his consent when he knows I can keep you ? " pressed Andrés. " Why don't you ask him when he comes ? I think he is not badly disposed to me already. I have taken great pains to be polite to him—and, besides, I like him. He puzzles me, but I like him very much."

" My papá is as good as bread," asserted María. " He always wants me to be happy. But, naturally, he does not like the idea of my getting married. What a pity we cannot have him to live with us ! You see, there is my mother. She is a very jealous woman ; she will not want him to come away from her."

María's light mention of her family ties chilled and depressed Andrés ; he felt them like a net in which he might very easily get entangled. He wanted María, consumedly, but he did not want her family. His short life had been passed in utter freedom, and he saw no reason to wish it otherwise. He hated being reminded of her superiority to him in this matter of family : he wanted to exclude everything but himself and María from his calculations.

It was cold at the window—being now October—and she shivered a little. Two girls from the other cabaret, La Montillana, passed and greeted Andrés familiarly across their shoulders. One of them winked and made a broad jest, which, to María's surprise, he returned, in no way discomposed by it. She frowned and bit her lip.

" Do you know those girls ? "

" No, of course not," he lied, understanding she did not wish him to know them, although not seeing her reason for it. He merely thought she was jealous of his knowing others beside herself.

" Then why did they speak to you ? "

He shrugged his shoulders and laughed. His laughter puzzled her ; it held knowledge of so many things of which she was ignorant ; it made him, in some way, inhabitant of a world in which she had no place. And the moonlight did the rest—the cold, white moonlight of a half-moon that seemed to float restlessly between the uneven roofs. It changed him from the youth she knew into a black-and-white stranger, who frightened her with his resemblance to something she had forgotten. His face, black and white and thin, seemed rather to grin than to smile at her through the reja : pressing close, with its glittering teeth, with its bone-white fingers that clutched the bars. She made a half-movement of recoil.

" María mía ! You wouldn't leave me ? It's the first chance we've ever had—you wouldn't waste our fine chance, María ? "

" What do you mean ? " she gasped.

" Open your door for me to-night ! I beg you, María ! What's the harm in it ? We're novios ; later on we'll be married—when I am earning a great deal of money no one will want to prevent us. María queridísima, can't you feel it too ? It's a night of the moon—a night for lovers to be together. Listen. I promise you—some day I'll buy you a lovely carmen, and we'll look at the moon through the leaves of the orange-trees. But to-night there's just your little room, and your warm bed, and your arms. Don't refuse me, María of my heart ! "

" I hate the moon. I don't ever want to look at it ! " She made the sign of the cross upon her breast. " For me it's bad luck."

" But why ? "

" Because of something I once heard." She refused to tell him more.

" Open the door, María. When we are together I will make you forget there is anything in the world but good luck—for you and me ! We'll be a king and queen together —we'll only have to say what we want and it will come true." His fantasy broke down in a rush of primitive emotion that brought a tremor into his voice. " Anda," he muttered, and shook the bars.

" I can't. I'm locked in. My aunt has the key ! "

" Por Dios ! Are you telling me the truth ? "

" The truth of the truth," she assured him.

He swore under his breath ; the sweat beaded his brows.

" Can't you steal it ? "

" How can I ? She sleeps with my uncle ; the key's under their pillow."

" You're right," he said laconically. " The moon brings us mala suerte." He lifted his face, angry and ironical, to the moonlight, and broke into a bitter laugh. " That's what it is ! La luna tuerta : a moon with only one eye."

She gave a muffled cry and buried her face. Baffled, he pressed his lips to her fingers and tried to soothe her.

" What is it, María mía ? What are you frightened of ? You don't really believe in those silly old sayings ? Why, you must be a gipsy," he teased, trying to comfort her. " Por Dios, there's no denying things are against us at present. Listen. Do you love me as much as I love you ? Do you know what you look like to me—with the moon on your little silver face and that white thing you have on ? Like a white lily of Granada. Like—no, I have it—like the Patrona—the Blessed Mother of God. Ay, if I could have you for my little mother to-night, María ! Just to go to sleep with my head on your bosom. I am so sleepy. Tell me, would you like that as well ? "

Her eyes answered him.

" What could be more harmless ? " continued Andrés. " I swear "—he kissed his crossed thumb and forefinger— " I swear I regard you so highly I would not so much as kiss your little toes unless you gave me leave. Although I am all afire for you, I would treat you like a brother, just for the sake of being close to your side." He paused ; as she made no reply, he whispered, " Is that door really locked ?"

" On the Virgin of the Angustias, sí señor ! "

" You swear it ? "

" I have sworn."

He went limp with frustration. Suddenly overcome with weariness and his recent celebrations, he yawned and lurched against the wall. " Oh, well," he muttered indistinctly. " I shall have to look for some girl who is kinder than you, María."

" What are you saying ? " she cried in horror.

" How can we go on this way ? I see you every day—just enough to keep me always in torment. I cannot sleep for thinking about you. I only live by waiting for the minutes when we meet. I might as well do away with myself as continue in this fashion."

It was only a few days later that fate played into the hands of the lovers in a way not to be foreseen by even the vigilance of Dolores. The house was fairly well filled with guests, when a novillada—the last of the season—was announced for the Sunday, and someone had evidently recommended the bull-fighters to put up at the Casa Fermín. Like many of the more respectable fondas, the Casa Fermín did not particularly care for catering for the personnel of the bull-ring.

" What's the use ? " grumbled Dolores, having concluded, with concealed reluctance, with the representatives who had called on her, an agreement for the rooms. " They want to pay less than everybody else, and expect twice as much attention. They keep the servants up all night, and bring who they like in with them. And the regular people grumble. Don Natálio said last time he couldn't get to sleep until six in the morning, and he's been with us five years—we don't want to lose him. But what are respectable working people, who have to be in their offices by seven o'clock, going to do about it ? For a famous matador one would try to make the best of it, but for these canalla—— ! "

" Perhaps they will become famous one day," said Carmela's daughter, " and then they will come back and spend a great deal of money here, and make it worth your while."

" Tonta ! When a man is making his fortune he does not want to spend it where there is no one to watch him doing

it. I once had one of El Gallo's picadores here ; he told me
Gallo had recommended him, because years ago, when the
house belonged to Luis's parents, Gallo himself had stayed
here. No ; the men with money go up the hill, to the
Washington Irving or the Palace. All the rewards one gets
for entertaining bull-fighters are hard work, damage to
property, and, very likely, trouble over the bill. And the
dirty habits they have ! " said Dolores, pulling a face.
" The rooms have to be scrubbed from floor to ceiling after
they have gone."

" I'd like to see the bull-fight," said María innocently ;
privately she thought Andrés might be going ; the seats
for the novilladas were always cheaper than those for the
corridas, and it could easily be contrived that they should
sit, if not together, at least in sight of one another.

" I shall have to let the room which is yours for the night,"
said Dolores, ignoring the remark. " That little room by the
door won't hold the baskets and all the paraphernalia !
You will either have to sleep there, or you must go to my
mother's. How it vexes me to have to inconvenience you
for these canalla ! "

" Do not let it worry you in the least," said María
politely. " I shall sleep just as well in another bed for the
night." But the room had, alas, no reja ! She was done out
of her evening conversation with Andrés. It had only a
little window, opening on the patio—too public a spot for
the conduct of a love-affair. Round about ten o'clock María
chafed in the sitting-room, among the plush furniture,
imagining Andrés tapping at her reja, being answered by
the deep voice of a man, or, more probably, by silence :
for, having eaten, the bull-fighters had gone out to their
favourite taverns.

The house had been in an uproar all the evening. María
caught glimpses of hard-bitten individuals with Cordobés

hats or slouch caps pushed sideways on their heads, who
carried toothpicks, apparently as a kind of insignia, between
their gold-filled teeth ; the dining-room was filled with the
reek of cheap " puros," and dirty bundles were piled in the
passages until carried by the grumbling servants to the
toreros' rooms.

" I'm going to bed," announced María, yawning, a little
after eleven. She felt ready to cry. Ever since the arrival of
the cuadrilla her aunt had forbidden her to stir out of the
three communicating rooms which made up the family
apartment. Dolores accompanied her to the little room
whose one window looked into the patio, and gave a
suspicious look round before slamming and bolting the
shutters. " I ought to have sent you to your grandmother's,"
she said vexedly. " What's going to happen, I should like
to know, if you want anything in the night ? " As María
usually slept from the moment she touched her pillow to
the second she was called, the question did not appear to
her important. She was only afraid that to-night she would
sleep past the hour when Andrés, returning from Las
Estrellas, passed through the patio on his way to bed. How
glad he would be to see her—not having had a glimpse of
her since the midday meal, which the family took in the
dining-room ; when, across the tables of shabby, middle-
aged lodgers, two pairs of young eyes met in a glass—María
being always carefully placed with her back to the room—
and exchanged pitiful promises.

It was only when the two women had kissed one another
good night that the key of the little room was found to be
missing. " Blessed Mother of God," prayed María, while
Dolores, distracted, was hunting for it, " don't let her find
it, blessed Virgin Mary ! " " You must pull the chest of
drawers across in front of the door," said Dolores returning.
" And don't you dare to move it, whatever you hear !

God knows what Carmela would say," she bemoaned herself. " Or your father either—letting you sleep by yourself in a room without a lock on the door ; and all these strangers in the house. Swear you won't open until I come for you in the morning ! "

María obediently raised her clasped hands and crossed thumbs, but her kiss was made quickly in the air. Her aunt did not notice it. When the door was closed : " Now ! Let me hear you put the chest against it now ! " cried Dolores, from outside.

The chest was very heavy, and made a great deal of noise in moving on the marble floor. María panted and grew red in the face. " Closer—closer ! " cried Dolores, having tried the door and found it would open about an inch. " That's as close as it will go," gasped María, at last. " Good night—sleep well ! " they called to one another. Dolores's heels went tapping away down the passage.

She was trembling from head to foot. Very slowly she removed all her clothes, carefully poured water into the bowl, and washed all her body. The combing of her hair took a long while—there was so much of it. Like Dolores's, it fell almost to the backs of her knees ; twisted, it made a formidable rope—a rope to strangle a man. In the middle of her preparations María suddenly sat quite still. It had occurred to her that she should be feeling wicked. She was deceiving her aunt, and she was preparing an act which would grievously hurt her father, when he came to know of it. But the act in itself was not a wicked one ; she and Andrés were novios. Some day there was no doubt they would be married. She was only doing what many another girl did with the full knowledge of her family. If anything came of this, the only result would be that she and Andrés would have to be publicly betrothed, and that, surely, would be a good thing. Perhaps it was the only way to make her family believe they were really in earnest : that it was not just a foolish boy-and-girl romance.

Having decided this with her conscience, María knelt down and said her prayers to the little moulded Virjen de las Angustias mounted on a tortoise-shell plaque which her aunt had given her : not forgetting to thank her for having caused Dolores to lose the key—surely a sign of divine approval !

She then began to move the chest again. The strokes of midnight had just sounded ; the cuadrilla had just returned, having evidently decided for an early night in view of the fight on the morrow. The noise they made, their shouts along the passage that brought the weary waiter shuffling, the loud voices of their friends—women among them— helped to drown the noise the chest made as she edged it, an inch at the time, from its former position. She had some fear that her aunt would come to try the door again and see if she was all right, and, to avoid discovery, wedged a chair between the door and the back of the chest, so that the former was as tightly closed as before. Her fear was not ungrounded, for presently she saw the handle turning.

" You are there, María ? " " Yes," she cried, trembling, from the farther side of the room. " Then, por Dios, put out the light ! It is high time you were asleep." " Very well, aunt," replied María meekly, and snapped down the button. But the white line of the moonlight, showing at the edges of the shutters in the darkness, caused her to put it on again as soon as she knew her aunt was gone. She did not want the moon, her enemy, to take part in her long vigil. She must at all costs keep awake, for Andrés, who did not know where she was sleeping, would certainly not rap on her shutters.

She sat upright in her bed, wrapped in her blankets, for the night was very chill ; at intervals her head fell against the wall.

CHAPTER IV

THE FATHER

PEOPLE WERE TALKING a lot about Aurelio López. In the casino, on the doorsteps, and in the market the gossip rustled, as it had rustled in the old days ; under the bright white glare of the moon, that changed the blood-red pimientos into black and the whitewashed façades into blue, heads came together at the passing of Aurelio López.

" There's something wrong with Aurelio ; he's gone crazy ; it's the loss of that girl of his has driven him crazy. Loss ? The way you talk she might be dead ! He's only got to take the tramway into Granada. There's more behind that than meets the eye, you can be sure. She knows something, that Doña Carmela ! Do you remember that business of Conchita López ? Calla ! Well, didn't that happen, ten—fifteen years ago ? A woman capable of that can do other things as well. Say what you like, she's the richest person in the town. One does not rake up old indiscretions about a person like that ! "

Aurelio was, indeed, a little crazy. He had begun to look crazy ; people turned to watch him as he went by, with a smile on his lips. The smile was for his invisible María, his ever-present companion, whose light steps ruffled the dust at his side. When spoken to, he returned greetings with the greatest gentleness—in a soft voice that held a hush, as though he were listening for something, as though he dreaded to drown a voice to which he was already listening. A sort of sorry beneficence emanated from him, as though the misfortunes of other people filled him with a profound pity and understanding, having partaken in them all.

And a still stranger thing, in the opinion of Agujasierra, was that he and Carmela were now often to be seen together. The women said jealously, " It's a perpetual Holy Thursday for her ! "—meaning that Carmela could get out of Aurelio whatever she pleased, a privilege only enjoyed once a year by other women, upon the eve of Good Friday, when, however errant had been his fancy for the rest of the year, every husband paid solemn tribute to the demands of his household.

The only moments when Aurelio's anger against Carmela revived were when she paraded her motherly complacency towards the girl she had driven out of her home. And in a sense it pleased him she should do this : it preserved his pride of family, the external unity of the casa upon which, like every Spaniard, he set great store—the more because he himself contributed little to it.

" Yes, indeed," he had heard her say, while measuring a litre of wine into a bottle brought by a customer, " it was not at all suitable for a girl like María to waste her time in a place like this. We all want opportunities for our daughters, do we not, señora ? " she added, surreptitiously spinning the proffered peseta to see if it was a good one before proffering change.

" I suppose she will be finding herself a fine novio," hinted the neighbour with a wink. " Between ourselves, señora, I never thought that Mario Gallego's boy was much of a catch for the daughter of a López." It had become the fashion to flatter Carmela ; a curious form of deference surrounded this woman whom nobody liked, but who had so perseveringly put herself at the head of their little community.

" That is as it may be," returned Carmela discreetly.

" At all events, she has plenty of time to look about her. My sister will certainly not encourage anything foolish, and, after the way she has been brought up, María is not the kind of girl to throw herself away on a good-looking ne'er-do-well."

It dawned on Aurelio, listening, that Carmela had actually persuaded herself of her own good motives towards María, and that she was using them to enhance her position among the neighbours. This was the hardest thing Aurelio had to forgive.

Up in the thyme and wild lavender, where, like windswept blossoms, the dance of butterflies rose and fell, where only the rustle of lizards in the parched grass broke the silence, he struggled with forgiveness. With all his heart he desired to forgive Carmela, for, unless he could empty his heart of bitterness towards her, what was the use of his sacrifice ? And, in her triumph, she was, for a little while, completely hateful to him ; for she was openly triumphant, smiling, singing, embarrassing him by her attentions to his bodily comfort, clearly bent upon showing him how happy and pleasant a home he had got now there were only the two of them to share it. And gradually these outward manifestations died down, and she became quietly satisfied, busy about her work in house or tavern, or rocking in her armchair during the siesta hours. Active or passive, she had been but a dim and restless entity in his gloaming of bereavement ; he did not for a while perceive a certain complacent comeliness that was dawning upon her, even a recrudescence of vanity, which led her to order new dresses, to visit the dentist and have replaced, after seventeen years, the teeth she had lost after María's birth.

Lost in his mourning for María, he saw nothing. For he mourned her as though she were dead. The María he visited every week was not the one who had danced barefooted among the thyme for him ; it was another María, whose heart was already given to a stranger. And because, above all things on earth, he desired the happiness even of this other María, he had done nothing—none of the wise, worldly things—to intervene between her love and herself. It seemed to him that, having sacrificed her to Carmela, the least he could do now was to sacrifice himself to her. Into whatever thorny paths her love might lead her, her father's feet must follow her. All that remained for him was to stand by and watch, as he had watched when she was a little thing, to save her from hurting herself by falling.

He had never told Carmela of the girl's love-affair, for there was no hope of Carmela sympathising with her daughter—she who had so ardently espoused the cause of Carlos Gallego. The boy on whom María's choice had fallen—what use in thinking of him ? Love dissolved all standards. If he was capable of making María happy—and how could one know even that when they were both so young ?—there could be no more to say. If not, she had her father's arms to return to, with little harm done. Seeing him constantly, under Dolores's care, she would learn, or feel, something ; for the moment she was drowning in love for him. Her eyes, which for so long had held her father's image, now held this youth's—well, it was natural. Why fight with nature ?

His lost, his beloved, María ! But along the mountain ridges, treading the escarpments with flying feet, laughing from a shadow and playing some intangible game of hide-and-seek among the clumps of grass, went her lovely ghost. In the wind that lifted the hair upon his temples he began to feel her presence ; her light spirit was blown across the parched roots until he could see each blade bending, as it had bent beneath her little trampling feet. A dozen Marías came to comfort him, sweet wraiths of her childhood, that transported Aurelio into a region of pure bliss beyond anything he had ever experienced when her material presence was at hand. They touched him with their delicate fingers, wove about him in the air a mystic radiance, filled him with subtle and sacred sensations, with far-off exultations that transcended the limitations of understanding. He delivered himself to them; he dissolved in them ; he allowed them to purify him.

And gradually their influence cleared him of his bitterness towards Carmela. Of what, after all, had she robbed him ? He had his visionary María ; he was in her and she in him ; their fleshly separation only drew them more closely together in spirit. His fatherhood extended itself, assumed a mysterious power and intimacy that had been wholly lacking from their relationship in latter years, when her womanhood clove her apart from him. In her company, as in that of an angel, he could return to Carmela, could resume his strange and sterile relationship with the inexplicable woman who, after her long struggle, had finally obtained what she believed to be supremacy over him.

He knew that she thought she had conquered him ; he was willing that she should have the happiness of thinking it. She was incapable of a higher happiness ; she could not pass with him through love's gate into the presence of God, because in her love was not : a jealousy of possession, a sour satisfaction in having made good her claim took the place of it.

But they were friendly together ; quieter, perhaps more contented than they had ever been, even during the first stages of their love. Her interest in the tavern prevented her from making any exorbitant demands upon him. She allowed him now to help her in the tavern, rather as one allows a child to pretend it is baking, or dusting a room. In a little while after María's departure, since her possession of him became undisputed, she ceased to trouble about anything in connection with him. Her nature had reverted completely to that of her mother, Doña Marta, who, in the making of money, had no time to spare for personal or sentimental considerations. She had at last got Aurelio to herself, and, like a child with a toy for which it has pestered its parents so long that by the time it gets it the interest and value of the thing is gone, she had become in a sense indifferent to him. He was there, part of the furniture of her house, her undisputed property. She had no sexual or other need of him. Her whole soul was filled with the clinking of duros.

Had he left her, it would hardly, save for the gossip it would have occasioned, have distressed her. But she nodded her head, sometimes, to see him sitting quietly in a corner of the tavern instead of disappearing up the mountain-side ; his presence was the visible sign of her triumph. It did not even annoy her to overhear his conversation, which was always of María. He talked of her as though none of the neighbours had ever seen her : describing minutely every detail of her behaviour and appearance to the murmurs of " Ya lo creo ! " " Digo, hombre ! " respectfully contributed by listeners who truly believed now that Aurelio López had gone out of his mind. He became dithyrambic, a poet in the service of his mistress.

Hardly could a lover have conceived a more fantastic, more unlikely portrait of his mistress than the vision of his María that shaped itself in the words of Aurelio. An ordinary listener would certainly have failed to identify the coquettish, commonsensical little María López with the figure, half human, half divine, created by her father in her image. He shaped this figure delicately, like an etcher with his needle ; boldly, like a painter with his brush ; powerfully, like a sculptor with his chisel, so that at last, in some extraordinary fashion, the living María, remembered by them all as a very pretty but in no wise extraordinary young woman, became canonised—assumed the qualities of sainthood during her very lifetime ; and even the playmates of María, although puzzled at first, and inclined to be incredulous, began to wonder whether they had entertained an angel unawares.

In one respect only did Carmela betray what may have been, *au fond*, her feelings ; she now spoke of María invariably as " your daughter." Many people noticed it. And, for the rest, she was now sunk, irrevocably submerged, in making money out of the tavern. She herself could not have explained, any more than she could have described, the sensual pleasure in fingering the perra-gordas as they passed into her pocket, or the joyful heaviness of that pocket at the close of day. She had money, and she had Aurelio ; these two were enough to ensure her the soundness of her night's rest.

With the tourists she was beginning to have a slightly bad name ; you had to keep your eye skinned when you went to the López posada ; you got charged ten and twelve pesetas for wine at eight-fifty the bottle, and twenty was a ludicrous sum to pay for a fourth- or fifth-rate guitarrista. Aurelio was suspected of standing in with Carmela's piracy —that half-simple, half-canny stuff was good business ; Aurelio talked and Carmela emptied pockets—an excellent partnership ! Had they known of it, the Agujasierrans would have rocked with laughter. Aurelio was God's blessed fool, whose riches lay in his poverty. There were one or two who remarked, privately, it was as well he had never been made alcalde.

He was, in a remote, half-conscious fashion, very happy. His whole life was filled with love.

Love is the measure of the heart's Felicity ;
The more 'tis filled with love the happier thou wilt be.

It was very cold when he next went down to Granada. Carmela had insisted upon buying him a cloak—its fronts faced with green plush, its folds of fine, dark blue cloth— in which, when he was enveloped, Aurelio looked very venerable.

" Papá mío ! How elegant ! How distinguished you look ! " María was enchanted when she saw him.

" Let us go for a walk," she begged him, later ; her manner, while they sat talking in the house, had been oddly nervous. Smiles came and went quickly on her face ; once or twice a look that was almost puzzled drew her brows into a frown. He thought, " How beautiful she is, how rare ! No wonder this young man has fallen in love with her ; I must not be angry with him about it." Dolores was in bed ; she had been ill almost ever since the cold weather started, but María had stoutly refused to go to her grandmother's. " If you are sick María must go to my mother's," Carmela had written. " How can you look after her properly if you are laid away in bed ? " María, when shown the letter, had cried out upon it.

" What barbarity ! Of course I shall not go. Who is to look after you if I am not here ? Those servants, they will leave you alone all day, and my uncle has no more sense than a donkey," she declared ; and had stood by her word, caring for Dolores tenderly, so that the sick woman had come to depend on her in every particular, and the two were more closely than ever drawn together. Even so, María had not confided in her about Andrés. No one must know before her father. It was this she had resolved to tell him, as they sat for a moment on the low parapet which, from the Alhambra, looks down upon the Albaícin and the surrounding hills.

" See, there is the very road up which thy father used to drive the goats when he was a youth," said Aurelio, mildly reminiscent. " Just up there, near San Bartolomé, was the house of your great-aunt, and there I first saw——." " Your mother," he was going to add, when the odd thought struck him that in no sense was Carmela the mother of María. Save by the physical accident of birth, the girl had never known motherhood. He lifted his cloak and folded it around her, tenderly, to keep her from the wind that came bitingly past the rose-red walls, as a mother might have done. He felt her tremble against his side.

" Papá mío, I have something to tell you," she began. " You know that Andrés and I have been loving one another ever since I came to Granada ? Do not be angry with me, papá mío, nor with Andrés either. We could not help it. And now we are really novios."

As the full meaning of her words came to him, Aurelio felt his heart die in his breast. After a silence, he said :

" This is a very serious thing, my beloved."

" Ay, papá, I know it is ! " said María, shedding some tears of relief at the mildness of Aurelio's words. " But it had to be that way. You know Andrés cannot afford to get married for a long time yet—and we know it is useless to ask mamá for money. So we just did the best we could. Do not blame my aunt ; she has known nothing about it. You see," she said, abandoning herself to a luxury of confession, " she locked me up in my room every night, but one night when there were a lot of people I had to sleep in another room, and after that—well, Andrés has a friend who makes keys, and he gave Andrés a piece of wax to take an impression of the lock . . ." She stopped, appalled by the grey pallor which had overspread Aurelio's face. " Do not be so hurt, papá mío, I implore you ! I cannot bear the pain of seeing you look like that. Of course you will help us. I have clung to you in my mind as to the tablets of salvation ! " she assured him passionately. The words brought some bitter consolation to him, even in his pain.

" So you have both been deceiving us," he said heavily.

" Oh, papá, what could we do ? It was no use asking if we could be betrothed ; we are both so young, and Andrés has nothing—nothing in the world. I have told him to meet us up here," she said hurriedly. " Here he comes, now. I pray you, papá mío, on my knees, to be good to him ! "

Andrés came quickly towards them across the open space. His hands were in his pockets, his thin shoulders hunched beneath his coat, his head driven down into the wind. His face, when he raised it to Aurelio's, was thin, white, sharpened by fear and anxiety. He had not wished, so soon, to share their secret with María's father ; it was she who had insisted, for reasons she had not imparted to Andrés. The two men looked at one another silently. At last Aurelio rose and put his hand on the other's shoulder. " My son," he said, " you have behaved very ill."

Andrés shuddered—partly because he was chilled through and through, not possessing an overcoat, and partly because Aurelio's gentleness was so much worse than anything he had expected. He looked with the eyes of a whipped dog at the man who had called him son. Aurelio had seen the shudder ; María's head was covered with the velo, the ends of which were snugly tucked into the fur collar of her coat, a present from her grandmother. He lifted his arm, and, with a gesture of infinite compassion, laid it across the shoulders of Andrés, so that the latter was shielded from the wind.

" Come," he said mildly. " It is too cold for us to talk out here. There is a little tavern near the pensions——"

Andrés began to sob ; the three of them walked quickly past the palace of Cárlos Quinto, and found the small dark wine-shop which goes by the name of the Casa de Apolonario, in memory of the composer Angel Barrios, whose father gave him that name. It was, fortunately, empty. Aurelio ordered red wine for the three of them ; they clasped their frozen fingers round the glasses and drank. Andrés drained his glass at a gulp. The wine loosened his tongue. He caught at Aurelio's sleeve, as they sat at a little distance from the counter, and spoke almost in a whisper, although, with her customary delicacy, the dueña had retired into her little room behind the wine-shop.

" I know that I am nothing, that I am utterly worthless ; but, I swear to you upon the grave of my mother, it will not always be so."

" Is your mother dead, then ? " asked Aurelio, looking at him kindly.

" I have not the least idea," said Andrés, momentarily discomposed. " But so far as I am concerned the last rites have been said over her. I never saw her in my life."

Aurelio drew patiently from the boy the story of his birth ; he knew, from María, that Andrés was an orphan, but wished to hear from the boy's own lips what he knew of his parenthood. Andrés, as he mumbled the ignoble story, could have wished María had not been there, following every word with her great glowing eyes. It was difficult to cast the glow of romance upon the past which he had managed to conjure for María ; not knowing Aurelio's simplicity, he was prepared for suspicion and unbelief ; his lying was not so good as usual. The one fact he left un-touched was the fact of his rearing in the foundling hospital

—what was the use of lying about that ? He had no relations to produce, no background to match María's ; he stood to be accepted on his own naked worth, and it was curious how little that stood for in this interview with his novia's father. He came as quickly as possible to the few facts which were not discreditable.

" But it will not be long, señor, before I am in a position to support a wife ; I——"

" How many years have you ? " asked Aurelio mildly.

" I have nineteen," lied Andrés boldly ; at least on the matter of his age it would be difficult to disprove him. He saw, from María's nod, that she approved of the exaggeration.

" It is young, but many boys marry at that age," concurred Aurelio gravely.

" And on less expectations than I," boasted Andrés, now more at ease, since he felt he had gained a point. This father of María's was, as she had said, as good as bread. A rush of emotion caused him to lay his hand on Aurelio's own. The latter looked down upon it ; a curious feeling came across him of having seen such a hand before, although when and where he could not remember. " I am madly in love with her," muttered Andrés, " and it is not my fault that I have nothing in the world. How could I say that to anyone but you, señor ? From the first time we talked together she has done nothing but tell me of your goodness, of your wisdom and understanding. I feel already as though you were my father. Do not refuse to let me be your son ! "

" What man," said Aurelio, out of a dream, " would refuse a son ? But how am I to know you will be a son to me ? If you would be my son, you must first show yourself capable of being to this my only daughter as a brother. I am a man, and, like all men, I have loved women. But in that easier way, that lover's way, that you yourself have known. It was not in me, when I was a young man, to love them in any other way ; is it in you ? "

Andrés was mute.

" Youth thinks only of itself," went on Aurelio. " You are both children ; it is right you should think of yourselves. But you must also think of each other. No one said these things to me when I was young ; it is only since I became old that they have come to me ; some day, when you are old, you may remember them, for now they are just empty words. You only want to enjoy each other, to find happiness in each other's youth. Dio' mío, is it not right that this should be your desire, before the dark night of knowledge comes upon you both ? "

María gave a little cry, and caught her father's other hand. The pair of them sat looking up at Aurelio ; in their two youthful faces was the one passion, the one plea. He turned his head away from it. Everything in his soul opposed, without reason, their combined appeal ; but he distrusted his own judgment, because he knew that his love, his desire to keep her for his own, adulterated all his thoughts.

" You have come to me too late," he said sadly. " You have taken your lives in your own hands."

" Then, papá, you will help us ? " cried María, speaking for the first time.

" How ? " he said.

" You can ask my mother——" began María. He silenced her with a look.

" I have at least this in my favour," cried Andrés, " I am not an idler ! I am very ambitious, señor ! I shall never rest until I have made a position for myself which will command everybody's respect."

" It will be time enough then to talk of the future," said Aurelio, with a sudden coldness. He held out his hand.

" Do me the favour to give me the key to my daughter's room."

Andrés changed colour, and shot a glance of reproach at María, who was completely outfaced by this unexpected demand of Aurelio's. Andrés stammered :

" You refuse to allow us to be novios ? "

" I refuse to allow you to go on enjoying my daughter in secret," retorted Aurelio, with an implacable gesture. " There are many men," he added, " who would kill you for what you have done."

" But——"

" The key." Andrés produced it, shamefaced, from his pocket, and handed it to Aurelio. The latter looked at it as though it were something unclean. " What is the use ? " he said, as though to himself. " What is done is done. I will take her away."

A cry came from both.

" I shall die without Andrés, papá ! "

" What wrong have we done ? "—fiercely—from Andrés. " We regard ourselves as solemnly betrothed to each other. When we are of age, no one can prevent our marrying each other."

" We can go before the judge," cried María, who had evidently talked it over with Andrés, " and get an order from him without having to ask anybody's permission."

Aurelio turned upon her a look of illimitable sadness. " Once thy father was thy judge."

She burst into tears, and, raising his hand to her lips, began to kiss it passionately. Andrés, his pride stung by her capitulation, launched his final bolt.

" I am not as worthless as you suppose, señor ! " he cried. " I grant you the cabaret was not much, though many a man does less for his living than I did for my money ! But good luck has come my way at last. I have got an engagement at the theatre, for the Sunday after next. Perhaps that convinces you that my work is worth something," he ended, with a foolish, offended dignity that, despite himself, touched Aurelio's heart. Andrés's boast conveyed little to him ; there was no clear distinction between the cabaret and the theatre in his mind, but he remembered one paid for one's seat in the theatre, and this, probably, lent the performance a dignity not associated with cabaret. The one occasion on which he had visited the theatre came back to him with a fearful distinctness : all of his life, like a slow river, seemed to have started from that night ; all that came before it was difficult to remember, and slightly unreal, like a remembered tale of childhood. How, thinking of that night, could he blame these two for what had passed between them ? Had not the same sacred urge which had mastered him driven them into each others' arms ? Something that went beyond a man's will, beyond his power to control ?

It was many years since he had heard from her, from his partner of that night's rapture. Her letters had come once a year for a few years—telling him nothing, obviously written only in accordance with her promise—and then had ceased. He had not even regretted their cessation. Their bald, polite phrases had nothing in common with the woman he remembered, they could do nothing to illuminate her memory for him. In the end, he had even opened them reluctantly. She had never sent him the promised address to which he might write to her. So much the better.

He said something kind, congratulatory, to the boy, who by his manner showed he considered the praise lukewarm. Vanity drove him, however, to drag a folded paper out of his pocket, which, with a glance at María, he held out towards her father. Only the lowest line of the print showed.

" María has not seen this yet," he said proudly. " It was only given to me this afternoon."

A theatre bill, at whose foot, in suitably small print that gave the measure of insignificance of the artiste, the words : " The brilliant comedian, *Andrés*, from the cabaret Las Estrellas." But what mattered the smallness of the letters in the glory of beholding one's name, for the first time, in print ?

María, gasping with excitement, was looking over his shoulder as Aurelio slowly and mechanically unfolded the paper. He could feel himself impelled to do this, impelled to read each name as, in larger and larger print, it mounted to the principal. He knew what that name was when he had seen but the bases of the letters ; he stared at it stupidly, knowing it, yet unable to attach it to the image within his mind.

" Maravilla del Monte, the stupendous and world-famous artiste, in her repertoire."

" They couldn't get La Estreso," the slightly contemptuous voice of Andrés was saying. " She must be a long way past her best, this del Monte. Folks here say they remember her twenty years ago—she was very good then. But what can a woman do after she's lost her youth ? "

María, who had read the name, was afraid to look at her father. The conversation she had heard on the stairs outside the widow Herédia's room came back to her. She longed, and was afraid to see this woman, after whom she was called

CHAPTER V

FULL CIRCLE

"Do me the favour to see these lights are attended to ; and don't forget to sprinkle the insect powder in all the corners before you unpack the dresses."

"Sí, señora. Jesú, qué frío ! "

"You don't expect the management to have the consideration to turn on the heating for a mere rehearsal ? We're in Granada, girl, not Madrid. And also—let me remind you of something you appear to have forgotten : that, although the patrons, who have paid for their seats, are worth a little warmth, a little comfort, the artistes who provide the amusement, being mere cattle, must not expect concessions to their physical desires. Look ! We have walls !—a roof ! What more do cattle need ? Mix me some more of that mouthwash," said the speaker sharply. " My throat feels as though it would burst." Picking up a handglass from the bench, she opened her mouth widely, and looked into its crimson arch between the double row of excellent teeth that showed, considering all things, small traces of the dentist's attentions.

Having concluded her inspection, she touched an eyelash, drew a flattened curl a little more forward on her cheek-bone, and added a light touch of powder at the corner of her nostrils. What a difference these small things made ! They almost disguised the traces of an all-night journey, if they could not restore the one quality most needed by a woman—her long-past youth ! She blinked her eyes, moved her head to get rid of that stiff anxiety that came into her face in unguarded moments—a hard, handsome, rapacious face that had still the art of assuming so many different expressions. A thick perfume shook itself out of the folds of an elegant coat of imitation fur as she threw back the lapels, and, with her hands on her hips, expanded her chest in a tested movement of allure. On the bench lay an expensive-looking handbag ; a pair of immaculate gloves, in reservation for appearance in the street, waited to be drawn over the tiny hands with their scarlet lacquered nails. Cattle ! She laughed shortly at the memory of her own words ; then changed her expression swiftly as a rap came on the dressing-room door.

" And here is Señor Gómez ! Good morning, Don Fernando ; you are well ? It delights me to hear it. What a long time since we met—when I was acting in this very theatre. You find changes ? "

The manager bent stiffly to kiss her extended fingers ; he was not interested in changes so long as his artistes were capable of drawing their public. They faced each other, a look of cold, professional scrutiny passed between them, quickly, like a knife thrust, under cover of their smiles. Hers said : " Yes, you wanted La Estreso, didn't you ? Young, pretty, impudent, of a famous theatrical family. She is very ' fashionable,' just at the minute ; but, my dear sir, you know you must pay for fashion. You are wondering if I know my business—I, who was filling the music-halls before La Estreso was born ! You are wondering on what pretext to suggest to me I should take a little less than the agreed percentage ; and you are wondering what I shall look like on the stage at night. Fool—as though on top of a long railway journey any woman is capable of showing what she can be and do. Perhaps you will have a surprise, my friend—I warn you ! "

His said : " These agents are all the same—they fill you up with cock-and-bull yarns to place their clients. She must be over fifty—and in this light she looks it. What's the use of experience ? Oliwoo has spoiled the public taste for all that. So long as a woman is young and has her figure they are satisfied. That's a lie about Estreso being sick ; she's either had a better offer, or she's got a lover. . . . If I lose on these three performances, I'll claim damages."

He addressed her with a great parade of flattery.

" Permit me to congratulate you, señora, upon your adoption of a new style ! How few of our artistes to-day have the requisite flexibility."

" Shall I say, the times forced the change upon me ? " she answered carelessly. " And as for a new style—hardly that ! I have returned to my original *métier*—shall we put it that way ? The wheel has come full circle ; I received my training for the stage in the class of work to which I have now returned."

" And I dare say you find it agreeable—reminiscent ? "

" An artiste has little time for reminiscences, señor," she retorted, seeing perfectly the trend of his suggestion. " Those are for later on—when one has time, perhaps too much time, at one's disposal. I, fortunately, have not reached the stage." That has scotched him, she thought, with satisfaction. I have given him to understand I am busy, successful, and in great demand ; he will not now have the impertinence to say anything about the percentage. " I hope you have engaged good support for me," she continued. " There are a good many artistes who do not care to be too strongly supported—the danger of rivalry always seems to be present in their minds. For my part, I do not care for appearing in an inferior programme ; it gives me a feeling of unequal balance, it destroys my sense of artistic symmetry."

She has sufficient assurance, thought Gómez ; at her age

she would certainly have a right to be anxious about rivals. He hastily replied that the others were all people of experience.

" I am glad of that," she answered. " You will forgive me for mentioning the matter ; but you yourself know the custom in the provincial towns—especially if the star is a little expensive. One understands that it is a temptation to the management to economise on the other artistes. But we are both agreed that this is a very false form of economy. For one thing, it destroys the confidence of the public, which does not pay to stand about in the lobbies, waiting for the star to appear ; and, speaking for myself, it gives one a very uncomfortable feeling to find oneself isolated in the company of raw beginners, or of old, worn-out failures whose inclusion in the programme should rather be regarded as an act of charity than seriously expected to contribute to the entertainment of the public."

Impressed, although unwillingly—for, as she had suspected, he had intended to try her with a suggestion of a lower percentage—by her grand manner, Gómez said hastily : " Do not allow me to inconvenience you for a moment ; but when you are at liberty the band is at your service ; the rest of the artistes are now trying over their numbers, but everything waits upon your convenience."

" A thousand thanks, señor. If you will have the kindness to send someone for the band parts of my songs, there will be no delay." As he bowed, and the door closed behind him, she gave a laugh. " Cattle ! Yes, that's the way to treat them. What would you have gathered, Rosario, from our conversation ? "

The woman who was shaking out the dresses, and hanging them on their pegs in the order of the evening's requirements, turned with a smile to Maravilla.

" Por Dios, mujer ! That that Don Fernando ought to be down on his marrowbones at the very least ! "

" That I am accustomed only to the very best—in company, in payment, in treatment ? " said Maravilla rapidly. " That I have only to take my choice of the most important engagements ? That my date cards are full ; that nothing short of a fortunate accident put me at his disposal in the present instance ? Yes, I think I conveyed all that ! A few years ago it was the truth."

" Mujer, it will be the truth again ! La Estreso hasn't got everything her own way yet. All those years of yours in the drama have given you something the rest of them haven't got," said the maid staunchly.

" I don't know ; it seems to me sometimes that my type of work is dated," murmured Maravilla, easing the gloves carefully over her fingers. She would not go down to rehearsal in the careless disarray affected by many women of the theatre ; as the star, it behoved her to look rich, famous—overpowering ! She would receive the homage of the other artistes haughtily, as if it was her due. One was accepted at one's own valuation. She had seen that in the case of other people—in the case of Emilia Mera. In the theatre one must not be modest, self-effacing, diffident of one's powers. Well, she was none of these things naturally, so there was no need for her to affect them.

Her gloves were on ; but she still sat, resting her hands on the white cloth which the maid had hastily spread upon the bench.

" While I am on the stage, you had better go out and look for a hotel. For the love of God try to find a fairly respectable one ! Tell them to have my bed ready ; after I have eaten I will go to sleep. A room on the patio, fairly high up. See what arrangement you can come to about the price."

" I will do the best I can ; I don't know Granada."

" Nor I."

" I thought you had been here before ? "

" Eighteen years ago. One hardly knows the place. And for three nights, during the feria. A friend and I had rooms in a little back street . . . "

" What is the matter, señora ? "

" Why do you ask ? "

" Pues—look at the colour of your face ! If I were you I should put on some of that pink stuff. Don't try to deceive me—there's something that is upsetting you. What's the use of worrying ? We only live a day at a time ; God takes care of the future, and what is past is gone," said the woman kindly.

" The past is not necessarily gone because it is over, Rosario," replied Maravilla, forcing a smile, and holding out her hand for the box of rouge which the maid picked out of a tin for her. " Now I shall soil my gloves ! What a fool you are. Some people's past is always with them. If I looked sad, or sick, for a moment, it was because this place reminded me of a decision I once made——"

" We can all make wrong decisions," offered Rosario, with intent to comfort. Maravilla flung the box of rouge at her.

" Idiot ! What I regret is not the decision, but the fact that I didn't keep it."

" Madre mía——"

" Open the door ; don't you hear someone is knocking ? It is for the band parts ; give them the portfolio—let them sort them out for themselves. It really won't make the least difference if the bassoon gets the first violin's part, and the French horn finds himself with the drums ! The effect will be quite the same. Positively, I should be discomposed by a theatre band that was capable of interpreting my accompaniments ! " She picked up the throat-wash which Rosario had prepared, gargled, rinsed, and spat the residue into the basin. " If I had kept my word on that occasion," she said, reverting to her former subject, " I should not now be working for my living. I might, in fact, be a rich widow with a house in Cádiz ! "

" Jesú María Santísima ! What were you thinking of ? "

" You may well ask ! I allowed myself to be carried away by the wrong kind of influences. The worst of the artistic nature is that it is too easily affected by its surroundings, by the people with whom it comes in contact. One grows out of it, of course—but the chances do not come one's way again."

" Madre mía, what a pity. But cheer up, señora ; one never knows what lies ahead of us. Actresses are not like ordinary people—what about that young gentleman at Bilbao ? You need only have given him a glance——"

" Calla ! I don't need you to tell me all that. Forgive me ; I dare say it will come to that in the end."

" And, for the love of God, would it be such a bad end ? I hope, when it comes, you'll think of me."

" Now that's enough nonsense for the present. What are you thinking about ? Old women don't attract young lovers—they *buy* them ! If I had only a little resignation !

" Rosario, I once knew an angel. De veras. Madre mía de mi alma, why are there not more of them ? We acted together for years—in this very theatre we acted together. I was the leading woman, and she—the irony of it—had to play small parts and support me. She, who knew more of her art than I shall know if I live to twice her age—and I do not say a thing of that kind lightly, as you know. When I left the company she wept ; she gave me the most precious thing she had—it had travelled with her everywhere. I knew she loved me by her giving it to me. How slow we are to believe in love of that kind !

" I tell you, Rosario, there is something holy in people who love the country—the fields, the air, the grass—as Emilia Mera loved it. She tried to teach me, but I could not learn her lesson. I could not see what the fields and the air could have for a woman like myself. I only wanted ease, luxury, money. Emilia would, I think, have been happy in a little farm. She died—when I was in Brazil."

" Pobrecita ! " Rosario's eyes filled with the facile tears of her class.

" I think, sometimes, that every good impulse I had during those years came to me through Emilia Mera. When she had gone——"

" Por Dios, señora——"

" You are right," said Maravilla, hastily drying her own eyes before the tears which had gathered there ran over upon the mascara of her lashes. " I shall look well, going down to rehearse with these traces of the past on me ! Now—look at me. Do I look well ? Do I strike the eye as an important person ? I must remember to do as little as possible. Emilia used to tease me sometimes about letting myself go ' all out ' at rehearsals. ' Play on your technique,' she used to say. ' Remember that everyone has only a certain amount of emotion ; reserve yours for your public.' But I took a joy in playing to my fellow-actors ; in giving them as much as I gave my public—no, sometimes more. I was very often better at rehearsal than I was at night. I owe some of my engagements to that ! But this kind of work is different ; one is alone ; one owes nothing to any-one. One lowers one's dignity by giving it all away to a few bandsmen, a handful of spectators. I shall just walk through my numbers——"

The stage was dusty, empty, and bitterly cold. The bandsmen were blowing on their fingers, wrapping them-selves in their mufflers, slipping out at intervals for cups of coffee. A ballet dancer had just finished rehearsing ; standing in the wings she was slipping her feet out of her worn practice-shoes ; her arms were blue with cold. Her eyes met Maravilla's with envy as the latter came on to the stage, very rich, very prosperous-looking in the coat which, under the few electric bulbs, looked like the richest sable ; her shoes, her gloves elegant—very much the Madrid star, patronising, for a caprice, a provincial hall. An excellent entrance, which took by surprise a few people who had been whispering that La Maravilla was certainly done for by this time, and that Gómez must have been out of his mind to engage her ; which brought the bandsmen who were seated to their feet, and the others hurrying to their places.

She looked round her rather wistfully. It would have been pleasant to recognise a face, to have had a personal greeting from someone. The stage hands stood apathetically ; they were only engaged for three nights ; the house was now a cine. The bandsmen were all young fellows, who might, perhaps, have heard her name—no more. She felt like a returned ghost seeking a familiar and reassuring hand. How absurd, how bad, professionally, to feel like that ! She must not allow it to be apparent.

Only as she came insolently down towards the line of the footlights did she notice a young man, who, at her approach, hurried diffidently towards the wings with a piece of music in his hands.

" Olá, niño ! " Her voice recalled him. " You were trying your numbers ? Do not let me stop you ! Come, we are all fellow-artistes ; there is no reason to be so humble." What a fool I am, she was thinking. Of course I should stand upon my dignity, impose my fame upon them, make them conscious that I am the star ! What extraordinary spirit had entered into her that she was now giving way to an insignificant person who was just brought along to fill a corner of the programme ? She felt soft, uncertain, doubtful of herself ; not of herself as artiste—that, never—but of her *self*, that self which threatened at any moment to betray her by floating away into the past. She wanted time to recover herself, to resume her *tenue*.

Andrés, blushing to the roots of his hair, turned and bowed deeply to the star. He had never before found himself close to any famous person of the theatre, and for all his glibness in catching a tone of disparagement from his associates, who joked about La Maravilla and had said she would probably appear on crutches, he was for the moment completely overwhelmed. Her hard, assured stare, contrasted with the kindliness of her word, robbed him, momentarily, of his own self-assurance. Everything about her—the movements of her hands, her way of standing, the modulations of her voice—spoke of her experience. A woman of that age who could still head a programme must have something rare about her. Her *forte*, they said, was impersonations, character studies, little sketches of town life—the very style he hoped, in time, to make his own.

" Come, continue," she said, with a patronising gesture. " Why waste time ? Your music is on the stands ; I will watch you. The work of young people always interests me, and you, from your age, cannot yet have a great deal of experience. Perhaps some of mine may be of service to you."

She turned and left the stage. Instinctively her steps led her down the passage which led to the auditorium ; in the bútacas were gathered a few spectators—Pressmen, their friends, and the casuals who, for some reason, feel it adds to their importance to come to a rehearsal. She avoided them all ; she went upstairs to one of the palcos, where she sat down, alone in the chilly darkness, and surrendered herself to the memories which, from the moment of her arrival in Granada, had been thrusting themselves against the barrier of her will. Looking down upon the stage, it seemed to be herself that she saw there.

It was not often that Maravilla thought of her lovers ; the days of love were over, and she did not find the pleasure taken by some women in turning over the wrack left by those tides.

There were few towns touched in her travels which did not carry some indistinct memory—rarely agreeable—of an amorous incident ; but, for reasons known only to herself, every moment of a certain night in Granada was registered upon her mind in colours as bright and clear as they had been eighteen years ago. She would have given much to have dismissed them : they filled her less with remembered rapture than their consequences filled her with shame and pain.

She made a movement of impatience ; to escape from her thought she leaned forward to give her full attention to Andrés, who had started the first of his numbers. To her surprise she found it—or him—interesting. His material was lamentable—the usual material of the third-rate comedian that appeals solely to the lowest section of the audience and usually empties the palcos—but he had a neat way of handling it ; he timed his preposterous jokes cleverly, and delivered them with a whimsical style of utterance that mitigated their grossness. He had the intimate manner of the cabaret performer, and his voice, when at last he come to his song, was pleasant ; his enunciation distinct. Maravilla was very interested ; he had either been very well trained—which seemed unlikely—or he had a natural instinct for the stage, which was even more interesting. She began to get excited ; all her impersonal delight in her art leapt to encourage the young performer.

Someone came into the palco behind her ; it was Gómez, who sat down beside her, took his cigar out of his mouth, and nodded towards the stage.

" That's something a little more than usual—no ? "

" Who is he ? " she asked eagerly.

" I picked him out of a cabaret here," boasted Gómez. " Before that, they say, he was with a travelling show ; and before that—quien sabe ? A waiter, so I've heard. Not so bad, is it ? "

" If he had something clever to do, instead of that—— ! What does he call himself ? "

" Andrés. I have never heard any other name."

" With a little teaching he would be excellent ; good enough for the drama. I shall tell him so." She thought excitably of people to whom she could introduce him, of managers to whom she might recommend him. The boy's thin, anxious face, his slightly hectic manner of nervousness, which he had visibly conquered during his performance, but which descended upon him as he hurried off the stage, appealed to some incalculable instinct she had not known herself to possess.

Andrés watched the great Maravilla del Monte go through her numbers with mingled feelings. He was too inexperienced to realise that she was saving herself for the night, giving no more than an indication of what she meant to do, for the benefit of the bandsmen who had to accompany her characterisations. He was disappointed, puzzled, and—hypnotised. It was like seeing a magnificent painting through a veil ; but now and then, as through a rent in the veil, shot forth such a ray of brilliance that he found himself gasping, doubting his eyesight, his understanding. It was not for him to realise that she was doing it on purpose : that each time the ray appeared it was directed deliberately at him ; that the woman who directed it had calculated to a nicety its effect upon its object. Maravilla knew that in this her original *métier* she was a much finer artiste than she had ever been in the legitimate drama. For the latter her style had been too broad, too florid. She held to her original intention of not cheapening herself by giving away her whole performance at the rehearsal, but, for some reason for which she was totally unable to account, she found herself unable to resist giving this boy a taste of her quality. It was partly a matter of vanity, for, remembering other beginners, she thought it possible he would misinterpret her restraint ; but why she should trouble herself about his misinterpretation was a thing inexplicable to herself, as it would have been to anyone else save probably Andrés, with his youthful conceit.

" The curtain rises at ten," the artistes were told, as they prepared to leave the theatre.

" Olá, niño ; come here and speak to me," said Maravilla. She was acting on impulse. It was sheer folly to hang about the ice-cold theatre, with a fatigued body and a empty stomach that predisposed one to the pulmonía which is the dread of the artiste ; she dragged the collar of her coat more closely about her throat, noticing that he had only the thinnest of jackets—a paper-weight smartness—to protect him from the cold. If she were only a rich woman she would buy him an overcoat to cover his ridiculous americano ! " You know, you are very good—really extraordinarily good. But you must not always be satisfied to present rubbish."

Andrés smiled, only partly understanding ; he had never thought of his songs as rubbish. They were the kind of thing people liked—although probably in a town like Sevilla, or in Madrid, the audiences wanted something better. What was " better " ? He supposed he would find out in time.

" Who has taught you ? What experience have you had ?" she was asking him.

" I have taught myself, señora. I worked in a cabaret for a time, but it's closed down ; Granada isn't big enough to support two places of the kind. It isn't a good town for artistes."

" That is clear enough. So what are you going to do ?

" I want to go to Madrid."

" Have you any friends ? Any people who can help you ? "

" No, señora," answered Andrés, with a note of pride in his voice.

" No one ? " she insisted. He shook his head, smiling.

" No one at all. I haven't any parents, and I have looked after myself since I was twelve years old."

" Madre mía. But you belong to the theatre ? Your parents—one of them, at least, was an actor ? Don't tell me I'm wrong. Genius doesn't generate itself, you know— perhaps we will not say genius, but there is something in your work, something that can't be taught, that can only be born in the person—a matter of inheritance. From where did you get that ? "

" I haven't the least idea, señora."

" What ? You did not know your parents ? "

" No. I'm a foundling." He spoke defiantly.

The blood rushed suddenly to her eyes ; she felt moisture breaking out all over her body. The condition was not strange to her : she had reached the time of life when women are troubled with sudden accesses of heat and cold, and swimmings in the head, and faintnesses. She told herself that her condition was due to this ; but a question forced itself to her lips, and was only held back by sheer strength of will. What was to be gained by asking that question ? Was she prepared to hear the answer ? These must be answered before she asked it. Her eyes, the only living things in her face, which had become a mask, plunged into his, seeking reassurance. There was nothing there to give her half-acknowledged suspicion any groundwork ; no trait of feature or colouring which associated itself in any way with others that held for her a special meaning. The olive skin, soft and smooth with youth, the languid, almond-shaped eyes were alike so common they amounted to a disguise for the multiple variations of the human soul. The narrow, light framework of the body held no distinguishing characteristics by which one could name it, and say, " In this way So-and-so is built." She struggled against an onslaught of imagination which invariably comes to the assistance of a half-suspicion.

The brain of Andrés was revolving his opportunity. It was not every day one came by such chances ; it might be that fortune would never again put in his way so obvious a solution of his difficulties.

" If you could advise me——" he stammered. She cried sharply :

" To what ? How ? "

" If I get to Madrid : who to go and see—what to do."

She looked at her wrist-watch ; she wanted nothing, now, but to escape from his presence, to be alone with her thoughts, her fears, her suspicions. . . . But surely the latter were absurd ?

" Ask me on another occasion ; I am tired—and hungry. You have somewhere to eat ? " The question was irrepressible.

" At my lodgings, señora——"

" Oh—you have money for lodgings ? "

" I live with the aunt of my novia."

" Which is the way out of this place ? " she interrupted.

" With your permission, I will conduct you——"

" Wait ; my maid is waiting for me. I have to find out where we are stopping . . ."

" Don't give yourself the trouble to mount the stairs, señora. I will find her and bring her to you."

She heard his feet go flying up the stairs as she sat on the chair he had set for her. She felt faint, sick, afraid. A reluctance she felt to be wholly unnatural prevented her asking the question her conscience informed her it was her duty to ask. Trying to rally herself, she grimaced at the thought of how differently the situation would have been treated on the stage—of the eagerness with which the heroine would clasp her long-lost child to her bosom. That was, according to dramatic convention, the obvious reaction.

" He walks like me ; he speaks like me ; he has my tricks with his head and hands." This way lay madness. Her question unasked, what proof had she that Andrés was her son ? How far was treacherous imagination leading her, since she had opened the door to it ? The hackneyed theory was that, in such a moment of encounter, some mutual instinct drew mother and child together : what instinct had she had, or the boy either, in their moment of meeting ? Nothing. All she now felt was built upon an ambiguous possibility, which she herself lacked courage to crystallise into fact.

Strange that, in all the years that had passed, this possibility had never once occurred to her ; how should it ? A thing so improbable in a world so wide : a weakly new-born child, dealt with by its distracted mother in the only way her imagination could devise in the midst of her professional demands. " Up to the hour before you were born, I was on the stage ; four hours afterwards, I was in the train with the company, which had its next engagement at two days' distance from the town where you were born. Could I have exposed you to that ? Could I have borne to have watched you dying in my hands, unable to afford the nourishments which alone would have saved your life ? God knows I had treated you badly enough before you saw the light of day : hiding you, denying you, because if I had acknowledged you neither of us would have had enough to eat ! " Thus she had justified to herself her own

action ; but how could she face this child whom she had
deserted ? How explain to him her motives, the need
which had driven her, or the bitterness—long dead—she
had felt towards the innocent thwarter of her schemes ?
How could she say, " I am your mother," and assume in
a moment all the responsibilities of motherhood which in
the first place she had renounced ?

" Por Dios, señora, you have the face of death ! Take my
arm, lean on me. This accursed place has given you your
death of cold," muttered Rosario, as she found her mistress
hunched up on the chair, her face leaden in colour, buried
in the collar of her coat.

" Andrés." With great difficulty, after the midday meal,
María had contrived an opportunity to speak to him.
Dolores, who was still weak, had gone to lie down, but
María knew she was watched, and spied upon, by every
member of the household. Latterly she had begun to
wonder if Dolores's suspicions had been roused ; on several
occasions she had surprised a piercing inquiry in her aunt's
eyes, and had nervously to turn her head away. Sooner or
later, now, Dolores would have to know, and no doubt she
would be very angry ; but María's every instinct warned
her to keep her secret to herself as long as possible. Not
even Andrés must know until it was quite certain ; but
after nearly two months——— ?

He had made signs to her, during the meal, that he
wanted to speak to her, so, greatly daring, she had stolen
back to the dining-room after the tables had been cleared
and the lodgers had mostly gone about their various business. Andrés had risen from his own place ; his own room
was too bitterly cold to invite him to repose during the
daytime, so he had moved to sit at the family table, under

which was a brasero ; he had crossed his arms on the table, and put his head down on them ; he was nearly asleep.

María crossed the room nervously. Old Don Natálio would take no notice ; the other, a stranger, favoured her with the inevitable stare, but was too occupied in picking his teeth and cleaning his nails—both of which offices he performed with the same implement—to offer further attentions. She touched Andrés on the shoulder ; he started, looked up, and beamed.

" María de mi alma——"

" Cállate ! We are not alone," she whispered.

He jumped to his feet, flinging an impatient glance at the others, bit his thumb-nail, and put his mouth close to her ear.

" We can't talk here ; come to my room."

" Por Dios, Andrés ! "

" Well, it won't be for the first time."

" But in the daytime——"

" Tell them you're going to sleep—because of the theatre to-night—and slip up the back stairs."

After an interval, nerve-racking for them both, she slipped through the door of the little attic-room ; she slid the bolt behind her, stood facing him, and trembling.

" Come, María mía ; it's so cold, we'd better get into bed."

With the blankets dragged round their shoulders, they sat together, pressed side by side, in each other's arms : kissing each other with soft, small kisses, as though the enormity of their action scared the desire out of them, and left them with nothing but a gentle, innocent affection for each other. María's kisses suddenly stopped ; she stared at the wall at the foot of Andrés's bed, at an empty nail.

" Why—she's gone ! "

" Of course she's gone—down to the theatre. You don't

suppose I'm going to make my first appearance without La Divina Pastora to look after me ? "

" But she isn't your patrona ! "

" What does that matter ? She's always been with me, everywhere. I'm superstitious about her."

" You've got the medal I gave you ? "

He opened his shirt, and showed her the little silver disc pinned inside the breast : Nuestra Señora de las Angustias, the miraculous Virgin of Granada.

" Doña Dolores gave me another. I'm as well rigged up for medals as though I were a bullfighter going into the ring. You shall see—I'll beat all of them to-night. La Maravilla spoke to me this morning ; she thinks a lot of me, I can tell you."

" What is she like ? " María had an almost morbid longing to see this woman who was so strangely connected with her own life. She wondered what Andrés would say if she told him ; but some obscure feeling of loyalty towards Aurelio had sealed her lips. She had never even told Andrés that her name was really Maravilla ; ever since that overheard conversation at the widow Herédia's she had suffered from a curious self-consciousness of the name by which she was baptised ; she was glad that another had been found for her, and that she was always called by it. Although she had always meant to let Andrés into the secret of her real name, it had become impossible from the day on which La Maravilla was first mentioned between them.

" Buena persona," answered Andrés. " Listen, María. I believe she's going to give me the money to go to Madrid."

María gave a cry, and clutched him.

" You are not going to Madrid ! "

" Pues ! You know I always meant to go to Madrid. How else am I to earn money, and make it possible for us to get married ? "

" I won't allow you to go to Madrid ! " she sobbed, holding him against her bosom. A flash of masculine impatience made him wriggle a little in her arms.

" But, María mía. You must be reasonable. We've each got to look after ourselves until I can look after both of us. It's not as though your people are doing anything to help."

" It is not mi padre's fault he can't help us ! "

" I dare say not ; although, after the way he talked to us the other day, I must say I expected him to come and see me at the theatre to-night. He says he's not altogether against me ; so he might have shown a little interest——"

" You don't understand anything about it ! " cried María, flaming, as usual, at any hint of adverse criticism of Aurelio. " Mi pobre papá ! " she thought tenderly. " Dio' mío, but he must have been terribly in love with that woman ! " She was rather glad Aurelio was not coming ; she would certainly have been tormented by a jealous fear that the bygone passion, which now she so well understood, would revive. How sad that she could not tell him she knew all about it ; fold him in her arms, and let the sympathy of understanding which only experience brings console him for all the sorrows of the past. " You must not go away to Madrid and leave me all alone," she reiterated. " What do you suppose I am to do without you ? "

" It will not be very agreeable for me either, will it ? Thinking of you here, all by yourself—perhaps finding another novio."

" Never—upon the cross ! "

" You swear it ? "

" Andrés mío, how can you ask such a thing ? "

" I'd come back and kill him," he threatened savagely. She shivered with delight.

" Of course you would. *Don't* go, Andrés mío ! "

" You don't care if I'm famous or not ? "

" I don't care for anything, except having you near me."

" Even if we never get married ? We can't expect your aunt to keep me for ever, you know. Especially if she finds out——"

" She won't, until I tell her. But, Andrés mío, I shall have to tell her, and everybody, very soon," whispered María.

" What do you say ? " He stiffened ; grew sharp with attention.

" I may be going to have a baby."

" Por Dios ! " He was frozen.

" Aren't you glad ? It's seven weeks——"

" Are you sure ? "

" Quite sure. They'll have to let us be betrothed properly then. And you won't have to go away and leave me just when I'm going to have a little baby, will you ? "

He muttered something, giving her a perfunctory caress. Secretly, he was horrified. Her family would be furious ; he would almost certainly be prevented from going to Madrid—that meant he would be tied to this dead-end of a Granada, or, worse, to María's hill-village, for the rest of his life. The future looked like melting in his hands. His mind worked rapidly.

" María mía." He adored her, of course ; but why, oh, why, had she got to have a baby when they were both so young ? In his affairs with other girls nothing like this had happened ; he had never so much as dreamed of its happening with María. " If that's the case," he said slowly, " we shall have to do something. You will have to come away with me." The moment the words were out of his mouth, he perceived, with hideous distinctness, how the addition of a woman and a child was going to complicate his future. God ! And he had not one to consult, no one to turn to for advice or help—he was alone in the world ! There was only one thing to do—the thing which people like him did when they got into difficulties : to run away.

" Come with you to Madrid ? But what would mi papá say ? "

" You are right. It would not do at all."

" So you see we must stay here ; and some day we shall have a lovely little baby of our very own. And when I have him to keep me company," said María artfully, " then you can go away for a little while and make money for us both——"

" Why did you tell me this now ? " he cried wildly.

" Now ? What difference does it make—now or another time ? "

" You will look well if you have ruined my performance to-night ! " he cried, with the actor's egotism.

" But how should that be, Andrés mío ? You have got two things to be proud of : of me, sitting in the palco and clapping my hands every time you do anything, and of this "—she took his hand and pressed it to her body—" of which you are the father ! What a fine night for you ! "

He got out of the bed and began to pull on his shoes.

" Where are you going ? "

" I'm going to walk a little. You don't understand—this has made me nervous ; as though my nerves weren't enough on end already. You have a lot to learn, María, before you are fit to be an artiste's wife ! " he flung at her savagely.

" But I don't understand," said María, so pitifully that he caught her in his arms and crushed his mouth to hers.

" Of course you don't understand, hijita de mi alma ! No more do you understand how much I love you. I love you ; I could eat you ; one of your eyelashes is more dear to me than—than the sight of my eyes ! It destroys me to think of parting with you——"

" But you aren't going to part with me," she cried.

" Of course not. Never. Never in my life." But he knew

it was a lie, and the tears glittered upon his lashes. His lovely, darling María ! He ought never to have loved her —he ought to have seen from the beginning it was no use for him to fall in love with a girl of her class. There were plenty of others—plenty. A sob broke from him ; he roughly put her arms aside and rushed from the room.

She cried a little ; but when she had crept back to her own room her serenity revived in taking out and shaking the dress Dolores had made for her to wear at the theatre : of black, because of their mourning for Angustias Herédia, but all little frills and tucks and cut pieces—such a dress as never had been seen in Agujasierra ; it would have given her pleasure to wear it there !

CHAPTER VI

THE THEATRE

IT WAS SUNDAY NIGHT, and, to the comfort of the artistes, the theatre was moderately full. An audience composed mainly of men filled the floor and the two tiers of palcos. A great deal of whistling and shouting betrayed the impatience of the cheaper parts of the house that the show should begin. As usual, the curtain was late in rising ; it was nearly twenty minutes past ten.

To his horror, Andrés had found he was to open the proceedings : as befitted the most inexperienced—and, by implication, the worst—of the artistes, he was sent on to receive the ironic applause of the galleries, to fill in the time while the palcos slowly received their quota of the important and sophisticated people whose interest in the entertainment began and ended with the star.

The palms of his hands were soaking ; his tongue clove to the roof of his mouth ; the crude make-up which he had chosen to contribute to his comedy was running down his face long before his call came. He stood in the wings, his knees knocking together, waiting for the band to finish the overture. He had to go on in silence ; the first ten minutes of his number consisted of patter, interspersed by some foolish actions and a jiggling little dance that led into his song. For the first time his material struck him as inadequate : supposing they did not laugh ? Supposing he got the bronca for his efforts ? He had seen no one to give him a word of encouragement ; the stage hands were profoundly indifferent, the stage-manager only interested in his timing, the other artistes sunk in their individual egotism. He had not, since arriving in the theatre, caught a glimpse of La Maravilla. He felt intensely outside of it all : the unwanted amateur, encroaching on ground reserved for other people. He was fearfully impressed by the stage itself, by its appointments, its mysterious lights and pulleys, its painted canvases, its shadowed recesses.

He could feel a helpless panic taking possession of him ; his muttered prayers, the contact of María's medal upon his flesh, gave him no sort of confidence. What he needed was the presence of some familiar object : something that he knew, that was familiar among all this strangeness. Suddenly turning tail, he ran at full speed away from the wings, took, with a series of bounds, the stairs to the dressing-rooms, and, a moment later, was back, panting, with the required object in his arms. The mere contact of the worn frame, of the broken glass, as his fingers traced the crack, of the odd little painting of La Divina Pastora, gave him what he needed. This had been with him in all his wanderings : it was the only thing that had accompanied him through all his short, troubled life. He pressed his lips to the rosy, painted face of the Virgin, and placed the frame carefully in a dark corner beside the proscenium. He was quite calm ; as the curtain rolled up, hissing, into its mysterious hiding-place, he walked into the lights as though he had been doing precisely that thing every night of his life.

The white blur of faces at first dazzled him ; he stood, for a moment, confused by them. This was very different from the cabaret, where, by stretching out one's hand, one could touch almost every member of the audience. It was different from the scrofulous little show, where stage and auditorium alike partook of the illumination of the big arc-lamp hung from the middle of the tent. He raised his head, startled, and almost at once saw María, leaning upon the edge of her palco, beaming at him, Dolores beside her, and standing behind them, smoking a cigar, Don Luis, who had come, inevitably, to escort his womenfolk. But who was the fourth in the box—sitting apart from the rest, with a stillness that seemed to merge his figure into the woodwork which formed its background ?

Andrés had a shock not altogether pleasant in recognising María's father. He must have come unexpectedly ; but why ? She had so definitely stated that he would not be there. He seemed queerly out of place, with his Cordobés hat on his head, his hands clasped on the handle of a stick.

The long pause that succeeded his appearance had roused the not too friendly attentions of the audience ; he pulled himself together, and delivered his first line.

After a while he became so confident that he actually was able to look about him while doing his business. Stage work he found to be almost child's play after the rough-and-tumble to which he had been accustomed. He smiled up at María, but caught her watching her father with an anxious and loving expression.

Glancing into the wings, he saw La Maravilla standing there, motionless, with her eyes apparently fixed on him. At first this gave him a thrill of pleasure, that she should pay him the compliment of coming down before her call to watch him ; but, the next time he looked at her, he saw that her eyes were not on him ; instead, they looked directly across his head, their glance struck deep into the darkness of the auditorium. At whom was she gazing ? Her face was perfectly still ; the colour she had put upon it made it seem like a painting against its shadowy background. But her eyes had a terrible life in them. She was looking—that is, she seemed to be looking—straight up at the box in which María was sitting ; but why should she ? What was there there to rivet her cold, her almost terrible, attention ?

As the curtain began to come down, Maravilla moved sharply, and her foot struck against something. There was a tinkle of glass ; she bent, automatically, to see what had fallen : glass in the wings meant danger to the artistes. She picked up an old picture-frame, with some fragments of glass in it. With it in her hands, she became immovable. Her question was answered.

" Por Dios, señora, what is wrong with you ? Ojalá, that we had never come to Granada ! There's something evil in the place—you look all the time as if you were seeing ghosts."

" I am. Give me the lipstick." With the firm, apparently heedless, sweep of old, she outlined the blurred contours of her lips.

" Well, I must say I've never seen anyone do that like you do it before ! " said Rosario admiringly. " And without a look in the glass."

" Listen. While I am on the stage I want you to find that young man's dressing-room ; that young fellow—you know the one I mean. Tell him that I want to see him ; tell him to be sure not to leave the theatre without my seeing him."

" Now, don't you forget it doesn't do to be too generous," grumbled Rosario, with a jealous look at her mistress.

" Will you do me the favour to mind your own business ? "

" Oh, I know what you are—a duro here, a duro there, to people who haven't done anything but pick up your handkerchief ! I suppose, like all these young artistes, he's been telling you he's hard up ? "

" Another word and I will have you put out of the theatre. Quick, get me a glass of cognac before I go on ; my nerves are in ribbons to-night."

" *That*'s not like you," muttered Rosario, as she ran to do her mistress's bidding.

Since the moment he took his seat in the palco, Aurelio had never moved. He felt himself to be the victim of some great tide that swept him hither and thither in its ebb and flow without the smallest personal volition. What, save fate itself, could have brought him down to Granada, when he had intended to stay at home and postpone his usual visit to María until later in the week ? It was Carmela who had come to him, with—

" See, Aurelio ; I want to make my mother a little present. She is very fond of olives, and the last that I pickled myself are nearly gone. She will be very much annoyed if she thinks I have forgotten her taste for them."

So trivial a request should have been easy to dismiss, or at least to postpone ; there was no particular reason why Doña Marta should have her olives on that especial Sunday, but Carmela had the stone jar in her hands, and added sharply :

" You will be catching the usual tramcar ; see you don't forget them when you set off."

Her calm, and perfectly reasonable, assumption that he was following his usual practice of visiting María took the power of explanation out of his lips. If he were to say he was not going, her suspicions would inevitably be aroused. " Why not ? What is this ? What secret have you and María got between you ? " She had been so unexpectedly reasonable about his visits to María, had so consistently forborne to remark upon them, or to put difficulties in his way, that he felt a great reluctance to rousing her curiosity in the present instance. Besides, what harm could be done by his taking the jar of olives to Doña Marta, calling in upon María, and catching the last tram, which left the Puerta

KM

Real at five o'clock—the procedure which he had regularly followed since María went to Granada. The fact that Granada had suddenly shrunk to a small shell enclosing one figure only—that of Maravilla—existed, of course, only in his imagination. Supposing they should meet, after so many years, how many were the chances of their recognising each other ? And if they did so, what harm in it ?

But during the whole of the journey his heart drummed against his ribs ; in the streets of Granada it seemed impossible to keep his eyes from plunging deep into those of every stranger—so that women shrank away from the wild-looking countryman.

María was delighted to see him—so unexpectedly. It seemed to him once or twice that she had a great deal to say ; that her words came nervously, in great volume ; that she seemed anxious to prevent his talking, his asking questions. She said little of Andrés—and that little in connection with his appearance at the theatre. But for the first time in his life he wanted to escape, even from his María ; he had a feeling of danger, of something that threatened the difficult calm which had succeeded the long struggle of his life.

For once, his sister-in-law's husband was at home : a man with whom Aurelio had little in common, but who, for some unknown, masculine reason, elected to accompany him to the tramway when he had made his adieux. Don Luis Fermín, hat on the side of his head, and, as usual, lightly elevated with wine, utilised the journey to entertain Aurelio with an account of his latest mistress. Aurelio listened patiently, bored in his soul, and conscious all the time of that obscure anxiety which, he felt, would only be alleviated when the tram started on its journey to the mountains.

The terminus, usually fairly crowded at the hour of the

evening tram, was strangely deserted. Aurelio looked about him, puzzled. A couple of loungers, seeing his uncertainty, called out to him, " Are you waiting for the tramway, hombre ? It's out of order ; there's nothing running until to-morrow morning." So common a factor of Granada locomotion raised no excitement in an accustomed people. Don Luis smote his companion on the shoulder.

" There you are ! What could be better, from your point of view or María's ? A little holiday, a change—one can have too much of the connubial life, no ? And out in your part of the world—hombre, you must get sick of it ! I know what those pueblos are—everyone knowing everyone else's business ! Granada is bad enough, but it's not so bad for a stranger. You can make a fine night of it, and no one any the wiser. It couldn't have fallen out better—in fact, it's very rarely these accidents happen at the moment one could do with them ! You will, of course, accompany us to the theatre ; we have a palco—yes, Dolores insisted on it. These family parties are a nuisance, but when they happen the only thing is to make the best of them. And having one of the artistes in the house—well, it becomes an obligation, no ? Not that I shall be sorry to see the end of him. Lodgers who don't pay for their rooms are better out of the way. Still, it's no use arguing with women. And perhaps we both know someone who would be sorry to see him gone ? You don't intend that to be taken seriously, do you, hombre ? "

What was the use of arguing ? There was nothing to be done. The memory of a night when he had walked from Granada to Agujasierra shot like a dart into Aurelio's mind. Such feats were not for one's later years—and, moreover, Carmela would say he was mad to attempt it. Nor would it be possible to stay in Granada without going to the theatre. What excuse could one offer for slighting the hospitality of the Fermíns and, doubtless, grievously disappointing his María ? But he was conscious of a faint feeling of puzzled surprise at her manner of receiving the announcement. He saw her go first white, then red, and she shot at him a queer, furtive glance which did not seem to belong to his María. " Now you will be satisfied—now you have your father to go with you ! " said Dolores ; and she answered hurriedly, " Claro, I am satisfied," and made an excuse to go out of the room. All of these things would have impressed him more deeply had he not been conscious, all the time, of being the plaything of a fate more powerful and more unscrupulous than any he had so far encountered.

In the theatre, time was not. He sat as though stunned, and from his weatherbeaten body eighteen years slipped away. He became an empty shell, or a watch-case in which, with a loud, echoing reverberation, ticked his heart.

He barely saw Andrés's performance : would have been wholly unaware of it, had it not been for the excited pressure of María's hand upon his knee, of her panting whispers : " Did you see that, papá ?—Was not that very good ?— Do you hear how they are clapping ? " He barely caught the warning and ironical glance of Dolores's beautiful eyes across his daughter's head. " Yes, that must be good, hija —that must be good," he murmured to satisfy her, when the laughter and applause reached the far region in which his spirit had taken refuge. Once or twice, at a lewder sally which made the women take refuge behind their fans, Don Luis gave a chuckle. He leaned heavily on Aurelio's shoulder. " But wait until you see La Maravilla ! I saw her once or twice in Sevilla when she was a girl. After that she took to acting in plays—I never cared for the drama. But you see, she's found it best to return to her former line. Digo, hombre ! She was formidable in those days. Well, we shall see, shan't we ? "

A vertigo seized him when the curtain rose for the third time. (The second artiste on the programme had been a dancer, to whom he paid as little attention as to Andrés.) He was not aware of María's hand withdrawn from his knee : of the stiff, conscious line of her head and neck, both averted from him. He knew nothing until he saw Don Luis leaning over his daughter, and heard his husky inquiry—" Well, young lady, what do you think of your namesake ? "—and met María's eyes, brilliant and burning, gazing full into his. In that moment seemed to take place the apotheosis of their intimacy; his own eyes said, " Forgive me ! " and hers, " I love you ! " No two lovers could have exchanged a deeper, a more understanding, regard.

But in between lay a space of confusion, of attempted adjustments, of spiritual travail, as his mind struggled to link the past with the present : to identify the solitary figure that took such a regal command of the stage with the being, human and super-human, that his soul remembered.

It may have been partly his closeness to the stage, partly the experience of his later years, that left little room in the mind of Aurelio, then, for illusion. In place of that celestial figure, he saw, clearly, a hard, handsome actress, making the most of charms that were visibly waning, smiling through reddened lips, exerting the utmost lure of brilliant eyes upon a palco full of middle-aged men on the immediate right of the stage, a Cordobés hat upon her head, a rose between her teeth, a shawl so arranged as to outline in the most becoming fashion a figure which had kept its lissomeness, if not its slender contours, as La Maravilla opened her programme with a national number.

Now, as before, he had no means of judging of the quality of her performance ; its finer points—and when did the performances of La Maravilla lack those ?—were totally lost upon him. His sex made its utterly mechanical response, as it proceeded, to the demands she made upon the sex of every man in the audience ; his dry lips even parted in a smile, of which he was not conscious, at one or two of her jests that brought a roar and cries of " Olé, la Maravilla ! " from the house. But much of what she said—her quick, topical allusions, her witty generalisations—was lost upon him ; it belonged to a world outside the knowledge of a mountain villager.

He did not perceive the delicacy and beauty of her impersonation of a fashionable woman having her hair dressed, or the raking irony of her " Ladies in Church," or her dashing " Bullfighter." He was puzzled and amused by her study of two old women gossiping at a well. Much of her work was, indeed, completely above the heads of her audience ; it was the kind of thing that Raquel Meller has made famous in foreign countries. Granada applauded, but reserved its wilder enthusiasm for her modern topical songs —the broader the better—and her Spanish costumes.

She was a stranger. A kind of relief dawned upon him. Without knowing it, Aurelio drew a deep, audible breath that was almost a groan.

But as the curtain started to come down she threw a momentary direct glance up at his box, and in an instant revived all the doubts, fears, and uncertainties of the night they had spent together.

" I was abominable. I deserved to be hissed from the stage."

" What are you saying, mujer ? They went mad over you."

" These provincial fools ! What do they know ? You're right ; brilliance is wasted on them. Well, I gave them just what they deserve, to-night ! "

" I believe there's someone in front ! I've never seen you like this before," commented Rosario.

" Madre mía ! Yes, if you want to know, there is ' someone in front.' And not in front alone. Por Dios, must I be tormented in this fashion ? "

" An old lover ? " pressed Rosario, greatly thrilled.

" Hold your tongue, woman ! Did you give my message ? "

" But naturally I did, señora. Will he be escorting you home ? "

" Are you out of your mind ? Since when have I let myself be escorted home by young men of the theatre ? "

" Jesú, mujer ! I'm not talking of him. The caballero in front."

" If you mention that once again I shall throw a bottle at you. What did he say ? "

" What should he say ? " retorted the woman sulkily. " He asked what time would best suit your convenience, and I said when you had changed your dress for your second appearance. I supposed you didn't want to hang round at the end of the show."

" Very well. When you have shown him in, you can take these letters and post them—not in an estanco ; I don't trust the collections. You can take them up to the general office——"

" And suppose your call comes when I'm out ? "

" I don't need your arm to help me down the stairs, do I ? Collect my things, and follow me down as quickly as you can."

Andrés stood shyly at the door ; he was still in the ridiculous garments of his second appearance ; was breathless from his efforts, and conscious—this time, definitely—of having been a success.

She did not turn towards him ; she sat with her back to him, devouring with her eyes every inch of his reflection, which was opposite to her in the glass. Just like that she herself must have appeared in her youth : running off the stage, breathless with excitement, to burst into her mother's dressing-room to boast of her triumphs ; beautiful, young, and eager, confident of the future, brave and adventurous, seeing the world as a thing to be conquered, fame as a certainty, almost within reach.

Yes ; she would tell him. But not here. Not now. Her eyes lost their hardness, became passionately tender, as her future resolved itself—no longer a struggle for herself but for him ! Every ounce of weight that his mother's reputation could contribute in his favour should be at his disposal. Her lips broke into a smile as she thought of what this would mean to him : the miraculous smoothing of paths ; the opening of doors which had once seemed irrevocably closed ; the priceless opportunities sought in vain by young people, equally gifted, who had no recommendations and no guarantors for their talents. Her own sun might be setting : she could watch the extinction of its rays with equanimity in the dawning of a new day. She could always struggle along, with an engagement here and there, a little entertaining in cabarets, an odd comedy part in a third-rate company. And all she had—all she earned—should be dedicated to him, until he needed it no longer.

Nor would she allow him to tax himself with her maintenance when that time came. What claim had she on him—she who, for his own good, but also for her own convenience, had deserted him as an infant ? All that she could do, she owed to him for her act in putting him into the world ; he owed her nothing—not even the conventional duty of son to mother, since she had never been a mother to him.

Thank God—thank God that even in these days of her decline her name still stood for something that was not

forgotten in the world of the theatre : that world she knew
so intimately in all its branches. . . .

" You wanted to speak to me, señora ? "

" Come in." In her effort to steady her voice, its notes
grew harsh. She still kept her back to him. " What was that
you said—something about going to Madrid ? "

" That is what I wish, señora." The boy's voice, lacking
her control, trembled. " You can see for yourself, there is
nothing for a person in Granada. When to-morrow and the
next day are over I shall be without anything—again ;
unless they take me on at La Montillana. I shan't much
like that—after being here ! "

" And what will you do in Madrid ? "

" Look for work, I suppose," he said uncertainly.

" Indeed ! Anda, niño ! Do you suppose work is to be
found at every street corner ? "

" No—but there are theatres ; managers to see."

" You don't know what you're talking about," she told
him harshly. " How do you think you are going to see
managers ? They don't sit about at café tables, waiting to
be pestered by young men with a turn for the stage."

" Agents, then." He turned a little sullen under her
teasing.

" You can afford agents' fees ? You are prepared to put
yourself on their books ? "

" There must be ways of doing these things ; other people
do them," he retorted. Her tone changed ; she swung
round in her chair, and faced him ; he was startled by the
tenderness of her expression.

" Yes, niño ; you are right. There are ways, but you have
to learn them. There is one of the ways." She handed him
her card, on which she had scribbled a few words. " You
may find that useful when you start your hunting."

" A thousand thanks, señora ! " He caught her hand and

kissed it impulsively. She drew it away with a shudder, and picked up her purse from the bench. Thank God, there was, for once, money in it. She had, as usual, stipulated for a part of her salary in advance, and had also, before coming to Granada, drawn a little of what remained of her savings of the last few years. It was strange what had made her begin to save. Never in her life, until her return from the Argentine, had she saved a penny ; her mother's death, shortly before she took to the drama (had her mother lived, she might not have been permitted that excursion), had left her without obligations. Now it seemed as though there must have been some hidden intention in that saving. She drew from the purse three folded notes, and handed them to him. He blushed and trembled in taking them.

" God will repay you, señora ! And I—when I am earning money," he stammered.

" I make one stipulation only. That when I come back to Madrid you will seek me out," she said. " My address is on that card ; it is not in a very smart or imposing quarter—— But that has nothing to do with the matter. You will write to me there—you can read ? And write ? " she added quickly. It was possible he could not do either. What care, what schooling, had he had ? To her relief, he answered proudly :

" Naturally I can, señora ! "

" Then you will write, telling me where to find you, as soon as you get to Madrid. I shall be back in a month or less. You will swear to that ? "

He lifted his clasped hands and crossed thumbs in the gipsy fashion. She frowned.

" On something better than that. On something you hold in esteem. On your picture of La Divina Pastora."

He looked at her in astonishment.

" It was I who broke it."

" No, it was broken before," he corrected her. " I can easily put the bits back in the frame. Yes, La Divina Pastora—that's a thing I've got ; it was left with me—I suppose my mother left it—at the foundling hospital. It brings me luck—at least I think it does. Yes, I'll swear on that, if you wish me to, señora."

She thought, " There is no need to make him swear ; he knows the value of keeping me in sight." She understood the quick, bird-like, predatory glance he gave her when she had given him her card ; knew the way that young beginners cling to their benefactors until they are shaken off—or until they find someone more beneficent ! Yes, that was her only danger : that Andrés would find someone more celebrated—and, therefore, still more useful—than herself to help him. But he had sworn, and that, and what she had to tell him, made her safe. She would not, however, tell him in Granada—risk the information spreading, the reestablishment of some claim. . . . What would he say, supposing she took him by the hand, and, pointing to the palco, said, " There is your father ? "

When she had gone down for her second appearance, Andrés stood still, fingering the notes in his hand. His fingers trembled ; he had never had so much money before in his life. In imagination he was already in Madrid ; *why not be there in fact ?* What was to be gained by his finishing his engagement at Granada ? The sooner he got away the better—this opinion was strengthened by the appearance of María's father. Supposing she should take it into her head to tell him, to-night, about the baby ? The idea appalled him. There was a train that left Granada at midnight for Madrid ! By making a bolt immediately, he could surely catch it. He could write—explain to her. But how if, by breaking his three-night contract with Gómez, he should happen to offend, not the manager, but

La Maravilla ? That would be, with a vengeance, biting off his nose to spite his face !

His one single hope was to get at María immediately : warn her for the present to keep her mouth shut, say nothing to her, of course, about his plans, but get away quietly on Tuesday night after the performance. He thrust the notes hurriedly in his pocket ; he went back to his own dressing-room. Already there was something furtive in his movements—something that always moved below the surface of the mind of a young man whose living had depended wholly on his wits.

CHAPTER VII

PARENTS AND CHILDREN

WITH ALL the Andalucían love of gaiety, Dolores had prepared a little fiesta : there were sugared cakes, almonds, and sweet wine. " Look, is it what your mother would have done for you on such an occasion ? But mind now : no indiscretions. You understand what I refer to ? Things are only at their beginnings. Ojalá that all may go well with you, my son, in the end ! " She ran her fingers through the boy's hair with a loving, maternal gesture. " For all your meek looks, I'm not so sure you're not thoroughly bad underneath ! You and that little minx of a María ! Take care, the pair of you, you don't get me into trouble. And now," she cried, throwing open the door into her private room, " here is our hero of the night, here is our famous artiste ! What honour for the house ! Do me the favour, Don Natálio, to fill the glasses." Don Natálio, the doyen of the Casa Fermín, had been invited to join the family party, although he had not been to the theatre : in the absence of her husband—for, when the curtain came down, Don Luis had, as usual, gone about his own affairs— Dolores had felt the need of someone to do the honours of the feast she had lovingly prepared.

Andrés stood, smiling awkwardly, holding his glass. He would rather have been celebrating in a tavern with some of his own companions, but he had returned with the others in the hope of getting a word with María before she went to bed. There seemed small chance of it in the crowded little sitting-room, with María smiling with radiant shyness from the curve of her father's arm, with all eyes fixed upon himself, and the harsh glare of the light revealing the slightest change of expression upon all their faces. The compliments, the remarks, the flow of badinage, all proceeded from Don Natálio and Dolores : seemingly outside their glittering ambience sat the two from the mountains, the father and daughter, linked together by their mysterious intimacy, a little overcome by their recent bizarre experience. Andrés felt that intimacy as a thing to be feared, a thing which threatened him, from which, at all costs, he must secure himself. If only she would keep her mouth shut until Tuesday ! But she was looking at him now as if she could eat him ! She did not seem to care that her lips and her eyes were revealing things that are not supposed to exist between young lovers before their betrothal. Ordinarily such looks as she gave him would have contributed to his self-esteem ; on the present occasion they were too dangerous.

Suddenly she rose from her father's side. She joined Andrés and, in front of them all, put her hand through his arm.

" Now come, what is this ? " cried her aunt, with an alarmed look at Aurelio. Ignoring her :

" Papá mío. I want you to say something to Andrés. I want you to tell him he mustn't go to Madrid," she said boldly.

" Now—María ! " muttered Andrés, not knowing where to look.

Aurelio lifted his eyes, which had been fixed on the ground.

" What is it my daughter says ? "

" Now, Aurelio, don't pay any attention to this foolish girl ! " cried Dolores hastily. " She has a head full of nonsense ! Come," she added sharply to her niece, " is this a way to behave yourself in front of people ? What has it got to do with you where Andrés goes or what he does? He has to earn his living, and to-night he has made a fine beginning. No one must stand in his way."

" Come," said María, urging Andrés by his arm towards her father, as though, for her, the other people in the room had ceased to exist. " Papá mío, we have no secrets, have we ? You know we are only waiting your permission to be betrothed. There is no reason to wait any longer—is there, Andrés ? Andrés is going to be rich and famous, papá, and he must have someone to look after him."

" Cállate, niña," said Aurelio gently. " These things are for the future. You are both of you children——"

His words were interrupted by María's falling on her knees before him ; with her small, strong hands she gripped her father's thin knee-caps through the stuff of the trousers ; her eyes, uplifted, sped their message to his stricken heart before her whispered words were spoken :

" Can a child have a child, papá ? "

Andrés felt his limbs turning to water ; the room spun round him ; he waited for some outcry, some violence of action on the part of Aurelio ; none came.

" No," said Aurelio slowly. . . . Then, with a look of inexpressible reproach which passed from the one to the other, " You have both defeated me."

" Pues—Aurelio ! " wailed Dolores. He turned his haggard glance on her.

" Well ? It had to come some time. Who is to blame, if not myself ? It is better she should marry the one whom she loves, is it not ? "

" What will her grandmother say ? What will Carmela say ? "

" What have they done, either of them, to entitle them to say anything ? What do they know of my child's heart, of her wants, her wishes, her thoughts—which have been mine ever since she could speak to tell them to me ? This thing is for ourselves and no one else. Do you think it is easy for a father to put his feelings on one side ? When I lose her I lose everything ; I have no longer any reason for being. But what should I be if I let that come between her and her happiness ? She herself knows, as she has known from her babyhood, that her father's only desire is that she shall be happy. But you, my son, you did not know it ; and you have done very wrong by us. Take care that God does not repay you for what you have brought on her. You have much to atone for ; see that you atone for it."

Andrés stood mum ; his face was green with misery ; he felt as though he might be going to be sick. Dolores, weeping, sank into a chair. " And to think you should repay me in this fashion for all I have done for you ! And how can he marry her ? " she cried indignantly. " What has he besides the clothes he stands up in—and those, very likely, not paid for ? "

María, ignoring it all, was stroking and patting her father's face.

" You have forgiven us ? You have forgiven your María ? "

" It is I who should be asking for forgiveness—that God may grant it ! See how she confides in me. Ah, my son, if you ever come to know that confidence, you are more blessed than the holy saints themselves. How lovely is my little child, how good ! " he murmured, returning her caresses.

" But you are crazy, Aurelio ! The boy comes from nowhere at all. God knows it is not for me to make a reproach of it ; you will forgive me, niño. But he does not even know who his parents are ! My family won't care for that."

" We are all born alike, of a man and a woman. It makes

little difference by what door a child enters the world,"
said Aurelio.

" That is all very well," said Dolores more gently, " but
the world does not look kindly upon these things. You know
yourself there's a difference between walking in through the
door and stealing in through a broken window ! There is
nothing for it now, I suppose, but to let them be betrothed.
God knows how these things should have happened, with
all the pains I took. Thankless—deceitful—the pair of you !
She'll have to go home while I make my peace as well as
may be with my mother. I shall never hear the end of it
from her. I hope no one here thinks I had anything to do
with it."

María turned pale and bit her lip. She had not thought
of this solution of the situation. She turned imploring eyes
upon Aurelio, who, stunned, as he always was, by the
impact of fact upon his world of the spirit, only nodded
his head and agreed.

" Yes, she will have to come home."

" But, papá—— ! "

He sighed. He could feel upon himself once more the
compulsion to act, to arrange, to assert himself, which was
so foreign to his nature. But he realised that it was not
enough, now, to declare himself in the young couple's
favour ; whatever it might cost him, he must secure her
future safety and happiness. Betrothal ; marriage ; a home
with her parents, until her domestic situation resolved itself—those were what he owed to her. Carmela must be
brought to see this. . . .

" Perhaps I could go to my grandmother's for a while,"
suggested María timidly. " And Andrés could come with
me——"

" Por Dios, where do you get such ideas ? Do I know my
mother or do I not ? " cried Dolores.

" We will all three go home to-morrow," said Aurelio dully.

" Now, Aurelio ! You know the boy has his work to do——"

" And it would be better you should see my mother first," said María anxiously.

He agreed, after a pause, that it was better so. The clock struck three ; old Don Natálio, too old and selfish willingly to involve himself in the affairs of other people, had long since gone, mumbling some excuse, to his room ; their four faces were white with fatigue and strain.

" María must go to bed ! " said Dolores. " And you ! " She turned to Andrés and enveloped him in her look of bitter reproach. " Well, you have a bed like the rest of us. Go to it—and may shame steal the sleep from your pillow ! "

" Por Dios, señora, what have I done ? Is it a crime to fall in love ? The fact that I'm nameless doesn't rob the nature from me——"

" Be silent, shameless one ! Haven't you brought enough dishonour on my house ? "

He hung his head ; waited for a moment indecisively before María before muttering to her, " Good night, María."

She sprang up and took him by the arms.

" Well, aren't you glad it's over ? Do not pay too much attention to my aunt—she trusted us, and we have behaved very badly, but she will forgive us by and by. Didn't I tell you mi papá was as good as bread ? Aren't you happy to think it will all be arranged for us ? You won't need to go away now, will you, until the baby is born ? " she whispered. " You understand, alma mía, that I want you near me all the time until the baby comes. We'll be so happy at home ! My mother won't be so jealous when she sees

I have someone to take my attention away from papá. And she is bound to be pleased about the baby."

" Yes—I understand. Let me go, María. We'll—we'll talk about it to-morrow," he stammered.

" You love me ? " she whispered.

" Si te quiera ! " He gave her a quick, nervous pressure, made as though to kiss her—a movement she evaded.

" Andrés—por Dios ! Shall I ask papá for the key ? There's no reason now——"

" No—no ! "

" Then to-morrow will do."

" Come, María," said Dolores. " Say good night to your father."

Aurelio had risen heavily from his seat ; his bowed figure was turned towards them both. He drew the boy towards him, and, with his hands on Andrés's shoulders, looked long into his eyes.

" You have made yourself my son," he said slowly. " What do I know of you ? What have you in you that has made my daughter betray me ? I cannot see. But, then, I am foolish ; I am old. You two have between you the precious gift of youth. I should hate you ; but—I cannot tell why, my son—I love you. I can feel in you something that draws my love no less surely than the moon draws the tides after it. What can it be ? It is nothing of yourself, for I can see clearly what you are : you are vain, egoistical, unprincipled, and almost wholly worthless. The one thing that gives you worth is that my daughter loves you. But that by itself is not enough to account for this strange feeling that I have in my heart towards you.

" In a little while we shall know each other better. Yes, you can dedicate a few months to our knowing each other better. When one is so young, what is a month, a week, a year ? Your work can wait : you have other obligations to attend to for the present. And I—I must know to whom my daughter has given her heart."

"One does not expect to be punctual, but this is too much !" grumbled La Maravilla, dragging her fur coat about her uncovered shoulders. "At this rate one will be blue before one goes before the public !" She lit a cigarette impatiently. "You had better go across to the café and order them to send me in some coffee—and see it is covered !" she called after the retreating figure of the messenger. "And the curtain is supposed to go up at ten ! Why are audiences so stupidly patient ? One might think it were a tribute to the artistes if one did not know the temperament of these people—so slow, so apathetic !" Her thoughts were interrupted by a commotion which seemed to have broken out on the same floor. Accustomed to theatre brawls, she shrugged her shoulders and picked up a leather pad to polish her nails.

A loud rap on her door. "Se puede ? " cried a voice ; and, without waiting for permission, the dancer burst into the room. A *peignoir*, flung loosely across her shoulders, did not conceal the fact that she was in undress.

"Do you hear that ? " She was evidently in a violent passion. "They are asking me to go on first—to open the programme, if you please ! Whoever heard of such impertinence ? "

Maravilla again shrugged her shoulders ; she was too used to these struggles for precedence to be impressed.

"Entonces ! Do you by any chance suggest I should open it ? " she asked, with the dry superiority of the star.

"Mujer, por Dios ! But I refuse absolutely to be treated like a nobody," grumbled the other.

" You are right. They have no business to make alterations, to give beginners the positions of experienced artistes," said La Maravilla calmly : but her heart quickened a beat. Was it like that, then ? Had even Gómez, provincial ignoramus that he was, recognised the boy's merit by removing him from his position of ignominy at the beginning of the programme ?

" What are you saying ? They have made no alterations ! " said the dancer, in a tone of offence. " I would hardly expect that, even in a place of this sort. It is that that youth—that comedian, as he calls himself—has not turned up this evening. They only found out a few minutes ago——"

" What ? " said Maravilla, half rising from her chair.

" And Gómez had the coolness to suggest I should ' fill in ' for him ! I soon let him see I was not to be used for his convenience in that fashion ! He's sent out now to one of the cabarets——"

" But, por Dios, where has he gone ? "

" How should I know ? The audience is getting well out of hand, I can tell you that much ! Whoever turns up will have something to deal with."

Her teeth were chattering ; she began to walk up and down the narrow room. The other coolly seated herself in her chair. " I am not surprised you are annoyed. Who wouldn't be—at the prospect of being in this hole until two in the morning ? But you would not expect me to act otherwise, would you ? "

" Certainly not," replied Maravilla ironically.

The door had been left open, and the discomposed figure of Gómez appeared there, accompanied by another, a stranger to Maravilla.

" Well, what is this ? " she cried sharply.

" You do well to ask, señora ! It seems you have

something to do with it. This is what one gets for doing a good turn to these local good-for-nothings."

" I ? What are you talking about ? "

Gómez apparently made a great effort to control himself.

" Permit me to present my friend, Don Luis Fermín," he muttered. Don Luis, very much flattered at finding himself in the room of an actress—above all, of La Maravilla—tiptoed forward in his most fascinating manner, to bestow a kiss upon the fingers she absently extended to him.

" At your feet, señora ! What gratification it gives me to address so stupendous an artiste ! "

" A thousand thanks, señor. But what is this ? What have you—or I—to do with Andrés's disappearance ? "

Don Luis raised his shoulders, pursed his lips, and, with an expression of importance, drew an envelope from his pocket.

" It was not for you to know, señora, that the youth is the novio of my niece by marriage. Una cosa seria—they are to be married," he put in, in parenthesis. " It is not an agreeable thing for a young woman who is expecting to be married to receive a letter of that kind ! Particularly not," he added—but she was not listening—" in the circumstances. She got it this morning, on her return from the Mass."

" You might have let me know earlier," grumbled Gómez.

" Hombre ! One considers one's family first," returned Don Luis, in a tone of virtuous disapproval.

Maravilla had dragged the thin sheet of paper from the cover, and was devouring its contents. Some detached particle of her brain rendered account of the wrangling of the two men over her head.

" One does not find a ' turn ' so easily as that in Granada ! "

" I don't know about that. I had three women to deal with—my wife, my wife's mother, and the girl."

" A message could have been sent——"

" Are messengers always at hand ? The girl's father had to be informed ; he was half way up the sierras by then. It cost me ten pesetas to overtake the tramcar——"

" María de mi alma," read La Maravilla,—" When you get this I shall be on my way to Madrid. Forgive me, queridísima mía ! What were we to do ? There was no other remedy. Try to understand, María mía, that I could not come and live with your family out in the mountains—not even for a week. I have my career to think of, and now I have made a beginning I must not let anything stand in my way. Granada is no use to me ; I could never earn enough money here to keep us, and it is no use my living on your parents in an out-of-the-way place like Agujasierra. I am not the only person who thinks highly of my art, María mía, or who expects much of me. La Maravilla has given me the money to go to Madrid with, and she has promised to help me to get on. María mía, you know this is a great thing for me— that an important and famous person like that should interest herself in my career. With her influence I shall jump to the top in half the time it would take me if I were to struggle on by myself. I do not forget what you told me, but one never knows with these things ; it may not happen after all, and perhaps for now it would be better if it did not. María mía, I adore you with my body and my soul——"

She lifted her haggard head.

" I see how I am responsible. I am very sorry for this." Gómez shrugged his shoulders. " You know, with these people, it is not wise to put money in their hands before they have earned it ; they have no sense of obligation. And besides, he was conceited enough, without your adding to it."

" Your niece is suffering, señor ? " She turned to Don Luis.

" What would you have, señora ? When one is in love——" He sighed sentimentally.

" Poor girl. But what he says is the truth, señor. There are no opportunities here for artistes. Young people are ambitious ; it is right it should be so——"

She turned the envelope idly in her fingers ; the direction for the first time caught her eye. Señorita Doña María López Moreno. Her heart missed a beat. No. *No.* That could not be. There was no name in Spain more common than López. She swallowed a lump in her throat ; her fingers went icy cold.

The roar of the impatient audience penetrated to the dressing-room. Gómez hurried out to deal with it, meeting, in the doorway, the waiter who brought the coffee, followed by Rosario. Maravilla seized the glass and drained it, scalding though it was. Her make-up suffered ; she snatched a powder-puff and began automatically to repair the damage.

" Tell me about your niece, señor." She cleared her throat. " And pardon my forgetfulness ! A chair, Rosario ; and then you can go downstairs and tell me what is going on."

Don Luis seated himself with pleasure. One did not often get behind the scenes ; it was said the artistes objected. The general turmoil caused by Andrés's flight had done him a good turn. He had had enough to put up with for one day ! That was what came of taking one's wife's relations into one's house. He had no desire to talk about María, of whom he knew next to nothing, but one subject was as good as another to start a conversation !

" La pobrecita ! It is indeed a misfortune for her. The señora will sympathise—as a woman ; she is embarazada."

The woman's cold lips moved soundlessly.

" In a formal family like my wife's, these things are taken seriously. The betrothal has not yet been announced."

He was startled to find the hand of La Maravilla on his arm. Dios, what a clutch she had ! Like steel claws. A woman's hand should not be like that. He looked down reproachfully on the small white fingers with their scarlet nails.

" Señor, tell me, por Dios—what is the name of her father ? "

" Aurelio López Méndez," replied Don Luis, when he had recovered from his astonishment.

" She's past her best." " Dios, how old she is ! Quite a skeleton ! " " There's something lifeless in her performance." " Shall we go out ? " " What—and waste our money ? Mujer ! " " She hardly seems to have strength to crawl across the stage ! " " Gómez should know better than to insult his public with such worn-out performers."

" Here's something to make you open your eyes ! " muttered Don Luis, as he crept into the room where Aurelio sat beside his now sleeping María. At long last she had worn herself out with weeping ; she had fallen asleep with her head on his arm ; her small face, colourless save for the twin black arcs of her brows, was white as the pillow on which her hair was scattered. Don Luis pressed his hand on Aurelio's shoulder, and, as the latter looked up, favoured him with a wink. " Hombre, the President of the Republic will be sending for you next ! It's all right ; you can trust to my absolute discretion. Dolores shall not know anything of this."

" Of what ? "

" Of your going to the Hotel Internacional. Pull yourself together ! Don't you hear what I am saying ? La Maravilla is asking for you."

Aurelio made a vehement gesture of refusal ; his eyes returned to the bed. Don Luis nudged him sharply.

" Come, you can't refuse a woman like that. It would not be caballero. There you are, you see ! What did I tell you ? If you would only spend a little more time in Granada, no one knows what adventures would come your way. A man is only as old as he feels——"

" Leave me alone ; I am not going out of the house."

" Now, don't take offence, hombre, at a little harmless teasing. I tell you the message is a genuine one. I let her read the letter ; es una mujer muy simpática. If that young one is to be found, she will do it. She recognises her obligations——"

The porter at the hotel eyed him sleepily. " La Maravilla ? No, she's not come in yet. Have a seat ; it won't be long before she is here. There was some trouble down at the theatre to-night—one of the artistes didn't turn up ; perhaps that's made the rest of them late." Aurelio, accustomed to the omniscience of Agujasierra about all local happenings, found nothing strange in the way news spreads in Granada.

He did not recognise—how should he ?—the figure which crawled through the doorway a little later : the bowed shoulders, the feeble step of the woman who had flaunted her charms before him on the previous night. She loosened the collar of her coat sufficiently to let him see the lined, grey face, the loose red mouth, with the colour smeared at the corners. She did not speak ; her eyes told him to follow her. He did so, without a word.

In her room, she seemed to recover some of her usual bearing. She took off her coat and flung it on the broad white bed ; went to a chest and drank thirstily of lukewarm water. Then she thrust her fingers through her disordered hair, as though to relieve herself of its weight, and, turning to him, held out her hand.

" After eighteen years ! " she said, with meaning.

He took her hand, puzzled ; his brain, filled with the suffering of María, failed to identify her with the past.

How strange, how sad, she thought, that two people who had together sounded the utmost depths of intimacy could, after a few years, meet as strangers, with no single reverberation from the past in their pulses. Agitation and apprehension—and she had suffered both—died on a rustling sigh that lifted the sparkling cross on her bosom. It was a sigh partly of regret, partly of relief. Yes, she had been right. She knew she had been right when she saw this man standing before her in his rustic clothing ; his face worn, dead-looking, patient and simple : the latter-day version of an ardent lover come to dust. The mountains had laid their seal upon his brow ; his uncertainties and aspirations had vanished in the sobriety of middle age. That " something misplaced " which her questing imagination had found in him at their first encounter had worn itself away, leaving the slow, contemplative countryman, engrossed in his ties of family. Looking at him, she could see, as in a miniature painting, all that his life had been.

Madre mía, how could she have been so mad as to dream, even for a moment, of uniting her life with such a one ?

How right had been Emilia Mera—how right in with-holding just that fraction of encouragement which would have precipitated her into a lifetime of regret ! " You are a creature of luxury " : yes, but also a creature of the theatre. " We are all victims," she thought ; " there is no escape for us from our destiny." Hate it as she might, she had also to adore this fearful organisation that had made and broken and made her again. Its dust was in her blood. She could never have known peace even in the life she had planned for herself—the life so strangely and unconsciously thwarted by the man who stood before her now.

How would he take the news she had to give him ? She must control herself, not allow hysteria to gain the upper hand. It was rather like killing a meek, sacrificial animal that, all unknowingly, offers its throat to the knife.

" I should have known you in the street," she said, forcing a smile. " And that is more than you can say for yourself."

" The human being is the copybook of Time, señora," answered Aurelio, wondering how she could expect him to know her, this woman whom he had never before seen. " Sometimes the pen writes smoothly, and sometimes the points are crossed."

She made a muttered exclamation, turning to the glass.

" This pen was broken," she repeated, almost inaudibly. " Well, have you nothing to ask me ? Have you no interest in what has happened to me since last we met ? "

A creeping uneasiness showed itself in his features ; he lifted his hand to them, as though aware of it.

" The señora must forgive me if——" She interrupted him.

" Tell me about yourself ! For God's sake, let us not be strangers ! "

How could she reveal herself to him, to a man who stood

before her like a servant, in an attitude of respect? How could she speak to him of that living past unless this false barrier, which the years had built, was broken down? She began to tremble; she could see her knees shaking under her silk gown.

" What is there to tell? " said Aurelio wonderingly. " It is not to people like myself that things happen. I eat, I sleep, I walk. Are these things that one can talk about? "

" You have a wife, a daughter," she reminded him.

" Yes. Perhaps," he ventured, " you yourself have a family, señora? "

" Por Dios, do not keep on saying señora to me, as though I——" She checked herself. " How old is your daughter? When was she born? "

What chord had she touched that drew across his face the blind and baffled look that cried out to her like a warning? Her soul recoiled before it. His eyes were fixed on her, and, during a moment that seemed to both of them like eternity, she saw the past take hold of him. She felt her way-worn and weary flesh dissolving, and within its outline another shape take form: slim, captivating, naked, angel-devil—the lost one, Maravilla! And she saw his eyes take knowledge of it, while, victim of the same hallucination, his own figure straightened, his long-dead youth cried out to her. . . . She made a rough movement to dismiss it all.

" Come, have you forgotten the date of your daughter's birth? That is not very fatherly of you! " she rallied him.

" It was," he said slowly, " on a day—on a day when I was away from home. The day after I was with thee." Unconsciously he employed the familiar second person; a shiver went through her.

" Caramba. And her name? What did you call her? "

" Maravilla."

" . . . Were you mad? " she whispered, after a long pause.

"Thou knowest I was," he muttered. Time swung back; for both, the formal appointments of the hotel room vanished, and they were back between the grimy white-washed walls of a six-peseta boarding-house. An unshaded electric bulb ; a narrow, dishevelled bed. She was the first to recover her self-command.

" But you were indeed crazy, my poor friend ! That name —madre mía ! It was not even my own. It was bestowed by the public on a little girl who liked running on the stage and being clapped by the audience for her imitations of the real comedians. A name like Consuelo was much too important for a little girl like that. And as she grew older she discovered that, even in the serious theatre, it did not pay to discard a name that stood for useful associations in the memories of the agents and managers. But you—what a fool you were to have handicapped your daughter with a name like that ! Only, perhaps "—she could not restrain herself from adding it—" perhaps you thought of me some-times, when you called her by it ? "

" Many times," he answered, looking away from her.

" Do not regret it, my friend. God will repay you," she said, deeply moved. " No doubt you have other children : but she is your favourite, this girl. I can see it."

" I have no others ; the birth of this one left my wife barren."

" And she is your treasure—the little joy of your heart ! How you will spoil her—giving her all she asks for, and before she asks for it. How God has blessed you in giving you the charge of your own little child ! "

She moistened her dry lips.

" You remember——" she began. " You remember that —when we parted—I too had plans for my future."

" Yes, I remember."

" You do not ask me if they materialised ? "

" It is not for me to question the señora."

" Mother of God, do you want to send me quite out of my mind ? " cried Maravilla. " You remember—I had a rich admirer ; an old man who was so infatuated with me I had even hopes he would marry me. Listen to me while I tell you. I went to him very shortly after I left you. For several months—what luxury I tasted ! It was a dream —a madness. Every day he brought me fresh proofs of the esteem in which he held me. I might have been a princess— a queen ! Ah, the remembrance of those days is something to live on, when there seems to be nothing. Nothing.

" Are you listening ? He was very jealous, so he provided me with a señora de compañia. He must have paid her a great deal of money, for she was unwearying in the watch she kept upon me. How I loathed that woman ! And with good cause, for it was due to her that, a few months later, I found myself in the street, with nothing whatever between me and starvation. Figure to yourself : nothing—after everything. And worse than nothing."

" La pobretica. And had you no family ? No friends ? "

" My mother was dead. I had a friend—but I was too proud to look for her. What could she have done ? She was just an actress, like myself. She had given me a little picture when we parted—a little picture that had gone everywhere with her, until it had come to seem a part of herself. I saw it, for the first time after seventeen years, last night.

" Madre mía—how can I tell you ? I found work, of course ; it was not difficult—but I had to take the first thing that offered, because I was starving. My lover was very angry, very revengeful. He had given me nothing— because that woman, that devil, whom God will repay, had told him I was going to have a baby."

She had slipped to her knees ; her face was working,

her hands clasped and unclasped themselves. Upon her upturned face was all the bitter experience, all the tragic knowledge of her fifty years ; her face was terrible. The tears ran down it, furrowing their way into lines that by some strange effort of will she normally concealed.

" Forgive me ! In the name of God, forgive me ! What could I do ? I was working among strangers ; some of them suspected, but I dared not confide in them, because I would have lost my position in the company. They would never have believed I could go on working, concealing my child, right on till the end ! It was born—my baby was born—late one night, when I got back to my lodgings. All the time, through the evening's performance, I could feel it, knocking and turning, wanting to come out. It was torturing me. ' You must wait, my darling,' I said to it. ' You must wait until your mother is ready.'

" The next morning we were going on to another town. I had nothing for it to wear, nothing to feed it with. My starving breasts would not have kept it alive for two days. I covered it with a shawl and ran out of the house with it. There was a foundling hospital in the town—with a cradle in the wall. I put the child in and turned the cradle round . . ."

" Ay," said Aurelio heavily. " How bad is the world. How hard the life God gives some of us to live."

She looked at him in stupefaction.

" Is it possible you have not understood that the child was yours ? "

" Mine ? "

" Madre mía, how should it not be yours ? Had I not given you my word ? From the night I said farewell to you, I never took another lover until after the child was born. I swear it—by my dead mother."

It was Aurelio who was now stupefied. He said at last :

" Mujer . . . but you told me nothing. In none of your letters have you said one word——"

" Why should I tell you ? What could you have done, save curse me for deserting our child ? "

" Am I God ? " She shuddered away from his outstretched hand.

" Wait. I have more to tell you. Do not think that all the punishment, all the payment, was to be mine. Wait ! You shall have your share of it !

" I tried to forget. I give you my word I tried to forget ! Sometimes I thought of going back, of asking for my child, and taking it away with me. But what sort of a life was mine for a little baby ? And besides, who wants to employ an actress who trails a child with her wherever she goes ? It was different—it was the usual thing—in my mother's young days, when I was born. I had not enough money to put it to board—not then, nor for many years after. Ill fortune seemed to pursue me—there is no need to tell you, who cannot understand, about that. Until at last I got an engagement for the Argentine. And when I came back it was too late. I knew they do not keep the children in those places after they are old enough to earn their livings. Where to look for him ? "

" I had a son ? " said Aurelio, in a quiet voice of resignation. " You are right. I am punished. God punished me by depriving me of my son."

" Is that what you feel ? " She scrambled to her feet ; the two stood facing each other, with the weight of their years and sadness on them. " God has given your son back to you now ! Your son is your daughter's novio. Make what you choose of the gift."

Flinging the words at him, she buried her face in her hands, and broke into the uncontrollable, ugly weeping of a woman who has lost her youth. The room was filled

L M

with the noise of her weeping ; it went on for a long time

When at last she lifted her head, hardly daring to look at him, Aurelio was standing exactly as he had stood before. He might have been carved out of wood, or stone, so still was his body, his head, his eyes—that looked across her own head as though there were no limits to their vision. But the look that was on his face strangled the sobs in her throat.

He stood like a blind man ; his face had exactly that blend of patience and sensitiveness, of polite attention that may at any moment be distracted by one of those things which only the blind can see. An air of the mountains, delicate and remote, lingered about him. Where had she seen a face like Aurelio's ? She remembered : it was in a painting of the Ascension. Aurelio's face was that of the ascending Christ. Heaven opening was in his face ; he was God's son, being received into his Father's bosom.

Awestricken, she crept towards him ; she laid her hand on him—half fearfully.

" Well ? Have you nothing to say ? "

" How shall a man not be glad," said Aurelio, from his immense distance, " to know he has begotten a son ? "

" But—the rest ? For God's sake, are you more, or less, than human ? Do you understand that, because of what has happened, a child may come into the world ? "

" Who knows ? And if it does ? "

" May God forgive you ! " she cried, shuddering away from him. " The antique—the unmentionable sin ! "

" Who shall speak of sin in connection with it ? If we must talk of antiquity," said Aurelio slowly, " by whom did the sons of Adam conceive their children ? Was that accounted for sin ? These two, our children, have loved one another ; who is to blame for it ? If any, it is ourselves, not they, who have brought darkness upon their love.

They knew nothing, so how can they be guilty of sin?—
which is a state of knowledge of good and evil. And how
shall they suffer for their innocence? They are as innocent
as the blessed daylight, as the white crocuses that flower
in our mountains! How often, when she was little, I have
made her a crown for her innocence out of those crocuses.

" So innocent are they, that, had this matter lain simply
with ourselves—with them and with me—I should have
allowed them to continue in their God-given innocence.
Yes, reproach me if you will. I should have allowed them
to betroth themselves; they should have come back and
lived in happiness and innocence in the mountains. Why
not? A sin committed in ignorance is not a sin. No evil
can come of it. I am so sure of the mercy of God, I would
willingly take upon myself the burden of their actions, and,
in due time, should answer for it. But you? Mujer, what
bad thing possessed you that you made this impossible?"

" I ?" She was dumbfounded.

" Claro, that you are the one to blame for telling the
boy. We had it all settled that they were to be betrothed;
that the two of them were to come home and wait until
the child was born. It is because you have told him that
he has gone away."

She was shocked in the profoundest depths of her being.
In all the stormy ways of her life she had preserved her
faith in her religion, she had practised, so far as she found
it possible, her rule of a strict Catholic. Aurelio's calm
words were blasphemy to her. Never, in any condition,
would she have yielded to his suggestion that the relationship between their children should continue. She knew
next to nothing of eugenic reasons against it: she only
knew that such a relationship carried the condemnation
of the Church, and that, in conniving at it, she would be
risking her hereafter.

For this reason she chose to deceive him. Why should he not think that this was the reason of Andrés's departure ?—instead of the infinitely more ignoble one which, in the depths of her heart, she knew was the truth. It was well Aurelio should think in this way : it made the boy more wholly hers, for if he ever showed the intention of returning to María—against which she felt there were a million chances—she had but to tell him the truth. Ojalá that such a day might never come !

The night wore on, to the slow murmur of their voices. The dawn came slowly ; it revealed an untouched bed, two figures, grey as dust, that sat stiffly and looked in each other's faces, as though startled, each, to discover that the other had outlived the night.

CHAPTER VIII

MARÍA

"Olá, Aurelio! Hombre, is it you? A nice state your wife's been in—wondering what had become of you. Blessed be God, it's well to know nothing ill has befallen you."

As Aurelio descended from the tramcar at the mountain terminus, he was dimly conscious of the curious stares of the little knot of people who always made it their business to meet the tram when it arrived Probably none of them were meeting their friends ; only one or two were getting into the coach for the return journey. They were simply there because in the mountains the day is so long, and the arrival of some message from the outside world may give a fillip to the gossip which spins its slow thread from door to door.

He greeted them politely, but when some would have accompanied him on the long walk home—there were still between four and five kilometres to be covered before reaching the village—he made mild excuses. " With your permission—I have friends to meet." They watched him, wide-eyed, as he plunged over the side of the roadway, went lurching and trampling among the wire scrub, the boulders and brambles of the hill-side.

" For sure he is crazy—Aurelio López ! " They were not offended, as they would have certainly been had anyone else proffered so poor an excuse for declining their company. Meeting friends, indeed, down in the gully where the only living thing one encountered might be a scurrying rabbit, a snake, sliding with all possible haste under a slab of stone ! But, looking on him as an idiot, the hill-people had come to regard the actions of Aurelio with a kind of protective gentleness, within the limits of their own inter-pretation of the term. Beyond shouting a few derisive messages to his " friends," they made no attempt to inter-fere with him ; they merely hurried on, to be the first, if possible, to bring the news of Aurelio's return.

After scrambling a little way, he stood still, and lifted his head. The mountains were ranged about him, their silence compassed him, their height made an ant of him. He took off his hat, and a little current of wind lifted his thin hair. Every seam, every crack on their great, barren sides stood out with delicate distinctness, like violet veinings upon a leaf. The nearer ranges were brown, the farther amethyst : both colours very clear and pure, that revealed the details of their surface to the accustomed eyes of the hill-dweller. Here a little house, there a strip of shale, identified itself in his memory. The sky had a wintry silver, with little stacks of duller cloud ; a changeful mist, that thickened into smoke, poured with a strange, circular movement, down into the valleys, and withdrew itself to poise, as delicately as Ariel, upon some dizzy height. The savage, remote and austere beauty of the country among which he dwelt, which had never, as a young man, dawned upon Aurelio, drew from him now an unconscious act of praise, of identifica-tion with its solitudes, which laid balm upon his anguished mind.

" Here," he thought, " I am myself. No. I am more than myself. I am Man and God-in-Man. I am great as the almighty mountains, and humble as a grain of earth ; strong as a rock, and weaker than a broken twig."

He sat down upon a boulder which clung, as by a miracle,

to the bare hillside. Somewhere close at hand, but hidden, there was the noisy chatter of a hill stream. For a moment his mind emptied itself of all but instinct ; he was very thirsty. He rose, found the torrent, and lay prone to drink from it. The water was like ice ; he knew it had come from the upper snows.

In his pitiful love for María, he knew himself so strong that nothing could prevail against him. He had failed her once, but never again. Never again in his life would he suffer her to leave his side, or cease to watch over her and her child, whose claim upon his love and protection was such that the brain reeled in contemplating it. In yielding to Carmela on that one fatal occasion, he had done María a wrong which the rest of his life must be spent in expiating. In the face of all comers he would expiate it.

She had her home : a home to which she was no less entitled than the woman who had ousted her from it. She had her child, which she must be allowed to bear in peace and security under her own roof. No hand must be raised against her ; as for gossip—what harm did gossip do anybody ? She would not be the first Agujasierran girl to bear a fatherless child in the village ; and, as a López, would she not have every protection, every claim upon the toleration of those who might consider themselves in a position to be censorious ? Let them censure her ! He, her father, would show himself capable of dealing with any who dared to voice their censure within his hearing. As for her mother— at least Carmela was not inhuman. She could not withhold from her own flesh and blood that which, indeed, she had denied to a member of Aurelio's own family.

For Carmela he felt nothing but pity. His whole spirit shrank from the blow he was to deal the proud woman whose integrity was dearer to her than anything under heaven. How could he comfort her ? What could he do or say to palliate the draught he had to administer ? Imagination failed him. The one thing on which he had to depend was the strength of Carmela's character, which, having battled on her own behalf so many bitter years, might now assert itself in defence of her daughter. He drew, to his comfort, upon the recent memories of the way in which Carmela now spoke of María, but these availed him little. How could they, when the majority consisted of her vauntings of the virtues of the absent girl ?—her superiority, by implication, over the girls of the neighbourhood, whom María far exceeded in looks, in cleverness, and in her prospects for the future. It was a bitter well to draw upon ; he ceased to do so.

By threat, by self-assertion—these were the only means he could employ to assure the girl any sort of reception. And how alien a means to a man of Aurelio's temperament ! What threat could he employ to make Carmela receive her own daughter ? To turn her out of doors ? That would make a fine scandal—would bring the name of López into worse disfavour than any matter of an errant daughter could do. It would not go at all well with his brother's family at Atarfe. Apart from this, it was an act of which he knew himself wholly incapable.

To whom does a man owe most : to his wife, or to his child ? The immensity of the question confounded him. To the best of his ability he had fulfilled his dual obligation, up to the time when its duality defined itself to the extent of forcing a choice between the two. And then, obeying an instinct rather than a desire, he had determined his course of action in Carmela's favour, justifying it by telling himself what was indeed the truth—that his decision was for María's good. But had the decision been so pure, so free from hidden motive, as that ? How much of it was due to his own longing, at any price, for peace in his own home ?

The gospel of peace is enjoined upon mankind, for only through peace can the soul find its way to God. But how far is a man justified in sacrificing others to his desire for peace—even when the desire goes beyond desire : when it is drawn from the deepest roots of conviction in that man's soul ?

It came to this : that in support of his conviction Aurelio had sacrificed the thing dearest in the world to him. He stood aghast before the realisation of what he had done. Slowly he began to see in what his expiation lay : in a continual warfare—a continual watchfulness between his two women, to see that the weaker of them did not come to grief ; in the renunciation of all he had come to rely upon as essential to his own well-being : his mountain solitudes, his quiet ignoring of what went on in his own household, his relinquishment of initiative, and his life of contemplation —he had to give them all up ; he had to make for himself, more than a new life, a new personality.

Had he known more, had he not been filled, at the time, with that strange strength, that calmness of solitude, Aurelio would have known that what he proposed to do was beyond human possibility.

At midnight, as often happened in the cold evenings, the tavern was empty. Carmela was moving briskly about, setting bottles back on their shelves, counting the glasses. Aurelio sat where he had been sitting most of the evening— at the little round table, covered with American cloth, under which a brasero was softly subsiding into a little crater of grey ash. The tavern had been crowded when he made his appearance, and beyond saying, " So there you are ! " and giving him a look of penetrating curiosity, she had taken little notice of him. It was not often that, out of the

tourist season, they had forasteros at the tavern ; but, on
this particular night, one of the Granada guides had
brought out a party of English or American tourists who
had wanted to " see the mountains by moonlight." They
had driven out at sunset, and left only when the moon was
high—a pale, flat half-circle, like a broken silver coin,
above the topmost peaks. With their going, with the departure of the few hangers-on who always, on occasions like
these, remained to cadge drinks from the easy-going
tourists, with the good nights of the blind guitarrista and
his companion and the girl who had been ordered in by
Carmela to perform gipsy dances, silence like a soft, dark
blanket fell upon the town.

The keys turned sharply in their locks ; the wooden bars
clanked home. Then Carmela came and, sitting down
opposite Aurelio, remarked :

" And now perhaps you will tell me what you have been
up to." She did not speak too harshly ; it was curiosity, more
than anything else, that made her ask her question. For
experience had slowly forced upon her doubting soul that
Aurelio was incapable of deceiving her in the only way a
woman cannot forgive a man for deceiving her. Whatever
had kept him in Granada, it was not a woman. She had had
two busy days—had made more money than she usually
looked to make in a week during the winter. She actually
strangled a yawn, and rose to go to the coffee-machine and
see whether there was enough left to make a cup for herself
and Aurelio. She struck a match, relit the gas, and returned.

" Come, hombre, have you lost your tongue ? " she said,
in the good-humouredly slighting tone she now frequently employed to him.

His hands were clasped on the table in front of him ;
looking down at them, Aurelio began to speak.

He did not see the change in her face : how its latter-day

comeliness vanished into viperish lines. Her small, hard
hand drummed on the table, but he paid no attention to it.
As his tale proceeded, a vicious smile appeared on her
mouth, and, with a random movement that she herself was
almost unconscious of, she picked up the newspaper that
the guide had left behind and made as though she were
reading it. The coffee began to boil over. She rose, sending
her rocking-chair clacking back against the wall, and went
to attend to it, without speaking a word to him. She filled
two cups, brought them back to the table, and again picked
up the paper.

Aurelio looked up. At her strange occupation, he said
uncertainly, " Carmela ; did you hear ? María is going to
have a child ? "

She shrugged her shoulders.

" So much the worse for her. If she got herself in that way
with Dolores, Dolores can look after her. She does not
come here."

" Think what you are saying. She is your daughter."

" My daughter ? " Carmela gave a short laugh. " That
did well enough when she was a child. I am not wholly
without ordinary feelings of humanity. But now there is no
need to keep up the pretence any longer."

" What are you saying ? " said Aurelio, aghast.

She put down the paper and leaned towards him across
the table. On her face was so evil a smile that he recoiled
before it.

" Did you think I was so completely a fool, to be taken
in with a trick like that ? You and your family must have
had a poor idea of my intelligence. Do you think I didn't
know what happened," she went on rapidly, " when my
own poor creature died, and you put your mistress's child
in its place ? Bah ! what fools men are, to think a woman is
deceived like that ! Though I'm surprised at your family

for conniving at it. Those creatures ! Did you think it was
for nothing I drove Asunción and Conchita López out of
my house ? Didn't I see them sneering and jeering at me,
laughing because I was so easily taken in ? I've kept silent
long enough, for your sake ; but I swear if that girl crosses
my threshold I'll publish your shame in all the town ! Your
brother shall hear of it—we shall hear what the López
have to say when an interloper is forced upon them as one
of the family."

" But you are indeed mad ! " gasped Aurelio, utterly
taken aback. Suddenly, out of the past, came an echo :
the thin, clear voice of the widow Herédia : " But of course
she is a little mad. She married late, and it was late in life
for her to have a child. And besides—all her mother's
family do odd things when they get to a certain age. . . ."
Blessed saints of God ! Had this canker been growing in
Carmela's soul ever since the birth of the child, or had it
suddenly developed out of her present rage ? But she did
not appear to be in a rage ; there was something far more
sinister and fear-compelling in her quietness, in the white-
lipped, repressed way in which she had brought out her
preposterous accusation, than in all her former frenzies.
He sat frozen into silence, trying to think how he was to
counter it, how reach the spot of sanity which evidently
still controlled a brain diseased.

" The trouble I have taken," she was saying, " that no
one should suspect it, least of all my own family—for your
sake alone ! Ah, you can never say I have not taken care of
your reputation ! Granuja as you are, I have loved you,
and for that I have sacrificed my tenderest feelings. What
more can a woman do than sit by and watch her husband
lavish all his affection on his bastard, while he neglects her
as though she has no existence apart from ministering to his
comfort ? As for that ——" She used, in connection with

María's name, an epithet which, in any conjunction, would
have startled Aurelio upon Carmela's lips. It went through
him like a shot ; his beloved, his darling ! For a moment
he struggled with the awful temptation to fling the truth in
her face—to tell her that María was in truth her own child,
but that, since she would have it, his bastard, now living,
had been begotten on the night before María's birth : his
son, the father of María's child ! He strangled the words in
his throat, and caught up with a trembling hand the paper
which Carmela had been handling. His darling ! How was
he to protect her ?

Over him flowed, in ceaseless flood, Carmela's vitupera-
tions : not of himself, but of María. He had to hold himself
tightly not to strike the lying words from her lips. He had
to make himself deaf to them, to concentrate the full force
of his mind and being on the problem of what was to happen
to María : for, no matter what his powers of will or per-
suasion might effect, how could he bring her into this madhouse ?

His silence, his apparent ignoring of her words, so maddened Carmela that, in the end, with a kind of gasp, she
picked up the cup of coffee which stood between them and
flung its contents full in Aurelio's face. The heat had gone
from the liquid—there was nothing injurious in the act
beyond the affront to a man's dignity. The two of them rose
simultaneously, he wiping his face with the sleeve of his
coat, she gasping, glaring defiantly with eyes from which the
last vestiges of sanity had departed.

" You and your love ! As things are between you. I
should not be surprised at all if you yourself were responsible
for the girl's condition ! "

As he carried her, prisoned in his arms, into their bedroom, he was reminded of the day when she had made the
scene with the knife. Yes, more and more clearly he came

to see that, for possibly several years, certainly during the last six months, Carmela's reason had been failing her. He held her with a very careful gentleness. Compassion for her almost drove from his mind every other thought. As he laid her down, and, to prevent her struggling, stretched his body upon hers, the memory of her youth came to him, almost overwhelmingly : how lovely she had been, how enchanting, with her tart sayings that lent savour to the adorable gentleness of her ways. What a mistress, what a lover—poor Carmela ! Forgetting that she was not in a condition to understand what he said, he began speaking softly, close to her lips. He closed his eyes, because he could not bear to see her convulsed face. He began to use gentle words, to reassure her. But she raved on, struggling to free her arms from the pressure he exerted upon them. He shifted the pressure a little, upwards ; he did not wish to bruise her soft flesh.

And then he remembered his María, her need, her danger—her utter and desperate reliance upon him to make things safe for her. He saw her little face, from which the joy had departed like a candle blown out, and the bitter cry with which she had flung herself into his arms when they brought him back to her rang in his ears. Without knowing it, his clutch on Carmela again altered. He saw, heard, felt nothing but his María, and her cry to him to save and help her.

After a little while it seemed to him Carmela was very quiet. He himself—his arms and hands were stiff. He moved them, surprised. He felt the thick coil of Carmela's hair slip across his wrist. He wondered what his hands were doing up there.

Her body, under his, was very still and quiescent ; he remembered the other time when it had been still, but he had felt it palpitant with some evil emotion that repulsed his own. He moved to one side to relieve her of his weight, and said, " Carmela." She made no reply.

The only light in the room was that which streamed through the little reja from the tavern ; the bed was in darkness. He went to open the shutters. His limbs were shaking, and the latch clattered in his fingers. But at last they were open ; through the square emptiness, protected with wire netting, poured the hard white light of the moon directly upon the pillow where the head of Carmela lay. He crept towards the bed, wondering still at her silence. Was it possible that, on the heels of her frenzy, she had fallen asleep ? Her head was turned away from him ; the beautiful rope of her hair lay, partly untwisted, across her bosom. The bed was in great disorder.

. . . A little later he found himself unbolting the door. He stepped out into the market square, empty, white with moonlight. The irregular little houses, the town hall, the church tower, were all silvered with the same white magic ; an unearthly tranquillity lay upon the place. A cat went slinking rapidly between two patches of shadow.

The black peak of the Aguja went towering up behind the town. Along the edge of a sky, prickly with stars, palely luminous with their radiance, the mountains raised their black barricade of silence. Aurelio's feet echoed crisply on the cobbles. His mind was clear—clear as the stars. He was going to the house of the alcalde. Always the alcaldes were friends of the López. He would tell him the truth : that Carmela had become insane ; that in mastering her it had happened. There would no doubt be some trouble ; but in the end his reputation—the reputation of a López— would put things right.

With his hand raised to the knocker of the alcalde's door he paused to look back at his own house, on the farther side of the square. With the first sound of the knocker a